TWENTY YEARS AFTER

Alexandre Dumas

LIGHTYEAR PRESS

LAUREL, NEW YORK 11948

waited for the man to scoop out their ice cream, they watched the boy, licking furiously at one side of his tall ice-cream cone. Suddenly, the ice cream slid off the top of the cone and fell to the ground. The boy stared in dismay at the blob of ice cream, now spreading into a creamy puddinglike circle in the green grass.

"Country ice cream!" he muttered with a shrug of his shoulders. "Won't even stay on a cone." He turned and walked off.

CONTENTS.

TWENTY YEARS AFTER.

CHAPTER I.

THE PHANTOM OF RICHELIEU.

In a study of the Cardinal's Palace of Paris, since known as the Royal Palace, or, retaining the Frence title, as the *Palais Royal,* a man was sitting at a large writing table, bound in brass at the corners, and loaded with books and papers. His attitude was meditative. At sight of that pallid and bent brow in its musing, that scarlet simar so richly laced, by the loneliness of the ante-chambers and the silence there, scarcely broken by the measured tread of the guards on the threshold without, it might be believed that the phantom of the Prime Minister Cardinal Richelieu dwelt still in this study of his.

Alas! this is, in very deed, only the shadow of the great man. France enfeebled, the royal authority mocked at, the nobles again strong and turbulent, and enemies swarming over the frontier, all bore witness that Richelieu was no longer in the field.

This mere shadow of Richelieu was Mazarin, alone and feeling that he was weak.

"Foreign—Italian—these are their worst words of cowardly reproach," he muttered, "with which they assassinated, hanged, and made away with Concini and, if I gave them their way, they would assassinate, hang, and make away with me, in the same manner, although they have nothing to complain of, except a tax or two now and then.

"Favorites are never in fashion—but I am no ordinary favorite. Queen Elizabeth's, the Earl of Essex, 'tis true, wore a splendid ring, set with diamonds, given him by his royal mistress; whilst I—I have nothing but a simple circlet of gold, with a cypher on it and a date; but that ring has been blessed in the Chapel Royal, so the Queen will never banish me; and even were I obliged to yield to the populace, she would yield with me; if I flee, she will flee; and then we shall see how the rebels will get on without either King or Queen.

(3)

"Oh, were I not a foreigner! were I but a Frenchman! would I were even merely a gentleman!"

The position of the Cardinal was, indeed, critical, and several recent events added to his difficulties. Discontent had long pervaded the lower ranks of society in France.

One day—it was the morning of that when this story begins—the King, Louis XIV., then ten years of age, went in state, under pretext of returning thanks for his recovery from small-pox, to Notre Dame. He took the opportunity of calling out his guard, the Swiss troops, and the Musketeers, and he had planted them round the Palais Royal, on the quays, and on the Pont Neuf. After mass, the young monarch drove to the parliament house, where, upon the throne, he hastily confirmed not only the edicts which he had already passed, but issued new ones; each one—according to Cardinal de Retz, more ruinous than the others—a proceeding which drew forth a strong remonstrance from the chief president Mole—whilst President Blancmesnil and Councillor Broussel raised their voices in indignation against fresh taxes.

The King returned amidst the silence of a vast multitude to the Palais Royal. All minds were uneasy—most were foreboding—many of the people using threatening language.

At first, indeed, they were doubtful whether the King's visit to the parliament had been in order to lighten or increase their burdens; but scarcely was it known that the taxes were even to be increased, than cries of "Down with Mazarin!" "Long live Broussel!" "Long live Blancmesnil!" resounded through the city. All attempts to disperse the groups now collected in the streets, or to silence their exclamations, were vain. Orders had just been given to the Royal Guards, and to the Swiss Guards, not only to stand firm, but to send out patrols into the streets where the people thronged and were most vociferous, when the mayor of Paris was announced at the Palais Royal.

He was shown in directly: he came to say that if these offensive precautions were not discontinued, in two hours Paris would be under arms.

Deliberations were being held, when a lieutenant in the Guards, named Comminges, made his appearance with his clothes all torn, his face streaming with blood. The Queen, on seeing him, uttered a cry of surprise, and asked him what was going on.

As the mayor had foreseen, the sight of the guards had exasperated the mob. The tocsin was sounded. Comminges' account confirmed the mayor's. The authorities were not in a condition to contend with a serious revolt. Mazarin endeavored to circulate a report that troops had only been stationed on the quays, and on the Pont Neuf, on account of the ceremonial of the day, and that they would soon withdraw. In fact, about four o'clock they were all concentrated about the Palais Royal, the courts and ground floors of which were filled with Musketeers and Swiss Guards, and there awaited the event of all this disturbance.

Such was the state of affairs at the very moment when we introduced our readers into the study of Cardinal Mazarin— once Cardinal Richelieu's. All at once he raised his head: his brow slightly contracted, like one who has a resolution; taking up a silver whistle placed on the table near him, he whistled twice.

A door hidden in the tapestry opened noiselessly, and a man in black stood behind the chair on which Mazarin sat.

"Bernouin," said the Cardinal, not turning round, for, having whistled, he knew that it was his valet-de-chambre who was behind him, "what Musketeers are on duty in the palace?"

"The Black Musketeers, de Treville's company, under command of Lieutenant d'Artagnan."

"A man on whom we can depend, I hope."

"Oh, yes, my lord."

"Give me a uniform of these Musketeers, and help me to dress."

The valet went out as silently as he came in, and appeared in a few minutes, bringing the dress. When his master was completely dressed, he said:

"Bring M. d'Artagnan hither."

When left alone, the Cardinal looked at himself in the glass with self-satisfaction. Still young—for he was scarcely forty-six years of age—he possessed great elegance of form, and was above the middle height. He arranged his shoulder-belt, then looked with great complacency at his very beautiful hands, of which he took the greatest care; and throwing on one side the large kid gloves which he tried on at first, belonging to the uniform, he put on others of silk. At this instant the door opened.

"M. d'Artagnan," the valet-de-chambre announced.

A military officer strode in. He was a man under forty, of medium stature, but extremely well built, slender but sturdy: his eyes were lively and intelligent, and his black moustaches and chin beard somewhat grizzled, as always happens when life has been too gay or too grave, and particularly when it is a man of dark complexion.

Lieutenant Louis d'Artagnan took four steps into the cabinet well remembered from his visit to it in the late Cardinal's time, and, at first perceiving only one of his own men, gave him a stern look to identify him, when he recognized the Premier directly. He remained standing in a dignified but respectful posture, as became a man of good birth, who had in his life been frequently in the society of the highest nobles.

The Cardinal looked at him with a glance cunning rather than deeply, he examined him with attention, and, after a short silence, said:

"You are M. d'Artagnan?"

"I am he," replied the officer.

Mazarin gazed once more at a countenance full of intelligence, the excessive play of which had been subdued by age and experience; but d'Artagnan received the scrutiny like one who had formerly sustained many a look from eyes much more piercing than those whose investigation he bore now.

"Lieutenant," said the Cardinal, "I would like you to come with me, or—a better way of putting it—I should like to go with you."

"At your orders, monseigneur," responded the officer.

"I wish to visit in person the outposts which surround the Palais Royal; do you suppose there is any danger in so doing?"

"Danger, my lord!" asked d'Artagnan, with astonishment; "what danger?"

"I am told that there is a popular mutiny."

"The uniform of the King's Musketeers carries respect with it; and even if that were not the case, I would engage, with four of my men, to put to flight a hundred of these clowns."

"But do you know what happened to Comminges?"

"M. de Comminges is in the Guards, and not in the Musketeers——"

"Which means, I suppose, that the Musketeers are better soldiers than the Guards?" The Cardinal smiled as he spoke.

"Every one likes his own uniform best, my lord."

"Myself excepted;" and again Mazarin smiled; "for you perceive that I have left off mine, and put on yours."

"Plague take us! this is modesty," cried d'Artagnan. "Had I such a uniform as your Eminence, I protest I should be content; and I would take an oath never to wear any other——"

"Yes, but for to-night's adventure, I don't suppose it very safe. Give me my felt hat, Bernouin."

"How many men does your Eminence wish for escort?"

"You say that with four men you will undertake to disperse a hundred rabble; as we may encounter two hundred, take eight——"

"I am ready."

"I follow you. This way—light us down stairs, Bernouin."

The valet held a wax-light; the Cardinal took a key from his bureau, and, opening the door of the secret stairs descended into the palace-yard.

CHAPTER II.

A NIGHT PATROL.

IN ten minutes Mazarin and his party were traversing the street. The appeareance of the town denoted the greatest agitation. From time to time uproar came in the direction of the public markets. The report of fire-arms was heard, and occasionally church bells began to ring indiscriminately and at the caprice of the populace. D'Artagnan, meantime, pursued his way with the indifference of a man upon whom such acts of folly made no impression. The Cardinal envied his composure, which he ascribed to the habit of encountering danger. On approaching an outpost near the Barriere des Sergens, the sentinel cried out, "Who's there?" and d'Artagnan answered—having first asked the pass-word of the Cardinal—"Louis" and "Rocroy." After which he inquired if Lieut. Comminges were not the commanding officer. The soldier replied by pointing out to him an officer who was conversing, on foot, with his hand upon the neck of a horse on which the individual to whom he was talking sat. It was the officer whom d'Artagnan was seeking.

"Here is M. de Comminges," said d'Artagnan, returning to the Cardinal. He instantly retired, from a respectful delicacy; it was, however, evident that the Cardinal was recognized by both Comminges and the other officer on horseback.

"Well done, Guitaut," cried the Cardinal to the equestrian; "I see plainly, that notwithstanding the sixty-four years which have passed over your head, you are still the same man, active and zealous. What were you saying to this youngster?"

"My lord," replied Guitaut, "I was observing that the mob have suggested throwing up barricades in the Rues Saint Denis and Saint Antoine."

"And what was Comminges saying to you in reply, dear Guitaut?"

"My lord," said Comminges, "I answered that to compose a League, only one ingredient was wanting—in my opinion an essential one—a Duke of Guise—moreover, no one ever does the same thing twice over."

"No, but they mean to make a *Fronde*, as they call it," said Guitaut. "It seems that some days since, Counsellor Bachaumont remarked at the palace that rebels and agitators reminded him of schoolboys slinging stones from the moats round Paris, young urchins who run off the moment the constable appears, only to return to their diversion the instant that his back is turned. So they have picked up the word, and the insurrectionists are called 'Frondeurs,' and yesterday every article sold was, 'a la Fronde'—bread, hats, gloves, pocket-handkerchiefs, and fans,—but listen——"

At this juncture, a window opened, and a man, sticking out his head, began to sing:

> "A breeze of the Fronde
>   Did this morning begin;
> I warrant 'twill roar
>   Against Mazarin—
> This breeze of the Fronde
>   Will yet make a din."

"A saucy rogue!" growled Guitaut.

"My lord," said Comminges, who, irritated by his wounds, wished for revenge, and longed to give back blow for blow, "shall I fire off a ball to punish that jester, and to teach him not to sing so much out of tune in future?"

And, as he spoke, he put his hand on the holster of his uncle's saddle-bow.

"Certainly not—certainly not!" exclaimed Mazarin. "Diavolo! my dear friend, you are going to spoil everything—everything is going on famously. I know the French as well as if I had made them myself from first to last. They sing—let them pay the piper. During the League, about which Guitaut was speaking just now, the people chanted nothing except the mass, so everything went to destruction. Come, Guitaut, come along, and let's see if they keep watch at the Quinzo Vingts as at the Barriere des Sergens."

And, waving his hand to Comminges, he rejoined d'Artagnan, who instantly put himself at the head of his troop, followed by the Cardinal, Guitaut, and the rest of the escort.

"Just so," muttered Comminges, looking after Mazarin. "True, I forgot—provided he can get money out of the people, that is all he wants."

The street of Saint Honore, when the Cardinal and his party passed through it, was crowded by an assemblage, who, standing in groups, discussed the edicts of that memorable day.

D'Artagnan passed through the very midst of this discontented multitude, just as if his horse and he had been made of iron. Mazarin and Guitaut conversed together in whispers. The Musketeers, who had already discovered who Mazarin was, followed in profound silence.

D'Artagnan led the way to the hill of Saint Roch, where stood a guardhouse.

"Who is in command here?" asked the Cardinal.

"Villequier," said Guitaut.

"Diavolo, speak to him yourself, for ever since you were deputed by me to arrest the Duke de Beaufort, this officer and I have been on bad terms. He laid claim to that honor as captain of the Royal Guards."

Guitaut accordingly rode forward, and desired the sentinel to call Villequier.

"Ah! so you are here!" cried the officer, in a tone of ill-humor habitual to him; "what the devil are you doing here?"

"I wish to know—can you tell me, pray—is there anything fresh happening in this part of the town?"

"What do you mean? People cry out, 'Long live the King! down with Mazarin!'—that's nothing new—no, we've been used to those acclamations for some time."

"And you sing chorus," replied Guitaut, laughing.

"Faith, I've half a mind to do it. In my opinion the people are right: and cheerfully would I give up five years of my pay—which I am never paid, by the way—to make the King five years older."

"Really! And pray what is to come to pass supposing the King were five years older than he is?"

"As soon as ever the King becomes of age, he will issue his commands himself, and 'tis far pleasanter to obey the grandson of Henry IV, than the grandson of Pietro Mazarin. S'death! I would die willingly for the King; but supposing I happened to be killed on account of Mazarin, as your nephew was near being to-day, there could be nothing in Paradise—however well off I might have been in this world—that could console me."

"Well, well, M. de Villequier," here Mazarin interposed, "I shall take care that the King hears of your loyalty. Come, gentlemen," he addressed the troop, "let us return. All's well."

"Hello!" exclaimed Villequier; "so, Mazarin is here! so much the better. I have been wanting for a long time to tell him what I think of him. I'm obliged to you, Guitaut, for this opportunity."

He turned away, and went off to his post, whistling a tune then popular with the "Fronde," while Mazarin returned, in a pensive mood, towards the Palais Royal. All that he had heard from these three different men, Comminges, Guitaut, and Villequier, confirmed him in his conviction that in case of serious tumults, there would be no one on his side except the Queen, who had so often deserted her friends, that her support seemed very precarious. During the whole of this nocturnal ride, during the whole time that he was endeavoring to understand the various characters of Comminges, Guitaut, and Villequier, Mazarin was, in truth, studying more especially one man. This man—who had remained immovable when menaced by the mob—not a muscle of whose face was altered either by Mazarin's witticisms, or by the jests—seemed to the Cardinal a peculiar being, who, having participated in past events similar to those now occurring, was calculated to cope with those on the eve of taking place.

The name of d'Artagnan was not altogether new to Mazarin, who, although he had not arrived in France before the year 1634, or 1635, that is to say, about eight or nine years after the events which we have related in "The Three Musketeers," fancied that he had heard it pronounced, in reference to one who was said to be a model of courage, address and loyalty.

Possessed by this idea, the Cardinal resolved to know all about d'Artagnan immediately; of course he could not inquire from d'Artagnan himself who he was; so, on reaching the walls which surrounded the Palais Royal, the Cardinal knocked at a little door, and after thanking d'Artagnan, and requesting him to wait in the court-yard, he made a sign for Guitaut to follow him in.

"My dear friend," said the Cardinal, leaning, as they walked through the gardens, on his arm, "you told me just now that you have been twenty years in the Queen's service."

"Yes, 'tis true; I have," returned Guitaut.

"Now, my dear Guitaut, I have often remarked that in addition to your courage—which is indisputable, and to your fidelity—which is invincible, you possess an admirable memory. Hence, I brought you here to ask," returned Mazarin, "if you have taken any particular notice of our Lieutenant of Musketeers?"

"D'Artagnan? I do not care to notice him particularly; he's an old acquaintance, a Gascon. De Treville knows him, and esteems him greatly, and de Treville, as you know, is one of the Queen's greatest friends. As a soldier, the man ranks well; he did his duty, and even more than his duty, at the siege of Rochelle—as well as at Suze and Perpignan."

"But you know, Guitaut, we poor ministers often want men with other qualities besides courage; we want men of talent. Pray was not d'Artagnan, in the time of the Cardinal, mixed up in some intrigue from which he came out, according to report, rather cleverly?"

"My lord, as to the report you allude to"—Guitaut perceived that the Cardinal wished to make him speak out—"I know nothing but what the public knows. Consult some politician of the period of which you speak, and if you pay well for it, you will certainly get to know all you want."

Mazarin, with a grimace which he always made when spoken to about money—"People must be paid—one can't do otherwise," he said.

"There is one man who could inform you—if he would speak."

"Birds that can sing and won't sing, must be made to sing," observed the Italian.

"Well, it is Count de Rochefort, but he has disappeared these four or five years, and I have lost the run of him."

"*I* know, Guitaut," said Mazarin.

"Well, then, how is it that your Eminence complained just now of want of information on some points?"

"You think," resumed Mazarin, "that Rochefort——"

"He was Cardinal Richelieu's familiar spirit, my lord. I warn you however, his services will be expensive. The Cardinal was lavish to his underlings."

"Yes, yes, Guitaut," said Mazarin; "Richelieu was a great man, a very great man, but he had that defect. Thanks, Guitaut; I shall benefit by your advice this very evening."

Here they separated, and bidding adieu to Guitaut in the court of the Palais Royal, Mazarin approached an officer who was walking up and down within that enclosure.

It was d'Artagnan, who was waiting for him.

"Come hither," said Mazarin, in his softest voice. "I have an order to give you."

D'Artagnan bent low, and, following the Cardinal up the secret staircase, soon found himself in the study whence he had first set out.

The Cardinal seated himself before his bureau, and taking a sheet of paper, wrote some lines upon it whilst d'Artagnan remained standing imperturbable, and without showing either impatience or curiosity. He was like a military automaton acting (or, rather, obeying the will of others) upon springs.

The Cardinal folded and sealed his letter.

"M. d'Artagnan," he said, "you are to take this despatch to the Bastille, and to bring back here the person whom it concerns. You must take a carriage and an escort, and guard the prisoner carefully."

D'Artagnan took the letter, touched his hat with his hand, turned round upon his heel like a drill-sergeant and, a moment afterwards, was heard in his dry and monotonous tone, commanding, "Four men and an escort, a carriage and a horse." Five minutes afterwards the wheels of the carriage and the horses' shoes were heard resounding on the pavement of the court-yard.

CHAPTER III.

ONCE FOES.

D'ARTAGNAN arrived at the Bastille just as it was striking half-past eight. His visit was announced to the governor, who, on hearing that he came from the Cardinal, went to meet him, and received him at the top of the great flight of steps outside the door. The governor of the Bastille was Tremblay who received d'Artagnan with extreme politeness, and invited him to sit down with him to supper, of which he was himself about to partake.

"I should be delighted to do so," was the reply; "but if I am not much mistaken, the words, 'In haste,' are written on the envelope of the letter which I brought."

"You are right," said du Tremblay. "Halloa, major, tell them to order number 256 to come down stairs."

A bell sounded.

"I must leave you," said du Tremblay; "I am sent for to sign the release of the prisoner. I shall be happy to meet you again, sir."

"May the devil annihilate me if I return your wish!" murmured d'Artagnan, but sweetly smiling as he thought out the imprecation; "I declare I feel quite ill, after being only five minutes in the court-yard. Go to—go to! I should rather die upon straw, than hoard up five thousand a year by being governor of the Bastille."

He had scarcely finished this soliloquy before the prisoner arrived. On seeing him d'Artagnan could hardly suppress a start of surprise. The prisoner did not seem, however, to recognize the Musketeer as he stepped into the vehicle.

"Gentlemen," thus d'Artagnan addressed the four Musketeers, "I am ordered to exercise the greatest possible care in guarding the prisoner; and, since there are no locks to the carriage, I shall sit beside him. M. de Lillibonne, lead my horse by the bridle, if you please." As he spoke, he dismounted, gave the bridle of his horse to the Musketeer, and placing himself by the side of the prisoner, said, in a voice perfectly composed, "To the Palais Royal, at a full trot."

The carriage drove on, and d'Artagnan, availing himself of the darkness in the archway under which they were passing, threw himself into the arms of the prisoner.

"Rochefort!" he exclaimed; "you—is it you; you, indeed? I am not mistaken?"

"D'Artagnan!" cried Rochefort.

"Ah! my poor friend!" resumed d'Artagnan, "not having seen you for four or five years, I concluded that you were dead."

"I'faith," said Rochefort, "there's no great difference, I think, between a dead man and one who has been buried alive; now I have been buried alive, or very nearly so."

"And for what crime are you imprisoned in the Bastille?"

"You will not believe me: it was for theft in the night. I was with some young larks who snatched cloaks on the New Bridge, and brought the watch down on us all. I and another were on the statute of Henry Fourth when the archers hauled us off."

"I see that it was a mere pretext, but you will soon know the true charge, for I am taking you before the Premier. I had no idea I was sent for you."

"No idea—when you are the favorite's favorite!"

"Not a bit of it, my poor friend," replied the officer. "No, I am as poor a Gascon as when you came athwart me at Meung, two-and-twenty years ago—heigho! Just lieutenant, for my captaincy was not confirmed."

"What meanness! I infer that Mazarin has not changed."

"The same, except that he has married the Queen."

"Resist Buckingham, and yield to Mazarin."

"Just like the women," replied d'Artagnan, coolly.

"Like women—but not like queens."

"Good heavens, in love, queens are doubly women."

"Of course the Duke of Beaufort is still imprisoned, or he would have released me."

"My boy, it is more likely that you will liberate him."

"Any war on with Spain?"

"Not with Spain but with Paris. You may hear the guns of the citizens amusing themselves."

"Pooh! do you think they could do anything?"

"They might do well if they had a good leader."

"Oh, that I were free!"

"Don't be downcast. Since Mazarin has sent for you, it is because he wants you. I congratulate you! Many a long year has passed since anyone wanted to employ me; so you see in what a situation I am."

"Make your complaints known; that's my advice."

"Listen, Rochefort; let's make a compact. We are friends, are we not?"

"Egad! I bear the traces of our friendship—three cuts from your sword."

"Well, if you should be restored to favor, don't forget me."

"On the honor of a Rochefort; but you must do the like for me.

"Apropos, are we to speak about your friends as well— Athos, Porthos, and Aramis? or have you forgotten them?"

"Almost!"

"What's become of them?"

"I don't know, we separated, as you know. They are alive, and that's all I can say about them. From time to time I hear of them indirectly, but in what part of the world they are, devil take me if I know. No, on my honor, I have not a friend in the world but you, Rochefort."

"And the illustrious—what's the name of the lad whom I made a sergeant in the Piedmont regiment?"

"Planchet?"

"The illustrious Planchet. What's become of him?"

"I shouldn't wonder if he is not at the head of the mob at this very moment. He married a woman who keeps a grocer's store in the Rue des Lombards; for he's a lad that was always fond of sweetmeats; he's now a citizen of Paris. You'll see that that queer fellow will be sheriff before I shall be captain."

"Come, dear d'Artagnan, look up a little—courage. It is when one is lowest on the wheel of fortune, that the wheel turns round and raises us. This evening your destiny begins to change."

"Amen!" exclaimed d'Artagnan, stopping the carriage.

He got out and remounted his steed, not wishing to arrive at the gate of the Palais Royal in the same carriage with the prisoner.

In a few minutes the party entered the court-yard, and d'Artagnan led the prisoner up the great staircase, and across the corridor and ante-chamber.

"Tell M. d'Artagnan to wait outside—I don't require him yet," said the Cardinal.

Rochefort, rendered suspicious and cautious by these words, entered the apartment, where he found Mazarin sitting at the table, dressed in his ordinary garb, and as one of the prelates of the Church, his costume being similar to that of the priests, excepting that his scarf and stockings were violet.

As the door was closed, Rochefort cast a glance towards Mazarin, which was answered by one, equally furtive, from the minister.

There was little change in the Cardinal; still dressed with sedulous care, his hair well arranged and well curled, his person perfumed—he looked, owing to his extreme taste in dress, only half his age. But Rochefort, who had passed five years in prison, had become old in the lapse of years; the dark locks of this estimable friend of the defunct Cardinal de Richelieu were now white; the deep bronze of his complexion had been succeeded by a mortal paleness, which betokened debility. As he gazed at him, Mazarin shook his head slightly, as much as to say, "This is a man who does not appear to me fit for much."

After a pause, which appeared an age to Rochefort, Mazarin, however, took from a bundle of papers a letter, and, showing it to the count, he said:

"I find here a letter in which you sue for liberty, M. de Rochefort. Did you not once refuse to undertake a journey to Brussels for the Queen?"

"Ah! ah!" exclaimed Rochefort. "There is the true reason! Idiot as I am, though I have been trying to find it out for five years, I never found it out."

"Well, the Queen saw in your refusal nothing but a distinct refusal; she had also much to complain of you during the lifetime of the Cardinal!—yes,—her majesty the Queen——"

Rochefort smiled contemptuously.

"Since I was a faithful servant, my lord, to Cardinal Richelieu during his life, it stands to reason that now, after his death, I should serve you well, in defiance of the whole world."

"With regard to myself, M. de Rochefort," replied Mazarin, "I am not like Richelieu, all-powerful. I am but a minister, who wants no servants, being myself nothing but a servant of the Queen's. Now, the Queen is of a sensitive nature; hearing of your refusal to obey her, she looked upon it as a declaration of war; and as she considers you as a man of superior talent, and therefore dangerous, she desired me to make sure of you—that is the reason of your being shut up in the Bastille—but your release can be managed. I want friends. When I say I want, I mean the Queen wants them. I do nothing without her commands; pray, understand that—not like Richelieu, who went on just as he pleased—so I shall never be a great man, as he was, but, to compensate for that, I shall be a good man, M. de Rochefort, and I hope to prove it to you."

Rochefort knew well the tones of that soft voice, in which there was sometimes the hissing voice of a viper.

"I am disposed to believe your Eminence," he replied; "but have the kindness not to forget that I have been five years in the Bastille, and that no way of viewing things is so false as through the grating of a prison."

"Ah, M. de Rochefort! have I not told you already that I

had nothing to do with that? The Queen—cannot you make allowances for the pettishness of a queen and princess? As for me, I play my game fair and above board, as I always do. Let us come to some conclusion. Are you one of us, M. de Rochefort? Men of loyalty are scarce."

"I think so, forsooth," said Rochefort; "and when you find any of them you pack them off to the Bastille. However, there are plenty of them in the world, but you don't look in the right direction for them, my lord."

"Indeed! explain to me. Ah! my dear M. de Rochefort, how much you must have learned during your intimacy with the late Cardinal! Ah! he was a great man!"

"Like master, like man; the great duke was able to find trusty servants—dozens and dozens of them."

"He! the point aimed at by every poignard! Richelieu, who passed his life in warding off blows which were forever aimed at him!"

"But he *did* ward them off," said de Rochefort, "and the reason was, that though he had bitter enemies, he possessed also true friends. I have known persons," he continued,—for he thought he might avail himself of the opportunity of speaking of d'Artagnan—"who, by their sagacity and address, have deceived the penetration of Cardinal Richelieu; who, by their valor, have got the better of his guards and his spies; persons without money, without support, without credit, yet who have preserved to the crowned head its crown, and made the Cardinal sue for pardon.

"One is d'Artagnan, a Gascon, who saved his Queen, and made Richelieu confess, that in point of talent, address, and political skill, he was to him only a tyro."

"Tell me how it all happened."

"No, my lord, the secret is not mine; it is a secret which concerns the Queen. In what he did, this man had three colleagues, three brave men, such men as you are wishing for just now."

"You pique my curiosity, my dear Rochefort; pray tell me the whole story."

"That is impossible, but I will tell you a true story, my lord. Once upon a time there lived a Queen—a powerful monarch—who reigned over one of the greatest kingdoms of the universe; and a minister; and this minister wished much to injure the Queen whom once he loved too well. There came to the court an ambassador so brave, and magnificent, and elegant, that every woman lost her heart to him; and the Queen had even the indiscretion to give him certain ornaments so rare that they could never be replaced by any like them.

"As these ornaments belonged to the King, the minister persuaded his majesty to insist upon the Queen's appearing in them as part of her jewels, at a ball. There is no occasion to tell you, my lord, that the minister knew for a fact that these ornaments had been sent after the ambassador, who was far away, beyond seas. This great Queen was ruined, you see, lowered beneath her meanest subject, since her fall was from the height of her grandeur."

"That's true," commented the listener.

"But, my lord, four men made up their minds to save her. They were not princes or dukes, rich or powerful—but four swordsmen, who had stout hearts, strong arms, and keen blades. Off they went! The minister heard of their start, and set men along the highway to stay them from reaching their mark. Stay them—stay the whirlwind! Still, three of them were disabled by the numerous enemies; but one reached the seaport, killing or wounding all that opposed him, crossed the sea, and brought back to the sovereign the ornaments which she wore on the designated day, on her shoulder, which all but destroyed the minister. What do you say to this, my lord? magnificent! but I could tell a dozen more of their exploits."

"And was this d'Artagnan one of the Four?" queried the Italian, who had been thinking.

"Rather! he led the enterprise."

"And who were the others?"

"I leave it to M. d'Artagnan to name them, my lord."

"You doubt me, but I really want you—and him—and all such valuable aids. Come, you shall be my confidential agent, and in the first place go to watch over the Duke de Beaufort in Vincennes."

"The prison? that is only from one to another. Nay, my lord,—I am for fresh air. Employ me in any other way; employ me even actively—but let it be on the high roads."

"My dear M. de Rochefort," Mazarin replied, in a tone of raillery, "you think yourself still a young man—your spirit is still juvenile, but your strength fails you. Believe me, you ought now to take rest."

"I see, my lord, that I am to be taken back to the Bastille."

"You are sharp."

"I shall return thither, my lord, but you are wrong not to employ me."

"You? the friend of my greatest foes? don't suppose that you are the only person who can serve me, M. de Rochefort. I shall find many as able men as you are."

"I wish you may, my lord," replied de Rochefort.

He was then reconducted by the little staircase, instead of passing through the ante-chamber where d'Artagnan was waiting. In the court-yard the carriage and the four Musketeers were ready, but he looked around in vain for his friend.

"Ah!" he muttered to himself, "this materially changes matters, and if there be as thick a crowd in the street as when we came along, we will try to show old Mazzy that we are still good for something better than to look after prisoners."

Thereupon he skipped into the carriage as nimbly as if he were but twenty-five.

CHAPTER IV.

ANNE OF AUSTRIA AT FORTY-SIX.

WHEN left alone with Bernouin, Mazarin was, for some minutes, lost in thought. He had gained much information, but not enough.

"My lord, have you any commands?" asked Bernouin.

"Yes, yes," replied Mazarin. "Light me; I am going to the Queen."

Bernouin took up the candlestick and led the way.

There was a secret communication between the Cardinal's apartments and those of the Queen; and through this corridor Mazarin passed whenever he wished to visit Anne of Austria.

Anne was reclining in a large easy chair, her head supported by her hand, her elbow resting on a table near her. She asked, with some impatience, what important business had brought the Cardinal there that evening.

Mazarin sank into a chair, with the deepest melancholy painted on his countenance.

"It is likely," he replied, "that we shall soon be obliged to separate, unless you love me well enough to follow me into Italy."

"Why," cried the Queen; "how is that?"

"Because the whole world conspires to break our bonds. Now as you are one of the whole world, I mean to say that you also desert me."

"Cardinal!"

"Heavens! did I not see you the other day smile on the Duke of Orleans? or rather at what he said—'Mazarin is a stumbling block. Send him away and all will be well.'"

"What do you wish me to do?"

"Oh, madam—you are the Queen!"

"Queen forsooth, when I am at the mercy of every scribbler in the Palais Royal, who covers waste paper with nonsense, or of every country squire in the kingdom."

"Nevertheless, you have still the power of banishing from your presence those whom you do not like."

"That is to say, whom *you* do not like," returned the Queen.

"I!—persons whom *I* do not like!"

"Yes, indeed. Who ordered M. de Beaufort to be arrested?"

"An incendiary; the burden of whose song was his intention to assassinate me. My enemies, madam, ought to be yours, and your friends my friends."

"My friends, sir!" The Queen shook her head. "Alas! I have none. In vain do I look about me for friends."

"Do you know M. de Rochefort?" said Mazarin.

"One of my bitterest enemies—the faithful friend of Cardinal Richelieu."

"I know that, and we sent him to the Bastille," said Mazarin.

"Is he at liberty?" asked the Queen.

"No; still there—but I only speak of him in order that I may introduce the name of another man. Do you know M. d'Artagnan?" he added, looking steadfastly at the Queen.

Anne of Austria received the blow with a beating heart.

"Has the Gascon been indiscreet?" she murmured; then said aloud:

"D'Artagnan! stop an instant; that name is certainly familiar to me. D'Artagnan! there was a Musketeer who was in love with one of my women, poor young creature! she was poisoned on my account."

"That's all you know of him?" asked Mazarin.

The Queen looked at him, surprised.

"You seem, sir," she remarked, "to be making me undergo a course of interrogations."

"Which you answer according to your own fancy," replied Mazarin.

"Tell me your wishes, and I will comply with them."

The Queen spoke with some impatience.

"Endeavor to remember the names of those faithful servants who crossed the Channel, in spite of Richelieu—tracing the roads along which they passed by their blood—to bring back to your majesty certain jewels given by her to Buckingham."

Anne arose, full of majesty, and, as if touched by a spring, started up, and looking at the Cardinal with the haughty dignity which, in the days of her youth, had made her so powerful, "You insult me, sir," she said.

"I wish," continued Mazarin, finishing, as it were, the speech which this sudden movement of the Queen had cut short; "I wish, in fact, that you should now do for your husband what you formerly did for your lover."

"Again that accusation?" cried the Queen. "However, I swear I am not guilty; I swear it by——"

The Queen looked around her for some sacred object by which she could swear; and taking out of a cupboard, hidden in the tapestry, a small coffer of rosewood, set in silver, and laying it on the altar—

"I swear," she said, "by these sacred relics that Buckingham was not my lover."

"What relics are those by which you swear?" asked Mazarin, smiling. "I am incredulous."

The Queen untied from around her throat a small golden key which hung there, and presented it to the Cardinal.

"Open," she said, "sir, and look for yourself."

Mazarin opened the coffer; a knife covered with rust, and two letters, one of which was stained with blood, alone met his gaze.

"What are these things?" he asked.

"What are these things?" replied Anne, with queen-like dignity and extending towards the open coffer an arm, despite the lapse of years, still beautiful. "These two letters are the only letters that I ever wrote to him. That knife is the knife with which Felton stabbed him. Read the letters and see if I have lied or spoken the truth."

But Mazarin, notwithstanding said permission, instead of reading the letters, took the knife which the dying Buckingham had snatched out of the wound, and sent by Laporte to the Queen. The blade was red, for the blood had become rust; after a momentary examination, during which the Queen became as white as the cloth which covered the altar on which she was leaning, he put it back into the coffer with an involuntary shudder.

"It is well, madam; I believe your oath."

"No, no, read," exclaimed the Queen, indignantly; "read, I command you, for I am resolved everything shall be finished to-night, and never will I recur to this subject again. Do you think," she said, with a ghastly smile, "that I shall be inclined to re-open this coffer to answer any further accusations?"

Mazarin, overcome by this determination read the two letters. In one the Queen asked for the ornaments back again. This letter had been conveyed by d'Artagnan, and had arrived in time. The other was that which Laporte had placed in the hands of the Duke of Buckingham, warning him that he was about to be assassinated; this had arrived too late.

"It is well, madam," said Mazarin; "nothing can be said to this testimony."

"Sir," replied the Queen, closing the coffer, and leaning her head upon it, "if there is anything to be said, it is that I have always been ungrateful to the brave men who saved me—that I have given nothing to that gallant officer, d'Artagnan, you were speaking of just now, but my hand to kiss, and this diamond."

As she spoke she extended her beautiful hand to the Cardinal, and showed him a superb diamond which sparkled on her finger.

"It appears," she resumed, "that he sold it—he sold it in order to save me another time—to be able to send a messenger to the duke to warn him of his danger. He sold it to M. des Essarts, on whose finger I remarked it. I bought it from him, but it belongs to d'Artagnan. Give it back to him, sir; and since you have such a man in your service, make him useful.

"And now," added the Queen, her voice broken by her emotion, "have you any other question to ask me?"

"Nothing"—the Cardinal spoke in the most conciliatory manner—"except to beg of you to forgive my unworthy suspicions. I shall retire, madam; do you permit me to return?"

"Yes, to-morrow."

The Cardinal took the Queen's hand, and pressed it, with an air of gallantry, to his lips.

CHAPTER V.

THE GASCON AND THE ITALIAN.

WHEN he was alone, he opened the door of the corridor, and then that of the ante-chamber. There d'Artagnan was asleep upon a bench.

The Cardinal went up to him, and touched his shoulder. D'Artagnan started, awakened himself, and, as he awoke, stood up exactly like a soldier under arms.

"M. d'Artagnan," said the Cardinal, sitting down in an armchair, "you have always seemed to be a brave and an honorable man."

"Possibly," thought d'Artagnan; "but he has taken a long time to let me know his thoughts;" nevertheless, he bent down to the very ground in gratitude for Mazarin's compliment.

"M. d'Artagnan," continued Mazarin, "you performed sundry exploits in the last reign."

"Your Eminence is too good to remember that. It is true, I fought with tolerable success."

"I don't speak of your warlike exploits, monsieur," said Mazarin; "although they gained you much reputation, they were surpassed by others."

D'Artagnan pretended astonishment.

"I speak of certain adventures. I speak of the adventure referring to the Queen—of the diamond studs, of the journey you made with three of your friends."

"Ha, ho-o!" thought the Gascon; "is this a snare, or not? Let me be on my guard."

And he assumed a look of stupidity which the finest low comedians might have envied.

"Bravo," cried Mazarin, "they told me that you were the man I wanted. Come, let us see what you will do for me!"

"Everything that your Eminence may please to command me," was the reply.

"You will do for me what you have done for the Queen?"

"Certainly," d'Artagnan said to himself, "he wishes to make me speak out. But Richelieu could not do that, and this fox is not near as sharp, devil take him!" but all he said aloud was: "For a queen, my lord? I do not follow you."

"You don't comprehend that I want you and your three friends to be of use to me?"

"What friends, my lord?"

"Your three friends—the friends of former days."

"Of former days, my lord! In former days I had not only three friends, I had fifty; at twenty, one calls everyone one's friends."

"Well, sir," returned Mazarin; "prudence is a fine thing, but to-day you might regret having been too prudent."

"My lord, Pythagoras made his disciples keep silent for five years, that they might learn to hold their tongues."

"But you have been silent for twenty years, sir. Speak, now, for the Queen herself releases you from your promise, in token of which she commanded me to show you this diamond, which she thinks you know."

And so saying, Mazarin extended his hand to the officer, who sighed as he recognized the ring which had been given to him by the Queen on the night of the ball at the Hotel de Ville.

" 'Tis true. I remember well that diamond."

"You see, then, that I speak to you in the Queen's name. Answer me without acting as if you were on the stage—your interests are concerned in your doing so. Where are your friends?"

"I do not know, my lord. We have parted company this long time; all three have left the service."

"Where can you find them, then?"

"Wherever they are, that's my business."

"Well, your conditions."

"Money, my lord; as much money as what you wish me to undertake will require."

"The devil! Money! and a large sum!" said Mazarin.

"Richelieu!" thought d'Artagnan, "would have given me five hundred pistoles in advance."

"You will then be at my service?" asked Mazarin.

"If my friends agree. What are we to do?"

"Make your mind easy; when the time for action comes, you shall be in full possession of what I require from you; wait till that time arrives, and find out your friends."

"My lord, possibly they are not in Paris. I must, perhaps, make a long journey to find them òut. Traveling is dear, and I am only a poor lieutenant in the Musketeers, and my pay is three months in arrears; besides, I have been in the service for twenty-two years, and have accumulated nothing but debts."

Mazarin remained some moments in deep thought, as if he combated with himself; then, going to a large cupboard closed with a triple lock, he took from it a bag of silver, and weighing it twice in his hand before he gave it to d'Artagnan—

"Take this," he said, with a sigh, " 'tis for your journey."

D'Artagnan bowed, and plunged the bag into the depth of an immense pocket.

"Well, then, all is settled; you are to set off," said the Cardinal. "Oh, what are the names of your friends?"

"The Count de la Fere, formerly styled Athos; M. du Vallon, whom we used to call Porthos; the Chevalier d'Herblay—now the Abbé d'Herblay—whom we used to call Aramis——"

The Cardinal smiled.

"Younger sons," he said, "who enlisted in the Musketeers under feigned names in order not to lower their family names. Long rapiers, but light purses, you know."

"If, God willing, these rapiers should be devoted to the service of your Eminence," said d'Artagnan, "I shall venture to express a wish—which is, that, in its turn, the purse of your Eminence may become light, and theirs heavy—for with these three men, your Eminence may stir up all Europe, if you like."

"These Gascons," said the Cardinal, laughing, "almost best the Italians in effrontery."

"At all events," answered d'Artagnan, with a smile similar to the Cardinal's, "they beat them when they draw their swords."

He then withdrew, and as he passed into the court-yard he stopped near a lamp, and dived eagerly into the bag of money.

"Crown pieces only, silver! I suspected it. Ah, Mazarin! Mazarin! thou hast no confidence in me! so much the worse for thee—harm may come of it!"

Meanwhile the Cardinal was rubbing his hands in great satisfaction.

"A hundred pistoles! a hundred pistoles! for a hundred pistoles I have discovered a secret for which Richelieu would have paid a thousand crowns: without reckoning the value of that diamond"—he cast a complacent look at the ring, which he had kept, instead of restoring it to d'Artagnan—"which is worth, at least, ten thousand francs."

He returned to his room, and, after depositing the ring in a casket filled with brilliants of every sort—for the Cardinal was a connoisseur of precious stones—he called to Bernouin to undress him, regardless of the noises, or of the firing of guns which continued to resound through Paris, although it was now nearly midnight.

CHAPTER VI.

D'ARTAGNAN IN HIS FORTIETH YEAR.

YEARS have elapsed, many events have happened, alas! since, in our romance of "The Three Musketeers," we took leave of d'Artagnan. He had not failed in his career, but circumstances had been adverse to him. So long as he was surrounded by his friends, he retained his youth and the poetry of his character. His was one of those fine, ingenuous natures which assimilate themselves easily to the dispositions of others. Athos imparted to him his greatness of soul; Porthos, his enthusiasm; Aramis, his elegance. Had d'Artagnan continued his intimacy with these three men, he would have become a superior character. Athos was the first to leave him, in order that he might retire to a small property which he had inherited near Blois; Porthos, the second, to marry an attorney's wife; and lastly, Aramis, the third, to take orders, and become a priest. From that day, d'Artagnan felt lonely and powerless, without courage to pursue a career in which he could only distinguish himself on condition that each of his three companions should endow him with one of the gifts which each had received from heaven.

Notwithstanding his commission in the Musketeers, d'Artagnan felt completely solitary. For a time the delightful remembrance of Constance Bonacieux left on his character a poetic tinge, perishable, and, like all other recollections in the world, these impressions were, by degrees, effaced. A garrison life is fatal even to the most aristocratic organizations; and, imperceptibly, d'Artagnan, always in the camp, always on horseback, always in garrison, became a thorough soldier. His early refinement of character was not only not lost, but was even greater than ever; but it was now applied to the little, instead of to the great things of life—to the material condition of the soldier—comprised under the heads of a good lodging, a good table, a good hostess. These important advantages d'Artagnan found to his own taste in the Rue Tiquetonne, at the sign of the Nannygoat.

At the period of his first stay here, the landlady, a fair, fresh Fleming, about twenty-five, fell deeply in love with him. After some pranks in consequence of which the officer had drawn his sword several times against the jealous husband, this man had disappeared, forever deserting the home, but selling some casks of wine surreptitiously and carrying off all the money and his wife's jewelry. It was given out that he was dead, and his wife stoutly asserted this, as the idea of widowhood was sweet. In short, after three years of this connection, which d'Artagnan had no wish to break, as his hostess and the lodging became more enjoyable daily, for both were a credit to him, the woman had the exorbitant conceit to become his wife.

"For shame," retorted he; "to propose bigamy. You cannot really think of it, my darling."

"But I am quite sure that he is no more."

"He was a very vexatious chap, and will come back on purpose to get us hanged."

"No, for you are so skillful and brave that you can kill him if he turns up."

"Plague on't, that is only another means of getting hanged."

"So you reject my request?"

"I decidedly do, and with a relish!"

The buxom landlady was heart-broken. She wanted the dashing trooper not only as better-half, but as an idol, he was such a splendid fellow and had such a killing moustache.

Along in the fourth year of this arrangement, came the expedition into Franche-Comte, for which d'Artagnan was appointed to go, and he made his preparations. There was loud lamentation, ceaseless tears, and solemn promises to remain faithful forever—all these on the hostess's side, of course. The soldier was too great a nobleman to pledge anything. All he was thinking of was to add glory to his name. In this connection, d'Artagnan's courage was well known: he risked his body wastefully for his salary, and as he charged at the front of his company, he caught a bullet through his chest which made him measure his length upon the battlefield. He was seen to fall from his charger and not to rise again, so that he was reported dead, and all those likely to gain by his removal naturally repeated at venture that he was slain. But our hero was not the sort to let himself be killed as easily as this. After having remained in a swoon through the daytime on the field, the night's coolness revived him, and, gaining a hamlet, he knocked at a cottage door, and it opened to receive him.

Cured, cared for, until in better condition than ever, one fine morning he set out on the homeward road, and as soon as he was in the capital, he turned his steps to his former lodgings.

But in his room, the Musketeer found a suit of men's clothes hanging up, and he thought that the husband had come back.

He questioned of the new waiter and maid, for the mistress was out for a walk. With the master, they said, so the officer presumed that the lawful lord had come home, indeed.

"If I had some money," he reasoned, "I should take myself off —but I must wait and follow the hostess's advice, so as to baffle this awkward returned spirit."

He was finishing this monologue—a proof that the monologue is the natural resort of great minds in emergencies—when the maid, peering out at the door, suddenly called: "Here comes mistress, with the master."

D'Artagnan glanced up the street and beheld at the corner the landlady waddling along, hanging on the arm of a huge

Swiss guardsman, who swaggered with airs that pleasantly reminded the viewer of his old friend Porthos.

"Is that your master?" muttered the soldier. "It strikes me
he has grown tremendously."

He went and sat down in the large room where he must
meet the eye. On coming in the first, the hostess perceived him
and uttered a faint shriek. Upon this recognition, the officer
arose, ran to her and bussed her on her plump cheek. She
turned pale, and the Swiss started in stupefaction.

"Oh, lord, monsieur, is it you?" she inquired, in the greatest agitation. "What do you want?"

"I suppose the gentleman is your brother, or your cousin?"
returned the intruder, without departing from the line he had
traced: in pursuance farther of which he flung himself, without waiting for her answer, flat on the Helvetian, who submit-
ted to the hug with utmost placidity.

"Which did you say the man was?"

The only response from the hostess was in sobs.

"What is this Swiss?" demanded d'Artagnan.

"The gentleman intends to marry me," stammered the lady,
between two spasms.

"So your husband is really gone, eh?"

"What pishnessh ish dat of yoursh?" inquired the Swiss.

"A good deal, for the lady cannot marry without my consent,
and I am not going to give it to a Swiss Cheese;" such was the
Musketeer's answer.

The hearer became red as a poppy; he was in his resplend-
ent uniform, and the speaker was wrapped in a warworn military grey cloak: the former was over six feet, and the latter about five feet; and the Swiss thought he was at home and
the Frenchman an interloper.

"Will you get yourseluf out this of?" challenged the foreigner,
stamping like one who was really angry.

"Me? not a bit of it," replied d'Artagnan.

"Then he must be put out," remarked the waiter, who could
not understand so little a man disputing with so big a one.

"Oh, you begin to keep your place and don't you stir if you
want any ear left on you." So the officer, whose wrath was
also rising, pulled the interrupter's ear. "As for this illustrious descendant of William Tell, he must go and make
a bundle of his toggery, which is in the way in my rooms,
and go hunt for another house pretty quickly."

The Swiss laughed boisterously.

"Vy should I tepart?" he wanted to be informed.

"I see that you understand French," returned d'Artagnan,
"so come and take a walk with me, and I will explain the rest
of the mystery."

The landlady, who knew that the speaker was a famous
fencer, began to weep and tear her golden locks.

"Then, if you want him spared, send him off," said d'Artagnan.

"Booh, booh," said the Swiss, who had understood the invitation after time enough, "you mad must be to brobose to gross swords mit me."

"I am lieutenant of the King's Musketeers, and consequently your superior in rank," said the Frenchman, "but I waive all that since we are only at odds about our billet for the night. You know the custom to fight for the bed. Come right along, and whichever returns can have the room."

He dragged away the Swiss in spite of the wailing of the hostess, who at heart leaned towards her first lover, and yet was not sorry to have the proud Musketeer given a lesson for refusing her hand.

It was night when the two adversaries reached the Montmartre ditches, where the challenger politely asked the other to yield him up the room and keep away: but the Swiss shook his head and drew his sword.

"Then here you shall lie!" said d'Artagnan. "Cursed poor accommodation, but it is not my fault, and you have brought it on yourself."

He drew his blade now and crossed that of the foe. He had a strong wrist to contend with, but his suppleness was superior to mere force. The Swiss's point never once found the Musketeer's body, while he received a couple of stabs without feeling them from the cold; but soon loss of blood and the resulting weakness constrained him to sit down.

"I told you so," commented d'Artagnan; "you have got yourself into a nice mess by being pigheaded. However, you will come round in a fortnight. Stay where you are, and I will send your things here by the tavern-boy. Keep well till we meet again. By the way, let me recommend the Spinning Cat tavern, in the Rue Montorgueil, where the cheer is good if the hostess is not quite as luscious. Fare thee well!"

Returning merrily to the tavern, he did send the man his apparel, the boy finding him seated where he was left, stunned by the coolness of the victor. The hostess, the waiter, and the maid, showed the latter such esteem as Hercules must have met if he returned to earth to recommence his Twelve Labors.

"Now, fair Madeleine," said d'Artagnan, when they were alone, "you ought to have known the distance between a Swiss and a French nobleman. You have acted like the keeper of a low-down wine-shop, which is so much the worse for you as your conduct loses you my esteem and my custom. I drive the Swiss away to humble you; I take myself off because I cannot dwell where I despise. Hello, boy—carry my valise to the Hogshead of Love tavern, Rue des Bourdonnais. Good bye, madam."

In thus speaking, he was majestic and affectionate withal, so that the woman had to drop at his feet, beg for pardon, and retain him with gentle violence. Need we say more? the spit turned laden with roast meat—the frying-pan sputtered—the penitent Madeleine wept—the returned warrior felt hunger and cold—and love re-awoke in him: he forgave, and he remained.

Thus it is that Lieutenant d'Artagnan still lodged in the Nannygoat Inn.

CHAPTER VII.

AN OLD ACQUAINTANCE COMES TO HELP IN A QUANDARY.

In the evening, after his conversation with Mazarin, he returned to his lodgings, absorbed in reflection. His mind was full of the fine diamond which he had once called his own, and which he had seen on the minister's finger that night.

"Should that diamond ever fall into my hands again," such was his reflection, "I should turn it at once into money; I should buy, with the proceeds, certain lands around my father's chateau, which is a pretty place—well enough—but with no land to it at all except a garden about the size of the Cemetery des Innocents; and I should wait, in all my glory, till some rich heiress, attracted by my good looks, chose to marry me. Then I should like to have three sons; I should make the first a nobleman, like Athos; the second a good soldier, like Porthos; the third an excellent abbé, like Aramis. Faith! that would be a far better life than I lead now; but M. Mazarin is a mean wretch who won't dispossess himself of his diamond in my favor."

On entering the Rue Tiquetonne he heard a tremendous noise, and found a dense crowd near the house.

He was told that twenty citizens had attacked a carriage which was escorted by a troop of the Cardinal's bodyguard; but a reinforcement having come up, the assailants had been put to flight, and the leader had taken refuge in the hotel next to his lodgings; the house was now being searched.

In his youth, d'Artagnan had often headed the *bourgeoisie* against the military, but he was cured of all those hot-headed propensities; besides, he had the Cardinal's hundred pistoles in his pocket; so he went into the hotel without saying a word; he found Madeleine alarmed for his safety, and anxious to tell him all the events of the evening, but he cut her short by ordering her to put his supper in his room, and to give him with it a bottle of good Burgundy.

He took his key and his candle, and went upstairs to his bedroom. He had been contented, for the convenience of the house, to lodge on the fourth story; and truth obliges us even to confess that his chamber was just above the gutter and below the roof. His first care in entering it was to lock up, in an old bureau with a new lock, his bag of money, and then as soon as supper was ready, he sent away the waiter who brought it up, and sat down to table.

Not to reflect on what had passed, as one might fancy. No—d'Artagnan considered that things are never well done when they are not reserved to their proper time. He was hungry; he supped, he went to bed. Neither was he one of those who think that the silence of the night brings good counsel with it. In the night he slept, but in the morning, refreshed and calm, he was inspired with the clearest views of everything. It was long since he had had any reason for his morning's inspiration, but he had always slept all night long. At daybreak he awoke, and made a turn round his room.

"In '43," he said, "just before the death of the late Cardinal, I received a letter from Athos. Where was I then? Let me see. Oh! at the siege of Besancon! I was in the trenches. He told me—let me think—what was it? That he was living on a small estate—but where? I was just reading the name of the place when the wind blew my letter away—I suppose to the Spaniards; there's no use in thinking any more about Athos. Let me see,—with regard to Porthos, I received a letter from him, too. He invited me to a hunting party on his property in the month of September, 1646. Unluckily, as I was then in Bearn, on account of my father's death, the letter followed me there. I had left Bearn when it arrived, and I never received it until the month of April, 1647; and as the invitation was for September, 1646, I couldn't accept it. Let me look for this letter; it must be with my title-deeds."

D'Artagnan opened an old casket, which stood in a corner of the room, and which was full of parchments, referring to an estate, during a period of two hundred years lost to his family. He uttered an exclamation of delight, for the large handwriting of Porthos was discernable, and beneath it some lines traced by his worthy spouse.

D'Artagnan eagerly searched for the date of this letter; it was dated from the Chateau du Vallon.

Porthos had forgotten that any other address was necessary; in his pride he fancied that everyone must know the Chateau du Vallon.

"Devil take the vain fellow," said d'Artagnan. "However, I had better find him out first, since he can't want money. Athos must have become an idiot by this time from drinking. Aramis must be absorbed in his devotional exercises."

He cast his eyes again on the letter. There was a postscript.

"I write by the same courier to our worthy friend Aramis in his convent."

"In his convent! what convent?" There are about two hundred in Paris, and about three thousand in France; and then, perhaps, on entering the convent he has changed his name.

Ah! if I were but learned in theology, I should recollect what it was he used to dispute about with the Curate of Montdidier and the Superior of the Jesuits, when we were at Crêvecour; I should know what doctrine he leans to, and I should glean from that what saint he has adopted as his patron.

"Well, suppose I go back to the Cardinal and ask him for a passport into all the convents one can find; even into the nunneries? It would be a curious idea, and maybe I should find my friend under the name of Achilles. But, no! I should ruin myself in the Cardinal's opinion. Great people only thank you for doing for them what's impossible; what's possible, they say, they can do themselves, and they are right."

So he was perfectly ignorant either where to find Aramis any more than Porthos, and the affair was becoming a matter of great perplexity, when he fancied he heard a pane of glass break in his room window. He thought directly of his bag, and rushed from the inner room where he was sleeping. He was not mistaken; as he entered his bedroom a man was getting in by the window.

"Ah! you scoundrel," cried d'Artagnan, taking the man for a thief, and seizing his sword.

"Sir," cried the man. "In the name of heaven, put your sword back into the sheath, and don't kill me unheard. I'm no thief, but an honest citizen, well off in the world, with a house of my own. My name is—ah! but surely you are M. d'Artagnan?"

"And you—Planchet!" cried the lieutenant.

"At your service, sir," said Planchet, overwhelmed with joy; "and I'm still capable of serving you."

"Perhaps so," replied d'Artagnan. "But why the devil do you run about the house tops at seven o'clock in the morning in January?"

"Sir," said Planchet, "you must know; but, are you on good terms with M. de Rochefort?"

"Perfectly; one of my dearest friends, but he is in the Bastille!"

"That is to say, he was there," replied Planchet. "But in returning thither last night, as his carriage was crossing the Rue de la Ferronnerie, his guards insulted the people, who began to abuse him. The prisoner thought this a good opportunity for escape; he called out his name, and cried for help. I was there. I heard the name of Rochefort. I remembered him well. I said in a loud voice that he was a prisoner, and a friend of the Duke de Beaufort, who called for help. The people were infuriated; they stopped the horses, and cut the escort to pieces, whilst I opened the door of the carriage, and M. de Rochefort jumped out and was lost amongst the crowd. At this moment a patrol passed by. I was obliged to beat a retreat towards the Rue Tiquetonne; I was pursued, and took refuge in a house next to this, where I have been concealed till this morning on the top of the house, between two mattresses. I ventured to run along the gutters, and——"

"Well," interrupted d'Artagnan, "I am delighted that de Rochefort is free; but as for you, you have done a pretty thing, for the king's men will hang you if you fall into their clutches. Do you expect his officer to give you asylum?"

"Ah! sir, you know well I would risk my life for you."

"You may add that you have risked it, Planchet. I have not forgotten all I owe you. Sit down there, and eat in security. I see you cast expressive glances at the remains of my supper."

"Yes, sir; for all I've had since yesterday was a slice of bread and butter with preserve on it. Although I don't despise sweet things in proper time and place, yet I found that supper rather light."

"Poor fellow!" said d'Artagnan. "Well, come; set to."

"Ah, sir! you are going to save my life a second time," cried Planchet.

And he seated himself at the table and ate as he did in the merry days, whilst d'Artagnan walked to and fro, and thought how he could make use of Planchet under present circumstances. While he turned this over in his mind Planchet did his best to make up for lost time at the table.

At last he uttered a sigh of satisfaction, and paused, as if he had partially appeased his hunger.

"Come," said d'Artagnan, who thought that it was now a convenient time to begin his interrogations, "do you know where Athos is?"

"No, sir," replied Planchet.

"The devil you do not! Do you know where Porthos is?"

"No—not at all."

"And Aramis?"

"Not in the least."

"The devil! the devil! the devil!"

"But, sir," said Planchet, with a look of surprise, "I know where Bazin is,—he is a beadle in the Cathedral."

"Good, for he must know where his old master is."

D'Artagnan thought for a moment, then took his sword, and put on his cloak ready to go out.

"Sir," said Planchet, in a mournful tone, "do you abandon me thus to my fate! Think, if I am found out here the people of the house, who have not seen me enter it, must take me for a thief."

"True," said d'Artagnan. "Let's see. Can you speak any jargon?"

"I can speak Flemish."

"That will do capitally."

D'Artagnan opened the door, and called out to a waiter to desire Madeleine to come upstairs.

When the landlady made her appearance she expressed much astonishment at seeing Planchet.

"My dear landlady," said d'Artagnan, "I beg to introduce to you your brother, who is arrived from Flanders, and whom I am going to take into my service. Wish your sister good morning. Master Peter."

"Wilkom, suster," said Planchet.

"Goeden day, broder," replied the astonished landlady.

"This is the case," said d'Artagnan: "this is your brother, Madeleine; you don't know him, perhaps, but I do; he has arrived from Amsterdam. You must dress him up during my absence. When I return, which will be in about an hour, you must offer him to me as a servant, and, upon your recommendation, though he doesn't speak a word of French, I take him into my service. You understand?"

"That is to say, I guess your wishes; and that is all that's necessary," said Madeleine.

"You are a precious creature, my pretty hostess, and I'm obliged to you."

The next moment d'Artagnan was on his way to Nôtre Dame.

CHAPTER VIII.

THE DIFFERENT EFFECTS WHICH HALF A PISTOLE MAY PRODUCE UPON A BEADLE AND A CHORISTER.

D'ARTAGNAN congratulated himself upon having found Planchet again; for at that time an intelligent servant was essential to him; nor was he sorry that through Planchet, and the situation which he held in the Rue des Lombards, a connection might be commenced, at that critical period, with the class preparing to make war with the court party. It was like having a spy in the enemy's camp. In this frame of mind, grateful for the accidental meeting with Planchet, pleased with himself, d'Artagnan reached Nôtre Dame. He ran up the steps, entered the church, and addressing a verger who was sweeping the chapel, asked him if he knew Bazin.

"M. Bazin, the beadle," said the verger. "Yes; there he is, attending mass, in the chapel of the Virgin."

D'Artagnan nearly jumped for joy—he had despaired of finding Bazin; but now, he thought, since he held one of the threads, he should be pretty sure to reach the other end of the clue.

He knelt down just opposite to the chapel, in order not to lose sight of his man; and as he had almost forgotten his prayers, and had omitted to take a book with him, he made use of his time in gazing at Bazin.

Bazin wore his dress, it may be observed, with equal dignity and saintly propriety. It was not difficult to understand that he had gained the summit of his ambition. His person had undergone a change, analogous to the change in his dress; his figure was rounded, and, as it were, canonized.

The officiating priest was just finishing the mass, whilst d'Artagnan was looking at Bazin; he pronounced the words of the holy sacrament, and retired, giving the benediction, which was received by the kneeling communicants, to the astonishment of d'Artagnan, who recognized in the priest the Coadjutor himself, the famous Jean François Gondi, who at that time, having a presentiment of the part he was to play, was beginning to court popularity by almsgiving.

D'Artagnan knelt as well as the rest and received his share of the benediction, but when Bazin passed in his turn, with his eyes raised to heaven, and walking, in all humility, the very last, d'Artagnan plucked him by the hem of his robe.

Bazin looked down and started as if he had seen a serpent.

"M. d'Artagnan!" he cried; "Vade retro Satanas!"

"So, my dear Bazin," said the officer, laughing, "this is the way you receive an old friend."

"Sir," replied Bazin, "the true friends of a Christian are those who aid him in working out his salvation; not those who hinder him in so doing."

"I don't understand you, Bazin; nor can I see how I can be a stumbling-block in the way of your salvation," said d'Artagnan.

"You forget, sir, that you very nearly ruined forever that of my master; and that it was owing to you that he was very nearly being damned eternally for remaining a Musketeer, whilst his true vocation was for the church."

"My dear Bazin, you ought to perceive," said d'Artagnan, "from the place in which you find me, that I am much changed in everything. Age produces good sense, and, as I doubt not but that your master is on the road to salvation, I want you to tell me where he is, that he may help me to mine."

"Rather say—to take him back with you into the world. Fortunately, I don't know where he is."

D'Artagnan saw clearly that he should get nothing out of this man, who was evidently telling a falsehood, but whose falsehoods were bold and decided.

"Well, Bazin," said d'Artagnan, "since you do not know where your master lives, let us speak of it no more; let us part good friends. Accept this half-pistole to drink my health."

"I do not drink"—Bazin pushed away with dignity the officer's hand— " 'tis good only for the laity."

"Incorruptible!" murmured d'Artagnan; "I am unlucky;" and whilst he was lost in thought, Bazin retreated towards the sacristy, where he began conversing with the sacristan. Bazin was making with his spare, little, short arms, ridiculous gestures. D'Artagnan perceived that he was enforcing prudence with respect to himself.

D'Artagnan slipped out of the cathedral and placed himself

in ambuscade at the corner; it was impossible that Bazin could go out without his seeing him.

In five minutes Bazin made his appearance, looking in every direction to see if he were observed, but he saw no one. Tranquilized by appearances, he ventured to walk on. Then d'Artagnan rushed out of his hiding place, and arrived in time to see Bazin enter in the Rue de Calandre, a respectable-looking house; and this d'Artagnan felt no doubt, was the habitation of the worthy. Afraid of making any inquiries at this house, d'Artagnan entered a small tavern at the corner, and asked for a cup of hypocras. This beverage required a good half-hour to prepare it, and d'Artagnan had time, therefore, to watch Bazin unsuspected.

He perceived in the tavern a pert boy between twelve and fifteen years of age, whom he fancied he had seen not twenty minutes before, under the guise of a chorister. He questioned him; and as the boy had no interest in deceiving, d'Artagnan learned that he exercised from six o'clock in the morning until nine, the office of chorister; and from nine o'clock till midnight that of a waiter in the tavern.

Whilst he was talking to this lad, a horse was brought to the door of Bazin's house. It was saddled and bridled. Almost immediately Bazin came downstairs.

"Look!" said the boy, "there's our beadle going on a journey."

"And where is he going?" asked d'Artagnan. "Half a pistole if you can find out. Wait till he is set out, and then, marry, come up—ask, and find out. The half-pistole is ready;" and he showed one.

"I understand," said the child, with that jeering smile which marks especially the street boy. "Well, we must wait."

Five minutes afterwards, Bazin set off on a full trot, urging on his horse by the blows of an umbrella, instead of a riding-whip.

Scarcely had he turned the corner than the boy rushed after him like a blood-hound on full scent.

Before five minutes had elapsed he returned.

"Well!" exclaimed the boy; "the thing is done."

"Where is he gone?"

"The half-pistole is for me?"

"Doubtless; answer me."

"I want to see it. Give it me, that I may see that it is not false."

The artful lad took it to his master and got it changed, and returning as he pocketed the silver, he said: "He has gone to Noisy, which is his custom, whereupon he always borrows the butcher's horse."

"Is there a Jesuit monastery at Noisy?"

"A big one."

"What's your name?"

"Friquet."

D'Artagnan wrote down the child's name in his tablets.

"Please, sir," said the boy, "do you think I can get any more half-pistoles any way?"

"Perhaps," replied d'Artagnan.

And, having got out all he wanted, he paid for the hypocras, which he did not drink, and went quickly home.

CHAPTER IX.

D'ARTAGNAN, GOING TO A DISTANCE TO FIND OUT ARAMIS, DISCOVERS HIM RIDING BEHIND PLANCHET.

THE plan adopted by d'Artagnan was soon perfected. He resolved not to reach Noisy in the day, for fear of being recognized: he had therefore plenty of time before him, for Noisy is only three or four leagues from Paris, on the road to Meaux.

At about a league and a half from the city, d'Artagnan, finding that in his impatience he had set out too soon, stopped to give the horses breathing time. The inn was full of disreputable-looking people, who seemed as if they were on the point of commencing some nightly expedition.

D'Artagnan went up to the landlady—praised her wine—which was a horrible production—and heard from her that there were only two houses of importance in the village; one of these belonged to the Archbishop of Paris, and was at that time the abode of his niece, the Duchess of Longueville; the other was a convent of Jesuits, and was the property of these worthy fathers.

At four o'clock d'Artagnan recommenced his journey. He proceeded slowly, and in a deep reverie. Planchet was also lost in thought, but the subject of their reflections was not the same.

One word which their landlady had pronounced had given a particular turn to d'Artagnan's deliberations—this was the name of Longueville. Mdme. de Longueville was one of the highest ladies in the realm; she was also one of the greatest beauties at the court and was now connected by a bond of a political nature with the Princede Marsillac, the eldest son of old Rochefoucauld, whom she was trying to inspire with an enmity towards the Duke de Condé, her brother-in-law, whom she now hated mortally.

D'Artagnan thought of Aramis, who, without possessing any greater advantages than he had, had formerly been the lover of Mdme. de Chevreuse, who had been in another court what Mdme. de Longueville was in that day; and he wondered how it was that there should be in the world people who succeed in every wish—some in ambition, others in love—whilst others, either from chance or from ill-luck, or from some natural de-

fect or impediment, remain only halfway on the road towards
the goal of their hopes and expectations.

He was confessing to himself that he belonged to the latter
class of persons, when Planchet approached, and said:

"I will lay a wager, your honor, that you and I are thinking
of the same thing, of those desperate-looking men who were
drinking in the inn where we rested. They were assembled
there for some bad purpose; and I was reflecting on what my
instinct had told me, in the darkest corner of the stable, when
a man, wrapped in a cloak, and followed by two other men,
came in."

"Ha!"

"I listened, and I learnt that they were lying in wait for a
gentleman who would be in plain clothes, with a servant out
of livery, one who would use his sword if set upon. The chief
was styled Prince by the others, and he promised impunity
from the police."

"Well—what matters all that to us?" said d'Artagnan; "this
is one of those attempts that happen every day. We are unfortunately no longer in those times in which princes would
care to assassinate me. Those were good old days: never
fear—these people owe us no grudge."

"Well—we won't speak of it any more, then;" and Planchet
took his place in d'Artagnan's suite with that sublime confidence
which he had always had in his master, and which fifteen years
of separation had not destroyed.

At about half-past eight o'clock they reached the first houses
in Noisy; everyone was in bed, and not a light was to be seen
in the village. The obscurity was broken only now and then
by the dark lines of roofs of houses. Here and there a dog
barked behind a door, or an affrighted cat fled precipitately,
the only living creatures that seemed to inhabit the village.

Towards the middle of the town, commanding the principal
open space, rose a dark mass, separated from the rest of the
world by two lanes, and overshadowed in the front by enormous
lime trees. D'Artagnan looked attentively at the building.

"This," he said to Planchet, "must be the archbishop's palace, the abode of the fair Mdme. de Longueville; but the convent, where is that?"

"At the end of the village; I know it well."

"Well, then, Planchet, gallop up to it, whilst I tighten my
horse's girth, and come back and tell me if there is a light in
any of the Jesuits' windows."

In about five minutes Planchet returned.

"Sir," he said, "there is one window of the convent lighted
up."

"Hem! If I were a 'Frondeur,'" said d'Artagnan, "I should
knock here and should be sure of a good supper. If I were a
monk, I should knock yonder, and should have a good supper
there, too; whereas, 'tis very possible that between the   castle

and the convent, we shall sleep on hard beds, dying with hunger and thirst."

"Shall I knock?"

"Hush!" replied d'Artagnan: "the light in the window is extinguished."

"Do you hear nothing?" whispered Planchet.

"What is that noise?"

There came a sound like a whirlwind, and at the same time two troops of horsemen, each composed of ten men, sallied forth from each of the lanes which encompassed the house, and surrounded d'Artagnan and Planchet.

"Heyday!" cried d'Artagnan, drawing his sword, and taking refuge behind his horse; "are you not mistaken? is it us you wish to attack—us?"

"Here he is! we have him now," said the horsemen, rushing on d'Artagnan with naked swords.

"Don't let him escape," said a loud voice.

"No, my lord; be assured, we shall not."

D'Artagnan thought it was now time for him to join in the conversation.

"Hallo, gentlemen!" he called out in his Gascon accent, "What do you want?"

"You will soon know," shouted a chorus of horsemen.

"Stop, stop!" cried he whom they had addressed as "my lord;" " 'tis not his voice."

"Ah! just so, gentlemen! pray do people get into passions at random at Noisy? Take care, for I warn you that the first man that comes within the length of my sword—and my sword is long—I rip him up."

The chief of the party drew near.

"What are you doing here?" he asked, in a lofty tone, and like one accustomed to command.

"What are *you* doing here?" replied d'Artagnan.

"Be civil, or I shall beat you; for, although one may not choose to proclaim one's self, one insists on respect suitable to one's rank."

"You don't choose to discover yourself, because you are the leader of an ambuscade," returned d'Artagnan; "but with regard to myself, who am traveling quietly with my own servant, I have not the same reasons as you have to conceal my name!"

"Enough! enough! what is your name?"

"I shall tell you my name in order that you may know where to find me, my lord, or my prince, as it may suit you best to be called," said our Gascon, who did not choose to seem to yield to a threat. "Do you know M. d'Artagnan?"

"Lieutenant in the King's regiment of Musketeers?" said the voice. "If you are he, you have come to defend him we are after."

"I am not here to defend any but myself," retorted d'Artagnan, beginning to wax wroth.

"Never mind," grumbled the party leader, "this is beyond doubt a Gascon, and not our man. We shall meet again, Master d'Artagnan; let us go onwards, gentlemen."

And the troop, angry and complaining, disappeared in the darkness, and took the road to Paris. D'Artagnan and Planchet remained for some moments still on the defensive; then as the noise of the horsemen became more and more distant they sheathed their swords.

"You see, simpleton," said d'Artagnan to his servant, "that they wished no harm to us."

"But to whom, then?"

"I'faith! I don't know, nor care. What I care for now is to make my way into the Jesuits' convent; so, to horse, and let us knock at their door. Happen what will—devil take them—they won't eat us."

And he mounted his horse. Planchet had just done the same, when an unexpected weight fell upon the back of his horse, which sank down.

"Hey! your honor!" cried Planchet, "I've a man behind me."

D'Artagnan turned round and saw plainly, two human forms upon Planchet's horse.

" 'Tis then the devil that pursues us!" he cried, drawing his sword, and preparing to attack the new foe.

"No, no, dear d'Artagnan," said the figure, " 'tis not the devil, 'tis Aramis; gallop fast, Planchet, and when you come to the end of the village, go to the left."

And Planchet, with Aramis behind him, set off full gallop, followed by d'Artagnan, who began to think he was dreaming some incoherent and fantastic dream.

CHAPTER X.

A NICE KIND OF PRIEST.

At the extremity of the village Planchet turned to the left, in obedience to the orders of Aramis, and stopped underneath the window which had a light in it. Aramis alighted, and knocked three times with his hands. Immediately the window was opened, and a ladder of rope was let down from it.

"My friend," said Aramis, "if you like to ascend, I shall be delighted to receive you."

"Pass on before me, I beg of you."

"As the late Cardinal used to say to the late King—only to show you the way, sire." And Aramis ascended the ladder quickly, and reached the window in an instant.

D'Artagnan followed, but less nimbly, showing plainly that the mode of ascent was not one to which he was accustomed.

"Sir," said Planchet, when he saw d'Artagnan on the top of the ladder, "this way is easy for M. Aramis, and even for you; in case of necessity I might also climb up, but my two horses cannot mount the ladder."

"Take them to yonder shed, my friend," said Aramis, pointing to a building in the plain, "there you will find hay and straw for them, then come back here, knock thrice, and we will give you out some provisions. Marry, forsooth, people don't die of hunger here."

And Aramis, drawing in the ladder, closed the window.

D'Artagnan then looked around him attentively.

Never was there an apartment at the same time more war-like and more elegant. Exteriorly nothing in the room showed that it was the habitation of an abbé.

Whilst d'Artagnan was engaged in contemplation the door opened, and Bazin entered; on perceiving the Musketeer he uttered an exclamation which was almost despair.

"My dear Bazin," said d'Artagnan, "I am delighted to see with what wonderful composure you tell a lie even in a church!"

"Sir," replied Bazin, "I have been taught by the good Jesuit fathers, that it is permitted to tell a falsehood when it is told in a good cause."

"So far, well," said Aramis; "but we are dying of hunger. Serve us up the best supper you can, and especially give us some good wine."

Bazin bowed low, and left the room.

"Now we are alone, dear Aramis," said d'Artagnan, "tell me how the devil did you manage to light upon the back of Planchet's horse?"

"Eh! faith!" answered Aramis, "as you see, from Heaven."

"From Heaven!" replied d'Artagnan, shaking his head; "you have no more the appearance of coming from thence than you have of going there."

"My friend," said Aramis, with a look of conceit on his face which d'Artagnan had never observed whilst he was in the Musketeers, "if I did not come from Heaven, at least I was leaving paradise, which is almost the same."

"Here, then, is a puzzle for the learned," observed d'Artagnan; "until now they have never been able to agree as to the situation of paradise, which is at Noisy, upon the site of the archbishop's place. People do not go out from it by the door but by the window; one doesn't descend here by the marble steps of a peristyle, but by the branches of a lime tree; and the angel with a flaming sword who guards this elysium, seems to have changed his celestial name of Gabriel into that of the more terrestrial one of Prince de Marsillac."

Aramis burst into a fit of laughter.

"You were always a merry companion, my dear d'Artagnan," he said, "and your witty Gascon fancy has not deserted you. Yes, there is something in what you say; nevertheless, do not believe that it is Mdme. de Longueville with whom I am in love."

"A plague on't! I shall not do so. After having been so long in love with Mdme. de Chevreuse, you would not lay your heart at the feet of her mortal enemy!"

"Yes," replied Aramis, with an absent air, "yes, that poor duchess! I once loved her much, and, to do her justice, she was very useful to us. Eventually she was obliged to leave France. He was a relentless enemy, that confounded Cardinal," continued Aramis, glancing at the portrait of the old minister. "He had even given orders to arrest her, and would have cut off her head, had she not escaped with her waiting-maid—poor Kitty! The duchess escaped in man's clothes, and a couplet was made upon her"—and Aramis hummed:

> "We do not ride as well as you,
> Who in the regiment appear
> To bear right manfully the spear,
> As well as any trooper true."

"Bravo!" cried d'Artagnan, "you sing charmingly, dear Aramis. I do not perceive that singing masses has altered your voice."

"My dear d'Artagnan," replied Aramis, "you understand, when I was a Musketeer, I mounted guard as seldom as I could; now, when I am abbé, I say as few masses as I can. But to return to our duchess."

"Which? Chevreuse or Longueville?"

"Have I not already told you that there is nothing between me and the Duchess de Longueville? little flirtations, perhaps, and that's all. No, I spoke of the Duchess de Chevreuse; did you see her after her return from Brussels, after the King's death?"

"Yes, she is still beautiful."

"Yes," said Aramis, "I saw her also at that time, I gave her good advice, by which she did not profit. I ventured to tell her that Mazarin was the lover of Anne of Austria. She wouldn't believe me, saying, that she knew Anne of Austria, who was too proud to love such a worthless coxcomb. She since plunged into the cabal headed by the Duke of Beaufort; and the rogue arrested de Beaufort, and banished Mdme. de Chevreuse."

"You know," resumed d'Artagnan, "that she has had leave to return to France?"

"Yes, she is come back, and is going to commit some fresh folly or another; she is much changed."

"In that respect unlike you, my dear Aramis, for you are still the same."

"Yes," replied Aramis, "I have to be extremely careful of my appearance. Do you know that I am growing old; I am nearly thirty-seven."

"Mind, Aramis"—d'Artagnan smiled as he spoke—"since we are together again, let us agree on one point, what age shall we be in future? I was your junior by two or three years, and, if I am not mistaken, I am turned forty."

"Indeed! Then 'tis I who am mistaken, for you have always been a good chronologist. By your reckoning I must be forty-three, at least. Don't let it out, it would ruin me," replied the abbé.

"Don't be afraid, I shall not," said d'Artagnan.

"And now let us go to supper," said Aramis, seeing that Bazin had returned and prepared the table.

The two friends sat down and Aramis began to cut up fowls, partridges, and hams with admirable skill.

"The deuce!" cried d'Artagnan; "do you live in this way always?"

"Yes, pretty well. The Coadjutor has given me dispensations from fasting on account of my health; then I have engaged as my cook the cook who lived with Lafollome,—the famous epicure."

"If it be not an indelicate question," resumed d'Artagnan, "are you grown rich?"

"Oh, heavens! no. I make about twelve thousand francs a year, without counting a little benefice which the prince gave me."

"And how do you make your twelve thousand francs?—by your poems?"

"No, I write sermons, my friend."

"Oh, preach them?"

"No; I sell them to those of my cloth who wish to become great orators."

"Ah, indeed! and you have been tempted by the hopes of reputation yourself?"

"I should, my dear d'Artagnan, have been so, but Nature said 'No.' When I am in the pulpit if by chance a pretty woman looks at me, I look at her again; if she smiles, I smile also. Then I speak at random; instead of preaching about the torments of hell, I talk of the joys of paradise. An event took place in the Church of Saint Louis. A gentleman laughed in my face. I stopped short to tell him that he was a fool, the congregation went out to get stones to stone me with, but whilst they were away, I found means to conciliate those present, so that my foe was pelted instead of me. 'Tis true that he came the next morning to my house, thinking that he had to do with a priest—like other priests."

"And what was the end?"

"We met in the Place Royale—Egad, you know about it."

"Was I not your second?" cried d'Artagnan.

"You were—you know how I settled the matter!"

"Did he die?"

"I don't know. But, at all events, I gave him absolution

'in articulo mortis.' 'Tis enough to kill the body, without killing the soul."

A long silence ensued. Aramis was the first to break it.

"What are you thinking of, d'Artagnan?" he began.

"I was thinking, my good friend, that when you were a Musketeer you turned your thoughts incessantly to the Church, and now that you are an abbé you are perpetually longing to be a Musketeer."

" 'Tis true; man, as you know," said Aramis, "is a strange animal, made up of contradictions. Since I became a priest I dream of nothing but battles. I practice shooting all day long, with an excellent master whom we have here."

"How! here?"

"Yes, in this convent—we have always a 'war instructor' in a convent of Jesuits."

"Then you would have killed the Prince de Marsillac if he had attacked you singly?"

"Certainly," replied Aramis, "or at the head of twenty bravoes!"

"Well, dear Aramis, you ask me why I have been searching for you. I sought you in order to offer you a way of killing M. de Marsillac whenever you please—prince though he may be. Are you ambitious?"

"As ambitious as Alexander."

"Well, my friend, I bring you the means of being rich, powerful, and free, if you wish. Have you, my dear Aramis, thought sometimes of those happy days of our youth that we passed laughing, and drinking, and fighting each other for play?"

"Certainly—and more than once regretted them—'twas a happy time."

"Well, those happy days may return; I am commissioned to find out my companions, and I began by you—who were the very soul of our society."

Aramis bowed rather with respect than pleasure at the compliment.

"To meddle in politics," he exclaimed, in a languid voice, leaning back in his easy chair. "Ah! dear d'Artagnan! see how regular I live—and how easy I am here. I understand that Mazarin is, at this very moment, extremely uneasy as to the state of affairs; he is not a man of genius, as I thought; but of no origin—once a servant of Cardinal Bentivoglio, and he got on by intrigue. He is neither a gentleman in manner nor in feeling, but a sort of buffoon, a punchinello, a pantaloon. Do you know him?—I do not."

"Hem!" said d'Artagnan, "there is some truth in what you say,—but you speak of him, not of his party, nor of his resources."

"It is true—the queen is for him."

"Something in his favor."

"But he will never have the king."

"A mere child."

"A child who will be of age in four years. Then he has neither the parliament nor the people with him—they represent the wealth of the country; nor the nobles, nor the princes—who are the military power of France; but perhaps I am wrong in speaking thus to you, who have evidently a leaning to Mazarin."

"I!" cried d'Artagnan, "not in the least."

"You spoke of a mission."

"Did I?—I was wrong then—no, I said what you say—there is a crisis at hand. Well! let's fly the feather before the wind, let us join to that side to which the wind will carry it, and resume our adventurous life. We were once four valiant knights—four hearts fondly united; let us unite again, not our hearts, which have never been severed, but our courage and our fortunes. Here's a good opportunity for getting something better than a diamond."

"You are right, d'Artagnan; I held a similar project, but, as I have not your faithful and vigorous imagination, the idea was suggested to me. Every one nowadays wants auxiliaries; propositions have been made to me, and I confess to you frankly, that the Coadjutor has made me speak out."

"The Prince de Conti! the Cardinal's enemy?"

"No!—the king's friend."

"But the king will be at the head of the army on Mazarin's side."

"But his heart will be in the army commanded by the Duke de Beaufort."

"M. de Beaufort? He is at Vincennes."

"Did I name M. de Beaufort?" said Aramis.

"He or another. Anything may be done, if we can separate mother and child."

"Never!" cried d'Artagnan. "You, Aramis, know Anne of Austria better than I do. Do you think she will ever forget that her son is her safeguard, her shield, the pledge for her dignity, for her fortune, for her life? Should she forsake Mazarin she must join her son, and go over to the prince's side; but you know better than I do that there are certain reasons why she can never abandon Mazarin."

"Perhaps you are right," said Aramis thoughtfully; "therefore I shall not pledge myself."

"To them, or to us, do you mean, Aramis?"

"To no one.

"I am a priest," resumed Aramis. "What have I to do with politics? I am not obliged to read any breviary. I have a little circle of holy and pretty women; everything goes on smoothly; so certainly, dear friend, I shall not meddle in politics."

"Well, listen, my dear Aramis," said d'Artagnan; "your philosophy convinces me, on my honor. I don't know what devil of an insect stung me, and made me ambitious. I have a post by which I live; at the death of M. de Treville, who is old, I may be a captain, which is a very pretty position for a poor Gascon. Instead of running after adventures, I shall accept an invitation from Porthos; I shall go and shoot on his estate. Do you know if he has estates,—Porthos?"

"1 should think so, indeed. Ten leagues of wood, of marsk land and valleys; he is lord of the hill and the plain, and is now carrying on a suit for his feudal rights against the bishop of Noyon!"

"Good," said d'Artagnan to himself. "That's what I want to know. Porthos is in Picardy!"

Then aloud,—

"And he has taken his old family name of Vallon?"

"To which he adds that of Bracieux—an estate which has been a barony, by my troth."

"So that Porthos will be a baron."

"I don't doubt it. The 'Baroness Porthos' will be particularly charming."

And the two friends began to laugh.

"Adieu, then." And d'Artagnan poured out a glass of wine. "To old times," he said.

"Yes," returned Aramis. "Unhappily those times are passed."

"Nonsense! They will return," said d'Artagnan. "At all events, if you want me, remember the Rue Tiquetonne."

"And I shall be at the convent of Jesuits. From six in the morning to eight at night, come by the door. From eight in the evening until six in the morning, come by the window. Go then, my friend," he added, "follow your career; Fortune smiles on you; do not let her flee from you. As for me, I remain in my humility and my indolence. Adieu!"

"Thou liest, subtle one," said d'Artagnan to himself. "Thou alone, on the contrary, knowest how to choose thy object, and to gain it stealthily."

The friends embraced. They descended into the plain by the ladder. Planchet met them close by the shed. D'Artagnan jumped on his saddle, then the old companions in arms again shook hands. D'Artagnan and Planchet spurred on their horses and took the road to Paris.

But after he had gone about two hundred steps d'Artagnan stopped short, alighted, threw the bridle of his horse over the arm of Planchet, and took the pistols from his saddle-bow to fasten them to his girdle.

"What's the matter?" asked Planchet.

"This is the matter; be he ever so cunning, he shall never say that I was his dupe. Stand here, don't stir, turn your back to the road, and wait for me."

Having thus spoken, d'Artagnan cleared the ditch by the roadside, and crossed the plain so as to wind round the village. He had observed between the house that Mdme. de Longueville inhabited and the convent of Jesuits, an open space surrounded by a hedge.

The moon had now risen and he could see well enough to retrace his road.

He reached the hedge, and hid himself behind it; in passing by the house where the scene which w have related took place, he remarked that the window was again lighted up, and he was convinced that Aramis had not yet returned to his own apartment, and that when he did return there, he would not be alone.

In truth. in a few minutes he heard footsteps approaching, and low whispers.

Close to the hedge the steps stopped.

D'Artagnan knelt down near the thickest part of the hedge.

Two men—to the astonishment of d'Artagnan—appeared shortly: soon, however, his surprise vanished, for he heard the murmurs of a soft, harmonious voice; one of these two men was a woman disguised as a cavalier.

"Oh!" exclaimed the latter.

"What's the matter?" asked Aramis.

"Do you not see that the wind has blown off my hat?"

Aramis rushed after the fugitive hat. D'Artagnan took advantage of the circumstance to find a place in the hedge not so thick, where his glance could penetrate to the supposed cavalier. At that instant the moon, inquisitive, perhaps, like d'Artagnan, came from behind a cloud, and by her light d'Artagnan recognized the large blue eyes, the golden hair, and the classic head of the Duchess de Longueville.

Aramis returned, laughing; one hat on his head, the other in his hand; and he and his companion resumed their walk towards the convent.

"Good!" said d'Artagnan, rising and brushing his knees; "now I have thee—thou art a Frondeur, and the lover of Mdme. de Longueville."

CHAPTER XI.

LORD PORTHOS DU VALLON DE BRACIEUX DE PIERREFONDS.

Thanks to what Aramis had told him, d'Artagnan, who knew already that Porthos called himself du Vallon was now aware that he styled himself, from his estate, de Bracieux; and that he was, on account of his estate, engaged in a lawsuit with the bishop of Noyon.

At eight o'clock in the morning he and Planchet again left home for Compiègne.

The morning was beautiful, and in the early spring-time the birds sang on the trees, and the sunbeams shone through the misty glades, like curtains of golden gauze.

D'Artagnan, sick of the closeness of Paris, thought that when a man had three names of his different estates joined one to another, he ought to be very happy in such a paradise; then he shook his head, saying, "If I were Porthos, and d'Artagnan came to make to me such a proposition as I am going to make to him, I know what I should say to it."

As to Planchet, he thought of nothing.

At the extremity of the wood d'Artagnan perceived the road which had been described to him: and at the end of the road he saw the towers of an immense feudal castle.

"Oh! oh!" he said, "I fancied this castle belonged to the ancient branch of Orleans. Can Porthos have negotiated for it with the Duke de Longueville?"

"Faith!" exclaimed Planchet, "here's land in good condition; if it belongs to M. Porthos, I shall wish him joy."

"Zounds!" cried d'Artagnan, "don't call him Porthos, or even du Vallon: call him de Bracieux or de Pierrefonds; thou wilt ruin my mission otherwise."

As he approached the castle which had first attracted his eye, d'Artagnan was convinced that it could not be there that his friend dwelt; the towers, though solid, and as if built yesterday, were open and broken. One might have fancied that some giant had broken them with blows from a hatchet.

On arriving at the extremity of the castle, d'Artagnan found himself overlooking a beautiful valley, in which, at the foot of a charming little lake, stood several scattered houses, which, humble in their aspect, and covered, some with tiles and others with thatch, seemed to acknowledge as their sovereign lord a pretty castle, built about the beginning of the reign of Henry IV., and surmounted by some stately weathercocks. D'Artagnan felt now no doubt of this being the dwelling of Porthos.

The road led straight up to this château, which, compared to its ancestor on the hill, was exactly what a fop would have been beside a knight in steel armor. D'Artagnan spurred his horse on and pursued his road, followed by Planchet at the same pace.

In ten minutes d'Artagnan reached the end of an alley regularly planted with fine poplars, and terminating in an iron gate, the points and cross bars of which were gilt. In the midst of this avenue was a grandee dressed in green, and with as much gilding about him as the iron gate, riding on a tall horse. On his right hand and his left were two footmen, with the seams of their dresses laced. A considerable number of clowns were assembled, and rendered homage to their lord.

"Ah!" said d'Artagnan to himself, "can this be the Seigneur du Vallon de Bracieux de Pierrefonds? Well-a-day! how he is wrinkled since he has given up the name of Porthos!"

"This cannot be M. Porthos," observed Planchet, replying, as it were, to his master's thoughts. "M. Porthos was six feet high: this man is scarcely five."

"Nevertheless," said d'Artagnan, "the people are bowing very low to this person."

As he spoke he rode towards the tall horse—to the man of importance and his valets. As he approached he seemed to recognize the features of this individual.

"Lord!" cried Planchet, "can it be?"

At this exclamation the man on horseback turned slowly and with a lofty air; and the two travelers could see, displayed in all their brilliancy, the large eyes, the vermilion visage, and the eloquent smile of Mousqueton.

It was, indeed, Mousqueton—as fat as a pig, rolling about with health, puffed out with good living, who, recognizing d'Artagnan, and acting very differently from the hypocrite Bazin, slipped off his horse and approached the officer with his hat off; so that the homage of the assembled crowd was turned towards this new sun, which eclipsed the former luminary.

"M. d'Artagnan!" cried Mousqueton, his fat cheeks swelling out, and his whole frame perspired with joy. "Monsieur! oh! what joy for my lord and master Du Vallon de Bracieux de Pierrefonds!"

"You good Mousqueton! where is your master?"

"You are on his property."

"But how handsome you are—how fat! how you have prospered and grown stout!" D'Artagnan could not restrain his astonishment at the change which good fortune had produced upon the once famished one.

"Hey? yes, thank God, I am pretty well," said Mousqueton.

"But do you say nothing to friend Planchet?"

"How, my friend Planchet? Planchet, are you there?" cried Mousqueton, with open arms and eyes full of tears.

"My very self," replied Planchet; "but I wanted first to see if you were grown proud."

"Proud towards an old friend? never, Planchet!"

"So far so well," answered Planchet, alighting, and extending his arms to Mousqueton, and the two servants embraced with an emotion which touched those who were present, and made them suppose that Planchet was a great lord in disguise, so greatly did they estimate the position of Mousqueton.

"And now, sir," resumed the latter, when he had rid himself of Planchet, who had in vain tried to clasp his hands round his friend's back, "now, sir, allow me to leave you, for I could not permit my master to hear of your arrival from any one but myself; he would never forgive me for not having preceded you."

"This dear friend," said d'Artagnan, carefully avoiding to utter either the former name borne by Porthos, or his new one; "then he has not forgotten me?"

"Forgotten! he!" cried Mousqueton; "there's not a day, sir, that we don't expect to hear that you were made Marshal."

On d'Artagnan's lips there played one of those rare and melancholy smiles which seemed to come from the depth of his heart; the last trace of youth and happiness which had survived disappointment.

"And you—fellows," resumed Mousqueton, "stay near my lord, the Count d'Artagnan, and pay him every attention in your power, whilst I go to prepare my lord for his visit."

And mounting his horse, Mousqueton rode off down the avenue, on the grass, in an easy gallop.

"Ah! there!—there's something promising," said d'Artagnan. "No mysteries, no cloak to hide one's self in—no cunning policy here; people laugh outright, they weep for joy here. I see nothing but faces a yard broad; in short, it seems to me that Nature herself wears a holiday suit, and that the trees, instead of leaves and flowers, are covered with red and green ribbons, as on gala days."

"As for me," said Planchet, "I seem to smell, from this place even, a most delicate smell of roast meat, and to see the scullions in a row by the hedge, hailing our approach. Ah! sir, what a cook must M. Pierrefonds have, when he was so fond of eating and drinking, even whilst he was only called M. Porthos!"

"Say no more!" cried d'Artagnan. "If the reality corresponds with appearances, I'm lost; for a man so well off will never change his happy condition;—and I shall fail with him, as I have already done with Aramis."

CHAPTER XII.

WEALTH DOES NOT PRODUCE HAPPINESS.

D'ARTAGNAN passed through the iron gate, and arrived in front of the château. He alighted,—as he saw a giant on the steps. Let us do justice to d'Artagnan, that, independent of every selfish wish, his heart palpitated with joy when he saw that tall form and martial demeanor, which recalled to him a good and brave man.

He ran to Porthos and threw himself into his arms; the whole body of servants, arranged in a circle at a respectful distance, looked on with humble curiosity. Mousqueton, at the head of them, wiped his eyes. Porthos put his arm in his friend's.

"Ah! how delightful to see you again, dear friend," he cried, in a voice which was now changed from a baritone into a bass; "you've not then forgotten me?"

"Forget you! oh! dear du Vallon, does one forget the happiest days of one's youth—one's dearest friends—the dangers we have dared together? on the contrary, there is not an hour that we have passed together that is not present to my memory."

"Yes, yes," said Porthos, turning to give his moustache a curl which it had lost whilst he had been alone. "Yes, we did some fine things in our time, and we gave that poor Cardinal some skeins to unravel."

And he heaved a sigh.

"Under any circumstances," he resumed, "you are welcome, my dear friend; you will help me to recover my spirits; tomorrow we will hunt the hare on my plain, which is a superb tract of land, or we'll pursue the deer in my woods, which are magnificent. I have four harriers, which are considered the swiftest in the country, and a pack of hounds which are unequalled for twenty leagues round."

And Porthos heaved another sigh.

"But first," interposed d'Artagnan, "you must present me to Mdme. du Vallon."

A third sigh from Porthos.

"I lost Mdme. two years ago," he said, "and you find me still in affliction on that account. That was the reason why I left my Château du Vallon, near Corbeil, and came to my estate, Bracieux. Poor Mdme., her temper was uncertain, but she came at last to accustom herself to my ways and to understand my little wishes."

"So you are free now—and rich?"

"Alas!" replied Porthos, "I am a widower, and have forty thousand francs a year. Let us go to breakfast "

"I shall be happy to do so; the morning air has made me hungry."

"Yes," said Porthos, "my air is excellent."

They went into the château; there was nothing but gilding. A gilt table ready set out, awaited them.

"You see," said Porthos, "this is my usual style."

"Devil take me!" answered d'Artagnan, "I wish you joy of it. The king has nothing like this."

"No," answered Porthos; "I hear it said that he is very badly fed by Cardinal Mazarin. Taste this cutlet, my dear d'Artagnan; 'tis off one of my sheep."

"You have very tender mutton, and I wish you joy of it," said d'Artagnan.

"Yes, the sheep are fed in my meadows, which are excellent pasture."

"Give me another cutlet."

"No, try this hare, which I killed yesterday in one of my warrens."

"Zounds! what a flavor!" cried d'Artagnan; "ah! fed on thyme only."

"And how do you like my wine?" asked Porthos; "it is fine, isn't it?"

"Capital."

"Home-growth, though, from a slope on the south there, yielding twenty hogsheads." But he sighed again, the fifth time, for his guest kept tally.

"You seem to be snug—what makes you sigh?"

"My dear fellow," replied Porthos; "to be candid with you, I am not happy."

"You not happy, Porthos? You, who have a château, meadows, hills, woods—you who have forty thousand francs a year—you not happy?"

"My dear friend, all those things I have, but I am alone in the midst of them."

"Surrounded, I suppose, only by clod-hoppers, with whom you could not associate."

Porthos turned rather pale, and drank off a large glass of wine.

"No; but just think, there are paltry country squires who have all some title or another, and pretend to go back as far as Charlemagne, or at least to Hugh Capet. When I first came here, being the last comer, it was to me to make the first advances. I made them, but, you know, my dear friend, Mdme. du Vallon——"

Porthos, in pronouncing these words, seemed to gulp down something.

"Mdme. du Vallon was of doubtful gentility. She had in her first marriage (I don't think, d'Artagnan, I am telling you anything new), married a lawyer; they thought that 'sickening'; you can understand that's a word bad enough to make one kill thirty thousand men. I have killed two, which has made people hold their tongues, but has not made me their friend. So that I have no society—I live alone; I am sick of it—my mind preys on itself."

D'Artagnan smiled. He now saw where the breastplate was weak, and prepared the blow.

"But now," he said, "that you are a widower, your wife's connections cannot injure you."

"Yes, but understand me; not being of a race of historic fame, like the de Coucys, who were content to be plain sirs, or the Rohans, who didn't wish to be dukes, all these people, who are all counts, go before me at church, in all the ceremonies, and I can say nothing to them. Ah! if I were merely a——"

"A baron, don't you mean?" cried d'Artagnan, finishing his friend's sentence.

"Ah!" cried Porthos; "would I were but a baron!"

"Well, my friend, I am come to give you this very title, which you wish for so much."

Porthos gave a jump which shook all the room; two or three bottles fell and were broken. Mousqueton ran thither, hearing the noise.

Porthos waved his hand to Mousqueton to pick up the bottles.

"I am glad to see," said d'Artagnan, "that you have still that honest lad with you."

"He's my steward," replied Porthos; "he will never leave me. Go away now, Mouston."

"So he's called Mouston," thought d'Artagnan. "Mousqueton is too long a word to pronounce."

"Well," he said aloud, "let us resume our conversation later —your people may suspect something—there may be spies about. You can't suppose, Porthos, what I have to say relates to important matters."

"Devil take them, let us walk in the park," answered Porthos, "for the sake of digestion."

"Egad," said d'Artagnan, "the park is like everything else, and there are as many fish in your pond as rabbits in your warren; you're a happy man, my friend, but I must frankly tell you that you must change your mode of life."

"How?"

"Go into harness again, gird on your sword, run after adventures, and leave, as in old times, a little of your fat on the roadside."

"Ah! hang it!" said Porthos.

"I see you are spoiled, dear friend, you are corpulent, your arm has no longer that movement of which the late Cardinal's Guards had so many proofs."

"Ah! my fist is strong enough, I swear," cried Porthos, extending a hand like a shoulder of mutton.

"Are we then to go to war? Against whom?"

"Are you for Mazarin, or for the princes?"

"I am for no one."

"That is to say you are for us. Well, I tell you that I come to you from the Cardinal."

This speech was heard by Porthos in the same sense as if it had still been in the year 1640, and related to the great Cardinal.

"Ho! ho! what are the wishes of his Eminence?"

"He wishes to have you in his service. Rochefort has spoken of you—and since, the Queen—and, to inspire us with confidence, she has even placed in Mazarin's hands that famous diamond—you know about it—that I had sold to M. des Essarts, and of which I don't know how she regained possession."

"But it seems to me," said Porthos, "that she ought to give it back to you."

"So I think," replied d'Artagnan; "but kings and queens are strange beings, and have odd fancies; nevertheless, since it is they who have riches and honors, one is devoted to them."

"Yes, one is devoted to them," repeated Porthos; "and you, to whom are you devoted, now?"

"To the King, the Queen, and to the Cardinal; moreover, I have answered for your devotion also; for, notwithstanding your forty thousand francs a year, and, perhaps even for the very reason that you have forty thousand francs a year, it

seems to me that a little coronet would do well on your carriage, hey?"

"Yes, indeed," said Porthos.

"Well, my dear friend, win it—it is at the point of our
swords. We shall not interfere with each other—your object
is a title; mine money. If I can get enough to rebuild Artagnan,
which my ancestors, impoverished by the Crusades, allowed to
fall into ruins, and to buy thirty acres of land about it, it is all
I wish. I shall retire and die tranquilly there."

"For my part," said Porthos, "I wish to be made a baron."

"You shall be one."

"And have you not seen any of our other friends?"

"Yes, I have seen Aramis."

"And what does he wish? To be a bishop?"

"Aramis," answered d'Artagnan, who did not wish to un-
deceive Porthos, "Aramis, fancy! has become a Jesuit, and lives
like a bear. My offers could not rouse him."

"So much the worse! He was a clever man—and Athos?"

"I have not yet seen him. Do you know where I shall find
him?"

"Near Blois. He is called Bragelonne. Only imagine, my dear
friend. Athos, who was of as high birth as the Emperor, and
who inherits one estate which gives him the title of count,
what is he to do with all those dignities—Count de la Fère,
Count de Bragelonne?"

"And he has no children with all these titles?"

"Ah!" said Porthos, "I have heard that he had adopted a young
man who resembles him greatly."

"What, Athos? Our Athos, who was as virtuous as Scipio?
Have you seen him?"

"No."

"Well, I shall see him to-morrow and tell him about you;
but I am afraid that his liking for wine has aged and degraded him."

"Yes, he used to drink a great deal," replied Porthos.

"And then he was older than any of us," added d'Artagnan.

"Some years only. His gravity made him look older."

"Well, then, if we can get Athos, all will be well. If we cannot, we will do without him. We two are worth a dozen."

"Yes," said Porthos, smiling at the remembrance of his former
exploits; "but we four altogether would be equal to thirty-six;
more especially as you say the work will not be easy. Will it
last long?"

"Two or three years, perhaps."

"So much the better," cried Porthos. "You have no idea,
my friend, how my bones ache since I came here. Sometimes,
on a Sunday, I take a ride in the fields, and on the property of
my neighbors, in order to pick up some nice little quarrel, which
I am really in want of, but nothing happens. Either they respect
or they fear me, which is more likely; but they let me trample

down the clover with my dogs, insult and obstruct everyone, and I come back still more weary and low-spirited—that's all. At any rate, tell me—there's more chance of fighting at Paris, is there not?"

"In that respect, my dear friend, it's delightful. No more edicts, no more of the Cardinal's Guards, no more bloodhounds. Underneath a lamp, in an inn, anywhere, they ask, 'Are you one of the Fronde?' All unsheathe, and that's all that is said. The Guise killed Coligny in the Place Royale, and nothing was said of it."

"Well, then, I decide I shall fight heart and soul for Mazarin; but he must make me baron."

"Zounds!" said d'Artagnan, "that's settled already. I answer for your barony."

On this promise being given, Porthos, who had never doubted his friend's assurance, turned back with him toward the castle.

CHAPTER XIII.

WHILE PORTHOS WAS DISCONTENTED, MOUSQUETON WAS COMPLETELY SATISFIED.

As they turned towards the castle, d'Artagnan thought of the miseries of poor human nature, always dissatisfied with what it has, always desirous of what it has not.

In the position of Porthos, d'Artagnan would have been perfectly happy, and, to make Porthos contented, there was wanting —what?—five letters to put before his three names, and a letter coronet to paint upon the panels of his carriage!

"I shall pass all my life," thought d'Artagnan, "in seeking for a man who is really contented with his lot."

Whilst making this reflection, chance seemed, as it were, to give him the lie direct. When Porthos had left him to give some orders, he saw Mousqueton approaching. The face of the steward, despite one slight shade of care, light as a summer cloud, seemed one of perfect felicity.

"Here is what I am looking for," thought d'Artagnan; "but alas! the poor fellow does not know the purpose for which I am here."

He then made a sign for Mousqueton to come to him.

"Sir," said the servant, "I have a favor to ask you. Do not call me 'Mousqueton,' but 'Mouston.' Since I have had the honor of being my lord's steward, I have taken the last name as more dignified, and calculated to make my inferiors respect me. You, sir, know how necessary subordination is in an establishment of servants."

D'Artagnan smiled. Porthos lengthened out his names— Mousqueton cut his short.

"Well, my dear Mouston," he said, "rest satisfied. I will call you Mouston."

"Oh!" cried Mousqueton, reddening with joy; "if you do me, sir, such an honor, I shall be grateful all my life—'tis too much to ask."

D'Artagnan was secretly touched with remorse—not at inducing Porthos to enter into schemes in which his life and fortune would be in jeopardy—for Porthos, in the title of baron had his object and reward; but poor Mousqueton, whose only wish was to be called Mouston—was it not cruel to snatch him from the delightful state of peace and plenty in which he was?

He was thinking on these matters when Porthos summoned him to dinner.

Whilst desert was on the table the steward came in to consult with his master upon the proceedings of the next day, and also with regard to the shooting party which had been proposed.

"Tell me Mouston," said Porthos—"are my arms in good condition? my military weapons?"

"Yes, my lord—I think so, at any rate."

"Make sure of it; and if they want it, have them rubbed up. See to the horses. Clean up, or make some one else clean my arms. Then take pistols with thee and a hunting knife."

"Are we going to travel, my lord?" asked Mousqueton, rather uneasy.

"Something better still, Mouston."

"An expedition, sir?" asked the steward, whose roses began to change into lilies.

"We are going to return to the service, Mouston," replied Porthos, still trying to restore his moustache to the military curl that it had lost.

"Into the service—the king's service?" Mousqueton trembled; even his fat smooth cheeks shook as he spoke, and he looked at d'Artagnan with an air of reproach; he staggered, and his voice was almost choked.

"Yes and no. We shall serve in a campaign, seek out all sorts of adventures; return, in short, to our former life."

These last words fell on Mousqueton like a thunderbolt. It was these terrible former days which made the present so delightful; and the blow was so great that he rushed out, overcome, and forgot to shut the door.

The two friends remained alone to speak of the future, and to build castles in the air. The good wine which Mousqueton had placed before them gave to d'Artagnan a perspective shining with quadruples and pistoles, and showed to Porthos a blue ribbon and ducal mantle; they were, in fact, asleep on the table when the servants came to beg them to go to bed.

Mousqueton was, however, a little consoled by d'Artagnan,

who the next day told him that in all probability war would always be carried on in the heart of Paris.

The friends took leave of each other on the very border of the estate of Pierrefonds, to which Porthos escorted his friend.

"At least," d'Artagnan said to himself, as he took the road to Villars-Cotterets, "at least I shall not be alone in my undertaking. That devil, Porthos, is a man of immense strength; still, if Athos joins us, well—we shall be three of us to laugh at Aramis—that little coxcomb with his good luck."

At Villars-Cotterets he wrote to the Cardinal:—

"MY LORD,
          I have already one man to offer to your Eminence, and he is well worth twenty. I am just setting out for Blois. Count de la Fère inhabits the castle of Bragelonne, in the environs of that city."

CHAPTER XIV.

TWO ANGELIC FACES.

THE road was long, but the horses upon which d'Artagnan and Planchet rode had been refreshed in the well-supplied stables of the Lord of Bracieux; the master and servant rode side by side, conversing as they went, for d'Artagnan had, by degrees, thrown off the master, and Planchet had entirely ceased to assume the manners of a servant. Planchet was, in truth, no vulgar companion in these new adventures; he was a man of good sense. Without seeking danger, he never shrank from an attack; in short, he had been a soldier, and arms ennoble a man; it was, therefore, on the footing of friends, that d'Artagnan and Planchet arrived in the neighborhood of Blois.

Going along, d'Artagnan, shaking his head, said:

"I know that my going to Athos is useless and absurd; but I owe this step to my old friend, a man who had in him materials for the most noble and generous of characters."

"Oh, M. Athos was a noble gentleman," said Planchet, "was he not? Scattering money about him as Heaven scatters hail. 'Tis a noble gentleman!"

"Yes, true as Gospel," said d'Artagnan, "but one single fault has swallowed up all these fine qualities."

"I remember well," said Planchet—"he was fond of drinking."

"And now," replied d'Artagnan, "behold the sad spectacle that awaits us. We shall find him changed into a bent-down old man, with red nose, and eyes that water; we shall find him extended on some lawn, whence he will look at us with a languid eye, and, perhaps not recognize us. God knows, Planchet, that I should fly from a sight so sad, if I did not wish to show my respect for the illustrious shadow of what was once the Count de la Fère, whom we loved so much."

Planchet shook his head and said nothing.

"And then," resumed d'Artagnan, "to this decrepitude is probably added poverty—for he must have neglected the little that he had, and the dirty scoundrel, Grimaud, more taciturn than ever, and still more drunken than his master—stay, Planchet, all this breaks my heart to think of."

"I fancy myself there, and that I see him staggering and hear him stammering," said Planchet, in a piteous tone, "but at all events, we shall soon know the real state of things, for I think those lofty walls, reddened by the setting sun, are the walls of Blois."

At this moment one of those heavy ox-carts which carry the wood cut in the fine forests of the country to the ports of the Loire, came out of a bye-road full of ruts, and turned on that which the two horsemen were following. A man carrying a long goad with which he urged on his slow team, was walking with the cart.

"Ho! friend," cried Planchet.

"What's your pleasure, gentlemen?" replied the peasant, with a purity of accent peculiar to the people of that district.

"We are looking for the house of M. de la Fère," said d'Artagnan.

The peasant took off his hat on hearing this revered name.

"Gentlemen," he said, "the wood that I am carting is his. I cut it in his copse, and am taking it to the castle."

D'Artagnan determined not to question this man; he did not wish to hear from another what he had himself said to Planchet.

"The castle," he said to himself; "what castle? Ah, I understand: Athos is not a man to be thwarted; he has obliged his peasantry, as Porthos has done his, to call him 'my lord,' and to call his paltry place a castle. He talked tall—our dear Athos—after drinking."

D'Artagnan, after asking the man the right way, continued his route, agitated, in spite of himself, at the idea of seeing once more that singular man whom he had so truly loved, and who had contributed so much by his advice and example to his education as a gentleman. He slackened the pace of his horse, and went on, his head drooping as if in deep thought.

Soon as the road turned, the la Vallière castle appeared in view, then, a quarter of a mile further, a white house, encircled in sycamores, was visible at the further end of a group of trees, which spring had powdered with a snow of flowers.

On beholding this house, d'Artagnan, calm as he was in general, felt an unusual disturbance within his heart—so powerful during the whole course of his life were the recollections of his youth. He proceeded, nevertheless, and came opposite to an iron gate, ornamented in the taste which marked the works of that period.

Through the gate were seen kitchen-gardens carefully attended to, a spacious court-yard, in which neighed several horses held by valets in various liveries, and a carriage drawn by two horses.

"We are mistaken," said d'Artagnan; "this cannot be the house of Athos. Good heavens! suppose he is dead, and that this property now belongs to some one who bears his name. Alight, Planchet, and inquire, for I confess I have not courage to do so."

Planchet alighted.

"Thou must add," said d'Artagnan, "that a gentleman who is passing by wishes to have the honor of paying his respects to the Count de la Fère, and if thou art satisfied with what thou hearest, then mention my name!"

Planchet obeyed these instructions. An old servant opened the door and took in the message which d'Artagnan had ordered Planchet to deliver, in case that his servant was satisfied that this was la Fère whom hey sought. Whilst Planchet was standing on the steps before the house he heard a voice say:

"Well, where is this gentleman, and why do they not bring him here?"

This voice—the sound of which reached d'Artagnan—reawakened in his heart a thousand sentiments, a thousand remembrances that he had forgotten. He sprang hastily from his horse, while Planchet, with a smile on his lips, was advancing towards the master of the house.

"But I know him—I know the lad yonder," said Athos, appearing on the threshold.

"Oh, yes—my lord you know me, and I know you. I am Planchet—Planchet, whom you know well." But the honest servant could say no more, so much was he overcome by this unexpected interview.

"What, Planchet, is M. d'Artagnan here?"

"Here I am, my friend, dear Athos!" cried d'Artagnan in a faltering voice, and almost staggering from agitation.

At these words a visible emotion was expressed on the beautiful countenance and calm features of Athos. He rushed toward d'Artagnan, with his eyes fixed upon him, and clasped him in his arms. D'Artagnan, equally moved, pressed him also close to him, while tears stood in his eyes. Athos then took him by the hand and led him into the drawing-room, where there were several people. Everyone rose.

"I present to you," he said, "the Chevalier d'Artagnan, lieutenant of His Majesty's Musketeers, a devoted friend, and one of the most excellent and bravest gentlemen that I have ever known."

D'Artagnan received the compliments of those who were pres-

ent in his own way; and whilst the conversation became general,
he looked earnestly at Athos.

Strange! Athos was scarcely aged at all! His long dark hair,
scattered here and there with grey locks, fell elegantly over his
shoulders with a wavy curl; his voice was still youthful, as if
only twenty-five years old; and his magnificent teeth, which he
had preserved white and sound, gave an indescribable charm to
his smile.

Meanwhile, the guests, seeing that the two friends were longing to be alone, prepared to depart, when a noise of dogs barking resounded through the court-yard, and many persons said
at the same moment:

"Ah! 'tis Raoul come home."

Athos, as the name of Raoul was pronounced, looked in-
quisitively at d'Artagnan, in order to see if any curiosity was
painted on his face. But d'Artagnan was still in confusion
and turned round almost mechanically, when a fine young man
of fifteen years of age, dressed simply, but in perfect taste,
entered the room, raising, as he came, his hat, adorned with a
long plume of red feathers.

Nevertheless, d'Artagnan was struck by the appearance of
this new personage. It seemed to explain to him the change in
Athos; a resemblance between the boy and the man explained
the mystery of this regenerated existence. He remained listening and gazing.

"Here you are home again, Raoul," said the count.

"Yes, sir," replied the youth, with deep respect, "and I have
performed the commission that you gave me."

"But what's the matter, Raoul?" said Athos, very anxiously.
"You are pale and agitated."

"Sir," replied the young man; "it is on account of an accident
which has happened to our little neighbor."

"Mdlle. de la Vallière?"

"She was walking with her nurse Marceline, in the place
where the woodmen cut the wood, when, passing on horseback,
I stopped. She saw me also, and in trying to jump from the
end of a pile of wood on which she had mounted, the poor child
fell, and was not able to rise again. She has, I fear, sprained
her ankle, and I come, sir, to ask your advice."

"But where is Mdlle. Louise?" asked the count.

"I have brought her here, sir, and I have deposited her in the
charge of Charlotte, who, till better advice comes, has put the
foot into iced water."

The guests now all took leave of Athos, excepting the old
Duke de Barbé, who, as an old friend of the family of la Vallière, went to see little Louise, and offered to take her to Blois
in his carriage.

"You are right, sir," said Athos. "She will be better with her
mother. As for you, Raoul, I am sure it is your fault; some
giddiness or folly."

"No, sir, I assure you," muttered Raoul, "it is not."

"Oh, no, no, I declare it is not!" cried the young girl, while Raoul turned pale at the idea of his being, perhaps, the cause of her disaster.

"Nevertheless, Raoul, you must go to Blois, and you must make your excuse and mine to Mdme. de Saint-Remy, her mother."

The youth looked pleased. He again took in his strong arms the little girl, whose pretty golden head and smiling face rested on his shoulder, and placed her gently in the carriage, then, jumping on his horse with the elegance and agility of a first-rate esquire, after bowing to Athos and d'Artagnan, he went off close by the door of the carriage, in the irside of which his eyes were incessantly riveted.

CHAPTER XV.

AT THE CASTLE OF BRAGELONNE.

WHILE this scene was going on, d'Artagnan remained with open mouth and confused gaze. Everything had turned out so differently to what he had expected, that he was stupefied with wonder.

Athos, who had been observing him and guessing his thoughts, took his arm, and led him into the garden.

"Whilst supper is being prepared," he said, smiling, "you will not, my friend, be sorry to have the mystery which so puzzles you cleared up.

"You are surprised at what you see here?"

"Extremely."

"But above all things, *I* am a marvel to you? Would you not have known me again, in spite of my eight-and-forty years of age?"

"I do not find you the same person at all."

"Ah, I understand," cried Athos, with a slight blush. "Everything, d'Artagnan, even folly, has its limit."

"Then your means, it appears, are improved, you have a capital house, your own, I presume? You have a park, horses, servants."

Athos smiled.

"Yes; I inherited this little property when I quitted the army, as I told you. The park is twenty acres—twenty, comprising kitchen-gardens and a common. I have two horses—I don't count my servant's bung-tailed nag. My sporting dogs consist of two pointers, two harriers, and two setters. And then all this extravagance is not for myself," added Athos, laughing.

"Yes, I see, for the young man Raoul," said d'Artagnan.

"You guess right, my friend; this youth is an orphan, deserted by his mother, who left him in the house of a poor country priest. I have brought him up.

"This child has caused me to recover what I had lost. I had no longer any wish to live for myself. I have lived for him. I have corrected the vices th⁻t I had. I have assumed the virtues that I had not. Precept is much, example is more. I may be mistaken, but I believe that Raoul will be as accomplished a gentleman as our degenerate age could display."

The remembrance of My Lady, a Frenchwoman, who had won this title by marrying an English noble, although Athos, her husband, was alive, and whom the four friends had doomed to death for her manifold crimes, recurred to the Musketeer.

"And are you happy?" he said to his friend.

"As happy as it is allowed to one of God's creatures to be on this earth; but say out all you think, d'Artagnan, for you have not done so."

"You are too bad, Athos; one can hide nothing from you," answered d'Artagnan. "I wish to ask you if you ever feel any emotions of terror resembling——"

"Remorse! I finish your phrase—yes and no. I do not feel remorse, because she, I believe, deserved her punishment. I do not feel remorse, because, had we allowed her to live, she would have persisted in her work of destruction. But I do not mean, my friend, that we were right in what we did. Perhaps all blood that is shed demands an expiation. Hers has been accomplished; it remains, possibly, for us to accomplish ours."

"I have sometimes thought as you do, Athos."

"She had a son, that unhappy woman. Have you ever heard of him?"

"Never."

"He must be about twenty-three years of age," said Athos, in a low tone. "I often think of that young man, d'Artagnan."

"Strange! for I had forgotten him," said the lieutenant.

Athos smiled—the smile was melancholy.

"And her brother-in-law, Lord Winter—do you know anything about him?"

"I know that he is in high favor with Charles I."

"The fortunes of that monarch are now at a low ebb. He shed the blood of Strafford: that confirms what I said just now—blood will have blood: and the Queen?"

"Henrietta of England is at the Louvre."

"Yes, and I hear in the greatest poverty. Her daughter during the bitterest cold, was obliged, for want of fire, to remain in bed. Why did she not ask from any one of us a home instead of from Mazarin? She should have wanted for nothing."

At this instant they heard the sound of horses' feet.

" 'Tis Raoul, who is come back," said Athos; "and we can now hear how the poor child is. Well," he added, "I hope the accident has been of no consequence?"

"They don't know yet, sir, on account of the swelling; but the doctor is afraid some muscle may be injured."

At this moment a youth, half-peasant, half-footboy, came to announce supper.

Athos led his guests into a dining room of moderate size, the windows of which opened on one side on the garden—on the other on a hothouse, full of magnificent flowers.

D'Artagnan glanced at the dinner service. The plate was magnificent, old, and belonging to the family. "Let us sit down to supper. Call Charles," he added, addressing the boy who waited.

"My good Charles, I particularly recommend to your care Planchet, the lackey of M. d'Artagnan. He likes good wine; now you have the key to the cellar—he has slept a long time on a hard bed, so he won't object to a soft one—take care of him, I beg of you." Charles bowed and retired.

"You think of everything," said d'Artagnan; "and I thank you for Planchet, my dear Athos."

Raoul started on hearing this name, and looked at the count to be quite sure that it was he thus addressed.

"That name sounds strange to you," said Athos, smiling; "it was my by-name when M. d'Artagnan, two other gallant friends, and myself performed some feats of arms at the siege of La Rochelle, under the deceased Cardinal. My friend is still so kind as to address me by that dear old appellation which makes my heart glad when I hear it."

"'Tis an illustrious name," said the lieutenant, "and had, one day, triumphal honors paid to it."

"What do you mean, sir?" inquired Raoul.

The Musketeer could not refrain from relating one of the episodes in which he and his host figured in that Odyssey of gallantry and bravery called "The Three Musketeers."

"D'Artagnan does not tell you, Raoul," said Athos, in his turn, "that he was reckoned one of the best swordsmen of his time—a thigh of iron, a wrist of steel, a sure eye, and a glance of fire—that's what his adversary met with from him. He was eighteen, only three years older than you are, Raoul, when I saw him at this work—pitted against tried men."

"And was M. d'Artagnan the conqueror?" said the young man, with glistening eyes.

"I killed one man, I believe," replied d'Artagnan, with a look of inquiry directed to Athos; "another I disarmed, or wounded. I don't remember which——"

"Wounded," said Athos; "oh you were a strong one."

The young man would willingly have prolonged this conversation all night, but Athos pointed out to him that his guest must need repose. D'Artagnan would fain have declared that he was not fatigued; but Athos insisted on his retiring to his chamber, conducted thither by Raoul.

CHAPTER XVI.

ATHOS AS A DIPLOMATIST.

D'ARTAGNAN retired to bed—not to sleep but to think over all that he had heard that evening. As he was good-hearted, and had once had for Athos a liking, which had grown into a sincere friendship, he was delighted at thus meeting a man full of intelligence and moral strength, instead of a wretched drunkard. He admitted, without annoyance, the continued superiority of Athos over himself, devoid as he was of that jealousy which might have s ddened a less generous disposition: he was delighted also that the high qualities of Athos appeared to promise favorable for his mission. Nevertheless, it seemed to him that Athos was not, in all respects, sincere and frank. Who was the youth whom he had adopted, and who bore so great a resemblance to him? What could explain Athos' having re-entered the world, and the extreme sobriety which he had observed at table? The absence of Grimaud, his old valet, whose name had never once been uttered by Athos, gave d'Artagnan uneasiness. It was evidently either that he no longer possessed the confidence of his friend, or that Athos was bound by some invisible claim, or that he had been forewarned of the lieutenant's visit.

Resolved to seek an explanation of all these points on the following day, d'Artagnan, in spite of his fatigue, prepared for an attack, and determined that it should take place after breakfast. He determined to cultivate the good will of the youth Raoul, and, either whilst fencing with him, or out shooting, to exact from his simplicity some information which would connect the Athos of the old times with the Athos of the present. But d'Artagnan, quite disposed to adopt a subtle course against the cunning of Aramis, or the vanity of Porthos, was ashamed to equivocate with the truehearted, open Athos.

There was now perfect stillness in the house, except footsteps, up and down in the chamber above,—as he supposed, the bedroom of Athos.

"He is walking about and thinking," thought d'Artagnan, "but of what? It is impossible to know; everything else might be guessed, but not that."

At length, Athos went to bed, apparently, for the noise ceased.

Silence, and fatigue together, overcame d'Artagnan, and sleep overtook him also. He was not, however, a good sleeper. Scarcely had dawn gilded his window-curtains than he sprang out of bed and opened the windows. Somebody, he perceived, was in the court-yard, but moving stealthily. True to his custom of never passing anything over that was within his power to know, d'Artagnan looked out of the window and perceived the close red coat and brown hair of Raoul.

D'Artagnan saw him ride by like a dart, bending, as he went, beneath pendant flowery branches of the maple trees and acacias. The road, as d'Artagnan had observed, was the way to Blois.

"So!" thought the Gascon, "he is a young blood who has already his love affair, who doesn't at all agree with Athos in his hatred to the fair sex. He's not going to hunt, for he has neither dogs nor arms; he's not going on a message, for he goes secretly. Why does he go in secret? Is he afraid of me, or of his father? for I am sure the count is his father. By Jove! I shall know about that soon, for I shall speak out to Athos."

Day was advanced as the Gascon went downstairs. Scarcely had he descended the last step than he saw Athos, bent down towards the ground, as if he were looking for a coin in the dust.

"Good day to you; have you slept well?"

"Excellently well, Athos; but what are you looking for? are you a tulip fancier?"

"My dear friend, if I were, you should not laugh at me for being so. I was looking anxiously for some iris roots which I planted here, close to this reservoir, and which some one has trampled upon this morning. These gardeners are the most careless people in the world; in bringing the horse out of the water, they've allowed him to walk over the border."

D'Artagnan began to smile.

"Ah! you think so, do you?"

"Who went out this morning?" Athos asked uneasily. "Has any horse got loose from the stable?"

"Not likely," answered the Gascon; "these marks are regular."

"Where is Raoul?" asked Athos; "how is it that I have not seen him?"

"Hush!" exclaimed d'Artagnan, putting his finger on his lips; and he related what he had seen, watching Athos all the while.

"Ah! he's gone to Blois; the poor boy—to inquire after little la Vallière; she has sprained her foot, you know. Don't you see that Raoul is in love?"

"Indeed! with whom? with a child of seven years old?"

"Dear friend, at Raoul's age the heart is so ardent that it must expand towards some object or another, fancied or real; well, his love is half one—half the other. She is the prettiest little creature in the world, with flaxen hair, blue eyes—at once saucy and languishing."

"But what say you to Raoul's fancy?"

"Nothing; I laugh at Raoul; but this first desire of the heart is imperious."

" 'Tis want of occupation; you do not employ Raoul, so he takes his own way of employing himself."

"Exactly so; therefore I think of sending him away from this place, though it will break his heart. So long as three or four years ago, he used to adorn and adore his little idol, whom he will some day fall in love with in good earnest, if he remains here. The parents of little la Vallière have for a long time perceived and been amused at it; but now they begin to look grave about it.

"Nonsense, however, Raoul must be diverted from this fancy. I think I shall send him to Paris."

"So!" thought d'Artagnan; and it seemed to him that the moment for attack had arrived. "Suppose," he said, "we chalk out a career for this young man. I want to consult you about something. Do you not think it is time to enter into service, for you, to include him?"

"But are you not still in the service? you—d'Artagnan?"

"I mean into active service. Our former life—has it still no attraction for you? should you not be happy to begin anew, in my society, and Porthos', the exploits of our youth?"

"On whose side?" asked Athos, fixing his clear, benevolent glance on the countenance of the Gascon. "Listen, d'Artagnan. There is but one person—or rather, one cause—to whom a man like me can be useful—the King's."

"Exactly," answered the Musketeer.

"Yes, but let us understand each other," returned Athos, seriously. "If by the cause of the King you mean that of Mazarin, we do *not* understand each other."

"I don't say, exactly," answered the Gascon, confused.

"Come, d'Artagnan, don't let us play a cunning game; your hesitation, your evasion, tell me at once on whose side you are; for that party no one dares openly to recruit, and when people recruit for it, it is with downcast head and low voice."

"Ah, my dear Athos!"

"You know that I am not alluding to you; you are the pearl of brave and bold men. I speak of that spiteful and intriguing Italian—of the pedant who has tried to put on his own head a crown which he stole from under a pillow—of the scoundrel who calls his party the party of the King—who wants to send the princes of the blood to prison, not daring to kill them, as our great Cardinal—our Cardinal did—of the miser who weighs his gold pieces, and keeps the clipped ones for fear, though he is rich, of losing them at play next morning—of the impudent fellow who insults the Queen, as they say—so much the worse for her—and who is going, in three months, to make war upon us, in order that he may retain his pensions—is that the master whom you propose to me? Thanks, d'Artagnan."

"You are more impetuous than you were," returned d'Artagnan.

"Age has warmed, not chilled your blood. Who told you that that was the master I proposed to you? Devil take it," he muttered to himself, "don't let me betray my secrets to a man not inclined to receive them well."

"Well, then," said Athos, "what are your schemes? what do you propose?"

"Zounds! nothing can be more natural; you live on your estate, happy in your golden means. Porthos has, perhaps, sixty thousand francs income. Aramis has always fifty duchesses who are quarreling for the priest, as they quarrelled formerly for the Musketeer; but I—what have I in the world? I have worn my cuirass for these twenty years, kept down in with inferior rank, without going forward or backward, without living. In fact, I am dead. Well! when I meet a master who wants to revive me a little, you throw a wet blanket over me by decrying him as an impudent fellow—a miser—a bad master! By Jove! I'm of your opinion; but find me a better one, or give me the means of living."

Athos was, for a few moments thoughtful.

"Good! d'Artagnan is for Mazarin," he said to himself.

From that moment he became very guarded.

On his side d'Artagnan was more cautious also.

"You spoke to me," Athos resumed, "of Porthos; what does he wish for?"

"To be a baron."

"Ah! true! I forgot," said Athos, laughing.

"'Tis true," thought the Gascon, "where has he heard it? Does he correspond with Aramis? Ah! if I knew that he did, I should know all."

The conversation was interrupted by the entrance of Raoul.

"Is our little neighbor worse?" asked Athos, seeing a look of vexation on the face of the youth.

"Ah, sir!" replied Raoul, "her fall is a very serious one; and without any apparent injury, the physician fears that she will be lame for life."

"That is terrible," said Athos.

"And what makes me wretched, sir, is that I am the cause of this misfortune."

"There's only one remedy, dear Raoul—that is, to marry her as a compensation," remarked d'Artagnan.

"Ah, sir!" answered Raoul, "you joke about a real misfortune; that is cruel, indeed."

The good understanding between the two friends was not in the least altered by the morning skirmish. They breakfasted with a good appetite, looking now and then at poor Raoul, who, with moist eyes and a full heart, scarcely ate at all.

After breakfast two letters arrived for Athos, who read them with deep attention; whilst d'Artagnan could not restrain himself from jumping up several times, on seeing these epistles, in one of which, having a very strong sight, he perceived the

strong writing of Aramis. The other was in a feminine hand,
long and crossed.

"Come," said d'Artagnan to Raoul—seeing that Athos wished
to be alone—"come, let us take a turn in the fencing gallery,
that will amuse you."

The amusement was rather one-sided, for the Musketeer, in
return for a couple of touches, had buttoned full on the youngster a score of hits.

In a quarter of an hour Athos joined them; and, at the
same moment, Charles brought in a letter for d'Artagnan,
which a messenger had just desired might be instantly delivered.

It was now the turn of Athos to take a sly look.

D'Artagnan read the letter with apparent calmness, and said,
shaking his head,—

"See, dear friend, what an army is; my faith, you are, indeed
right not to return to it. Tréville is ill—so my company can't
do without me; there! my leave is at an end!"

"Do you go back to Paris?" asked Athos quickly.

"Egad! yes; but why don't you come there also?"

Athos colored a little and answered,—

"Should I go, I shall be delighted to see you there."

"Hello, Planchet!" cried Gascon from the door, "we must
set out in ten minutes; give the horses some hay."

Then turning to Athos, he added,—

"I seem to miss something here. I am real sorry to go away
without having seen Grimaud."

"Grimaud!" replied Athos. "I was surprised you did not ask
after him. I have lent him to a friend——"

"Who will understand the signs he makes?" asked d'Artagnan.

"I hope so."

The friends embraced cordially; d'Artagnan pressed Raoul's
hand.

"Adieu, then, to both, my good friends," said d'Artagnan;
"may God preserve you! as we used to say when we said good
bye to each other in the late Cardinal's time."

Athos waved his hand, Raoul bowed, and d'Artagnan and
Planchet set out.

The count followed them with his eyes—his hand resting on
the shoulders of the youth, whose height was almost equal to
his own; but, as soon as they were out of sight, he said,—

"Raoul—we set out to-night for Paris."

"Eh!" cried the young man, turning pale.

"You may go and offer your adieux and mine to Mdme. de
Saint-Remy. I shall wait for you here till seven."

The young man bent low, with an expression of sorrow and
gratitude mingled, and retired to saddle his horse.

As to d'Artagnan, scarcely, on his side, was he out of sight, than he drew from his pocket a letter which he read over again.

"Return immediately to Paris—J. M."

"The epistle is laconic," said d'Artagnan; "and if there had not been a postscript, probably I should not have understood it; but, happily, there is a postscript."

And he read this sustaining postscript, which made him forget the abruptness of the letter.

"P. S. Go to the King's treasurer at Blois; tell him your name, and show him this letter; you will receive two hundred pistoles."

"Assuredly," said d'Artagnan; "I like this piece of prose, and the Cardinal writes better than I thought. Come, Planchet, let us pay a visit to the King's treasurer, and then set off."

"Towards Paris, sir?"

"Towards Paris."

And both set out on as hard a trot as their horses could go.

CHAPTER XVII.

THE DUKE OF BEAUFORT.

THE circumstances which had hastened the return of d'Artagnan to Paris were the following :—

During the whole five years in which Duke de Beaufort had been in prison, not a day had passed in which the Cardinal had not felt a secret dread of his escape. It was not possible, as he well knew, to confine for the whole of his life the grandson of Henry IV., especially when this prince was scarcely thirty years of age. But, however and whensoever he did escape, what hatred he must cherish against him to whom he owed his long imprisonment; who had taken him rich, brave, glorious, beloved by women, feared by men, to cast off from his life its happiest years; for it is not existence, but merely life, in prison. Meanwhile, Mazarin redoubled the watch over the duke. But, like the miser in the fable, he could not sleep near his treasure. Often he woke in the night, suddenly, dreaming that he had been robbed of Beaufort. Then he inquired about him, and had the vexation of hearing that the prisoner played, drank, sang—but that whilst playing, drinking, singing, he often stopped short, to vow that Mazarin should pay dear for all the amusements he had forced him to enter into at Vincennes.

So much did this one idea haunt the Cardinal, even in his sleep, that when, at seven in the morning, Bernouin came to arouse him, his first words were:—"Well—what's the matter? Has Lord de Beaufort escaped from Vincennes?"

"I do not think so, my lord," said Bernouin; "but you will

hear about him, for his special guard La Ramée is here, and awaits the commands of your Eminence."

"Tell him to come in," said Mazarin, arranging his pillows, so that he might receive him sitting, in bed.

The officer entered—a large fat man, with a good physiognomy. His air of perfect serenity made Mazarin uneasy.

"Approach, sir," said the Cardinal.

The officer obeyed.

"Do you know what is said here?"

"No, your Eminence."

"Well, that Lord de Beaufort is going to escape from Vincennes, if he has not done so already."

The officer's face expressed complete stupefaction. He opened, at once, his great eyes and his little mouth, to inhale better the joke that his Eminence deigned to address to him, and ended by a burst of laughter, so violent, that his great limbs shook in his hilarity as they would have done in a fever.

"Escape! my lord—escape! Your Eminence can not then know where M. de Beaufort is?"

"Yes, I do, sir; in the donjon of Vincennes."

"Yes, sir; in a room, the walls of which are seven feet thick, with grated windows, each bar being as thick as my arm."

"Sir," replied Mazarin, "with perseverance one may penetrate through a wall—with a watch-spring one may saw through an iron bar."

"Then my lord does not know that there are eight guards about him—four in his chamber, four in the ante-chamber—and they never leave him."

"But he leaves the room, he plays at tennis in the Mall?"

"Sir, those amusements are allowed; but if your Eminence wishes it, we will discontinue the permission."

"No, no," cried Mazarin, fearing that should his prisoner ever leave his prison he would be the more exasperated against him if he thus entrenched his amusements,—he then asked with whom he played.

"My lord—either with the officers of the guard, with the other prisoners, or with me."

"Humph!" said the Cardinal, beginning to feel more comfortable. "You mean to say, then, my dear M. la Ramée——"

"That unless M. de Beaufort can contrive to metamorphose himself into a little bird, I answer for him."

"Take care—you assert a great deal," said Mazarin. "M. de Beaufort told the guards who took him to Vincennes, that he had often thought what he should do in case he were put into prison, and that he had found out forty ways of escaping."

"My lord—if among those forty there had been one good way, he would have been out long ago."

"Come, come; not such a fool as I fancied!" thought Mazarin. "But when you leave him, for instance?"

"Oh! when I leave him! I have, in my stead, a bold fellow

who aspires to be His Majesty's special guard. I promise you, he keeps a good watch over the prisoner. During the three weeks that he has been with me, I have only had to reproach him with one thing—being too severe with the prisoners."

"And who is this Cerberus?"

"A certain Master Grimaud, my lord."

"And what was he before he went to Vincennes?"

"He was in the country, as I was told by the person who recommended him to me."

"And who recommended this man to you?"

"The steward of the Duc de Grammont."

"He is not a gossip, I hope?"

"Lord a-mercy, my lord! I thought for a long time that he was dumb; he answers only by signs. It seems his former master accustomed him to that. The fact is, I fancy he got into some trouble in the country from his stupidity, and that he wouldn't be sorry in the royal livery to find impunity."

"Well, my dear M. la Ramée," replied the Cardinal, "let him prove a firm and faithful keeper, and we will shut our eyes upon his rural misdeeds, and put on his back a uniform to make him respectable, and in the pockets of that uniform some pistoles to drink to the king's health."

Mazarin was large in his promises—quite different to the taciturn Grimaud, so be-praised by La Ramée; for he said nothing, and did much.

It was now nine o'clock. The Cardinal, therefore, got up, perfumed himself, dressed, and went to the Queen to tell her what had detained him. The Queen, who was scarcely more afraid of Beaufort than the Cardinal himself, and who was almost as superstitious as he was, made him repeat word for word all La Ramée's praises of his deputy. Then, when the Cardinal had ended,—

"Alas! sir! why have we not a Grimaud near every prince?"

"Patience!" replied Mazarin, with his Italian smile; "that may happen one day; but in the meantime—I shall take precautions."

And he wrote to d'Artagnan to hasten his return.

The captive, who was the source of so much alarm to the Cardinal, and whose prospective escape disturbed the repose of the whole court, was wholly unconscious of the terrors which he caused.

He had found himself so strictly guarded, that he soon perceived the fruitlessness of any attempt at escape. His vengeance, therefore, consisted in uttering curses on the head of Mazarin; he even tried to make some verses on him, but soon gave up the attempt.

After having failed in poetry, M. de Beaufort tried drawing. He drew caricatures with a piece of charcoal, of the Cardinal; and as his talents did not enable him to produce a very good likeness, he wrote under the picture, that there might be no doubt of the original—"Portrait of the Illustrious Coxcomb Mazarin." M. de Chavigny, the governor of Vincennes, of course, thought proper to threaten his prisoner that if he did not give up drawing such pictures, he should be obliged to deprive him of all means of amusing himself in that manner. To this M. de Beaufort replied, that since every opportunity of distinguishing himself in arms was taken from him, he wished to make himself celebrated in the fine arts; since he could not be a Bayard, he would become a Raphael, or a Michael Angelo. Nevertheless, one day when M. de Beaufort was walking in the meadow, his fire was put out, his coal taken away, and all means of drawing completely destroyed.

The poor duke swore, fell into a rage, yelled, and declared that they wished to starve him to death; but he refused to promise that he would not make any more drawings, and remained without any fire in the room all the winter.

His next act was to purchase a dog from one of his keepers. With this animal, which he called Pistache, he was often shut up for hours alone, superintending, as everyone supposed, its education. At last, when Pistache was sufficiently well trained, M. de Beaufort invited the governors and officers of Vincennes to attend a performance of the intelligent canine in his cell. But as the creature displayed capers which, as interpreted by his master were pantomimic satires against the Cardinal, they did not please, and three days afterwards, he was found poisoned.

Then the duke said openly that his dog had been killed by a drug with which they meant to poison him; and one day after dinner, he went to bed, calling out that he had pains in his stomach, and that Mazarin had poisoned him.

This fresh impertinence reached the ears of the Cardinal, and alarmed him much. The donjon of Vincennes was considered very unhealthy, and Mdme. de Rambouillet had said that the room in which the Marshal Ornano and the Grand Prior de Vondme had died was worth its weight in arsenic—a bonmot which had great success. So the prisoner was henceforth to eat nothing that was not previously tasted, and La Ramée was, in consequence, placed near him as a taster.

Every kind of revenge was practiced upon the duke by the governor, in return for the insults of the innocent Pistache.

At last his patience was exhausted. He assembled his keepers, and, notwithstanding his well-known difficulty of utterance, addressed them as follows:

"Gentlemen! will you permit a grandson of Henry IV. to be overwhelmed with insults and ignominy? As my grandfather used to say—I once reigned in Paris; do you know that? I had the King and Monsieur the whole of one day in my care. The Queen at that time liked me, and called me the most honest man in the kingdom. Gentlemen and citizens, set me free; I shall go to the Louvre, and strangle Mazarin. You shall be my bodyguard. I will make you all captains, with good pensions!—on—march forward!"

But, eloquent as he might be, the eloquence of the grandson of Henry IV. did not touch those hearts of stone; not one man stirred, so Beaufort was obliged to be satisfied with calling them rascals, and cruel foes.

La Ramée, the duke's dinner guest, by compulsion—his eternal keeper—the shadow of his person; but La Ramée—gay, frank, convivial, fond of play, a great hand at tennis—had but one defect in the duke's eyes—he was incorruptible.

One may be a jailer or a keeper, and at the same time a good father and husband. La Ramée adored his wife and children, whom now he could only catch a glimpse of from the top of the wall, when, in order to please him, they used to walk on the opposite side of the moat. 'Twas too brief an enjoyment, and La Ramée felt that the gaiety of heart which he had regarded as the cause of that health (of which it was, perhaps, rather the result) would not long survive such a mode of life.

He accepted, therefore, with delight, an offer made to him by his friend, the steward of the Duc de Grammont, to give him a substitute; he also spoke of it to M. de Chavigny, who promised that he would not oppose it in any way—that is, if he approved of the person proposed.

We consider it as useless to draw a physical or moral portrait of Grimaud: if—as we hope—our readers have not wholly forgotten "The Three Musketeers," they must have preserved a clear idea of that estimable individual—who is wholly unchanged—except that he is twenty years older, an advance in life that has made him only more silent; although, since the alteration that had been working in himself, Athos had given Grimaud permission to speak.

But Grimaud had for twelve or fifteen years preserved an habitual silence, and a habit of fifteen or twenty years' duration becomes a second nature.

CHAPTER XVIII.

GRIMAUD BEGINS HIS FUNCTIONS.

GRIMAUD thereupon presented himself with his smooth exterior at the donjon of Vincennes. Now Chavigny piqued himself on his infallible penetration; for that which almost proved that he was the son of Richelieu was everlasting pretension; he examined attentively the countenance of the applicant for the place, and fancied that the contracted eyebrows, thin lips, hooked nose, and prominent cheek-bones of Grimaud, were favorable signs. He addressed about twelve words to him; Grimaud answered in four.

"There's a promising fellow, and I have found out his merits," said M. de Chavigny. "Go," he added, "and make yourself agreeable to M. la Ramée, and tell him that you suit me in all respects."

Grimaud had every quality which could attract a man on duty who wishes to have a deputy. So, after a thousand questions which met with only a word in reply, La Ramée, fascinated by his sobriety in speech, rubbed his hands, and engaged Grimaud.

"My orders?" asked Grimaud.

"They are these: never to leave the prisoner alone; to keep away from him every pointed or cutting instrument—and to prevent his conversing any length of time with the keepers."

"Good," answered Grimaud; and he went straight to the prisoner.

The duke was in the act of combing his beard which he had allowed to grow as well as his hair, in order to reproach Mazarin with his wretched appearance and condition. But having, some days previously, seen from the top of the donjon, Mdme. de Montbazon pass in her carriage, and still cherishing an affection for that beautiful woman, he did not wish to be to her what he wished to be to Mazarin; and, in the hope of seeing her again, had asked for a leaden comb, which was allowed him. The comb was to be a leaden one, because his beard, like that of most fair people, was rather red; he therefore dyed it when he combed it out.

As Grimaud entered he saw this comb on the tea table; he took it up, and, as he took it, he made a low bow.

The duke looked at this strange figure with surprise. The figure put the comb in his pocket.

"Ho—hey! what's that?" cried the duke, "and who is this creature?"

Grimaud did not answer, but bowed a second time.

"Are you dumb?" cried the duke.

Grimaud made a sign that he was not.

"What are you, then? Answer! I command!" said the duke.

"A keeper," replied Grimaud.

"Keeper!" reiterated the duke; "there was nothing wanting in my collection except this gallows-bird. Hallo! La Ramée —some one!"

La Ramée ran in haste to obey the call.

"Who is this wretch who takes my comb and puts it in his pocket?" asked the duke.

"One of your guards, my prince—a man full of talent and merit—whom you will like, as I and M. de Chavigny do, I am sure."

"Why does he take my comb?"

"Why do you take my lord's comb?" asked La Ramée.

Grimaud drew the comb from his pocket, and passing his

fingers over the large teeth, pronounced this one word—
"Pointed!"

"True," said La Ramée.

"What does the animal say?" asked the duke.

"That the king has forbidden your lordship to have any piercing instrument."

"Are you mad, La Ramée?—you yourself gave me this comb."

"I was very wrong, my lord; for in giving it to you I acted in opposition to my orders." The duke looked furiously at Grimaud.

"I perceive that that creature will become odious to me," he muttered.

Grimaud, nevertheless, was resolved, for certain reasons, not at once to come to a full rupture with the prisoner; he wanted to inspire, not a sudden repugnance, but a good, sound, and steady hatred; he retired, therefore, and gave place to four guards who, having breakfasted, could attend on the prisoner.

A fresh practical joke had now occurred to the duke. He had asked for craw-fish for his breakfast on the following morning: he intended to pass the day in making a small gallows, and hang one of the finest of these fishes in the middle of his room— the red colors evidently conveying an illusion to the Cardinal— so that he might have the pleasure of hanging Mazarin in effigy, without being accused of having hung anything except a craw-fish.

The day was employed in preparations for the execution. Everyone grows childish in prison; but the character of M. de Beaufort was particularly disposed to become so. In the course of his morning's walk he collected two or three twigs and found a small piece of broken glass, a discovery which delighted him. When he came home he formed his handkerchief into a running noose.

Nothing of all this escaped Grimaud, but La Ramée looked on with the curiosity of a father who thinks that he may perhaps get an idea of a new toy for his children; the guards regarded it all with indifference. When everything was ready—the gallows hung in the middle of the room—the loop made—and when the duke had cast a glance upon the plate of craw-fish, in order to collect the finest specimen among them, he looked around for his piece of glass—it had disappeared.

"Who has taken my piece of glass?" asked the duke, frowning.

Grimaud made a sign to denote that he had done so.

"How! you, again! Why did you take it?"

"Yes—why?" asked La Ramée.

Grimaud, who held the piece of glass in his hand, said:
"Cutting."

"True, my lord!" exclaimed La Ramée. "Ah! deuce take it! we have got a precious lad."

"M. Grimaud!" said the duke, "for your sake, I beg of you, never come within the reach of my fist!"

"Hush! hush!" cried La Ramée, "give me your gibbet, my lord, I will shape it out for you with my knife."

And he took the gibbet and shaped it out as neatly as possible.

"That's it," said the duke; "now make me a little hole in the floor whilst I go and fetch the culprit."

La Ramée knelt down and made a hole in the floor; meanwhile the duke hung the craw-fish up by a thread. Then he put the gibbet in the middle of the room, bursting with laughter.

La Ramée laughed also, and the guards laughed in chorus; Grimaud, however, did not even smile. He approached La Ramée, and showing him the craw-fish, hung up by the thread, "Cardinal!" he said.

"Hung by his Highness, the Duke of Beaufort!" cried the prisoner, laughing violently, "and by Master Jacques Chrysostom La Ramée, the King's commissioner."

La Ramée uttered a scream of horror, and rushed towards the gibbet, which he broke at once, and threw the pieces out of the window. He was going to throw the craw-fish out also, when Grimaud snatched it from his hands.

"Good to eat!" he said; and he put it into his pocket.

This bit so enchanted the duke that, at the moment, he forgave Grimaud for his part in it; but on reflection, he hated him more and more, being convinced that he had some bad motive for his conduct.

The prisoner happened to remark among the guards one man, with a very good countenance, and he favored this man the more, as Grimaud became more and more odious to him.

One morning he took this man on one side and had succeeded in speaking to him, when Grimaud entered, saw what was going on, approached the duke respectfully, but took the guard by the arm.

"Go away," he said.

The guard obeyed.

"You are insupportable," cried the duke: "I shall beat you."

Grimaud bowed.

"I shall break every bone in your body," cried the duke.

Grimaud bowed, and stepped back.

"Mr. Spy," cried the duke, more and more enraged, "I shall strangle you with my own hands."

And he extended his hands towards Grimaud, who merely thrust the guard out, and shut the door behind him. At the same time he felt the duke's arms on his shoulders, like two iron claws; but instead either of calling out or defending himself, he placed his forefinger on his lips, and said in a low tone: "Hush!" smiling as he uttered the words.

A gesture, a smile, and a word from Grimaud, all at once, were so unusual, that his highness stopped short, astounded.

Grimaud took advantage of that instant to draw from his vest a charming little note, with an aristocratic seal, and presented it to the duke without a word.

The duke, more and more bewildered, let Grimaud loose, tore open the note, passed his hands over his eyes, for he was confused, and read:

"MY DEAR DUKE: You may entirely confide on the brave lad who will give you this note; he has consented to enter into the service of your keeper, and to shut himself up at Vincennes with you, in order to prepare and assist your escape, which we are contriving. The moment of your deliverance is at hand; have patience and courage, and remember that in spite of time and absence, all your friends continue to cherish for you the sentiments that they have professed. Yours wholly, and most affectionately,   "MARIE DE MONTBAZON."

"P. S. I sign my full name, for I should be vain if I could suppose that after five years of absence you would remember my initials."

The poor duke became perfectly giddy. What for five years he had been waiting,—a faithful servant—a friend—a helping hand—seemed to have fallen from Heaven just when he expected it the least.

"Oh, dearest Marie! she thinks of me, then, after five years of separation! Heavens! there is constancy!" Then turning to Grimaud, he said:

"And you, my brave fellow, consent to aid me?"

Grimaud nodded.

"What then shall we do? how proceed?"

"It is now eleven," answered Grimaud. "Let my lord at two o'clock ask leave to make up a game at tennis, with La Ramée, and let him knock two or three balls over the ramparts."

"And then?"

"Your highness will approach the walls and call out to a man who works in the moat to pitch them back again."

"I understand," said the duke.

Grimaud made a sign that he was going away.

"Hold!" cried the duke, "will you not accept any money from me?"

"I wish my lord would make me one promise."

"What? speak!"

"'Tis this—when we escape together, that I shall go and be always first; for if my lord should be overtaken and caught there's every chance of his being brought back to prison, whereas, if I'm caught, the least that can befall me—is to be hung."

"True; on my honor as a gentleman, it shall be as you suggest."

"Now," resumed Grimaud, "I've only one thing more to ask, that your highness will continue to detest me."

"I shall try," said the duke.

At this moment La Ramée, after the interview which we have described with the Cardinal, entered the room. The duke had thrown himself—as he was wont to do in moments of dullness and vexation—on his bed. La Ramée cast an inquiring look around him.

"Well, my lord," said La Ramée, with his rude laugh—"you still set yourself against this poor fellow?"

"So 'tis you, La Ramée; in faith 'tis time you came back again. I threw myself on the bed, and turned my nose to the wall that I mightn't break my promise and strangle Grimaud. I feel bored beyond everything to-day."

"Then let us have a match in the tennis court!" exclaimed La Ramée.

"I protest, my dear La Ramée," said the duke, "that you are a charming person, and that I would stay forever at Vincennes, to have the pleasure of your society."

"My lord," replied La Ramée, "I think if it depended on the Cardinal, your wishes would be fulfilled; my lord, you are a hobby nightmare."

The duke smiled with bitterness.

"Ah, La Ramée! if you would but accept my offers! I would make your fortune. I shall no sooner be out of prison than I shall be master of Paris."

"Pshaw! pshaw! I cannot hear such things said as that; I see, my lord, I shall be obliged to fetch Grimaud."

"Rather than that let us go and have a game of tennis, La Ramée."

"My lord—I beg your highness's pardon—but I must beg for half an hour's leave of absence. M. Mazarin is a prouder man than your highness, though not of such high birth: he forgot to ask me to breakfast."

"Well, shall I send for some breakfast here?"

"No, my lord; I must tell you that the confectioner who lived opposite the Castle—Father Marteau, as they called him—sold his business a week ago to a confectioner from Paris, an invalid, ordered country air for his health.

"This new-comer, your highness, when he saw me stop before his shop, where he has a display of things which would make your mouth water, my lord, asked me to get him the custom of the prisoners in the donjon. 'I bought,' says he, 'the business of my predecessor, on the strength of his assurance that he supplied the Castle; whereas, on my honor, M. de Chavigny, though I've been here a week, has not ordered so much as a tartlet.' So, my lord, I am going to try his pasties; and, as I am fasting, you understand, I would, with your highness's leave——" And La Ramée bent low.

"Go, then, my boy," said the duke; "but remember, I only allow you half an hour."

"May I promise your custom to the successor of Father Marteau, my lord?"

"Yes—if he does not put mushrooms in his pies—thou knowest that mushrooms from the Vincennes wood are fatal to my family."

La Ramée went out, but in five minutes one of the officers of the guard entered, in compliance with the strict orders of the Cardinal, that the prisoner should never be left one moment.

CHAPTER XIX.

IN WHICH THE CONTENTS OF THE PASTIES ARE DESCRIBED.

IN half an hour La Ramée returned full of glee, like most men who have eaten, and more especially drunk, to their heart's content. The pasties were excellent, and the wine delicious.

The weather was fine, and the game at tennis took place in the open air.

At two o'clock the tennis balls began, according to Grimaud's directions to take the direction of the moat, much to the joy of La Ramée, who marked fifteen whenever the duke sent a ball to the moat; and very soon balls were wanting, so many had gone over. La Ramée then proposed to send some one to pick them up. But the duke remarked that it would be losing time; and going near the rampart himself and looking over he saw a man working in one of the numerous little gardens which were cleared out by the peasants on the opposite side of the moat.

"Hello, friend!" cried the duke.

The man raised his head and the duke was about to utter a cry of surprise. The peasant, the gardner, was Rochefort, whom he believed to be in the Bastille.

"Well! what's wanted up there?" said the man.

"Be so good as to send us back our balls," said the duke.

The gardener nodded and began to throw up the balls, which were picked up by La Ramée and the guard. One however, fell at the duke's feet; and seeing that it was intended for him, he put it into his pocket.

La Ramée was in ecstasies at having beaten a prince of the blood.

The duke went indoors, and retired to bed, where he spent, indeed, the greater part of the day, as they had taken his books away. La Ramée carried off all his clothes, in order to be certain that the duke would not stir. However, the duke contrived to hide the ball under his bolster, and as soon as the door was closed, he tore off the cover of the ball with his teeth, and found underneath it the following letter:

"MY LORD:—Your friends watch over you, and the hour of your deliverance draws near. Ask to-morrow to have a pie made by the new confectioner opposite the Castle, and who is no other than Noirmont, your former servant. Do not open the pie till you are alone. I hope you will be satisfied with its stuffing.

"Your highness's most devoted servant,
"In the Bastille, as elsewhere,
"DE ROCHEFORT."

The duke, who had latterly been allowed a fire, burned the letter, but kept the ball, and went to bed, hiding the ball under his bolster. La Ramée entered: he smiled kindly on the prisoner, for he was an excellent man who had taken a great liking to the captive prince. He endeavored to cheer him up in his solitude.

"Ah, my friend!" cried the duke, "you are so good; if I could but go as you do, and eat pasties and drink Burgundy at the house of Father Marteau's successor!"

"'Tis true, my lord," answered La Ramée, "that his pasties are famous, and his wine magnificent."

"Good," said the duke to himself; "it seems that one of master La Ramée's seven deadly sins is gluttony."

Then aloud:

"Well, my dear La Ramée! the day after to-morrow is a holiday."

"Yes, my lord; Pentecost."

"Will you give me a lesson in gastronomy, the day after to-morrow?"

"Willingly, my lord."

"But tête-à-tête. The guards shall go to sup in the canteen—we'll have supper here, under your direction."

"Humph!" said La Ramée.

The duke watched the countenance of La Ramée with an anxious glance.

"Well, on condition that Grimaud should wait on us at table."

Nothing could be more agreeable to the duke; however, he had presence of mind enough to exclaim:

"Send your Grimaud to the devil! he'll spoil my feast. I see you distrust me."

"My lord, the day after to-morrow is Pentecost, and a magician has predicted that Pentecost would not pass without your highness being out of Vincennes."

The duke shrugged his shoulders.

"Well, then," with a well-acted good humor, "I allow of Grimaud, but no one else—you must manage it all. Order whatever you like for supper—the only thing I specify is one of those pies; and tell the confectioner that I will promise him my custom if he excels this time in his pies—not only now, but when I leave my prison."

"Then you think you shall leave it?" said La Ramée.

"The devil!" replied the prince; "surely at the death of Mazarin. I am fifteen years younger than he is. At Vincennes, 'tis true, one lives faster——"

"My lord," replied La Ramée, "my lord——"

"Or one dies sooner, so it comes to the same thing."

La Ramée was going out. He stopped, however, at the door for an instant.

"Whom does your highness wish me to send to you?"

"Any one, except Grimaud."

"The officer of the guard, then? with his chess-board?"

"Yes."

Five minutes afterwards the officer entered, and the duke seemed to be immersed in the sublime combinations of chess.

It was midnight before he went to sleep that evening, and he awoke at daybreak. Wild dreams had disturbed his repose. La Ramée found him so pale and fatigued, that he inquired whether he was ill.

"What is the matter with your highness?" he asked.

" 'Tis thy fault, thou simpleton," answered the duke. "With your idle nonsense yesterday, about escaping, you worried me so, that I dreamed that I was trying to escape, and broke my neck in doing so."

La Ramée laughed.

"Come," he said, " 'tis a warning from Heaven. Never commit such an imprudence as to try to escape, except in your dreams. Listen! your supper is ordered."

"You told him it was for me?"

"Yes; and he said he would do his best to please your highness."

"Good!" exclaimed the duke, rubbing his hands.

"Devil take it, my lord! what a gourmand you are becoming. I haven't seen you with so cheerful a face these five years."

At this moment Grimaud entered, and signified to La Ramée that he had something to say to him.

The duke instantly recovered his composure.

"I forbade that man to come here," he said.

" 'Tis my fault," replied La Ramée; "but he must stay here whilst I go and see M. de Chavigny, who has some orders to give me."

And La Ramée went out. Grimaud looked after him; and when the door was closed he drew out of his pocket a pencil and a sheet of paper.

"Write, my lord," he said, "All is ready for to-morrow evening. Keep watch from seven till nine. Have two riding horses quite ready. We shall descend by the first window in the gallery."

"Sign, my lord. Now, my lord, give me, if you have not lost it, the ball—that which contained the letter."

The duke took it from under his pillow, and gave it to Grimaud. Grimaud gave a grim smile.

"Now," said the duke, "tell me what this famous raised pie is to contain."

"Two poignards, a knotted rope, and a chokepear."

"Yes, I understand,—we shall take to ourselves the poignards and the rope," replied the duke.

"And make La Ramée eat the pear," answered Grimaud.

"My dear Grimaud, you speak seldom, but when you do, one must do you justice—your words are of gold."

CHAPTER XX.

ONE OF MARIE MICHON'S ADVENTURES.

WHILST these projects were being formed by Beaufort and Grimaud, the Count de La Fère and the Viscount de Bragelonne were entering Paris by the Rue du Faubourg Saint Marcel.

They stopped at the Fox, in the Rue du Vieux Colombier, a tavern known for many years by Athos, and asked for two bed-rooms.

"You must dress yourself, Raoul," said Athos. "I am going to present you to some one. I wish you to look well, so arrange your dress with care."

"I hope, sir," replied the youth smiling, "that there's no idea of a marriage for me; you know my engagement to Louise?"

Athos, in his turn, smiled also.

"No, don't be alarmed—although it is to a lady that I am going to present you—and I am anxious that you should love her."

"What age is she?" inquired the Viscount de Bragelonne.

"My dear Raoul, learn once for all, that that is a question which is never asked. When you can find out a woman's age by her face it is useless to ask it; when you cannot do so it is indiscreet."

"Is she beautiful?"

"During sixteen years she was deemed not only the prettiest but the most graceful woman in France."

This reply reassured the viscount. A woman who had been a reigning beauty for sixteen years could not be the subject of any scheme for him. He retired to his toilet. When he reappeared, Athos received him with the same parental smile as that which he had often bestowed on d'Artagnan—but a more profound tenderness for Raoul was now visibly impressed upon his face.

Athos cast a glance at his feet, hands, and hair—those three marks of race.

"Come," murmured Athos, "if she is not proud of him, she will be hard to please."

It was three o'clock in the afternoon. The two travelers proceeded to the Rue St. Dominique, and stopped at the door of a magnificent hotel, surmounted with the arms of De Luynes.

" 'Tis here," said Athos.

He entered the hotel, and ascended the front steps, and addressing the footman who waited there in a grand livery, asked if the Duchess de Chevreuse was visible, and if she could receive the Count de la Fère?"

The servant returned with a message to say that though the duchess had not the honor of knowing M. de la Fère, she would receive him. He was accordingly announced.

Mdme. de Chevreuse, whose name appears so often in our story—"The Three Musketeers"—without her actually having appeared in any scene, was still a most beautiful woman. Although about forty-four or forty-five years old, she scarcely seemed thirty-eight. She was the same mad creature who threw over her amours such an air of originality as to make them almost a proverb in her family.

She was in a little boudoir looking upon a garden, and hung with blue damask, adorned with red flowers, with a foliage of gold; and reclined upon a sofa, her head supported on the rich tapestry which covered it. She held a book in her hand, and her arm was supported by a cushion.

As the footman announced the strangers, she raised herself a little and peeped out, with some curiosity.

Athos appeared dressed in violet-colored velvet, trimmed with the same color. His shoulder-knots were of burnished silver; his mantle had no gold or embroidery on it, and a simple plume of violet feathers adorned his hat; his boots were black leather: and at his girdle hung that sword with a magnificent hilt that Porthos had often admired. Splendid lace formed the falling collar of his shirt, and lace fell also over the tops of his boots.

In his whole person he bore such an impress of high condition, that Mdme. de Chevreuse half rose from her seat when she saw him, and made him a sign to sit down near her. He obeyed, the servant disappeared, and the door was closed.

There was a momentary silence, during which these two persons looked at each other attentively.

The duchess was the first to speak.

"Well, sir! I am waiting to hear what you wish to say to me—with impatience."

"And I, madam," replied Athos, "am looking with admiration."

"Sir," said Mdme. de Chevreuse, "you must excuse me, but I long to know to whom I am talking. You belong to the court, doubtless, yet I have never seen you at court. Have you been in the Bastille by any mischance?"

"No, madam, I have not; but perhaps I am on the road to it."

"Ah! then tell me who you are, and get along with you," replied the duchess, with the gaiety which made her so charming, "for I am sufficiently in bad odor there already, without compromising myself still more."

"Who I am, madam? My name has been mentioned to you— the Count de la Fère—you do not know that name. I once bore another which you knew; but you have certainly forgotten it."

"Tell it me, sir."

"Formerly," said the count, "I was Athos."

Mdme. de Chevreuse looked astonished. The name was not wholly forgotten, but mixed up and confused with some old recollections.

"This Athos was one of three young Musketeers, named Porthos, and——"

He stopped short.

"And Aramis," said the duchess, quickly.

"And Aramis; you have not forgotten that name."

"No," she said: "poor Aramis; a charming man, elegant, discreet, and a writer of poetry verses. I am afraid he has turned out ill," she added.

"He has; he is."

"Ah, what a misfortune!" exclaimed the duchess, playing carelessly with her fan. "Indeed, sir, I thank you; you have recalled one of the most agreeable recollections of my youth."

"Will you permit me, then, to recall another to you? Aramis was intimate with a young needlewoman from Tours, a cousin of his, named Marie Michon."

"Ah, I knew her!" cried the duchess. "It was to her he wrote from the siege of Rochelle, to warn her of a plot against the Duke of Buckingham."

"Exactly so; will you allow me to speak to you of her?"

"If," replied the duchess, with a meaning look, "you do not say too much against her."

"You encourage me, madam. I shall continue," said Athos; and he began his narrative.

He alluded to events long gone by; a sorcerer rather than mere man. These disclosures were succeeded by an exclamation of joy from Mdme. de Chevreuse.

"He is here! my son! the son of Marie Michon! But I must see him instantly."

"Take care, madam," said Athos, "for he knows neither his father nor his mother."

"You have kept the secret! you have brought him to see me, thinking to make me happy. Oh, thanks! thanks! sir," cried

Mdme. de Chevreuse, seizing his hand, and trying to put it to her lips, "you have a noble heart."

"I bring him to you, madam," said Athos, withdrawing his hand, "hoping that, in your turn, you will do something for him; till now I have watched over his education, and I have made him, I hope, an accomplished gentleman; but I am now obliged to return to the dangerous and wandering life of party faction. To-morrow I plunge into an adventurous affair in which I may be killed. Then it will devolve on you to push him on in that world where he is called on to occupy a place."

"Be assured," cried the duchess, "I shall do what I can. I have but little influence now, but all that I have shall be his. As to his little fortune——"

"As to that, madam, I have made over to him the estate of Bragelonne, my inheritance, which will give him ten thousand francs a year, and the title of viscount;—and now I will call him."

Athos moved towards the door; the duchess held him back.

"Is he handsome?" she asked.

Athos smiled.

"He resembles his mother."

And he opened the door, and desired the young man to come in.

The duchess could not forbear uttering a cry of joy on see-ing so handsome a young cavalier, who surpassed all that her pride had been able to conceive.

"Come here," said Athos. "The duchess permits you to kiss her hand."

The youth approached with his charming smile, and his head bare, and, kneeling down, kissed the hand of the Duchess de Chevreuse.

"Sir," he said, turning to Athos, "was it not in compassion to my timidity that you told me that this lady was the Duchess de Chevreuse, and is she not the Queen?"

"No," said the duchess, extending her hand to him; "no; unhappily I am not the Queen, for, if I were, I should do for you at once all that you deserve: but let us see; whatever I may be," she added, her eyes glistening with delight, "let us see what profession you wish to follow."

Athos, standing, looked at them both with indescribable pleasure.

"Madam," answered the youth in his sweet voice, "it seems to me that there is only one career for a gentleman—that of the army. I have been brought up by my lord with the intention, I believe, of making me a soldier; and he gave me reason to hope that, at Paris, he would present to me some one who would recommend me to the favor of the prince."

"Yes, I understand it well. The Prince de Marsillac, my old friend,—shall recommend your young friend to Madame de Longueville, who will give him a letter to her brother, the prince, who loves her too tenderly not to do what she wishes immediately."

"Well, that will do charmingly," said the count; "but may I beg that the greatest haste may be made, for I have reasons to wish the viscount not to sleep longer than to-morrow night in Paris."

"Do you wish it known that you are interested about him?"

"Better for him, in future, that he should be supposed never to have seen me."

"Oh, sir!" cried Raoul.

"You know, Bragelonne," said Athos, "I never act without reflection."

"Well, Count, I am going instantly," interrupted the duchess, "to send for the Prince de Marsillac, who is, happily, in Paris just now. What are you going to do this evening?"

"We intend to visit the Abbé Scarron, for whom I have a letter of introduction, and at whose house I expect to meet some of my friends."

"'Tis well; I shall go there also, for a few minutes," said the duchess; "do not quit his parlor until you have seen me."

Athos bowed, and took his departure.

CHAPTER XXI.

AT THE ABBÉ SCARRON'S.

THERE stood, in the Rue des Tournelles, a house known by all the sedan-chairmen and footmen of Paris, and yet, nevertheless, this house was neither that of a great lord nor of a rich man. There was neither dining, nor playing of cards, nor dancing in that house. Nevertheless, it was the rendezvous of all the great world, and all Paris went there. It was the abode of little Scarron.

There, in the home of that witty abbé, there was incessant laughter; there all the news of the day had their source, and were so quickly transformed, misrepresented, and converted, some into epigrams, some into falsehoods, that everyone was anxious to pass an hour with little Scarron, listening to what he said, and reporting it to others.

At seven o'clock Athos and Raoul directed their steps to the Rue des Tournelles; it was stopped up by porters, horses, and footmen. Athos forced his way through and entered, followed by the young man. The first person that struck him on his entrance was Aramis, planted near a great chair on castors, very large, covered with a canopy of tapestry, under which there moved, enveloped in a quilt of brocade, a little face, rather young, rather merry, but somewhat pallid,—whilst its eyes never ceased to express a sentiment at once lively, intellectual and amiable. This was the Abbé Scarron, always laughing, joking, complimenting—yet suffering—and scratching himself with a little switch.

Around this kind of rolling tent pressed a crowd of gentlemen and women. The door opened and Mdme. de Chevreuse was announced. Everyone rose. Scarron turned his chair towards the door; Raoul blushed; Athos made a sign to Aramis, who went to hide himself in the inclosure of a window.

In the midst of all the compliments that awaited her on her entrance, the duchess seemed to be looking for some one; at last she found out Raoul, and her eyes sparkled; she perceived Athos, and became thoughtful; she saw Aramis and gave a start of surprise behind her fan. He had drawn near to the Coadjutor, who, smiling all the while, had contrived to drop some words into his ear. Raoul, following the advice of Athos, went towards them. Athos had now joined the other two, and they were in deep consultation as the youth approached them.

"'Tis a rouleau by M. Voiture that M. l'Abbé is repeating to me," said Athos in a loud voice, "and I confess I think it incomparable."

Raoul stayed only a few minutes near them, and then mingled in the group around Mdme. de Chevreuse.

"Well, then," asked Athos, in a low tone, as soon as the three friends were unobserved, "to-morrow?"

"Yes, to-morrow," said Aramis quickly, "at six o'clock, at St. Mande."

"Who told you?"

"The Count de Rochefort."

"Tell the Count de la Fère to come to me," said Mdme. de Chevreuse, "I want to speak to him."

"And I," said the Coadjutor, "want it to be thought that I do *not* speak to him. I admire, I love him—for I know his former adventures—but I shall not speak to him until the day after to-morrow."

"And what then?" asked Mdme. de Chevreuse.

"You shall know to-morrow evening," replied the Coadjutor, laughing.

Athos then drew near her.

"Count," said the duchess, giving him a letter, "here is what I promised you: our young friend will be extremely well received."

"Madam, he is very happy in owing any obligation to you."

Mdme. de Chevreuse rose to depart.

"Viscount," said Athos to Raoul, "follow the duchess; beg her to do you the favor to take her arm in going downstairs, and thank her as you descend."

The invalid disappeared soon afterwards, and went into his sleeping-room; and one by one the lights were extinguished.

Contrary to the custom of a man so firm and decided, there was this morning in his personal appearance something slow and irresolute. He was evidently occupying himself in preparations for the departure of Raoul; after employing nearly an hour in these cares, he opened the door of the room in which the viscount slept, and entered.

The sun, already high, penetrated into the room through the window, the curtains of which Raoul had neglected to close on the previous evening. He was still sleeping, his head gracefully reposing on his arm.

Athos approached and hung over the youth in an attitude full of tender melancholy; he remembered that the first part of his life had been embittered by a woman, and he thought with alarm of the influence which love might possess over so fine, and at the same time, so vigorous an organization as that of Raoul.

In recalling all that he had suffered, he foresaw all that Raoul would suffer; and the expression of the deep and tender compassion which throbbed in his heart was pictured in the moist eye with which he gazed on the young man.

At this moment Raoul awoke, without a cloud on his face, without weariness or lassitude; his eyes were fixed on those of Athos, and he, perhaps, comprehended all that passed in the heart of the man who was awaiting his awakening as a lover awaits the awakening of his mistress, for his glance, in return, had all the tenderness of infinite love.

"You are there, sir," he said respectfully.

"Yes, Raoul," replied the count. "How do you feel?"

"Perfectly well; quite rested, sir."

"You are still growing," Athos continued, with that charming and paternal interest felt by a grown man for a youth.

"Oh, sir! I beg your pardon," exclaimed Raoul, ashamed of so much attention; "in an instant I shall be dressed."

Athos then called Olivain.

"Everything," said Olivain to Athos, "has been done according to your directions; the horses are waiting."

"And I was asleep!" cried Raoul; "whilst you, sir, you had the kindness to attend to all these details. Truly, sir, you overwhelm me with benefits!"

"Therefore you love me, a little, I hope," replied Athos, in a tone of emotion.

"Oh, sir! God knows that I love and revere you."

"See that you forget nothing!" said Athos, appearing to look about him that he might hide his emotion.

"No, indeed, sir," answered Raoul.

The servant then approached Athos, and said hesitatingly: "M. le Viscount has no sword."

"'Tis well," said Athos. "I will take care of that."

They went downstairs, Raoul looking every now and then at the count to see if the moment of farewell was at hand, but

Athos was silent. When they reached the steps, Raoul saw three horses.

"Oh, sir! then you are going with me?"

"I shall conduct you part of the way," said Athos.

They set out, passing over Point Neuf; they pursued their way along the quay and went along by the walls of the Grand Châtelet. They proceeded to the Rue St. Denis.

Along the road the count gave his son lessons in war and the exercises of gentlemen, but with a delicacy which never offended the susceptibilities of youth.

They arrived that very moment at the town gate, guarded by two sentinels.

"Here comes a young gentleman," said one of them, "who seems as if he were going to join the army."

"How do you find that out?" inquired Athos.

"By his manner, sir, and his age; he's the second to-day."

"Has a young man, such as I am, gone through this morning, then?" asked Raoul.

"Faith, yes, with a haughty presence and fine equipage, such as the son of a noble house would have."

"He was to be my companion on the journey, sir," cried Raoul. "Alas! he cannot make me forget what I lose!"

Thus talking, they traversed the streets, full of people on account of the fête, and arrived opposite the old cathedral where the first mass was going on.

CHAPTER XXII.

ST. DENIS.

"Let us alight, Raoul," said Athos. "Olivain, take care of our horses, and give me my sword."

The two gentlemen then went into the church. Athos gave Raoul some of the holy water. A love as tender as that of a lover for his mistress dwells, undoubtedly, in some paternal hearts for a son.

"Come, Raoul," he said, "let us follow this man."

The verger opened the iron grating which guarded the royal tombs, and stood on the topmost steps, whilst Athos and Raoul descended. The depths of the sepulchral descent were dimly lighted by a silver lamp, on the lowest steps; and just below this lamp there was laid, wrapt in a large mantle of violet velvet, worked with fleur-de-lis of gold, a catafalque resting upon trestles of oak.

The young man, prepared for the scene by the state of his own feelings, which were mournful, and by the majesty of the cathedral, which he had passed through, had descended in a slow and solemn manner, and stood with his head uncovered before

these mortal spoils of the last king, who was not to be placed
by the side of his forefathers until his successor should take
his place there; and who appeared to abide on that spot, that
he might thus address human pride, so sure to be exalted by the
glories of a throne; "Dust of the earth! I await thee!"
There was a profound silence.

Then Athos raised his hand, and pointing to the coffin,—

"This temporary sepulchre is," he said, "that of a man of
feeble mind; yet whose reign was full of great events; because
over this king watched the spirit of another man, even as this
lamp keeps vigil over this coffin, and illumines it. He whose
intellect was thus supreme, was, Raoul, the actual sovereign;
the other, nothing but a phantom to whom he gave a soul; and
yet, so powerful is majesty amongst us, this man has not even
the honor of a tomb even at the feet of him in whose service
his life was worn away. Remember, Raoul, this! If Richelieu
made the king, by comparison, small, he made royalty great.
The palace of the Louvre contains two things—the king, who
must die; royalty, which dieth not. The minister, so feared, so
hated by his master, has descended into the tomb, drawing after
him the king, whom he would not leave alone on earth, lest
he should destroy what he had done. So blind were his con-
temporaries that they regarded the Cardinal's death as a deliverance; and I, even I, opposed the designs of the great man who
held the destinies of France in his hands. Raoul, learn how to
distinguish the king from royalty; the king is but a man;
royalty is the gift of God. Whenever you hesitate as to whom
you ought to serve, abandon the exterior, the material appearance, for the invisible principle: for the invisible principle is
everything. Raoul, I seem to read your future destiny as through
a cloud. It will be happier, I think, than ours has been. Different in your fate to us—you will have a king without a minister, whom you may serve, love, respect. Should the king prove
a tyrant, for power begets tyranny, serve, love, respect royalty, that Divine right, that celestial spark which makes this
dust still powerful and holy, so that we—gentlemen, nev02the-
less, of rank and condition—are as nothing in comparison with
that cold corpse extended here."

"I shall adore God, sir," said Raoul. "I shall respect royalty,
I shall serve the king, and I shall, if death be my lot, hope to
die for the king, for royalty, and for God. Have I, sir, comprehended your instructions?"

Athos smiled.

"Yours is a noble nature," he said, "here is your sword."

Raoul bent his knee to the ground.

"It was worn by my father, a loyal nobleman. I have worn
it in my turn, and it has sometimes not been disgraced when the
hilt was in my hand, and the sheath at my side. Should your
hand still be too weak to use this sword, Raoul, so much the

better. You will have more time to learn to draw it only when it ought to be used."

"Sir," replied Raoul, putting the sword to his lips as he received it from the count, "I owe everything to you, and yet this sword is the most precious gift you have made me. I shall wear it, I swear to you, as a grateful man should do."

" 'Tis well—arise, embrace me."

Raoul rose, and threw himself with emotion into the count's arms.

"Adieu," faltered the count, who felt his heart die away within him; "adieu, and think of me."

"Oh! for ever and ever!" cried the youth; "oh! I swear to you, sir, should any harm happen to me, that your name shall be the last I shall utter—the remembrance of you, my last thought."

Athos hastened upstairs to conceal his emotion, and regained, with hurried steps, the porch where Olivain was waiting with the horses.

"Olivain," said Athos, showing the servant Raoul's shoulder belt; "tighten the buckle of this sword, which falls a little too low. You will accompany M. le Viscount till Grimaud has rejoined you. You know, Raoul, Grimaud is an old and zealous servant. He will follow you."

"Yes, sir," answered Raoul.

"Now to horse, that I may see you depart."

Raoul obeyed.

"Raoul," said the count; "my dear boy!"

"Sir—my beloved protector!"

Athos waved his hand; he dared not trust himself to speak, and Raoul went away, his head uncovered. Athos remained motionless, looking after him until he turned the corner of the street.

Then the count threw the bridle of his horse into the hands of a peasant, mounted again the steps, went into the cathedral, there to kneel down in the darkest corner and to pray.

CHAPTER XXIII.

ONE OF THE FORTY METHODS OF ESCAPE.

THE game of tennis, which, upon a signal from Grimaud, M. de Beaufort had consented to play, began in the afternoon. The duke was in full force, and beat La Ramée completely.

Four of the guards, constantly near the prisoner, assisted in picking up the tennis balls. When the game was over, the duke, laughing at La Ramée for his bad play, offered these men some money to go and drink his health, with their four other comrades.

The guards asked permission of La Ramée, who gave it to

them, but not till the evening, however; until then he had business, and the prisoner was not to be left alone.

Six o'clock came, and, although they were not to sit down to table until seven o'clock, dinner was ready, and served up. Upon the side-board appeared the colossal pie with the duke's arms on it, and, seemingly cooked to a turn, as far as one could judge by the golden color which illumined the crust.

The rest of the dinner was to come.

Everyone was impatient, La Ramée to sit down to table—the guards to go and drink—the duke to escape.

Grimaud alone was calm as ever. One might have fancied that Athos had educated him with a forethought of this great event. There were moments when, looking at Grimaud, the duke asked himself if he was not dreaming, and if that marble figure was really at his service, and would become animate when the moment arrived for action.

La Ramée sent away the guards, desiring them to drink to the duke's health, and, as soon as they were gone, he shut all the doors, put the keys in his pocket, and showed the table to the prince with an air which meant——

"Whenever my lord pleases."

The prince looked at Grimaud—Grimaud looked at the clock—it was hardly a quarter past six. The escape was fixed to take place at seven o'clock. There were, therefore, three-quarters of an hour to wait.

The duke, in order to delay a quarter of an hour, pretended to be reading something that interested him, and said he wished they would allow him to finish his chapter. La Ramée went up to him and looked over his shoulder to see what book it was that had so singular an influence over the prisoner as to make him put off taking his dinner.

It was "Cæsar's Commentaries," which La Ramée had lent him, contrary to the orders of the governor; and La Ramée resolved never again to disobey those injunctions.

Meantime he uncorked the bottles, and went to smell if the pie was good.

At half-past six the duke arose, and said very gravely:

"Certainly, Cæsar was the greatest man of ancient times."

"You think so, my lord?" answered La Ramée.

"Yes."

"Well, as for me, I prefer Hannibal because he left no Commentaries," replied La Ramée, with his coarse laugh.

The duke offered no reply, but sitting down at table, made a sign that La Ramée should also seat himself opposite to him. There is nothing so expressive as the face of an epicure who finds himself before a well-spread table; so La Ramée, when receiving his plate of soup from Grimaud, presented a type of perfect bliss.

The duke smiled.

"Zounds!" he said; "I don't suppose there is a happier man at this moment in the kingdom than you are!"

"You are right, my lord Duke," answered the officer; "I don't know a pleasanter sight than a well-loaded table; and when, added to that, he who does the honors is the grandson of Henry IV., you will, my lord Duke, easily comprehend that the honor one receives doubles the pleasure one enjoys."

The duke bowed in his turn, and an imperceptible smile appeared on Grimaud's face, who kept behind La Ramée.

"My dear La Ramée," said the duke, "you are the only man who can turn a compliment as you do."

"No, my lord Duke," replied La Ramée, in the fulness of his heart; "I say what I think—there is no compliment in what I say to you——"

"Then you are attached to me?" asked the duke.

"To own the truth, I should be inconsolable if you were to leave Vincennes."

"A droll way of showing your affliction." The duke meant to say "affection."

"But, my lord," returned La Ramée; "what would you do if you got out? Every folly you committed would embroil you with the court, and they would put you into the Bastille, instead of Vincennes. Now, M. de Chavigny is not amiable, I allow; but M. du Tremblay is much worse."

"Indeed!" exclaimed the duke, who from time to time looked at the clock, the fingers of which seemed to move with a sickening slowness; "but what could you expect from the brother of a Capuchin monk, brought up in the school of Cardinal Richelieu?"

"Ah, my lord, it is a great happiness that the queen, who always wished you well, had a fancy to send you here, where there's promenade and a tennis court, good air, and a good table."

"In short," answered the duke, "if I comprehend you, La Ramée, I am ungrateful for having ever thought of leaving this place?"

"Oh! my lord Duke, 'tis the height of ingratitude; but your highness has never seriously thought of it?"

"Yes," returned the duke; "I must confess I do sometimes think of it."

"Still by one of your forty methods, your highness?"

"Yes—yes, indeed."

"My lord," said La Ramée, "now we are quite at our ease, and enjoying ourselves, pray tell me one of those forty ways invented by your highness."

"Willingly," answered the duke; "give me the pie!"

"I am listening," said La Ramée, leaning back in his arm chair, and raising his glass of Madeira to his lips, and winking his eye that he might see the sun through the rich liquid that he was about to taste.

The duke glanced at the clock. In ten minutes it would strike seven.

Grimaud placed the pie before the duke, who took a knife with a silver blade to raise the upper crust; but La Ramée, who was afraid of any harm happening to this fine work of art, passed his knife, which had an iron blade, to the duke.

"Thank you, La Ramée," said the prisoner.

"Well, my lord! this famous invention of yours?"

"Must I tell you," replied the duke, "on what I most reckon, and what I determine to try first?"

"Yes, that one! my lord."

"Well—I should hope, in the first instance, to have as a keeper an honest fellow, like you."

"And you have one, my lord—well?"

"Having then a keeper like La Ramée, I should try also to have introduced to me by some friend a man who would be devoted to me, and who would assist me in my flight."

"Come, come," said La Ramée, "not a bad idea."

"Isn't it? For instance, the former serving man of some brave gentleman, an enemy himself to Mazarin, as every gentleman ought to be."

"Hush—don't let us talk politics, my lord!"

"Then my keeper will begin to trust this man, and to depend on him; and then I shall have news from those without the prison walls."

"Ah, yes! but how can the news be brought to you?"

"Nothing easier—in a game of tennis. I send a ball into the moat; a man is there who picks it up; the ball contains a letter."

"The devil it does!" said La Ramée, scratching his head; "you are wrong to tell me that, my lord. I shall watch the men who pick up the balls."

The duke smiled.

"But," resumed La Ramée, "this is only one way of corresponding. 'Tis a good one, but not a sure one."

"Pardon me. For instance, I say to my friends, 'Be on a certain day, at a certain hour, at the other side of the moat, with saddle horses.' "

"Well, what then?"—La Ramée began to be uneasy—"unless the horses have wings to mount up to the ramparts and to come and fetch you."

"That's not needed. I have," replied the duke, "a way of descending from the ramparts."

"What?"

"A ladder of ropes."

"Yes—but," answered La Ramée, trying to laugh, "a ladder of ropes can't be sent round a ball like a letter."

"No; but it may come in another way—in a pie, for instance," replied the duke. "The guards are away. Grimaud is here alone; and Grimaud might be the man whom a friend has sent to second me in everything. The moment for my escape is fixed—seven o'clock. Well—at a few minutes to seven——"

"At a few minutes to seven?" cried La Ramée, the cold sweat on his brow.

"At a few minutes to seven," returned the duke, "I raise the crust of the pie. I find in it two poignards, a ladder of ropes and a gag. I clasp one of the poignards to La Ramée's breast, and I say to him, 'My friend, I am sorry for it, but if you stir or utter a cry you are a dead man!'"

The duke, in pronouncing these words, suited the action to the words. He was standing near the officer, and he directed the point of the poignard in such a manner, close to La Ramée's heart, that there could be no doubt in the mind of that individual as to his determination. Meanwhile, Grimaud, still mute as ever, drew from the pie the rope ladder and the gag.

La Ramée followed all these objects with his eyes; his alarm every moment increasing.

"Oh, my lord!" he cried, with an expression of stupefaction in his face; "you haven't the heart to kill me!"

"No; not if you do not oppose my flight."

At this moment the clock struck.

"Seven o'clock!" said Grimaud, who had not spoken a word.

La Ramée made one movement, in order to satisfy his conscience. The duke frowned; the officer felt the point of the poignard, which, having penetrated through his clothes, was close to his heart.

"Let us despatch," said the duke.

"My lord—one last favor."

"What? speak—make haste."

"Bind my arms, my lord, fast—that I may not be considered as your accomplice."

The duke undid his belt and gave it to Grimaud, who tied La Ramée in such a way as to satisfy him.

"Your feet also," said Grimaud.

La Ramée stretched out his legs, Grimaud took a napkin, tore it into strips, and tied La Ramée's feet together.

"Now, my lord," said the poor man, "let me have the choke pear. I ask for it; without it I would be tried in a court of justice because I did not call out. Thrust it into my mouth, my lord, thrust it in."

In a second La Ramée was gagged, and lay prostrate. Two or three chairs were thrown down, as if there had been a struggle. Grimaud then took from the pocket of the officer all the keys it contained, and first opened the door of the room in which they were, then shut it, and double-locked it, and both he and the duke proceeded rapidly down the gallery, which led to the little inclosure. At last they reached the tennis-court. It was completely deserted. No sentinels—no one at the windows.

The duke ran on to the rampart, and perceived, on the other

side of the ditch, three cavaliers with two riding horses. The duke exchanged a signal with them. It was well for him that they were there.

Grimaud, meantime, undid the means of escape.

This was not, however, a rope-ladder, but a ball of silk cord, with a narrow board, which was to pass between the legs and to unwind itself by the weight of the person who sat astride upon it.

"Go!" said the duke.

Instantly, Grimaud, sitting upon the board, as if on horseback, commenced his perilous descent.

The duke followed him with his eyes, with involuntary terror. He had gone down about three-quarters of the length of the wall when the cord broke. Grimaud fell—precipitated into the moat.

The duke uttered a cry, but Grimaud did not give a single moan. He must have been dreadfully hurt, for he did not stir from the place where he fell.

Immediately, one of the men who were waiting, slipped down into the moat, tied under Grimaud's shoulders the end of a cord, and the other two, who held the other end, drew Grimaud to them.

"Descend, my lord," said the man in the moat. "There are only fifteen feet more from the top down here, and the grass is soft."

The duke had already begun to descend. His task was the more difficult, as there was no board to support him. He was obliged to let himself down by his hands, and from a height of fifty feet. But, as we have said, he was active, strong, and full of presence of mind. In less than five minutes he arrived at the end of the cord. He was then only fifteen feet from the ground, as the gentleman below had told him. He let go the rope, and fell upon his feet, without receiving any injury.

He instantly began to climb up the slope of the moat, on the top of which he met de Rochefort. The other two gentlemen were unknown to him. Grimaud, in a swoon, was tied onto a horse.

"Gentlemen," said the duke, "I shall thank you later; now we have not a moment to lose. On, then! on! those who love me follow me!"

And he jumped on his horse, and set off on full gallop, drawing in the fresh air, and crying out, with an expression of face which it would be impossible to describe:

"Free! free! free!"

CHAPTER XXIV.

THE TIMELY ARRIVAL OF D'ARTAGNAN.

At Blois d'Artagnan received the money paid to him by Mazarin for any future services he might render the Cardinal.

From Blois to Paris was a journey of four days for ordinary travelers, but d'Artagnan arrived on the third day at the Saint Denis Bars. In turning the corner of the Rue Montmartre, in order to reach the Hôtel de la Chevrette, where he had appointed Porthos to meet him, he saw, at one of the windows of the hotel, his friend Porthos, dressed in a sky-blue waistcoat embroidered with silver, gaping till he showed all down his throat; whilst the people passing by admiringly gazed at this gentleman, handsome and rich, who seemed so weary of his riches and his greatness.

Porthos, seeing d'Artagnan, hastened to receive him on the threshold of the hotel.

"Ah! my dear friend!" he cried, "what bad stabling for my horses here!"

"Indeed;" said d'Artagnan; "I am most unhappy to hear it, on account of those fine animals."

"And I also—I was also wretchedly off," he answered, moving backwards and forwards as he spoke—"and had it not been for the hostess," he added, with his air of vulgar self-complacency, "who is very agreeable, and understands a joke, I should have got a lodging elsewhere."

"Yes, I understand," said d'Artagnan, "the air of La Rue Tiquetonne is not like that of Pierrefonds; but console yourself, I shall soon conduct you to one much better."

Then, taking Porthos aside:

"My dear du Vallon," he said, "here you are in full dress most fortunately, for I shall take you directly to the Cardinal's."

"Gracious me!—really!" cried Porthos, opening his great, wondering eyes. "A presentation?—indeed!"

"Does that alarm you?"

"No; but it agitates me."

"Oh! don't be distressed; you have not to deal with the other Cardinal; and this one will not oppress you by his dignity."

" 'Tis the same thing—you understand me, d'Artagnan—a court."

"There's no court now. Alas!"

"The Queen!"

"I was going to say, there's no longer a Queen. The Queen! Be assured we shall not see her."

"But you, my friend, are you not going to change your dress?"

"No, I shall go as I am. This traveling dress will show the Cardinal my haste to obey his commands."

They set out on Vulcan and Bayard, followed by Mousqueton on Phœbus, and arrived at the Palais Royal at about a quarter to seven. The streets were crowded, for it was a holiday—and the crowd looked in wonder at these two cavaliers; one as fresh as if he had come out of a band-box, and the other so covered with dust that he looked as though he had come from a field of battle.

Mousqueton also attracted attention; and as the romance of Don Quixote was then the fashion, they said that he was Sancho, who, after having lost one master, had found two.

On reaching the palace, d'Artagnan sent in to his Eminence the letter in which he had been ordered to return without delay. He was soon ordered to enter into the presence of the Cardinal.

"Courage!" he whispered to Porthos, as they proceeded.

"Do not be intimidated. Believe me, the eye of the eagle is closed forever. We have only the vulture to deal with. Hold yourself up stiff, and do not bend too low to this Italian; that might give him a poor idea of us."

"Good!" answered Porthos. "Good!"

Mazarin was in his study, working at a list of pensions and benefices, of which he was trying to reduce the number. He saw d'Artagnan and Porthos enter with pleasure, yet showed no joy in his countenance.

"Ah! you, is it? Lieutenant, you have been very prompt. 'Tis well. Welcome to ye."

"Thanks, my lord. Here I am at your Eminence's service, as well as M. du Vallon, one of my old friends, who used to conceal his nobility under the name of Porthos."

Porthos bowed to the Cardinal.

"A magnificent cavalier," remarked Mazarin.

Porthos turned his head to the left and to the right, and drew himself up with a movement full of dignity.

"The best swordsman in the kingdom, my lord," said d'Artagnan.

Porthos bowed to his friend.

Mazarin was fond of fine soldiers, as in later times, Frederick of Prussia used to be. He admired strong hands, broad shoulders, and steady eyes. He seemed to see before him the salvation of his administration, and of the kingdom, sculptured in flesh and bone. He remembered that the old association of Musketeers was composed of four persons.

"And your two other friends?" he asked.

Porthos opened his mouth, thinking it a good opportunity to put in a word in his turn; d'Artagnan checked him by a glance from the corner of his eye.

"They are prevented at this moment, but will join us later."

Mazarin coughed a little.

"And this gentleman, being disengaged, takes to the service willingly?" he asked.

"Yes, my lord, and from complete devotion to the cause, for M. de Bracieux is rich."

"Fifty thousand francs a year," said Porthos.

These were the first words he had spoken.

"From pure zeal?" resumed Mazarin with his artful smile, "from pure zeal and devotion, then? What does your friend wish for as the reward of his devotion?"

D'Artagnan was about to explain that the aim and end of the zeal of Porthos was, that one of his estates should be raised into a barony, when a great noise was heard in the ante-chamber; at the same time the door of the study was burst open, and a man, covered with dust, rushed into it, exclaiming:

"My lord! my lord the Cardinal!"

Mazarin thought that some one was going to assassinate him, and he drew back, pushing his chair on the castors. D'Artagnan and Porthos moved so as to plant themselves between the person entering and the Cardinal.

"Well, sir," exclaimed Mazarin, "what's the matter? and why do you rush in here as if you were going into a market-place?"

"My lord," replied the messenger, "I wish to speak to your Eminence in secret. I am M. du Poins, an officer in the guards, on duty at Vincennes."

Mazarin, perceiving by the paleness and agitation of the messenger that he had something of importance to say, made a sign that d'Artagnan and Porthos should retire.

When they were alone the man stammered:

"My lord, the Duke de Beaufort has contrived to escape from the castle of Vincennes."

Mazarin uttered a cry, and became paler than he who brought this news. He fell, almost fainting, back in his chair.

"Escaped? M. de Beaufort escaped?"

"My lord, from the top of the terrace, I saw him run off."

"And you did not fire on him?"

"He was beyond shot."

"Where was M. Chavigny?"

"Absent."

"And La Ramée?"

"He was found locked up in the prisoner's room, a gag in his mouth, and a poignard near him."

"But the man who was under him?"

"He was an accomplice of the duke's and escaped with him."

Mazarin groaned.

"My lord," said d'Artagnan, advancing towards the Cardinal, "it seems to me that your Eminence is losing precious time. It may still be possible to trace the prisoner. France is large; the nearest frontier is sixty leagues distant."

"And who is to pursue him?" cried Mazarin.

"I! Egad! if my lord orders me to pursue the devil, I would do so, and seize him by the horns and bring him back again."

"And I, too," said Porthos.

"Go, then, take what guards you find here, and pursue him."

"You command us, my lord, to do so?"

"And I sign my orders," said Mazarin, taking a piece of paper, and writing some lines, "M. du Vallon, your barony is on the back of de Beaufort's horse; you have nothing to do but to overtake it. As for you, my dear lieutenant, I promise you nothing; but if you bring him back to me, dead or alive, you may ask all you wish."

"To horse, Porthos!" said d'Artagnan, taking him by the hand.

"Coming," replied Porthos, with his sublime composure.

They descended the great staircase, taking with them all the guards that they found on the road, and crying out "To horse! To horse!" and they spurred on their horses, which set off along the Rue St. Honoré with the speed of a whirlwind.

"Well, baron! I promised you some exercise!" said the Gascon.

"Yes, my captain."

As they went, the citizens, awakened, left their doors, and the fierce dogs followed the cavaliers, barking. At the corner of the cemetery Saint Jean, d'Artagnan upset a man: it was too slight an occurrence to delay people so eager to get on. The troop continued its course as if their steeds were winged.

Alas! there are no unimportant events in this world! and we shall see, that this apparently slight one was near endangering the monarchy.

CHAPTER XXV.

AN ADVENTURE ON THE HIGH WAY.

The Musketeers rode the whole length of the road to Vincennes, and soon found themselves in sight of a village.

From the top of an eminence d'Artagnan perceived a group of people collected on the other side of the moat, in front of that part of the donjon which looks towards Saint Maur. He rode on, convinced that he should in that direction gain intelligence of the fugitive; and he learned from the people who composed the group, that the duke had been pursued without success; that his party consisted of four able men, and one wounded, and that they were two hours and a quarter in advance of their pursuers.

"Only four!" cried d'Artagnan, looking at Porthos; "baron, only four of them!"

Porthos smiled.

"And only two hours and a quarter before us, and we so well mounted, Porthos!"

Porthos sighed, for he thought of all that was awaiting his poor horses.

The troop then pursued their course with their wonted ardor; but some of them could no longer sustain this rapidity; three of them stopped after an hour's march, and one fell down.

D'Artagnan, who never turned his head, did not perceive it. Porthos told him of it in his calm manner.

"If we can only keep two," said d'Artagnan, "it will be enough, since the duke's troops are only four in number."

And he spurred his horse on.

At the end of another two hours the horses had gone twelve leagues without stopping, their legs began to tremble, and the foam that they had shed whitened the doublets of their masters.

"Let us rest here a minute to give these miserable creatures breathing time," said Porthos.

"Let us rather kill them! yes, kill them!" cried d'Artagnan; "I see fresh tracks; 'tis not a quarter of an hour since they passed this place."

In fact, the road was trodden by horses' feet, visible even in the approaching gloom of the evening.

They set out, but after a run of two leagues, Mousqueton's horse sank.

"Gracious me!" said Porthos, "there's Phœbus ruined."

"The Cardinal will pay you a hundred pistoles."

"I'm above asking."

"Let us set out then again, on a full gallop."

"Yes, if we can."

But at last the lieutenant's horse refused to go on; he could not breathe; one last spurt, instead of making him advance, made him fall.

"The devil!" exclaimed Porthos, "there's Vulcan foundered."

"Zounds!" cried d'Artagnan, "we must stop! Give me your horse, Porthos! What the devil are you doing?"

"By Jove, I am falling, or rather, Bayard is falling," answered Porthos.

All three then called out, "All's over."

"Hush!" said d'Artagnan.

"What is it?"

"I hear a horse, 'tis a hundred paces in advance."

There was, in truth, the neighing of a horse heard.

"Sir," said Mousqueton, "at a hundred steps from us there's a little hunting box."

"Mousqueton, my pistols."

"They are in my hand, sir."

"Porthos, keep yours in your holster. Now, we seize horses for the King's service."

"For the King's service," repeated Porthos.

"Then not a word, and to work!"

They went on, through the night, silent as phantoms; they saw a light shine in the midst of some trees.

"There is the house, Porthos," said the Gascon; "let me do what I please, and do you do what I do."

They glided from tree to tree, till they arrived at twenty steps from the house unperceived, and saw, by means of a lantern suspended under a hut, four fine horses. A groom was rubbing them down; near them were saddles and bridles.

"I want to buy horses," said d'Artagnan, approaching the groom.

"These horses are not for sale," was the reply.

"I take them, then," said the lieutenant.

And he took hold of one within his reach; his two companions did the same thing.

"Sir," cried the groom, "they have just come six leagues, and have only been unbridled about half an hour."

"Half an hour's rest is enough," replied the Gascon.

The groom called aloud for help. A steward appeared, just as d'Artagnan and his companions were prepared to mount. The steward wished to expostulate.

"My dear friend," cried the lieutenant, "if you say a word I will blow out your brains."

"But sir," answered the steward, "do you know that these horses belong to Lord de Montbazon?"

"So much the better; they must be good animals, then."

"Sir, I shall call my men."

"And I mine, I've ten guards behind me; don't you hear them gallop? and I'm one of the King's Musketeers; come, Porthos, come Mouston."

They all mounted as quickly as possible.

"Here! here!" cried the steward, "the house servants with the carbines!"

"On! on!" cried d'Artagnan; "there'll be shooting! on!"

They all set off, swift as the winds.

"Here!" cried the steward, "here!" whilst the groom ran to a neighboring building.

"Don't hurt your horse," said d'Artagnan to him, laughing.

"Fire!" replied the steward.

A gleam, like a flash of lightning, illumined the road, and, with the flash, was heard the whistling of balls, which were fired in the air.

"They fire like grooms," said Porthos; "in the time of the Cardinal, people fired better than that; do you remember the road to Crevecœur, Mousqueton?"

"Ah, sir! my left side still pains me."

"Are you sure we are on the right track, lieutenant?"

"Egad, didn't you hear—these horses belong to M. Montbazon: well, M. Montbazon is the husband of Lady Montbazon, and she is the mistress of the Duke de Beaufort."

"Ah! I understand," replied Porthos; "she has ordered relays of horses, and we are pursuing the duke with the very horses he has just left?"

"My dear Porthos, you are really a man of superior understanding," said d'Artagnan, with a look as if he spoke against his conviction.

"Pooh!" said Porthos, "I am what I am."

They rode on for an hour, till the horses were covered with foam and dust.

"Zounds! what is yonder?" cried d'Artagnan.

"You are very lucky, if you see anything in such a night as this," said Porthos.

"Something bright."

"I, too," cried Mousqueton, "saw it also."

"Yes, a dead horse," said d'Artagnan, pulling up his horse, which shied: "it seems that they also are broken-winded as well as ourselves."

"I seem to hear the noise of a troop of horsemen!" exclaimed Porthos, leaning over his horse's mane. "They appear to be numerous. Another horse!"

"Dead?"

"No, dying, saddled and bridled."

"Then 'tis the fugitives."

"Courage, we have them!"

"But, if they are numerous," observed Mousqueton, "'tis not we who have them, but they who have us."

"Nonsense!" cried d'Artagnan, "they'll suppose us to be stronger than themselves, as we're in pursuit—they'll be afraid, and disperse."

"Certainly," remarked Porthos.

"Oh! do you see?" cried the lieutenant.

"The sparks again! this time I, too, saw them," said Porthos.

"On! on! forward! forward!" cried d'Artagnan, in his stentorian voice, "we shall laugh over all this in five minutes."

And they darted on anew. The horses, excited by pain and emulation, raced over the dark road, in the midst of which was now seen a moving mass, more dense and obscure than the rest of the horizon.

CHAPTER XXVI.

THE COLLISION.

THEY rode on in this way for ten minutes. Suddenly, two dark forms seemed to separate from the mass, advanced, grew in size, and, as they grew larger and larger, assumed the appearance of two horsemen.

"Oh, oh!" cried d'Artagnan, "they're coming towards us."

"So much the worse for them," said Porthos.

"Who goes there?" cried a hoarse voice.

The three horsemen made no reply, stopped not, and all that was heard was the noise of swords, drawn from the scabbards, and of the cocking of the pistols, with which the two phantoms were armed.

"To the teeth," said d'Artagnan.

Porthos understood him and he and the lieutenant each one took from his left hand a pistol, and armed himself each in his turn.

"Who goes there?" was asked a second time. "Not another step, or you're dead men!"

"Stuff!" cried Porthos, almost choked with dust. "Stuff and nonsense! we have seen plenty of dead men in our time."

Hearing these words the two shadows blockaded the road, and by the light of the stars might be seen the shining of their arms.

"Back!" cried d'Artagnan; "or you are dead!"

Two shots were the only reply to this threat; but the assailants attacked their foes with such velocity that in a moment they were upon them; a third pistol shot was heard, aimed by d'Artagnan; and one of his adversaries fell. As to Porthos he slashed at his with such violence, that although his sword was thrust aside, the enemy was thrown off his horse, and fell about ten steps from it.

"Finish! Mouston—finish him!" cried Porthos. And he darted on, beside his friend, who had already begun a fresh pursuit.

"Well?" said Porthos.

"I've broken his skull," cried d'Artagnan. "And you——"

"I've only thrown him down; but hark!"

Another shot of a carbine was heard. It was Mousqueton, who was obeying his master's command.

"On! on!" cried d'Artagnan; "all goes well! we have the first throw."

"Ha! ha!" answered Porthos; "behold, other players appear."

And, in fact, two other cavaliers made their appearance detached, as it seemed, from the principal group; they again disputed the road.

This time the lieutenant did not wait for the opposite party to speak.

"Stand aside," he cried, "stand off the road."

"What do you want?" asked a voice.

"The duke!" Porthos and d'Artagnan roared out both at once.

A burst of laughter was the answer, but finished with a groan. D'Artagnan had, with his sword, cut the poor wretch in two who had laughed.

At the same time Porthos and his adversary fired at each other and d'Artagnan turned to him:

"Bravo!—you've killed him, I think."

"No, wounded his horse only."

"But what ails my horse?"

"He's falling down," replied Porthos.

In truth, the lieutenant's horse stumbled and fell on his knees; then a rattling in his throat was heard, and he lay down to die. D'Artagnan swore loud enough to be heard in the skies above.

"Does your honor want a horse?" asked Mousqueton.

"Zounds! want one?" cried the Gascon. "Rather!"

"Here's one, your honor——"

"How the devil have you two horses?" asked d'Artagnan, jumping on one of them.

"Their masters are dead! I thought they might be useful, so I took them."

Meantime Porthos had reloaded his pistols.

"Be on the alert!" cried d'Artagnan. "Here are two other cavaliers."

As he spoke two horsemen advanced at full speed.

"Ho! your honor," cried Mousqueton, "the man you upset is getting up."

"Why didn't you do as you did to the first man?" said Porthos.

"I was holding the horses, my hands were full, your honor."

A shot was fired at that moment and Mousqueton shrieked with pain.

"Oh! I'm hit in the other flank! exactly in the other! This hurt is just the fellow of that I had on the road of Amiens."

Porthos turned round like a lion—plunged on the dismounted cavalier, who tried to draw his sword; but, before it was out of the scabbard, Porthos, with the hilt of his, had hit him such a terrible blow on the head, that he fell like an ox beneath the butcher's knife.

Mousqueton, groaning, slipped down from his horse, his wound not allowing him to sit in the saddle.

On perceiving the cavaliers, d'Artagnan had stopped and charged his pistol afresh; besides, his horse, he found, had a carbine on the bow of the saddle.

"Here I am!" exclaimed Porthos. "Shall we wait, or shall we charge?"

"Let us charge them," answered the Gascon.

"Charge!" echoed Porthos.

They charged their horses upon the other cavaliers who were only twenty steps from them.

"For the King!" cried d'Artagnan.

"The King has no authority here!" answered a deep voice, which seemed to proceed from a cloud—so enveloped was the cavalier in a whirlwind of dust.

"So? the King's name is not a passport everywhere," replied the Gascon.

"See!" answered the voice.

Two shots were fired at once; one by d'Artagnan, the other by the adversary of Porthos. D'Artagnan's ball took off his enemy's hat. The ball fired by Porthos' foe went through the throat of his horse, which fell, groaning.

"Bah!" cried the voice, the tone of which was piercing and jeering—"this! 'tis nothing but a butchery of horses, and not a combat between men. To the sword, sir!—the sword!"

And he jumped off his horse.

"To our swords!—be it so!" replied d'Artagnan—"that's just what I want."

D'Artagnan, in two steps, was engaged with the foe, whom, according to his custom, he attacked impetuously, but he met this time with a skill and a strength of arm which made him pause. Twice he was obliged to step back; his opponent stirred not one inch. D'Artagnan turned, and again attacked him.

Twice or thrice blows were struck on both sides without effect; sparks were emitted from the swords like water spouting out.

At last d'Artagnan thought it about time to try one of his favorite feints in fencing. He brought it to bear, skilfully executed with the rapidity of lightning, and struck the blow with a force which he fancied would prove irresistible.

The blow was parried.

"S'death!" he cried, with his Gascon accent.

At this exclamation his adversary bounded back, and, bending his bare head, tried to distinguish in the gloom, the features of the lieutenant.

As to d'Artagnan, afraid of some feint, he still stood on the defensive.

"Have a care," cried Porthos to his opponent; "I've still two pistols charged."

"The more reason you should fire the first," cried his foe.

Porthos fired; a flash threw a gleam of light over the field of battle.

As the light was thrown on them, a cry was heard from the other two combatants.

"Athos!" exclaimed d'Artagnan.

"D'Artagnan!" ejaculated Athos.

Athos raised his sword—d'Artagnan lowered his.

"Aramis!" cried Athos—"don't fire!"

"Ha! ha! is it you, Aramis?" said Porthos.

And he threw away his pistol.

Aramis pushed his back into his saddle bag, and sheathed his sword.

"My son!" exclaimed Athos, extending his hand to d'Artagnan.

This was the name which he gave him in former days, in their moments of tender intimacy.

"Athos!" cried d'Artagnan, wringing his hands. "So you defend him! And I, who have sworn to take him dead or alive, I am dishonored—Ah!"

"Kill me!" replied Athos, uncovering his breast, "if your honor requires my death."

"Oh! woe's me!" cried the lieutenant; "only one man in the world could stay my hand; by a fatality that very man comes across my way. What shall I say to the Cardinal?"

"You can tell him, sir," answered a voice, which was a voice of high command in that battle-field, "that he sent against me the only two men capable of getting the better of four;—of fighting man to man, without discomfiture, against the Count de la Fère and the Chevalier d'Herblay, and of surrendering only to fifty men!"

"The prince!" exclaimed at the same moment Athos and Aramis, unmasking as they spoke; "The Duke de Beaufort," while d'Artagnan and Porthos stepped backwards.

"Fifty!" cried the Gascon and Porthos.

"Look around you, gentlemen, if you doubt the facts," said the duke.

The two friends looked to the right and left; they were encompassed by horsemen.

"Hearing the noise of the fight," resumed the duke, "I fancied you had about twenty men with you, so I came back with those around me, tired of always running away, and wishing to draw my sword for my own cause; but you are only two."

"Yes, my lord; but, as you have said, two equal to twenty," said Athos.

"Come, gentlemen, your swords," said the duke.

"Our swords!" cried d'Artagnan, raising his head and regaining his self-possession. "Never!"

"Never," added Porthos.

Some of the men moved towards them.

"One moment, my lord," whispered Athos; and he said something in a low voice.

"As you will," replied the duke. "I am too much indebted to you to refuse the first request. Gentlemen," he said to his escort, "withdraw. M. d'Artagnan, M. du Vallon, you are free."

The order was obeyed; d'Artagnan and Porthos then found themselves in the centre of a large circle.

"Now, d'Herblay," said Athos, "dismount and come here."

Aramis dismounted, and went to Porthos, while Athos approached d'Artagnan. All the four were together.

"Friends!" said Athos; "do you regret that you have not shed our blood?"

"No," replied d'Artagnan; "I regret to see that we, hitherto united, are opposed to each other. Ah! nothing will ever go well with us now!"

"Oh! Heaven! No, all is over!" said Porthos.

"Well—be on our side now," resumed Aramis.

"Silence, d'Herblay!" cried Athos; "such proposals are not to be made to gentlemen such as these. 'Tis a matter of conscience with them, as with us."

"Meantime, here we are, enemies!" said Porthos. "Grammercy! who would ever have thought it?"

D'Artagnan only sighed.

Athos looked at them both, and took their hands in his.

"Gentlemen!" he said, "this is a serious business, and my heart bleeds as if you had pierced it through and through. Yes, we are severed; there is the great—the sad truth! but we have not yet declared war; perhaps we shall have to make certain conditions, therefore a solemn conference is indispensable."

"For my own part, I demand it," said Aramis.

"I accept it," interposed d'Artagnan, proudly.

Porthos bowed, as if in assent.

"Let us choose a place of rendezvous," continued Athos, "and in a last interview, arrange our mutual position, and the conduct we are to maintain towards each other."

"Good!" the other three exclaimed.

"Will the Place Royale suit you?" asked d'Artagnan.

Athos and Aramis looked at each other.

"The Place Royale, Paris—be it so!" replied Athos.

"When?"

"To-morrow evening, if you please. At ten if that suits you—we shall be returned."

"Good."

"There," continued Athos, "either peace or war will be decided—our honor, at all events, will be secured."

"Alas!" murmured d'Artagnan, "our honor as soldiers is lost to us forever! Now, Porthos; now we must hence, to bear back our shame on our heads to the Cardinal!"

"And tell him," cried a voice, "that I am not too old to be still a man of action."

D'Artagnan recognized the voice of de Rochefort.

The duke disappeared, followed by his troop, who were soon lost in distance and darkness.

D'Artagnan and Porthos were alone with a man who held their two horses; they thought it was Mousqueton, and went up to him.

"What do I see?" cried the lieutenant. "Grimaud, is it you?"

Grimaud signified that he was not mistaken.

"And whose horses are these?" cried d'Artagnan. "Who has given them to us?"

"The Count de la Fère."

"Athos! Athos!" muttered d'Artagnan, "you think of everyone; you are, indeed, a gentleman! Whither are you bound to, Grimaud?"

"To join the Viscount de Bragelonne in Flanders, your honor."

They were taking the road towards Paris, when groans, which seemed to proceed from a ditch, attracted their attention.

"What is that?" asked d'Artagnan.

"It is I, Mousqueton," said a mournful voice, while a sort of shadow arose out of the side of the road.

"I will take care of Mousqueton," said Grimaud; and he gave his arm to his old comrade, whose eyes were full of tears, and Grimaud could not tell whether the tears were caused by his wounds, or by the pleasure of seeing him again.

D'Artagnan and Porthos went on, meantime, to Paris. They were passed by a courier, covered with dust, the bearer of a letter from the duke to the Cardinal, bearing testimony to the favor of d'Artagnan and Porthos.

Mazarin had passed a very bad night, when this letter was brought to him, announcing that the duke was free, and that he should henceforth raise up a mortal strife against him.

"What consoles me," said the Cardinal, after reading the letter, "is, that at least, in this chase, d'Artagnan has done me one good turn—he has destroyed Broussel. This Gascon is a precious fellow—even his mishaps are useful."

The Cardinal referred to that man whom d'Artagnan upset at the corner of the Saint Jean Cemetery in Paris, and who was no other than the Councillor Broussel.

CHAPTER XXVII.

THE FOUR OLD FRIENDS PREPARE TO MEET.

"Well," said Porthos, seated in the court-yard of the Hôtel de la Chevrette, to d'Artagnan, who with a long and melancholy face had returned from the Palais Royal, "did he receive you ungraciously, my dear friend?"

"I'faith, yes! a hideous brute, our Cardinal—what are you eating there, Porthos?"

"I am dipping a biscuit into a glass of Spanish wine—do the same."

"You are right. Gimblon, a glass of wine!"

"Well! how has all gone off?"

"Zounds! you know there's only one way of saying things; so I went in and I said: 'My lord, we were not the stronger party.'

"'Yes, I know that,' he said, 'but tell me the particulars.'

"You know, Porthos, I could not give him the particulars without naming our friends—to name them would be to commit them to ruin, so I merely said they were fifty and we were two.

"'There was firing, nevertheless, I heard,' he said; 'and your swords, they saw the light of day, I presume?'

"'That is, the starlight, my lord,' I answered.

"'Ah!' cried the Cardinal; 'I thought you were a Gascon, my friend.'

"'I am only a Gascon,' said I, 'when I succeed.' So the answer pleased, and he laughed."

"Well, not so bad a reputation as I feared," remarked Porthos.

"No, no, but 'tis the manner in which he spoke. Gimblon, another bottle of wine—'tis almost incredible what a quantity of wine these biscuits will hold."

"Hem—didn't he mention me?" inquired Porthos.

"Ah! yes, indeed!" cried d'Artagnan, who was afraid of disheartening his friend by telling him that the Cardinal had not breathed a word about him; "yes, surely! he said——'as to your friend, tell him that he may sleep in peace.'"

"Good, very good," said Porthos; "that means as clear as daylight that he intends still to make me a baron."

At this moment nine o'clock struck. D'Artagnan started.

"Ah yes," said Porthos; "there is nine o'clock. We have an appointment, you remember, at the Place Royale."

"Ah! stop! hold your peace, Porthos—don't remind me of it, 'tis that which has made me so cross since yesterday. I shall not go."

"Why?" asked Porthos.

"Why, suppose this appointment is only a blind? That there's something hidden beneath it?"

D'Artagnan did not believe Athos to be capable of a deception, but he sought an excuse for not going.

"We must go," said the superb lord of Bracieux, "lest they should say we were afraid. We, who have faced fifty foes on the high road, can well meet two in the Place Royale."

"Yes, yes, but they took part with the princes without apprising us of it—perhaps the duke may try to catch us in his turn."

"Nonsense! He had us in his power and let us go. Besides, we can be on our guard—let us take arms, and, let Planchet go with us with his carbine."

"Planchet is a Frondeur," answered d'Artagnan.

"Devil take these civil wars! one can no more reckon on one's friends than on one's footmen," said Porthos; "ah, if Mousqueton were here! there's one who will never desert me!"

"So long as you are rich! ah! my friend! 'tis not civil war that disunites us! It is that we are, each of us, twenty years older; it is that the honest emotions of youth have given place to the suggestions of interest—to the whispers of ambition—

to the counsels of selfishness. Yes, you are right—let us go, Porthos! but let us go well armed—were we not to go they would say we were afraid. Hello! Planchet, here! saddle our horses—take your carbine."

"Whom are you going to attack, sir?"

"No one—a mere matter of precaution," answered the Gascon.

"You know, sir, that they wished to murder that good Councillor Broussel, the father of the people, but he has been avenged. He was carried home in the arms of the people. His house has been full ever since. He has received visits from the Coadjutor, from Mdme. de Longueville, and the Prince de Conti—Mdme. de Chevreuse and Mdme. de Vendome have left their names at his door."

"How did you hear this?" inquired d'Artagnan.

"From a good source, sir—I heard it from Friquet."

"From Friquet? I know that name——"

"A son of M. de Broussel's servant, and a lad that I promise you, in a revolt, will not cast away his share to the dogs."

"Is he not a singing boy at Nôtre Dame?" asked d'Artagnan.

"Yes, that's he, patronized by Bazin."

"Ah, yes, I know."

"Of what importance is this reptile to you?" asked Porthos.

"Gad!" replied d'Artagnan; "he has already given me good information, and he may do the same again."

While all this was going on, Athos and Aramis were entering Paris by the Faubourg St. Antoine. They had taken some refreshments on the road, and hastened on that they might not fail at the rendezvous. Bazin was their only attendant, for Grimaud had stayed behind to take care of Mousqueton.

Scarcely had they reached the iron gate of the Place Royale, than they perceived three cavaliers, d'Artagnan, Porthos, and Planchet, the two former wrapped up in their military cloaks, under which their swords were hidden, and Planchet, his musket by his side. They were waiting at the entrance of the Rue St. Catherine, and their horses were fastened to the rings of the arcade. Athos, therefore, commanded Bazin to fasten up his horse and that of Aramis in the same manner.

Then they advanced, two and two, and saluted each other politely.

"Now, where will it be agreeable to you that we hold our conference?" inquired Athos, perceiving that the people were stopping to look at them, supposing that they were going to engage in one of those far-famed duels still extant in the memory of the Parisians—and especially the inhabitants of the Place Royale.

"The gate is shut," said Aramis, "but if these gentlemen like a cool retreat under the trees, and perfect seclusion,

I will get the key from the Rohan Townhouse, and we shall be well situated."

D'Artagnan darted a look into the obscurity of the place. Porthos ventured to put his head between the railings, to try if his glance could penetrate the gloom.

"If you prefer any other place," said Athos, in his persuasive voice, "choose for yourselves."

"This place, if M. d'Herblay can procure the key, is the best that we can have," was the answer.

Aramis went off at once, begging Athos not to remain alone within reach of d'Artagnan and Porthos; a piece of advice which he received with a contemptuous smile.

Aramis returned soon with a man who opened the gate, and Aramis faced round in order that d'Artagnan and Porthos might enter. In passing through the gate, the hilt of the lieutenant's sword was caught in the grating, and he was obliged to pull off his cloak; in doing so he showed the butt-end of his pistol, and a ray of the moon was reflected on the shining metal.

"Do you see?" whispered Aramis to Athos, touching his shoulder with one hand, and pointing with the other to the arms which the Gascon wore under his belt.

"Alas, I do!" replied Athos, with a deep sigh.

He entered third, and Aramis, who shut the gate after him, last. The two serving men waited without, but, as if they likewise mistrusted each other, kept their respective distances.

CHAPTER XXVIII.

THE·REUNION.

THEY proceeded silently to the centre of the Place; but as at this very moment the moon had just emerged from behind a cloud, it was considered that they might be observed if they remained on that spot, and they regained the shade of the lime-tree.

There were benches here and there—the four gentlemen stopped near them; at a sign from Athos, Porthos and d'Artagnan sat down, the two others stood in front of them.

After a few minutes of silent embarrassment, Athos spoke.

"Gentlemen," he said, "our presence here is a proof of our former friendship; not one of us has failed at this rendezvous; not one, has, therefore, to reproach himself."

"Hear me, Count," replied d'Artagnan; "instead of making compliments to each other, let us explain our conduct to each other, like men of right and honest hearts."

"I wish for nothing more; have you any cause of anger

against me or M. d'Herblay? If so, speak out," answered Athos.

"I have," replied d'Artagnan. "When I saw you at your château at Bragelonne, I made proposals to you, which you perfectly understood; instead of answering me as a friend, you played with me as a child; the friendship, therefore, that you boast of, was not broken yesterday by the shock of our swords, but by your dissimulation at your home."

"D'Artagnan;" said Athos, reproachfully.

"You asked for candor—there it is. You ask what I feel against you—I say it. And I have the same sincerity to show you, if you wish, M. d'Herblay; I acted in a similar way to you and you also deceived me; I reproach you with nothing, however; 'tis only because M. de la Fère has spoken of freindship that I question your conduct."

"And what do you find in it to blame?" asked Aramis, haughtily.

The blood mounted instantly to the temples of d'Artagnan, who rose, and replied:

"I consider it the conduct of a pupil of Jesuits."

On seeing d'Artagnan rise, Porthos rose also; these four men were, therefore, all standing at the same time, with a menacing aspect, opposite to each other.

Upon hearing d'Artagnan's reply, Aramis seemed about to draw his sword, when Athos prevented him.

"D'Artagnan," he said, "you come here to-night, still infuriated by our yesterday's adventure. I believe that your heart is sufficiently noble to enable a friendship of twenty years to be stronger than an affront of a quarter of an hour. Come, do you really think you have anything to say against me? say it then; if I am in fault, I will avow my fault."

The grave and harmonious tones of that beloved voice had still over d'Artagnan its ancient influence, while that of Aramis, which had become sharp and screaming in his moments of ill-humor, irritated him. He answered therefore:

"I think, that you had something to communicate to me at your château of Bragelonne, and that gentleman"—he pointed to Aramis—"had also something to tell me when I was at his convent. At this time I was not concerned in the adventure during which you barricaded the road that I was going; however, because I was prudent, you must not take me for a fool. If I had wished to widen the breach betweeen those whom M. d'Herblay chooses to receive with a rope ladder, and those he receives with a wooden ladder, I could have spoken out."

"What are you meddling with?" cried Aramis, pale with anger, suspecting that d'Artagnan had acted as spy on him, and had seen him with Mdme. de Longueville.

"I never meddle but with what concerns me, and I know how

to make believe that I haven't seen what does not concern me; but I hate hypocrites, and among that number, I place musketeers who are priests, and priests who are musketeers; and," he added, turning to Porthos, "here's a gentleman who is of the same opinion as myself."

Porthos, who had not spoken one word, answered merely by a word and a gesture.

He said, "Yes," and he put his hand on his sword. Aramis started back, and drew his. D'Artagnan bent forward, ready either to attack, or to stand on his defense.

Athos, at that moment, extended his hand with the air of supreme command which characterized him alone, drew out his sword and scabbard at the same time, broke the blade in the sheath on his knee and threw the pieces to his right. Then turning to Aramis, he said, "break your sword in two."

Aramis hesitated.

"It must be done," said Athos; then in a lower and more gentle voice, he added, "I wish it."

Then Aramis, paler than before, but subdued by these words, broke the flexible blade with his hands, and then, folding his arms, stood trembling with rage.

These proceedings made d'Artagnan and Porthos draw back. D'Artagnan did not draw his sword; Porthos put his back in the sheath.

"Never!" exclaimed Athos, raising his right hand to Heaven, "Never! I swear before God, who seeth us, and who in the darkness of this night heareth us, never shall my sword cross yours, never shall my eye cast a glance of anger, nor my heart a throb of hatred, to you. We lived together, we loved, we hated together; we shed and mingled our blood together, and, too, probably, I may still add, that there may be yet a bond between us closer even than that of friendship—perhaps the bond of crime; for we four, we once did condemn, judge, and slay a human being whom we had not any right to cut off from this world, although apparently fitter for hell than for this life. D'Artagnan, I have always loved you as my son. Porthos, we slept six years side by side; Aramis is your brother as well as mine, and Aramis has once loved you, as I love you now, and as I have ever loved you. What can Cardinal Mazarin be to us, who compelled such a man as Richelieu to act as he pleased? What is such or such a prince to us, who have fixed on the Queen's head the crown? D'Artagnan, I ask your pardon for having yesterday crossed swords with you; Aramis does the same to Porthos; now, hate me if you can, but, for my own part, I shall ever, even if you do hate me, retain esteem and friendship for you; repeat my words, Aramis, and then, if you desire it, and if they desire it, let us separate forever from our old friends."

There was a solemn, though momentary silence, which was broken by Aramis.

"I swear," he said, with a calm brow, and kindly glance, but in a voice still trembling with recent emotion, "I swear that I no longer bear animosity to those who were once my friends. I regret that I ever crossed swords with you, Porthos; I swear not only that it shall never again be pointed at your breast, but that in the bottom of my heart there will never in future be the slightest hostile sentiment; now, Athos, come."

Athos was about to retire.

"No! no! no! do not go away!" cried d'Artagnan, impelled by one of those irresistible impulses which showed the ardor of his nature, and the native uprightness of his character. "I swear that I would shed the last drop of my blood, and the last fragment of my limbs, to preserve the friendship of such a man as you, Athos—of such a man as you, Aramis." And he threw himself into the arms of Athos.

"My son!" exclaimed Athos, pressing him in his arms.

"And as for me!" said Porthos, "I swear nothing, but I'm choked—forsooth! If I were obliged to fight against you, I think I should allow myself to be pierced through and through, for I never loved anyone but you in the world;" and honest Porthos burst into tears, as he embraced Athos.

"My friends," said Athos, "this is what I expected from such hearts as yours—yes—I have said it, and I now repeat it! our destinies are irrevocably united, although we pursue different roads. I respect your convictions; and while we fight for opposite sides, let us remain friends. Ministers, princes, kings will pass away like a torrent; civil war, like a flame; but we—we shall remain; I have a presentiment that we shall."

"Yes," replied d'Artagnan, "let us still be Musketeers, and let us retain as our colors that famous napkin, of the bastion Saint Gervais—on which the great Cardinal had three fleur-de-lis embroidered."

"Be it so," cried Aramis. "Cardinalists, or Frondeurs, what matters it—let us meet again our capital seconds at a duel—our devoted friends in business—our merry companions in pleasure."

"And whenever," added Athos, "we meet in battle, at this word—'Place Royale!'—let us put our swords into our left hands, and shake hands with the right—even in the thick of the carnage."

"You speak charmingly," said Porthos.

"And are the first of men!" added d'Artagnan. "You excel us all!"

Athos smiled with ineffable pleasure.

"'Tis then all settled—gentlemen, your hands—are we not pretty good Christians?"

"Egad!" said d'Artagnan, "by Heaven—yes."

"We should be on this occasion, if only to be faithful to our oath," said Aramis.

"Ah, I'm ready to do what you will," cried Porthos—"to swear by Mahomet;—devil take me if I've ever been so happy as at this moment!"

And he wiped his eyes, still moist.

"Has not one of you a cross?" asked Athos.

Aramis smiled, and drew from his vest a cross of diamonds, which was hung around his neck by a chain of pearls. "Here is one," he said.

"Well," resumed Athos, "swear on this cross, which, in spite of its material, is still a cross, swear to be united in spite of everything, and forever, and may this oath bind us to each other—and even, also, our descendants! Does this oath satisfy you?"

"Yes!" said they all with one accord.

"Ah! traitor!" muttered d'Artagnan, leaning towards Aramis, and whispering in his ear, "you have made us swear on the crucifix of a Frondeuse."

CHAPTER XXIX.

THE RESCUE AT THE FERRY.

WE hope that the reader has not quite forgotten the young traveler whom we left on the road to Flanders.

In losing sight of his guardian, whom he had quitted, gazing after him in front of the royal Basilica, Raoul spurred on his horse, in order not only to escape from his own melancholy reflections, but also to hide from Olivain the emotion which his face might betray.

The aspect of external objects is often a mysterious guide communicating with the fibres of memory, which, in spite of us, will arouse them at times; this thread, like that of Ariadne, when once unraveled, will conduct one through a labyrinth of thought, in which one loses one's self endeavoring to follow that phantom of the past which is called recollection.

Now the sight of this château had taken Raoul back fifty leagues westward, and had caused him to review his life from the moment when he had taken leave of little Louise to that in which he had seen her for the first time; and every branch of oak, every weather-cock seen on a roof, reminded him, that instead of returning to the friends of his childhood, every instant removed him further from them, and that perhaps he had even left them forever.

With a full heart and burning head, he desired Olivain to lead on the horses to a little inn, which he observed by the wayside within gun-shot range, a little in advance of the place they had reached.

As for himself, he dismounted, remained under a beautiful group of chestnuts in flower, and bade Olivain send the host to him with writing paper and ink, to be placed on a table which he found there, conveniently ready for writing. Olivain obeyed and continued his road.

Raoul had been there about ten minutes, during five out of which he was lost in reverie, when there appeared within the circle comprised in his wandering gaze a rubicund figure, who, with a napkin round his body, and a white cap upon his head, approached him, holding paper, pen, and ink in hand.

"Ah! ah!" said the apparition, "every gentleman seems to have the same fancy, for, not a quarter of an hour ago, a young lad, well-mounted like you, as tall as you, and about your age, halted before this clump of trees, and had this table and this chair brought here, and dined here—with an old gentleman who seemed to be his tutor—upon a pie, of which they haven't left a mouthful, and a bottle of Mâcon wine, of which they haven't left a drop; but fortunately we have still got some of the same wine, and some of the same pies left, and if your worship will only give your orders——"

"No, friend," said Raoul, smiling, "I am obliged to you, but at this moment I want nothing but the things for which I have asked;—only I shall be very glad if the ink prove black, and pen good; upon these conditions, I will pay for the pen the price of the bottle, and for the ink the price of the pie."

"Very well, sir," said the host, "I'll give the pie and the bottle of wine to your servant, and in this way you will have the pen and ink into the bargain."

"Do as you like," said Raoul, who was beginning his experience with that particular class of society, who, when there were robbers on the high roads, were connected with them, and who, since highwaymen no longer exist, have advantageously supplied their place.

The host, his mind quite at ease about the bill, placed pen, ink, and paper upon the table. By a lucky chance the pen was tolerably good, and Raoul began to write. The host remained standing in front of him, looking with a kind of involuntary admiration at his handsome face, combining both gravity and sweetness of expression. Beauty has always been, and always will be, all-powerful.

"He's not a guest like the other one here just now," observed mine host to Olivain, who had rejoined his master to see if he wanted anything, "and your young master has no appetite."

"My master had appetite enough three days ago; but what can one do? he lost it the day before yesterday."

And Olivain and the host took their way together towards

the inn. Olivain, according to the custom of grooms contented with their places, related to the tavern-keeper all that he thought he could say about the young gentleman; and Raoul wrote to his father, after which he felt more composed. He looked around him to see if Olivain and the host were not watching him, while he impressed upon the paper, a mute and touching kiss, which the heart of Athos might easily divine on opening the letter.

During this time Olivain had finished his bottle and had eaten his pie; the horses also were refreshed. Raoul motioned the host to approach, threw a crown down on the table, mounted his horse, and posted his letter at Senlis. The rest that had been thus afforded to men and horses enabled them to continue their journey without stopping. At Verbérie, Raoul desired Olivain to make some inquiry about the young man who was preceding them; he had been observed to pass only three-quarters of an hour previously, but he was well mounted, as the tavern-keeper had already said, and rode at a rapid pace.

"Let us try to overtake this gentleman," said Raoul to Olivain; "like ourselves, he is on his way to join the army, and may prove agreeable company."

It was about four o'clock in the afternoon when Raoul arrived at Compiègne; there he dined heartily, and again inquired about the young gentleman who was in advance of them. He had stopped, like Raoul, at the hotel of the Bell and Bottle, the best at Compiègne, and had started again on his journey, saying that he should sleep at Noyon.

"Well, let us sleep at Noyon," said Raoul.

Olivain dared offer no opposition to this determination; but he followed his master grumbling.

"Go on, go on," said he, between his teeth, "expend your ardor the first day, to-morrow, instead of journeying twenty miles, you will do ten; the day after to-morrow, five, and in three days you will be in bed. There you must rest; all these young people are such braggarts."

It is easy to see that Olivain had not been taught in the school of the Planchets and the Grimauds. Raoul really felt tired, but d'Artagnan, that man of iron, who seemed to be made of nerve and muscle only, had struck him with admiration. Therefore, in spite of all Olivain's remarks, he continued to urge on his steed more and more, and following a pleasant little path, leading to a ferry, and which he had been assured shortened the journey by the distance of one league, he arrived at the summit of the hill, and perceived the river flowing before him. A little troop of men on horseback were waiting on the edge of the stream, ready to embark. But the rising ground soon deprived him of the sight of the travelers and when he had again attained a new height, the ferry-boat had left the shore, and was making for the opposite bank. Raoul, seeing that he could not arrive in time to cross the

ferry with the travelers, halted to wait for Olivain. At this
moment a shriek was heard which seemed to come from the
river. Raoul turned towards the side whence the cry had
sounded, and shaded his eyes from the glare of the setting
sun with his hand.

"Olivain!" he exclaimed, "what do I see below there?"

A second scream, more piercing than the first, now sounded.

"Oh, sir!" cried Olivain, "the rope which holds the ferry-boat
has broken, and the boat is drifting away. But what do I see
in the water? something struggling."

"Oh! yes," exclaimed Raoul, fixing his glance on one point
in the stream, splendidly illumined by the setting sun, "a horse,
a rider!"

"They are sinking!" cried Olivain in his turn.

It was true, and Raoul was convinced that some accident
had happened, and that a man was drowning; he gave his
horse its head, struck his spurs into its sides, and the animal,
urged on by pain, and feeling that he had space open before him,
bounded over a kind of paling which enclosed the landing-
place, and fell into the river, scattering to a distance waves of
white froth.

"Ah, sir!" cried Olivain, "what are you doing? Good God!"

Raoul was directing his horse towards the unhappy man in
danger.

"Leap, coward," cried Raoul, swimming on; then addressing
the traveler, who was struggling twenty yards in advance of
him, "courage, sir," said he, "courage, we are coming to your
aid."

"Too late!" murmured the young man, "too late!"

The water passed over his head, and stifled his voice in his
mouth.

Raoul sprang from his horse, to which he left the charge of
its own preservation, and in three or four strokes was at the
gentleman's side; he seized the horse at once by the curb, and
raised its head above water. The animal then breathed more
freely, and as if he comprehended that they had come to his
aid, redoubled his efforts. Raoul at the same time seized one
of the young man's hands, and placed it on the mane, at which
it grasped with the tenacity of a drowning man. Thus, sure
that the rider would not release his hold, Raoul now only directed his attention to the horse, which he guided to the opposite bank, helping it to cut through the water, and encouraging it with words.

All at once the horse stumbled against a ridge, and then
placed its foot on the sand.

"Saved!" exclaimed the man with gray hair, who sprang on
land in his turn.

"Saved," mechanically repeated the young gentleman, re-
leasing the mane, and gliding from the saddle into Raoul's
arms. Raoul was but ten yards from the shore; he bore the

fainting man there, and laying him down on the grass, unfastened the buttons of his collar, and unhooked his doublet. A moment later the gray-headed man was beside him. Olivain managed in his turn to land, after crossing himself repeatedly, and the people in the ferry-boat guided themselves as well as they were able towards the bank, with the aid of a hook which chanced to be in the boat.

Thanks to the attention of Raoul, and the man who accompanied the young gentleman, the color gradually returned to the pale cheeks of the dying man, who opened his eyes at first *be*wildered, but who soon fixed his glance upon the person who had saved him.

"Ah! sir," he exclaimed, "it was you I wanted; without you I was a dead man—thrice dead."

"But one recovers, sir, as you see," replied Raoul, "and we shall have had but a bath."

"Oh! my lord Count, what gratitude I feel!" exclaimed the man with gray hair.

"Ah, there you are, my good d'Arminges, I have given you a great fright, have I not? but it is your own fault; you were my tutor, why did you not teach me to swim better?"

"Oh, sir!" replied the old man, "had any misfortune happened to you, I should never have shown myself to the marshal again."

"I am the Count de Guiche," continued the young man; "my father is the Marshal de Grammont; and now that you know who I am, do me the honor of informing me who you are."

"I am the Viscount de Bragelonne," answered Raoul, blushing at being unable to name his father, as the other had done.

"Viscount, your countenance, your goodness, and your courage incline me towards you; my gratitude is already due to you —shake hands;—I ask your friendship."

"Sir," said Raoul, returning the count's pressure of the hand, "I like you already from my heart; pray regard me as a devoted friend, I beseech you."

"And now, where are you going, Viscount?" inquired de Guiche.

"To the army under the prince, Count."

"And I too!" exclaimed the young man, in a transport of joy. "Oh, so much the better; we shall fire off the first pistol shots together."

"It is well—be friends," said the tutor; "young as you both are, you were perhaps born under the same star, and were destined to meet. And now," continued he, "you must change your clothes; your servants, to whom I gave directions the moment they had left the ferry-boat, ought to be already at the inn. Linen and wine are both being warmed—come."

The young men had no objection to make to this proposition; on the contrary, they thought it an excellent one. They mounted again at once, while looks of admiration passed between them.

They were indeed, two elegant horsemen, with figures slight and upright—two noble faces, with open foreheads—bright and proud looks—loyal and intelligent smiles.

De Guiche might have been about eighteen years of age, but he was scarcely taller than Raoul, who was only fifteen.

CHAPTER XXX.

SKIRMISHING.

THE halt at Noyon was short, everyone there being wrapt in profound sleep. Raoul had desired to be awakened should Grimaud have arrived—but Grimaud did not arrive. Doubtless, too, the horses, on their parts, appreciated the eight hours of repose, and the abundant stabling which was granted to them. The Count de Guiche was awakened at five o'clock in the morning by Raoul, who came to wish him a good day. They had breakfast in haste, and at six o'clock had already gone ten miles.

The young count's conversation was most interesting to Raoul; therefore the count alone talked much. He criticised everybody humorously. Raoul trembled lest he should laugh among the rest at Mdme. de Chevreuse, for whom he entertained deep and genuine sympathy, but either instinctively, or from affection for the Duchesse de Chevreuse, he said everything possible in her favor. His praises increased Raoul's friendship for him twofold. The Queen herself was not spared, and Cardinal Mazarin came in for his share of ridicule.

The day passed away as rapidly as one hour. The count's tutor, a man of the world, and a "bon vivant," up to his eyes in learning, as his pupil described him, often recalled the profound erudition, the witty and caustic satire, of Athos to Raoul; but as regarded grace, delicacy, and nobility of external appearance, no one in these points was to be compared to the Count de la Fère.

The horses, which were better cared for than on the previous day, stopped at Arras at four o'clock in the evening. They were approaching the scene of war; and as bands of Spaniards sometimes took advantage of the night to make expeditions, even as far as the neighborhood of Arras, they determined to remain in this town until the morrow. The French army held all between Pont-à-Mare as far as Valenciennes, falling back upon Douai. The prince was said to be in person at Béthune.

The enemy's army extended from Cassel to Courtray; and as there was no species of violence or pillage which it did not commit, the poor people on the frontier quitted their isolated dwellings, and fled for refuge into the strong cities which held out shelter to them. Arras was encumbered with fugitives. An

approaching battle was much spoken of, the prince having manœuvred until that moment, only in order to await a reinforcement which had just reached him.
The young men congratulated themselves on having arrived
so opportunely. The evening was employed in discussing the
war; the grooms polished the arms; the young men loaded the
pistols in case of a skirmish, and they awoke in despair, having
both dreamt they arrived too late to participate in the battle.
In the morning it was rumored that Prince Condé had evac-
uated Béthune, and fallen back upon Carvin, leaving, however,
a strong garrison in the former city.
But as there was nothing positively certain in this report, the
young men decided to continue their way towards Béthune,
free, on the road, to diverge to the right, and to march to
Carvin if necessary.
The count's tutor was well acquainted with the country: he
consequently proposed to take a cross road, which lay between
that of Lens and that of Béthune. They obtained information
at Ablain, and a statement of their route was left for Grimaud.
About seven o'clock in the morning they set out. De Guiche,
who was young and impulsive, said to Raoul, "Here we are,
three masters and three servants. Our valets are well armed,
and yours seems to be tough enough."
"I have never seen him put to the test," replied Raoul, "but
he is a Breton, which promises something."
"Yes, yes," resumed de Guiche; "I am sure he can fire a musket when required. On my side, I have two very sure men, who
have been in action with my father. We, therefore, represent
six fighting men: if we should meet a little troop of enemies
equal or even superior in number to our own shall we charge
them, Raoul?"
"Certainly, sir," replied the viscount.
"Halloa! young people—stop there!" said the tutor, joining
in the conversation. "Zounds! how do you arrange my instructions, pray, Count? You seem to forget the orders I received to conduct you safe and sound to his highness, the
prince! Once with the army you may be killed at your good
pleasure; but, until that time, I warn you that in my capacity
of general of the army, I shall order a retreat, and turn my
back on the first red coat I see."
De Guiche and Raoul glanced at each other, smiling.
They arrived at Ablain without accident. There they inquired
and learned that the prince had quitted Béthune, and placed
himself between Cambria and La Venthie. Therefore, leaving
directions at every place for Grimaud, they took a cross road,
which conducted the little troop upon the bank of a small
stream flowing into the Lys. The country was beautiful, inter-
sected by valleys green as emerald. Every here and there they
passed little copses crossing the path which they were following. In the anticipation of ambuscade in these little woods, the

tutor placed his two servants at the head of the band, thus forming the advancing guard. Himself and the two young men
represented the body of the army, while Olivain, with his rifle
on his knee, and his eye on the watch, protected the rear.

They had observed for some time before them on the horizon a rather thick wood; and when they had arrived at a distance of a hundred steps from it, M. d'Arminges took his
usual precautions, and sent on in advance the count's two
grooms. The servants had just disappeared under the trees,
followed by the tutor, and the young men were laughing and
talking about a hundred yards off. Olivain was at the same distance in the rear, when suddenly there resounded five or six
musket-shots. The tutor cried halt; the young men obeyed,
pulling up their steeds, and at the same moment the two valets
were seen returning at a gallop.

The young men, impatient to hear the cause of the firing,
spurred on towards the servants. The tutor followed them behind.

"Were you stopped?" eagerly inquired the two youths.

"No," replied the servants," it is even probable that we have
not been seen; the shots were fired about a hundred steps in
advance of us, almost in the thickest part of the wood, and we
returned to ask your advice."

"My advice," said M. d'Arminges, "and, if needs be, my will
is, that we beat a retreat. There may be an ambuscade concealed in this wood."

"Did you see nothing there?" asked the count.

"I thought I saw," said one of the servants, "horsemen
dressed in yellow, creeping along the bed of the stream."

"That's it," said the tutor. "We have fallen in with a party
of Spaniards. Come back, sirs—back."

The two youths looked at each other, and at this moment a
pistol-shot and several cries for help were heard. Another
glance between the young men convinced them both that neither
had any wish to go back, and as the tutor had already turned
his horse's head they both spurred on forward, Raoul crying,
"Follow me, Olivain;" and Count de Guiche, "Follow, Urban
and Blanchet." And before the tutor could recover his surprise, they both disappeared into the forest. When they spurred
their steeds, they held their pistols ready also. Five minutes
after they arrived at the spot whence the noise had proceeded;
therefore, restraining their horses, they advanced cautiously.

"Hush," whispered de Guiche; "these are horsemen."

"Yes, three, but they have dismounted."

"Can you see what they are doing?"

"Yes, they appear to be searching a wounded or dead man."

"It is some cowardly assassination," said de Guiche.

"They are soldiers, though," resumed de Bragelonne.

"Yes, deserters; that is to say, highway robbers."

"At them!" cried Raoul. "At them!" echoed de Guiche.

"No, no! in the name of Heaven," cried the poor tutor.

But he was not listened to, and his cries only served to arouse the attention of the Spaniards.

The men on horseback at once rushed at the two youths, leaving the three others to complete the blunder of the two travelers; for, on approaching nearer, instead of one extended figure, the young men discovered two. De Guiche fired the first shot at ten paces, and missed his man; and the Spaniard, who had advanced to meet Raoul, aimed in his turn, and Raoul felt a pain in his left arm, similar to that of a blow from a whip. He let off his fire at but four paces. Struck in the breast, and extending his arms, the Spaniard fell back on the crup of his horse which, turning round, carried him off.

Raoul, at this moment, perceived the muzzle of a gun pointed at him, and remembering the recommendation of Athos, he, with the rapidity of lightning, made his horse rear as the shot was fired. His horse bounded to one side, losing its footing and fell, entangling Raoul's leg under its body. The Spaniard sprang forward, and seized the gun by its muzzle, in order to strike Raoul on the head by the butt-end. In the position in which Raoul lay, unfortunately, he could neither draw his sword from the scabbard, nor his pistols from their holsters. The butt-end of the musket hovered over his head, and he could scarcely restrain himself from closing his eyes, when, with one bound, de Guiche reached the Spaniard, and placed a pistol at his throat.

"Yield!" he cried, "or you are a dead man." The musket fell from the soldier's hands, who yielded at the instant.

De Guiche summoned one of his grooms, and delivering the prisoner into his charge, with orders to shoot him through the head if he attempted to escape, he leaped from his horse and approached Raoul.

"Faith, sir," said Raoul, smiling, although his pallor somewhat betrayed the excitement consequent on a first affair, "you are in a great hurry to pay your debts, and have not been long under any obligation to me. Without your aid," continued he, repeating the count's words, "I should have been a dead man—thrice dead."

"My antagonist took flight," replied de Guiche, "and left me at liberty to come to your aid. But you are seriously wounded! I see you are covered with blood!"

"I believe," said Raoul, "that I have got something like a scratch on the arm. If you will help me to drag myself from under my horse, I hope nothing need prevent us continuing our journey."

M. d'Arminges and Olivain had already dismounted, and were attempting to raise the horse, which struggled in terror. At last Raoul succeeded in drawing his foot from the stirrup, and his leg from under the animal, and in a second he was on his feet again.

"Nothing broken?" asked de Guiche.

"Faith, no, thank Heaven!" replied Raoul; "but what has become of the poor wretches whom these scoundrels were murdering?"

"I fear we arrived too late. They had killed them and taken flight, carrying off their booty. My two servants are examining the bodies."

"Let us go and see whether they are quite dead, or if they can be recovered," suggested Raoul. "Olivain, we have come into possession of two horses, but I have lost my own; take the best of the two for yourself and give me yours."

Saying this, they approached the spot where the victims lay.

CHAPTER XXXI.

THE REPULSIVE MONK.

Two men lay extended on the ground; one bathed in his blood, and motionless, with his face towards the earth; he was dead. The other leant against the tree, supported there by the two valets, and was praying fervently, with clasped hands and eyes raised to Heaven. He had received a ball in his thigh, which had broken the upper part of it. The young men first approached the dead man.

"He is a priest," said Bragelonne, "he has worn the tonsure. Oh the scoundrels! to lift their hands against a minister of God."

"Come here, sir," said Urban, an old soldier who had served under the Cardinal-duke in all his campaigns. "Come here, there is nothing to be done with him; whilst we may perhaps be able to save this one."

The wounded man smiled sadly. "Save me! oh no," said he; "but help me to die, you can."

"Are you a priest?" asked Raoul.

"No, sir."

"I ask, as your unfortunate companion appeared to me to belong to the church."

"He is the priest of Béthune, sir, and was carrying the holy vessels belonging to his church, and the treasure of the chapter, to a safe place, the prince having abandoned our town yesterday; and as it was known that bands of the enemy were prowling about the country, no one dared to accompany the good man, so I offered to do so.

"And, sir," continued the wounded man, "I suffer much, and would like, if possible, to be carried to some house."

"Where you can be relieved?" asked de Guiche.

"No, where I can confess myself."

"But perhaps you are not so dangerously wounded as you think," said Raoul.

"Sir," replied the wounded man, "believe me there is no time to lose; the ball has broken the thigh-bone, and entered the intestines."

"Are you a surgeon?" asked de Guiche.

"No, but I know a little about wounds, and mine is mortal. It is my soul that must be saved; as for my body, that is lost."

"Calm yourself, sir," replied de Guiche. "I swear to you that you shall receive the consolation that you ask. Only tell us where we shall find a house at which we can demand aid, and a village from which we can fetch a priest."

"Thank you, and God will reward you! about half a mile from this, on the same road, there is an inn! and about a mile further on, after leaving the inn, you will reach the village of Greney. There you must find the curate; or if he is not at home, go to the convent of the Augustins, which is the last house on the right in the village, and bring me one of the brothers. Monk or priest, it matters not."

"M. d'Arminges," said de Guiche, "remain beside this unfortunate man, and see that he is removed as gently as possible. The viscount and myself will go and find a priest."

"May Heaven prosper you!" replied the dying man, with an accent of gratitude impossible to describe.

The two young men galloped off in the direction mentioned to them, and ten minutes after reached the inn. Raoul without dismounting, called to the host, and announced that a wounded man was about to be brought to his house, and begged him in the meantime to prepare everything necessary for dressing his wounds. He desired him also, should he know in the neighborhood any doctor, surgeon, or operator, to fetch him, taking on himself the payment of the messenger. Raoul had already proceeded for more than a mile, and had begun to descry the first houses of the village, the red-tiled roofs of which stood out strongly from the green trees which surrounded them, when, coming towards them, mounted on a mule, they perceived a poor monk, whose large hat and grey worsted dress made them mistake him for an Augustine brother. Chance for once had seemed to favor them in sending what they were seeking for. He was a man about twenty-two or twenty-three years old, but who appeared to be aged by his ascetic exercises. His complexion was pale, not of that pallor which to Italians is a beauty, but a bilious, yellow hue; his light, colorless hair was short, and scarcely extended beyond the circle formed by the hat round his head, and his light blue eyes seemed entirely destitute of any expression.

"Sir," began Raoul, with his usual politeness, "are you an ecclesiastic?"

"Why do you ask me that?" replied the stranger, with a coolness which was barely civil.

"Because we want to know," said de Guiche, haughtily.

The stranger touched his mule with his heel, and continued his way.

In a second de Guiche had sprung before him and barred his passage. "Answer, sir," exclaimed he; "are you going to reply?"

"I am a priest," said the young man.

"Then, father," said Raoul, forcing himself to give a respect to his speech which did not come from his heart, "if you are a priest, then you have an opportunity, as my friend has told you, of exercising your vocation. At the next inn you will find a wounded man, who has asked the assistance of a minister of God, attended on by our servants."

"I will go," said the monk.

And he touched the mule.

"If you do not go, sir," said de Guiche, "remember that we have two steeds quite able to catch your mule, and the power of having you seized wherever you may be; and then I swear your trial will be short; one can always find a tree and a rope."

The monk's eyes again flashed, but that was all; he merely repeated his phrase, "I will go,"—and he went.

"Let us follow him," said de Guiche; "it will be the more sure plan."

"I was about to propose doing so," answered Bragelonne.

In the space of five minutes the monk turned round to ascertain whether he was followed or not.

"You see," said Raoul, "we have done wisely."

"What a horrible face that monk has," said de Guiche.

"Horrible!" replied Raoul, "especially in expression."

"What a misfortune for that poor wounded fellow to die under the hands of such a friar!"

"Pshaw!" said de Guiche. "Absolution comes not from him who administers it, but from God. However, let me tell you that I would rather die unshriven than have anything to say to such a confessor. You unshare of my opinion, are you not, Viscount? and I see you playing with the pommel of your pistol, as if you had a great inclination to break his head."

"Yes, Count, it is a strange thing, and one which might astonish you; but I feel an indescribable horror at the sight of that man. Have you ever seen a snake rise up in your path?"

"Never," answered de Guiche.

"Well, it has happened to me to do so in our Blaisois forests, and I remember that the first time I encountered one with its eyes fixed upon me, curled up, swinging its head, and pointing its tongue, that I remained fixed, pale, and as if fascinated, until the moment when the Count de la Fère——"

"Your father?" asked de Guiche.

"No, my guardian," replied Raoul, blushing.

"Very well——"

"Until the moment when the Count de la Fère," resumed

Raoul, "said, 'Come, Bragelonne, draw your sword;' then only I rushed upon the reptile, and cut it in two; just at the moment when it was rising on its tail and hissing ere it sprang upon me. Well, I vow I felt exactly the same sensation at the sight of that man when he said, 'Why do you ask me that?' and looked at me."

"Then you regret that you did not cut your servant in two morsels?"

"Faith, yes, almost," said Raoul.

They had now arrived in sight of the little inn, and could see on the opposite side the procession bearing the wounded man, and guided by M. d'Arminges. The youths rode up to the wounded man to announce that they were followed by the priest. He raised himself to glance in the direction which was pointed out, saw the monk, and fell back upon the litter, his face being lighted up by joy.

"And now," said the youths, "we have done all we can for you; and as we are in haste to join the prince's army we must continue our journey. You will excuse us, sir, but we are told that a battle is expected, and we do not wish to arrive the day after it."

"Go, my young sirs," said the sick man; "and may you both be blessed for your piety. God protect you and all dear to you!"

"Sir," said de Guiche to his tutor, "we will precede you, and you can rejoin us on the road to Cambrin."

The host was at his door, and everything was prepared, bed, bandages, and lint.

"Everything," said he to Raoul, "shall be done as you desire, but will you not stop to have your wound dressed?"

"Oh, my wound—mine—it is nothing," replied the viscount; "it will be time to think about it when we next halt; only have the goodness, should you see a horseman pass who should make inquiries about a young gentleman mounted on a chestnut horse, and followed by a servant, to tell him, in fact, that you have seen me, but that I have continued my journey, and intend to dine at Mazingarbe, and to stop at Cambrin. This cavalier is my attendant."

"Would it not be safer and more sure that I should ask him his name and tell him yours?" demanded the host.

"There is no harm in over-precaution. I am the Viscount de Bragelonne, and he is called Grimaud."

At this moment the wounded man passed on one side, and the monk on the other, the latter dismounting from his mule and desiring that it should be taken to the stables without being unharnessed.

"Come, Count," said Raoul, who seemed instinctively to dislike the vicinity of the Augustine; "come, I feel ill here," and the two young men spurred on.

The litter, borne by two servants, now entered the house.

The host and his wife were standing on the steps of the staircase, while the unhappy man seemed to suffer dreadful pain, and yet only to be anxious to know if he was followed by the monk. At the sight of this pale, bleeding man, the wife grasped her husband's arm.

"Well, what's the matter?" asked the latter; "are you going to be ill just now?"

"No, but look," replied the hostess, pointing to the wounded man; "I ask you if you recognize him?"

"In truth," cried the host, "misfortune has come upon our house; it is the executioner of Béthune!"

"The former executioner of Béthune!" murmured the young monk, shrinking back, and showing on his countenance the feeling of repugnance which his penitent inspired.

M. d'Arminges, who was at the door, perceived his hesitation.

"Sir monk," said he, "whether he is now or has been an executioner, this unfortunate being is no less a man. Render to him, then, the last service he will ask from you, and your work will be all the more meritorious."

The monk made no reply, but silently wended his way to the room where the two valets had deposited the dying man on a bed. D'Arminges and Olivain, and the two grooms, then mounted their horses, and all four started off at a quick trot to rejoin Raoul and his companion. Just as the tutor and his escort disappeared in their turn, a new traveler stepped on the threshold of the inn.

"What does your worship want?" demanded the host, pale and trembling from the discovery he had just made.

The traveler made a sign as if he wished to drink, pointed to his horse, and gesticulated like a man who is rubbing something.

"Ah!" said the host to himself, "this man seems dumb. And where will your worship drink?"

"There," answered the traveler, pointing to a table.

"I was mistaken," said the host; "he's not quite dumb. And what else does your worship wish for?"

"Have you seen a young man pass on a chestnut horse, followed by a groom?"

"The Viscount de Bragelonne?"

"Just so."

"Then you are called M. Grimaud?"

The traveler nodded.

"Well, then," said the host, "your young master has been here a quarter of an hour ago; he will dine at Mazingarbe, and sleep at Cambrin, which is two miles and a half from Mazingarbe."

"Thank you."

Grimaud was drinking his wine silently, and had just placed his glass on the table to be filled a second time, when a fearful scream resounded from the room occupied by the monk and the dying man. Grimaud sprang up.

"What is that?" said he; "whence that scream?"

"From the wounded man's room," replied the host; "the executioner of Béthune, who has just been brought in here, assassinated by the Spaniards, and who is now being confessed by an Augustine friar."

"The former ex-headman of Béthune?" muttered Grimaud; "a man between fifty-five and sixty, tall, strong, swarthy, black hair and beard?"

"That is he—do you know him?" asked the host.

"I have seen him once," replied Grimaud, a cloud darkening his countenance at the picture called up by his recollections.

At this instant a second scream, less piercing than the first, but followed by prolonged groaning, was heard.

"We must see what it is," said Grimaud.

If Grimaud was slow in speaking, we know that he was quick in action; he sprang to the door and shook it violently, but it was bolted on the other side.

"Open the door," cried the host, "open it instantly, monk!"

No reply.

"Unfasten it, or I will break in the panel," said Grimaud.

The same silence, and then, ere the host could oppose his design, Grimaud seized on some pincers which he perceived lying in a corner, and had forced the bolt. The room was inundated with blood, streaming through the mattresses upon which lay the wounded man, speechless,—the monk had disappeared.

"The monk!" cried the host; "where is the monk?"

Grimaud sprang towards the open window which looked into the court-yard.

"He has escaped by this means," exclaimed he.

"Do you think so?" said the host, bewildered; "boy, see if the mule belonging to the monk is still in the stable."

"There's no mule," replied the person to whom this question was addressed.

The host held up his hand, and looked around him suspiciously, whilst Grimaud knit his brows and approached the wounded man, whose worn, hard features awoke in his mind such awful recollections of the past.

"There can be no longer any doubt but that it is himself," he said.

"Does he still live?" inquired the inn-keeper.

Making no reply, Grimaud opened the poor man's jacket to feel if the heart beat, while the host approached in his turn; but in a moment they both fell back, the host uttering a cry of horror, and Grimaud becoming pallid. The blade of a dagger was buried up to the hilt in the left side of the executioner.

"Run—run for help!" cried Grimaud, "and I will remain beside him here."

The host quitted the room in agitation; and as for his wife, she had fled at the sound of her husband's cries.

CHAPTER XXXII.

GRIMAUD SPEAKS.

GRIMAUD was left alone with the executioner, who in a few moments opened his eyes.

"Help, help," he murmured; "oh, God! have I not a single friend in the world who will aid me either to live or to die?"

"Take courage," said Grimaud; "they are going to find help."

"Who are you?" asked the wounded man, fixing his half-opened eyes on Grimaud.

"An old acquaintance," replied Grimaud.

"You?" and the wounded man sought to recall the features of the person who was before him to his mind.

"One night, twenty years ago, my master fetched you from Béthune, and conducted you to Armentières."

"I know you well, now," said the executioner; "you are one of the four grooms. Where do you come from now?"

"I was passing on the road and drew up at this inn to rest my horse. They were relating to me how the executioner of Béthune was here, and wounded, when you uttered two piercing cries, upon hearing which, we ran to the door and forced it open."

"And the monk?" exclaimed the executioner; "did you see the monk who was shut in with me?"

"No, he was no longer here; he appears to have fled by that window. Was it he who stabbed you?"

"Yes," said the executioner.

Grimaud moved, as if to leave the room.

"What are you going to do?" asked the wounded man.

"He must be apprehended."

"Do not attempt it; he has avenged himself, and has done well. Now I may hope that God will forgive me, since my crime has been expiated."

"Explain yourself," said Grimaud.

"The women whom you and your masters made me kill— My lady, as you called her, she—was his mother."

Grimaud started, and stared at the dying man in a dull and stupid manner.

"His mother!" repeated he. "But does he know the secret, then?"

"I mistook him for a monk, and revealed it to him in confession."

"Unhappy man," cried Grimaud, whose face was covered with sweat, at the bare idea of the evil results which such a revelation might cause; "unhappy man, you named no one I hope?"

"I pronounced no name, for I knew none, except his mother's maiden name, and he recognized her; but he knows that his uncle was among her judges."

Thus speaking, he fell back exhausted. Grimaud, wishing to relieve him, advanced his hand toward the hilt of the dagger.

"Touch me not!" said the executioner; "if this dagger is withdrawn, I shall die."

Grimaud remained with his hand extended; then, striking his forehead, exclaimed: "Oh! if this man should ever discover the names of the others, my master is lost."

"Haste! haste to him, and warn him," cried the wounded man, "if he still lives; warn his friends too. My death, believe me, will not be the end of this terrible adventure."

"Where was the monk going?" asked Grimaud.

"Towards Paris."

"Who stopped him?"

"Two young gentlemen, who were on their way to join the army, and the name of one of whom I heard his companion mention, the Viscount de Bragelonne."

"And it was this young man who brought the monk to you. Then it was the will of God that it should be so, and this it is which is so awful," continued Grimaud; "and yet that woman deserved her fate; do you not think so?"

"On one's death-bed the crimes of others appear very small in comparison with one's own," said the executioner; and he fell back exhausted, and closed his eyes.

At this moment the host re-entered the room, followed not only by a surgeon, but by many other persons, whom curiosity had attracted to the spot. The surgeon approached the dying man, who seemed to have fainted.

"We must first extract the steel from the side," said he, shaking his head in a significant manner.

The prophecy which the wounded man had just uttered recurred to Grimaud, who turned away his head. The weapon, as we have already stated, was plunged into the body up to the hilt, and as the surgeon, taking it by the end, drew it from the wound, the wounded man opened his eyes, and fixed them in a manner truly frightful. When, at last, the blade had been entirely withdrawn, a red froth issued from the mouth of the wounded man, and a stream of blood sprang from the wound, when he at length drew breath; then, fixing his eyes on Grimaud, with a singular expression, the dying man uttered the last death rattle, and expired.

Then Grimaud, raising the dagger from the pool of blood which was gliding along the room—to the horror of all present—made a sign to the host to follow him, paid him with a generosity worthy of his master, and again mounted his horse.

Grimaud's first intentions had been to return to Paris, but he remembered the anxiety which his prolonged absence might occasion to Raoul, and, reflecting that there were now only two miles between Raoul and himself, that a quarter of an hour's ride would unite them, and that the going, returning, and explanation would not occupy an hour, he put spurs to his horse, and, ten minutes after, had reached the only inn of Mazingarbe.

Raoul was seated at table with the Count de Guiche and his tutor, when all at once the door opened, and Grimaud presented himself, travel-stained and dirty, still covered with the blood of the unfortunate executioner.

"Grimaud, my good Grimaud!" exclaimed Raoul, "here you are at last! Excuse me, sirs, this is not a servant, but a friend. How did you leave the count?" continued he; "does he regret me a little? Have you seen him since I left him? Answer, for I have many things to tell you, too; indeed, the last three days some odd adventures have happened,—but, what is the matter? how pale you are!—and blood, too! what is this?"

"It is the blood of the unfortunate man whom you left at the inn, and who died in my arms."

"In your arms?—that man! But know you who he was?"

"I know that he was the ex-headman of Béthune."

"You knew him? and he is dead?"

"Yes."

"Well, sir," said d'Arminges, "it is a common lot, and even a deathsman is not exempt from it. I had a bad opinion of him the moment I saw his wound, and, since he asked for a monk, you know that it was his own opinion, too, that death must ensue."

At the mention of the monk, Grimaud turned pale.

"Come, come," continued d'Arminges, "to dinner," for, like most men of his age and of his generation, he did not allow any emotion to interfere with a repast.

"You are right, sir," said Raoul. "Come, Grimaud, order some dinner for yourself, and when you have rested a little we can talk."

"No, sir, no," said Grimaud; "I cannot stop a moment; I must start for Paris again immediately. I can tell you but one thing, sir, for a secret you wish to know is not my own. You met this monk, you conducted him to the wounded man, and you had time to observe him, you would know him again were you to meet him?"

"Yes! yes!" exclaimed both the young men.

"Very well! if ever you meet him again, wherever it may be, whether on the high road or in the street, or in a church, anywhere, put your foot on his neck and crush him without pity, without mercy, as you would crush a viper; destroy him, and leave him not till he is dead; the lives of five men are not safe, in my opinion, as long as he lives!"

And without adding another word, Grimaud, profiting by the astonishment and terror into which he had thrown his auditors, rushed from the room. Ten minutes later the gallop of a horse was heard on the road—it was Grimaud on the way to Paris. When once in the saddle Grimaud reflected upon two things; firstly, that, at the pace he was going, his horse would not carry him ten miles, and secondly, that he had no money. But Grimaud's imagination was more prolific than his speech, and, therefore, at the first halt he sold his steed, and with the money obtained from the purchaser he took post-horses.

CHAPTER XXXIII.

A DINNER IN THE OLD STYLE.

THE second interview between the former Musketeers had not been so pompous and stiff as the first. It was held at a famous eating-house in the Rue de la Monnaie, of the sign of the Hermitage; for the following Wednesday, at eight o'clock in the evening precisely.

On that day, in fact, the four friends arrived punctually at the said hour, each from his own abode. Porthos had been trying a new horse; d'Artagnan came from being on guard at the Louvre; Aramis had been to visit one of his penitents in the neighborhood; and Athos, whose domicile was established in the Rue Guénegaud, found himself close at hand. They were therefore somewhat surprised to meet altogether at the door of the Hermitage.

The first words exchanged between the four friends, on account of the ceremony which each of them mingled with their demonstration, were somewhat forced, and even the repast began with a kind of stiffness. Athos perceived this embarrassment, and by way of supplying a prompt remedy, called for four bottles of champagne.

At this order, given in Athos' habitually calm manner, the face of the Gascon relaxed, and Porthos' brow was smooth. Aramis was astonished. He knew that Athos not only never drank, but that more, he had a kind of repugnance to wine. This astonishment was doubled when he saw Athos fill a bumper, and drink with his former gusto. His companions following his example, in an instant the four bottles were empty, and this excellent specific succeeded in dissipating even the slightest cloud which might have rested on their spirits. Now the four friends began to speak loud, scarcely waiting till one had finished for another to begin, and to assume each his favorite attitude on or at the table. Soon—strange fact —Aramis unfastened two buttons of his doublet, seeing which, Porthos unhooked his entirely.

Battles, long journeys, blows given and received, sufficed for the first subject of conversation; which then turned upon the silent struggles sustained against him who was now called the great Cardinal.

"Faith!" exclaimed d'Artagnan to his two friends, "you may well wish ill to Mazarin; for I assure you, on his side, he wishes you no good."

"Pooh! really?" asked Athos. "If I thought that the fellow knew me by my name, I would be re-baptized, for fear I should be thought to know him."

"He knows you better by your actions than by your name; he is quite aware that two gentlemen greatly aided the escape of M. de Beaufort, and he has instigated an active search for them, I can answer for it. This morning he sent for me to ask if I had obtained any information."

"And what did you reply?"

"That I had none yet; but that I was to dine to-day with two gentlemen, who would be able to give me some."

"You told him that?" said Porthos, his broad smile spreading over his honest face, "bravo! and you are not afraid?"

"No," replied Athos; "it is not the search of Mazarin that I fear."

"Now," said Aramis, "tell me a little what you do fear."

"Nothing for the present, at least in good earnest."

"And with regard to the past?" asked Porthos.

"Oh! the past is another thing," said Athos, sighing; "the past and the future."

"Are you afraid for your young Raoul?" asked Aramis.

"Well," said d'Artagnan, "one is never killed in a first engagement."

"Nor in a second," said Aramis.

"Nor in the third," returned Porthos; "and even when one is killed, one rises again, the proof of which is, that here we are!"

"No," said Athos, "it is not Raoul about whom I am anxious, for I trust he will conduct himself like a gentleman; and if he is killed—well—he will die bravely; but hold—should such misfortune happen—well——" Athos passed his hand across his pale brow.

"Well?" asked Aramis.

"Well, I shall look upon it as an expiation."

"Oh! ah!" said d'Artagnan; "I know what you mean."

"And I, too," added Aramis; "but you must not think of that, Athos; what is past is past."

"I don't understand," said Porthos.

"Beheading the woman."

"Oh, yes!" said Porthos; "true, I had forgotten it."

Athos looked at him intently.

"You have forgotten it, Porthos," said he.

"Faith! yes, it is so long ago," answered Porthos.

"This thing does not, then, weigh on your conscience?"

"Faith! no."

"And you, d'Artagnan?"

"I—I own that when my mind returns to that terrible period, I have no recollection of anything but the stiffened corpse of that poor Constance Bonacieux. Yes, yes," murmured he, "I have often felt regret for the victim, but never any remorse for the assassin."

Athos shook his head doubtfully.

"Consider," said Aramis, "if you admit divine justice and its participation in the beings of this world, that woman was punished by the will of Heaven. We are but the instruments— that is all."

"But as to free will, Aramis?"

"How acts the judge? He has a free will, and he condemns fearlessly. What does the executioner? he is master of his arm, and yet he strikes without remorse."

"The executioner!" muttered Athos, as if arrested by some recollection.

"I know that is terrible," said d'Artagnan; "but when I reflect that we have killed English, Rochellias, Spaniards, nay, even French, who never did us any other harm but to aim at us and to miss us, whose only fault was to cross swords with us, and not to be able to ward us off quick enough—I can, on my honor, find an excuse for my share for the murder of that woman."

"As for me," said Porthos, "now that you have reminded me of it, Athos, I have the scene again before me, as if I was there! My lady was there, as it were, in your place." (Athos changed color.) "I—I was where d'Artagnan stands. I wore a short sword, which cut like a Damascus—you remember it, Aramis, for you——"

"And you, Aramis?"

"Well, I think of it sometimes," said Aramis. "And I swear to you all three, that had the executioner of Béthune—was he not of Béthune?—yes, egad! of Béthune!—not been there, I would have cut off the head of the infamous being without remembering who I am, and even remembering it. She was a bad woman.

"And then," resumed Aramis, with a tone of philosophical indifference which he had assumed since he had belonged to the Church, and in which there was more atheism than confidence in God, "what is the use of thinking of all that? At the last hour we must confess this action, and God knows better than we can whether it is a crime, a fault, or a meritorious action. *I* repent of it? Egad! no! By honor, and by the holy cross, I only regret it because she was a woman."

"The most satisfactory part of the matter," said d'Artagnan, "is that there remains no trace of it."

"She left a son," observed Athos.

"Oh! yes; I know that," said d'Artagnan, "and you mentioned it to me; but who knows what has become of him? If the serpent be dead, why not its brood? Do you think that his uncle Winter would have brought up that young viper? Winter probably condemned the son as he had done the mother."

"Then," said Athos, "woe to Winter, for the child had done no harm."

"May the devil take me if the child be not dead," said Porthos. "There is so much fog in that detestable country, at least so d'Artagnan declares."

Just as this conclusion arrived at by Porthos was about probably to bring back hilarity to the faces now more or less clouded, footsteps were heard on the stair, and some one knocked at the door.

"Come in," cried Athos.

"Please your honors," said the host, "a person, in a great hurry, wishes to speak to one of you."

"To which of us?" asked all the four friends.

"To him who is called the Count de la Fère."

"It is I," said Athos, "and what is the name of the person?"

"Grimaud."

"Ah!" exclaimed Athos, turning pale. "Returned already? What has happened, then, to Bragelonne?"

"Let him enter," cried d'Artagnan, "let him come up."

But Grimaud had already mounted the staircase, and was waiting on the last step; so springing into the room, he motioned the host to leave it. The door being closed, the four friends waited in expectation. Grimaud's agitation, his pallor, the sweat which covered his face, the dust which soiled his clothes, all indicated that he was the messenger of some important and terrible news.

"Your honors," said he, "that woman had a child; that child has become a man; the tigress had a cub, the tiger has roused himself; he is ready to spring upon you—beware!"

Athos glanced around at his friends with a melancholy smile. Porthos turned to look at his sword which was hung up against the wall; Aramis seized his knife; d'Artagnan rose.

"What do you mean, Grimaud?" he exclaimed.

"That My lady's son has left England; that he is in France on his road to Paris, if he be not here already."

"The devil he is!" said Porthos. "Are you sure of it?"

"Certain!" replied Grimaud.

This announcement was received in silence. Grimaud was so breathless, so exhausted, that he had fallen back upon a chair. Athos filled a glass with champagne, and gave it to him.

"Well, and after all," said d'Artagnan, "supposing that he lives, that he comes to Paris, we have seen many other such. Let him come."

"Yes," echoed Porthos, stroking his sword, suspended to the wall, "we can wait for him, let him come."

"Moreover he is but a child," said Aramis.

Grimaud rose.

"A child!" he exclaimed. "Do you know what he has done —this child? Disguised as a monk, he discovered the whole history in confession from the executioner of Béthune, and having confessed him, after having learnt everything from him, he gave him absolution by planting this dagger into his heart. See, it is still red and wet, for it is not thirty hours ago since it was drawn from the wound."

And Grimaud threw the dagger on the table.

D'Artagnan, Porthos, and Aramis rose, and in one spontaneous motion rushed to their swords. Athos alone remained seated, calm and thoughtful.

"And you say he is dressed as a monk, as an Augustine monk, Grimaud? What sized man is he?"

"About my height," Grimaud said; "thin, pale, with light-blue eyes, and light hair."

"He did not see Raoul, I hope?" asked Athos.

"Yes, on the contrary, they met, and it was the viscount himself who conducted him to the bed of the dying man."

Athos rose, in his turn, without speaking—went, and unhooked his sword.

"Heigh, sir," said d'Artagnan, trying to laugh; "do you know we look very much like silly women! How is it that we four men who have faced armies without blinking, begin to tremble at the sight of a boy!"

"Yes," said Athos, "but this boy comes in the name of Heaven."

And they hastily quitted the inn.

CHAPTER XXXIV.

A LETTER FROM KING CHARLES THE FIRST.

THE reader must now cross the river Seine with us, and follow us to the door of the Carmelite Convent in the Rue St. Jacques. It is eleven o'clock in the morning, and the pious sisters have just finished saying a mass for the success of the armies of King Charles I. Leaving the church, a woman and a girl dressed in black, a widow and an orphan, have re-entered their cell.

The woman kneels on a painted wood and a short distance from her stands the girl, leaning against a chair, weeping.

The woman must have been handsome, but the traces of sorrow have aged her. The girl is lovely, and her tears only embellish her; the lady appears to be about forty years of age, the girl about fourteen.

"Oh, God!" prayed the kneeling supplicant, "protect my hus-· band, guard my son, and take my wretched life instead!"

"Oh, God!" murmured the girl, "leave me my mother!"

The two women who thus knelt together in prayer were the daughter and granddaughter of Henry IV., the wife and daughter of Charles I.

They had just finished their double prayer, when a nun softly tapped at the door of the cell.

"Enter, my sister," said the Queen.

"I trust your majesty will pardon this intrusion on her meditations, but a foreign lord has arrived from England, and waits in the parlor, demanding the honor of presenting a letter to your majesty."

"Oh! a letter! a letter from the King, perhaps. News from your father, do you hear, Henrietta—and the name of this lord?"

"Lord Winter."

"Lord Winter!" exclaimed the Queen, "the friend of my husband. Oh, let him come in!"

And the Queen advanced to meet the messenger, whose hand she seized affectionately, whilst he knelt down, and presented a letter to her contained in a gold case.

"Ah! my lord," said the Queen, "you bring us three things which we have not seen for a long timé. Gold, a devoted friend, and a letter from the King, our husband and master."

Winter bowed again, unable to reply from excess of emotion.

On their side the mother and daughter retired into the embrasure of a window to read eagerly the following letter:

"DEAR WIFE,—We have now reached the moment of decision. I have concentrated here at Naseby camp all the resources which Heaven has left me; and I write to you in haste from thence. Here I await the army of my rebellious subjects, and I am about to fight for the last time against them. If victorious, I shall continue the struggle; if beaten, I am completely lost. I shall try, in the latter case (alas! in our position, one must provide for everything), I shall try to gain the coast of France. But can they, will they receive an unhappy king, who will bring such a sad story into a country already agitated by evil discord? Your wisdom and your affection must serve me as guides. The bearer of this letter will tell you, madam, what I dare not trust to the risk of miscarrying. He will explain to you the steps which I expect you to pursue. I charge him also with my blessing for my children, and with the sentiments of my heart for yourself, dear wife."

The letter bore the signature, not of "Charles, King," but of "Charles—still king."

"And let him be no longer King!" cried the Queen. "Let him be conquered, exiled, proscribed, provided he still lives. Alas! in these days the throne is too dangerous a place for me to wish him to keep it! But, my lord, tell me," she continued, "hide nothing from me—what is, in truth, the King's position? Is it as hopeless as he thinks?"

"Alas! madam—more hopeless than he thinks."

"And now, my lord, that I see how sad the position of the King is, tell me with what you are charged on the part of my royal husband."

"Well then, madam," said Winter, "the King wishes you to try and discover the dispositions of the King and Queen towards him."

"Alas! you know the King is but still a child, and the Queen is a woman weak enough, too. Mazarin is everything here."

"Does he desire to play the part in France that Cromwell plays in England?"

"Oh, no! He is a subtle and cunning Italian, who, though he may dream of crime, dares never commit it; and unlike Cromwell, who disposes of both Houses, Mazarin has had the Queen to support him in his struggle with the Parliament."

"More reason, then, that he should protect a king pursued by his Parliament."

The Queen shook her head despairingly.

"If I judge for myself, my lord," she said, "the Cardinal will do nothing and will even, perhaps, act against us. The presence of my daughter and myself in France is already irksome to him; much more so would be that of the King. My lord," added Henrietta with a melancholy smile, "it is sad, and almost shameful, to be obliged to say that we have passed the winter in the Louvre without money, without linen—almost without bread, and often not rising from bed because we wanted fire."

"Horrible!" cried Winter; "the daughter of Henry IV., and the wife of King Charles! Wherefore did you not apply then, madam, to the first person you saw from us?"

"Such is the hospitality shown to a queen by the minister, from whom a king would demand it."

"But I heard that a marriage between the Prince of Wales and Mdlle. d'Orleans was spoken of," said Winter.

"Yes, for an instant I hoped it was so. The young people felt a mutual esteem; but the Queen, who at first sanctioned their affection, changed her mind, and the Duke d'Orleans, who had encouraged the familiarity between them, has forbidden his daughter to think any longer about the union. Oh, my lord!" continued the Queen, without restraining her tears, "it is better to fight as the King has done, and to die, as perhaps he will, than to live begging as I have."

"Courage, madam! courage! Do not despair! The interests of the French crown—endangered this moment—are to discourage civil rebellion in a nation so near to it. Mazarin, as a statesman, will understand the necessity of doing so."

"But are you sure," said the Queen doubtfully, "that you have not been forestalled by the Puritan?"

"By tailors, coachmakers, brewers. Ah! I hope, madam, that the Cardinal will not enter into negotiations with such men!"

"Ah! what wishes he himself?" asked Mdme. Henrietta.

"Solely the honor of the King—of the Queen."

"Well, let us hope that he will do something for the sake of their honor," said the Queen. "A true friend's eloquence is so powerful, my lord, that you have reassured me. Give me your hand, and let us go to the minister; and yet," she added, "suppose he refuse, and that the King loses the battle!"

"His majesty will then take refuge in Holland, where I hear that the Prince of Wales is."

"And can his majesty count upon many such subjects as yourself for his fight?"

"Alas! no, madam," answered Winter; "but the case is provided for, and I am come to France to seek allies."

"Allies!" said the Queen, shaking her head.

"Madam!" replied Winter, "provided I can find some old friends of former times, I will answer for anything."

"Come, then, my lord," said the Queen, with the painful doubt that is felt by those who have suffered much; "come, and may Heaven hear you."

CHAPTER XXXV.

CROMWELL'S LETTER.

At the very moment when the Queen quitted the convent to go to the Palais Royal, a young man dismounted at the gate of this royal abode, and announced to the guards that he had something of consequence to communicate to Cardinal Mazarin. Although the Cardinal was often tormented by fear, he was more often in need of counsel and information, and he was therefore sufficiently accessible. The true difficulty of being admitted was not to be found at the first door, and even the second was passed easily enough; but at the third watched, besides the guard and the doorkeepers, the faithful Bernouin, a Cerberus whom no speech could soften; no wand, even of gold, could charm.

It was, therefore, at the third door, that those who solicited or were bid to an audience, underwent a formal interrogatory.

The young man, having left his horse tied to the gate in the court, mounted the great staircase, and applied to Bernouin for admittance to the Cardinal for whom he said he bore a message from General Oliver Cromwell.

"Be so good as to mention this name to his Eminence, and to bring me word whether he will receive me—yes or no."

Saying which, he resumed the sullen and proud bearing peculiar at that time to the Puritans. Bernouin cast an inquisitorial glance at the young man, and entered the cabinet of the Cardinal, to whom he transmitted the messenger's words.

"What kind of a man?" said Mazarin——.

"A true Englishman, your Eminence. Hair sandy-red—more red than sandy; grey blue eyes—more grey than blue; and for the rest, stiff and proud."

"Let him give in his letter."

"His Eminence asks for the letter," said Bernouin, passing back into the ante-chamber.

"His Eminence cannot see the letter without the bearer of it," replied the young man; "but to convince you that I am really the bearer of a letter, see, here it is; and add," continued he, "that I am not a simple messenger, but an envoy extraordinary."

Bernouin re-entered the cabinet, and returning in a few seconds,—"Enter, sir," said he.

The young man appeared on the threshold of the minister's closet, in one hand holding his hat, in the other the letter. Mazarin rose. "Have you, sir," asked he, "a letter accrediting you to me?"

"There it is, my lord," said the young man.

Mazarin took the letter, and read it thus:

"Mr. Mordaunt, one of my secretaries, will remit this letter of introduction to his Eminence, Cardinal Mazarin, in Paris. He is also the bearer of a second confidential epistle for his Eminence.   "OLIVER CROMWELL."

"Very well, M. Mordaunt," said Mazarin, "give me the second letter, and sit down."

The young man drew from his pocket the second letter, presented it to the Cardinal, and sat down. The Cardinal, however, did not unseal the letter at once, but continued to turn it again and again in his hand; then, in accordance with his usual custom, and judging from experience that few people could hide anything from him, when he began to question them, fixing his eyes upon them at the same time, he thus addressed the messenger:

"You are very young, M. Mordaunt, for this difficult task of ambassador, in which the oldest diplomatists sometimes fail."

"My lord, I am twenty-three years of age; but your Eminence is mistaken in saying that I am young. I am older than your Eminence, although I possess not your wisdom. Years of suffering, in my opinion, count double, and I have suffered for twenty years."

"Ah, yes, I understand," said Mazarin; "want of fortune, per-

haps. You are poor—are you not?" Then he added to himself—"These English revolutionists are all beggars and ill-bred."

"My lord, I ought to have a fortune of three hundred a year,
but it has been taken from me."

"You are not then a commoner?" said Mazarin, astonished.

"If I bore my title I should be a lord. If I bore my name,
you would have heard one of the most illustrious in England."

"What is it, pray?" asked Mazarin.

"My name is Mordaunt," replied the young man, bowing.

Mazarin now understood that Cromwell's envoy desired to
retain his incognito. He was silent for an instant, and during
that time he scanned the young man even more attentively
than he had done at first. The messenger was unmoved.

"Devil take these Puritans," said Mazarin aside; "they are
cut out of marble." Then he added aloud, "But you have rela-
tives left to you?"

"I have one remaining, and three times I have presented myself to him to ask his support, and three times he has desired
his servants to turn me away."

"Oh, my dear M. Mordaunt," said Mazarin, hoping, by a
display of affected pity, to catch the young man in a snare,
"how extremely your history interests me! You know not,
then, anything of your birth, you have never seen your mother?"

"Yes, my lord; she came three times, while I was a child, to
my nurse's house; I remember the last time she came as well
as if it were to-day."

"You have a good memory," said Mazarin.

"Very, my lord!" said the young man, with such peculiar
emphasis that the Cardinal felt a shudder run through all his
veins.

"And who brought you up?" he asked again.

"A French nurse, who sent me away when I was five years
old, because no one paid her for me, telling me a kinsman's
name of whom she had heard my mother often speak."

"What became of you?"

"As I was weeping and begging on the high road, a minister
from Kingston took me in, instructed me in the Calvinistic
faith, taught me all he knew himself, and aided me in my researches after my family."

"And these researches?"

"Were fruitless; chance did everything."

"You discovered what had become of your mother?"

"I learnt that she had been assassinated by my relation, aided
by four friends, but I was already aware that I had been
robbed of all my wealth, and degraded from my nobility, by
King Charles I."

"Oh! I now understand why you are in the service of Cromwell; you hate the King."

"Yes, my lord, I do hate him!" said the young man.

Mazarin marked, with surprise, the diabolical expression with which the young man uttered these words; as, in general, ordinary countenances are colored by the blood—his face seemed dyed by hatred, and became livid.

"Your history is a terrible one, M. Mordaunt, and touches me keenly; but, happily for you, you serve an all-powerful master, he ought to aid you in your search; we have so many means of gaining information."

"My lord, to a hound of good breed it is only necessary to show but one end of a trail, that he may be certain to reach the other end."

"But this relative whom you mentioned—do you wish me to speak to him?" said Mazarin, who was anxious to make a friend about Cromwell's person.

"Thanks, my lord, I will speak to him myself; he will treat me better the next time I see him."

"You have the means, then, of touching him?"

"I have the means of making myself feared."

Mazarin looked at the man, but at the fire which shot from his glance, he bent down his head; embarrassed how to continue such a conversation, he opened Cromwell's letter. It was lengthy, and began by alluding to the situation of England, and announcing that he was on the eve of a decisive engagement with King Charles, and certain of success. He then adverted to the hospitality and protection afforded by France to Henrietta Maria, and continued:

"As regards King Charles, the question must be viewed differently; in receiving and aiding him, France will censure the acts of the English nation, and thus so essentially do harm to England, and especially to the progress of the Government which she reckons upon forming, so that such a proceeding will be equal to flagrant hostilities."

At this moment Mazarin became very uneasy at the turn which the letter was taking, and paused to glance under his eyes at the young man. The latter continued lost in thought. Mazarin resumed his reading of the General's worthy epistle, which ended by demanding perfect neutrality from France.

"A neutrality," it said, "which was solely to consist in excluding King Charles from the French territories, nor to aid a king so entirely a stranger, either by arms, money, or troops. Farewell, sir, should we not receive a reply in the space of fifteen days, I shall presume my letter has miscarried.

"OLIVER CROMWELL."

"M. Mordaunt," said the Cardinal, raising his voice, as if to arouse the thinker, "my reply to this letter will be more satisfactory to General Cromwell if I am convinced that all are ignorant of my having given one; go, therefore, and await it at Boulogne on the sea, and promise me to set out to-morrow morning."

"I promise, my lord," replied Mordaunt; "but how many days will your Eminence oblige me to await your reply?"

"If you do not receive it in ten days, you can leave."

Mordaunt bowed.

"It is not all, sir," continued Mazarin; "your private adventures have touched me to the quick; besides, the letter from Mr. Cromwell makes you an important person in my eyes as ambassador; come, tell me what can I do for you?"

Mordaunt reflected a moment, and, after some hesitation, was about to speak, when Bernouin entered hastily, and, bending down to the ear of the Cardinal, whispered to him:

"My lord, Queen Henrietta Maria, accompanied by an English noble, is just entering the Palais Royal at this moment."

Mazarin made a bound from his chair, which did not escape the attention of the young man, and repressed the confidence he was about to make.

"Sir," said the Cardinal, "you have heard me? I fix on Boulogne because I presume that every town in France is indifferent to you; if you prefer another, name it; but you can easily conceive that, surrounded as I am by influences from which I can escape alone by means of discretion, I desire your presence in Paris to be ignored."

"I shall go, sir," said Mordaunt, advancing a few steps to the door by which he had entered.

"No, not that way, I beg, sir," quickly exclaimed the Cardinal; "be so good as to pass by that gallery, by which you can gain the hall; I do not wish you to be seen leaving—our interview must be kept secret."

Mordaunt followed Bernouin, who conducted him through a neighboring chamber, and left him with a doorkeeper showing him the way out.

CHAPTER XXXVI.

HENRIETTA MARIA AND MAZARIN.

The Cardinal rose, and advanced in haste to receive the Queen of England. He showed the more respect to this Queen, deprived of all pomp, and without followers, as he felt some self-reproach for his own want of heart and his avarice. But suppliants for favor know how to vary the expression of their features, and the daughter of Henry IV. smiled as she advanced to meet one whom she hated and despised.

"Ah!" said Mazarin to himself, "what a sweet face! does she come to borrow money of me?"

And he threw an uneasy glance at his strong box; he even turned inside the bevel of the magnificent diamond ring, the brilliancy of which drew every eye upon his hand, which indeed was handsome and white.

"Your Eminence," said the august visitor, "it was my first

intention to speak of the affairs which have brought me here, to the Queen, my sister, but I have reflected that political matters are more especially the concerns of men. I am come to petition you, too happy should my prayer be heard favorably."

"I listen, madam, with interest," said Mazarin.

"Your Eminence, it concerns the war which the King, my husband, now sustains against his rebellious subjects. You are, perhaps, ignorant that they are fighting in England," added she, with a melancholy smile, "and that, in a short time they will fight in a much more decided fashion than they have done hitherto."

"I am completely ignorant of it, madam," said the Cardinal, accompanying his words with a slight shrug of the shoulders; "alas, our own wars have quite absorbed the time and the mind of a poor, incapable, and infirm minister like myself."

"Well, then, your Eminence," said the Queen, "I must inform you that Charles I., my husband, is on the eve of a decisive engagement. In case of a check—" (Mazarin made a slight movement) "one must foresee everything; in case of a check, he desires to retire into France, and to live here as a private individual. What do you say to this project?"

The Cardinal had listened without permitting a single fibre of his face to betray what he felt, and his smile remained as it ever was—false and flattering, and, when the Queen finished speaking, he said:

"Do you think, madam, that France, agitated and disturbed as it is, would be a safe refuge for a dethroned king? How will the crown, which is not too firmly set on the head of Louis IV., support a double weight?"

"This weight was not so heavy when I was in peril," interrupted the Queen, with a sad smile, "and I ask no more for my husband than has been done for me; you see that we are very humble monarchs, sir."

"Oh, you, madam, you," the Cardinal hastened to say, in order to cut short the explanations which he foresaw were coming, "with regard to you, that is another thing; a daughter of Henry IV., of that great, that sublime sovereign——"

"All which does not prevent you refusing hospitality to his son-in-law, sir! Nevertheless, you ought to remember that that great, that sublime monarch, when proscribed at one time, as my husband may be, demanded aid from England, and that England accorded it to him; and it is but just to say that Queen Elizabeth was not his niece."

"*Peccato!*" said Mazarin, writhing beneath this simple eloquence, "your majesty does not understand me; you judge my intentions wrongly, and that is because doubtless I explain myself ill in French."

"Speak Italian, sir; ere the Cardinal, your predecessor, sent our mother, Marie de Medicis, to die in exile, she taught us that language. If anything yet remains of that great, that sublime King Henry of whom you have just spoken, he would be much surprised at so little pity for his family being united to such a profound admiration of himself."

The perspiration hung in large drops upon Mazarin's brow.

"That admiration, on the contrary, so great, so real, madam," returned Mazarin, without noticing the change of language offered to him by the Queen, "that if the King, Charles I., whom Heaven protect from evil! came into France, I would offer him my house—my own house—but, alas! it would be but an unsafe retreat. Some day the people will burn that house, as they burnt that of Marshal d'Ancre. Poor Concini! and yet he but desired the good of the people."

"Yes, my lord, like yourself!" said the Queen ironically.

"Madam," cried Mazarin, more and more moved, "will your majesty permit me to give you counsel?"

"Speak, sir," replied the Queen; "the counsel of so prudent a man as yourself ought certainly to be good."

"Madam, believe me, the King ought to defend himself to the last, and not leave his kingdom. Absent kings are very soon forgotten; if he passes over to France his cause is lost."

"But then," persisted the Queen, "if such be your advice, and you have his interest at heart, send him some help of men and money, for I can do nothing for him: I have sold even to my last diamond to aid him. If I had a single jewel left, I should have bought wood this winter to make a fire for my daughter and myself."

"Oh, madam," said Mazarin, "your majesty knows not what you ask. On the day when foreign succor follows in the train of a king to replace him on his throne, it is an avowal that he no longer possesses the help and the love of his subjects."

"To the point, sir," said the Queen, "to the point, and answer me, yes or no; if the King persists in remaining in England, will you send him succor? If he comes to France, will you accord him hospitality? What do you intend to do?—speak."

"I will go this instant and consult the Queen, and we will refer the affair at once to the Parliament."

"With which you are at war, is it not so? You will charge Broussel to report it. Enough, sir, enough. I understand you, or rather, I am wrong. Go to the Parliament; for it was from this Parliament, the enemy of monarchs, that the daughter of the great, the sublime Henry IV., whom you so much admire, received the only relief this winter, which prevented her from dying of hunger and cold!"

And with these words Henrietta rose in majestic indignation, while the Cardinal, raising his hands clasped towards her, exclaimed, "Ah, madam, madam, how little you know me!"

"It signifies little," said Mazarin, when he was alone; "it gave me pain, and it is an ungracious part to play. But I have said nothing either to the one or the other. Bernouin!"

Bernouin entered.

"See if the young man with the black doublet and the short hair, who was with me just now, is still in the palace."

Bernouin went out, and soon returned with Comminges, who was on guard.

"Your Eminence," said Comminges, "as I was re-conducting the young man for whom you have asked, he approached the glass door of the gallery, and gazed intently upon some object, doubtless the picture by Raphael, which is opposite the door. He reflected for a second, and then descended the stairs. I believe I saw him mount on a grey horse and leave the palace court. But is not your Eminence going to the Queen?"

"For what purpose?"

"Guitaut, my uncle, has just told me that her majesty has received news of the army."

"It is well—I will go."

Comminges had seen rightly, and Mordaunt had really acted as he had related. In crossing the gallery parallel to the large glass gallery, he perceived Lord Winter, who was waiting until the Queen had finished her negotiation.

At this sight the young man stopped short, not in admiration of Raphael's picture, but as if fascinated at the sight of some terrible object. His eyes dilated, and a shudder ran through his body. One would have said that he longed to break through the wall of glass which separated him from his enemy; for if Comminges had seen with what an expression of hatred the eyes of this young man were fixed upon Winter, he would not have doubted for an instant but that the English lord was his mortal foe.

But he stopped—doubtless to reflect; for, instead of allowing his first impulse, which had been to go straight to Lord Winter, to carry him away, he leisurely descended the staircase, left the palace with his head down, mounted his horse, which he reined in at the corner of the Rue Richelieu, and with his eyes fixed on the gate, he waited until the Queen's carriage had left the court.

He did not wait long, for the Queen scarcely remained a quarter of an hour with Mazarin; but this quarter of an hour of expectation appeared a century to him. At last the heavy machine, called a coach in those days, came out, rumbling, and Winter, still on horseback, bent again to the door to converse with her majesty.

The horses started into a trot, and took the road to the Louvre, which they entered. Before leaving the convent of the Carmelites, Henrietta had desired her daughter to attend her at the palace, which she had inhabited for a long time, and which she had only left because their poverty seemed to them more difficult to bear in gilded chambers.

Mordaunt followed the carriage, and when he had watched it drive under the sombre arches, he went and stationed himself under a wall over which the shadow was extended, and remained motionless, like an equestrian statue.

CHAPTER XXXVII.

CHANCE OR PROVIDENCE.

"WELL, madam," said Winter, when the Queen had dismissed her attendants, "does the Cardinal refuse to receive the King? France refuse hospitality to an unfortunate prince? But it is for the first time, madam!"

"I did not say France, my lord, I said the Cardinal, and the Cardinal is not even a Frenchman."

"But did you see the Queen?"

"It is useless," replied Henrietta; "the Queen will not say yes when the Cardinal has said no. Are you not aware that this Italian directs everything, both indoors and out? Did you not observe the agitation in the Palais Royal, the passing to and fro of busy people? Can they have received any news, my lord?"

"Not from England, madam. I made such haste that I am certain of not having been forestalled. I set out three days ago, passing miraculously through the Puritan army, and I took post-horses with my servant Tony; the horses upon which we were mounted were bought in Paris. Besides, the King, I am certain, awaits your majesty's reply before risking anything."

"You will tell him, my lord," resumed the Queen, despairingly, "that I shall go and die by his side."

"Madam, madam!" exclaimed Winter, "your majesty abandons yourself to despair; and yet, perhaps, there still remains some hope."

"No friends left, my lord; no other friends left in the whole world but yourself! Oh God!" exclaimed the poor Queen, raising her eyes to Heaven, "have you indeed taken back all the generous hearts which existed in the world?"

"I hope not, madam," replied Winter, thoughtfully; "I once spoke to you of four men."

"What can be done with four men?"

"Four devoted, resolute men can do much, be assured, madam, and those of whom I speak have done much at one time."

"And these men were your friends?"

"One of them held my life in his hands, and gave it to me. I know not whether he is still my friend; but since that time I have remained his."

"Tell me their names, perhaps I have heard them mentioned, and might be able to assist you in finding them."

"One of them was called the Chevalier d'Artagnan."

"Oh! my lord, if I do not mistake, the Chevalier d'Artagnan is a lieutenant of the life guards; but take care, for I fear that this man is devoted entirely to the Cardinal."

"That would be a misfortune," said Winter, "and I shall begin to think that we are really doomed."

"But the others," said the Queen, who clung to this last hope as a shipwrecked man clings to the remains of his vessel, "the others, my lord!"

"The second—I heard his name by chance; for before fighting us, these four gentlemen told us their names; the second was called the Count de la Fère. As for the two others, I had so much the habit of calling them by their nicknames, that I have forgotten their real ones."

"My lord, they must be found; but what can four men, or rather three men, do!—for I tell you, you must not count on M. d'Artagnan."

"It will be one valiant sword the less, but there will remain still three, without reckoning my own; now four devoted men round the King to protect him from his enemies,—to be at his side in battle, to aid him in counsel, to escort his flight, are sufficient—not to make the King a conqueror, but to save him if conquered; and whatever Mazarin may say—once on the shores of France, your royal husband may find as many retreats and asylums as the sea-bird finds in storms."

"Seek them, my lord,—seek these gentlemen; and if they will consent to go with you to England, I will give to each a dukedom the day that we re-ascend the throne, besides as much gold as would pave Whitehall. Seek them, my lord. Seek them, I conjure you."

"I will search for them well, madam," said Winter, "and doubtless I shall find them—but time fails me. Has your majesty forgotten that the King expects your reply, and awaits it in agony?"

"Then, indeed, we are lost," cried the Queen, in the fulness of a broken heart.

At this moment the door opened, and the young Henrietta appeared; then the Queen, with that wonderful strength which is the heroism of a mother, repressed her tears, and motioned to Winter to change the subject of conversation.

"What do you want, Henrietta?" she demanded.

"My mother," replied the young princess, "a cavalier has just entered the Louvre, and wishes to present his respects to your majesty; he arrives from the army, and has, he says, a letter to remit to you on the part of the Marshal de Grammont, I think."

"Ah!" said the Queen to Winter, "he is one of my faithful adherents; but do you not observe, my dear lord, that we are so poorly served that it is my daughter who fills the office of introducer?"

"Madam, have pity on me," exclaimed Winter; "you break my heart!"

"And who is the cavalier, Henrietta?" asked the Queen.

"I saw him from the window, madam; he is a young man who appears scarcely sixteen years of age, the Viscount de Bragelonne."

The Queen, smiling, gave a nod; the young princess opened the door, and Raoul appeared on the threshold.

Advancing a few steps towards the Queen, he knelt down.

"Madam," said he, "I bear to your majesty a letter from my friend the Count de Guiche, who told me he had the honor of being your servant; this letter contains important news and the expression of his respect."

At the name of the Count de Guiche, a blush spread over the cheeks of the young princess, and the Queen glanced at her with some degree of severity.

"You told me that the letter was from Marshal de Grammont, Henrietta," said the Queen.

"I thought so, madam," stammered the young girl.

"It is my fault, madam," said Raoul. "I did announce myself in truth, as coming on the part of de Grammont; but being wounded in the right arm, he was unable to write, and therefore the Count de Guiche served as his secretary."

"There has been fighting, then?" asked the Queen, motioning to Raoul to rise.

"Yes, madam," said the young man.

"But no harm has happened to the young Count de Guiche?" she asked; "for not only is he our servant, as you say sir, but more; he is one of our friends."

"No madam," replied Raoul; "on the contrary, he gained great glory on that day, and had the honor of being embraced by his highness the prince on the field of battle."

The young princess clasped her hands; and then, ashamed of having been betrayed into such a demonstration of joy, she half turned away, and bent over a vase of roses, as if to inhale their odor.

"Let us see," said the Queen, "what the count says." And she opened the letter and read:

"MADAM,—Being unable to have the honor of writing to you myself, by reason of a wound which I have received in the right hand, I have commanded my son, the Count de Guiche, who with his father, is equally your humble servant, to write to tell you that we have just gained the battle of Lens, and that this victory cannot fail to give great power to the Cardinal Mazarin and to the Queen over the affairs of Europe. If her majesty will have faith in my counsels, she ought to profit by this event to address at this moment, in favor of her august husband, the court of France. The Viscount de Bragelonne, who will have the honor of remitting this letter to your majesty, is the friend of my son, to whom he owes his life; he is a gentleman in whom your majesty can confide entirely, in the case when your majesty may have some verbal or written order to forward to me.

"I have the honor to be, with respect, &c.,

"DE GRAMMONT."

At the moment, when mention occurred of his having rendered a service to the count, Raoul could not help turning his eyes toward the young princess, and then he saw in her eyes an expression of infinite gratitude to the young man; he no longer doubted that the daughter of King Charles the First loved his friend.

"The battle of Lens gained!" said the Queen; "they are lucky indeed for me—they can gain battles! Yes, Marshal de Grammont is right; this will change the aspect of affairs; but I much fear it will do nothing for ours, even if it does not harm them. This is recent news, sir," continued she, "and I thank you for having made such haste to bring it to me; without this letter I should not have heard it till to-morrow—perhaps after to-morrow—the last of all Paris."

"Madam," said Raoul, "the Louvre is but the second palace which this news has reached; it is as yet unknown to all, and I had sworn to the Count de Guiche to remit this letter to your majesty ere even I should greet my guardian."

"Your guardian! is he too a Bragelonne?" asked Lord Winter. "I knew formerly a Bragelonne—is he still alive?"

"No, sir, he is dead; and I believe it is from him that my guardian, whose near relation he was, inherited the estate from which I take my name."

"And your guardian, sir," asked the Queen, who could not help feeling some interest in the handsome young man before her, "what is his name?"

"The Count de la Fère, madam," replied the young man, bowing.

Winter made a gesture of surprise, and the Queen turned to him with a start of joy.

"The Count de la Fère!" cried Winter in his turn. "Oh, sir, reply, I entreat you—is not the Count de la Fère a noble, whom I remember, handsome and brave, a Musketeer under Louis XIII., and who must be now about forty-seven or forty-eight years of age?"

"Yes, sir, you are right in every respect."

"And who served under a nick-name?"

"Under the name of Athos. Latterly I heard his friend, M. d'Artagnan, give him that name."

"That is it, madam, that is the same. God be praised! And he is in Paris?" continued he, addressing Raoul; then, turning to the Queen—"We may still hope. Providence has declared for us, since I have found this brave man again in so miraculous a manner. And, sir, where does he reside, pray?"

"The Count de la Fère lodges in the Rue Guénegand, the Grand Roi Charlemagne Hotel."

"Thanks, sir. Inform this dear friend that I shall go and see him immediately."

"Sir, I obey this pleasure, if her majesty will permit me to depart."

"Go, M. de Bragelonne," said the Queen, "and be assured of our affection."

Raoul bent respectfully before the two princesses, and, bowing to Winter, departed.

The Queen and Winter continued to converse for some time in low voices, in order that the young princess should not overhear them; but the precaution was needless; she was in deep converse with her own thoughts.

Then, when Winter rose to take leave—

"Listen, my lord," said the Queen; "I have preserved this diamond cross which came from my mother, and this order of St. Michael, which came from my husband. They are worth about fifty thousand pounds. I had sworn to die of hunger rather than to part with these precious pledges; but now that this ornament may be useful to him or to his defenders, everything must be sacrificed to the hope of it. Take them, and if you need money for your expeditions, sell them fearlessly, my lord. But should you find the means of retaining them, remember, my lord, that I shall esteem you as having rendered the greatest service which a gentleman can render to a Queen; and in the day of my prosperity, he who brings me this order and this cross will be blessed by me and my children."

"Madam," replied Winter, "your majesty will be served by a man devoted to you. I hasten to deposit these two objects in a safe place, nor should I accept them if the resources of our ancient fortune were left to us; but our estates are confiscated, ready money is exhausted, and we are reduced to turn into resources everything we possess. In an hour hence I shall be with the Count de la Fère, and to-morrow your majesty shall have a definite answer."

The Queen tendered her hand to Lord Winter, who, kissing it respectfully, went out, traversing alone, unconducted, those large dark and deserted apartments, and brushing away tears which, hardened as he was by fifty years spent as a courier, he could not help shedding at the spectacle of this royal distress, so dignified and yet so intense.

CHAPTER XXXVIII.

UNCLE AND NEPHEW.

THE horse and servant belonging to Winter were waiting for him at the door; he sauntered towards his abode very thoughtfully, looking behind him from time to time to contemplate the dark and silent façade of the Louvre. It was then that he saw a horseman, as it were, detach himself from the wall and follow him at a little distance. In leaving the Royal Palace, he remembered to have observed a similar shadow.

"Tony," he said, motioning to his groom to approach, "did you remark that man who is following us?"

"Yes, my lord."

"Who is he?"

"I do not know, only he has followed your grace from the Palais Royal, stopped at the Louvre to wait for you, and now leaves the Louvre with you."

"Some spy of the Cardinal," said Winter to his aide. "Let us pretend not to notice that he is watching us."

And spurring on, he pursued the labyrinth of streets which led to his house. Lord Winter naturally returned to lodge near his ancient dwelling.

The unknown put his horse into a gallop.

Winter dismounted at his hotel, went up into his apartment, intending to watch the spy; but as he was about to place his gloves and hat on the table, he saw reflected in a glass opposite to him a figure which stood on the threshold of the room. He turned round, and Mordaunt was before him.

There was a moment of frozen silence between these two men.

"Sir," said Winter, "I thought I had already made you aware that I am weary of this persecution; withdraw, then, or I shall call, and have you turned out, as you were in London. I am not your uncle; I know you not."

"My uncle," replied Mordaunt, with his harsh and bantering tone, "you are mistaken; you will not have me turned out this time, as you did in London; you dare not. As for denying that I am your nephew, you will think twice about it, now that I have learnt some things of which I was ignorant a few days ago."

"And how does it concern me what you have learnt?" said Winter.

"Oh, it concerneth you much, my uncle, I am sure; and you will soon be of my opinion," added he, with a smile which sent a shudder through the veins of him whom he addressed. "When I presented myself before you for the first time in

London, it was to ask you what had become of my wealth; the second time it was to demand who had sullied my name; and this time I come before you to ask a question far more terrible than any other; to ask you, my lord, what have you done with your sister—your sister, who was my mother?"

Winter shrank from the fire of those scorching eyes.

"Your mother?" he said.

"Yes, my lord; my mother," replied the young man, advancing into the room till he was face to face with Lord Winter, and crossing his arms. "I have asked the headsman of Béthune," he said, his voice hoarse and his face livid with passion and grief, "and the headsman of Béthune gave me a reply. All is now explained; with this key the abyss is opened. My mother had inherited an estate from her husband, and you assassinated my mother; my name would have secured to me the paternal estate, and you have despoiled me of my name, you have deprived me of my fortune. I am no longer astonished that you knew me not. I am not surprised that you refused to recognize me. When a man is a robber, it is unbecoming to call him a nephew whom he has impoverished; when one is a murderer, to term that man whom he has made an orphan, a relative."

These words produced a contrary effect to what Mordaunt had anticipated. Winter remembered the monster that My lady had been; he rose, dignified and calm, restraining by the severity of his look the wild glances of the young man.

"You desire to fathom this horrible secret?" said Winter; "well, then, so be it. Know, then, what that woman was for whom to-day you come to call me to account. That woman had, in all probability, poisoned my brother, and in order to inherit from me she was about to assassinate me in my turn. I have proof of it. What say you to that?"

"I say that she was my mother."

"She caused the unfortunate Duke of Buckingham to be stabbed by a man who was, ere that, honest, good, and pure. What say you to that crime, of which I have the proof?"

"She was my mother!"

"On our return to France she had a young woman who was attached to one of her foes poisoned in the convent of the Augustines at Béthune. Will this crime persuade you of the justice of her punishment? of this I have the proofs!"

"Silence, sir—she still was my mother!" exclaimed the young man, his face running with sweat, his hair, like Hamlet's, standing upon his forehead, and raging with fury; "she was my mother! her crimes, I know them not—her disorderly conduct, I know it not—her vices, I know them not. But this I know, that I had a mother, that five men leagued against one woman, murdered her clandestinely by night—silently—like cowards. I know that you were one of them, my uncle, and that you cried louder than the others—'she must die.' Therefore I warn you—and listen well to my words, that they may be engraved on your memory, never to be forgotten—this murder, which has robbed me of everything—this murder, which has deprived me of my name—this murder, which has impoverished me—this murder, which has made me corrupt, wicked, implacable—I shall summon you to account for it first, and then those who were your accomplices—when I discover them!"

With hatred in his eyes, foaming at his mouth, and his fist extended, Mordaunt had advanced one more step—a threatening, terrible step—towards Winter. The latter put his hand to his sword, and said, with the smile of a man who for thirty years has jested with death:

"Would you murder me, sir? Then I shall recognize you as my nephew, for you are a worthy son of such a mother."

"No," replied Mordaunt, forcing all the veins of his face, and the muscles of his body to resume their usual places and to be calm; "no, I shall not kill you—at least, not at this moment, for without you I could not discover the others. But when I have found them, then tremble, sir. I have stabbed the headsman of Béthune—stabbed him without mercy or pity, and he was the least guilty of you all."

With these words the young man went out, and descended the stair sufficiently calm to pass unobserved; then, upon the lowest landing-place, he passed Tony leaning over the balustrade, waiting only for a call from his master to mount to his room.

But Winter did not call; crushed, enfeebled, he remained standing, and with listening ear; then only, when he heard the step of the horse going away, he fell back on a chair saying:

"My God, I thank thee that he knows me alone."

CHAPTER XXXIX.

PATERNAL AFFECTION.

WHILE this terrible scene was passing at Lord Winter's, Athos, seated near his window, his elbow on the table, and his head supported on his hand, was listening intently to Raoul's account of the adventures he met with on his journey, and the details of the battle.

Listening to the relation of those first emotions so fresh and pure, the fine, noble face of Athos betrayed indescribable pleasure; he inhaled the tones of that young voice as harmonious music. He forgot all that was dark in the past, and that was cloudy in the future. It almost seemed as if the return of this much-loved boy had changed his fear into hopes. Athos was happy—happy as he had never been before.

"And you took part in this great battle, Bragelonne?" said the former Musketeer.

"Yes, sir."

"And it was a hard one?"

"The Prince charged eleven times in person."

"He is a great commander, Bragelonne."

"He is a hero, sir; I did not lose sight of him for an instant. Oh! how fine it is to be called Count and to be worthy of such a name! He is as calm as at parade; as radiant as at a dance!"

"Well, very good; you will be the same, when the opportunity occurs—will you, Raoul?"

"I know not, sir, but I thought it was very fine and grand!"

"And the prince was pleased with you?"

"He told me so, at least, sir, when he desired me to return to Paris with M. de Châtillon, who was charged to carry the news to the Queen, and to bring the colors we had taken. 'Go,' said he, 'the enemy will not rally for fifteen days, and until that time I have no need of your service. Go and see those whom you love, and who love you, and tell my sister de Longueville that I thank her for the present she made me of you.' And I came, sir," added Raoul, gazing at the count with a smile of real affection, "for I thought you would be glad to see me again."

Athos drew the young man towards him, and pressed his lips to his brow, as he would have done to a young daughter.

"And now, Raoul," said he, "you are launched; you have dukes for friends, a marshal of France for a godfather, a prince of the blood as commander, and on the day of your return you have been received by two queens; it is rather well for a novice."

"Oh, sir!" said Raoul, suddenly, "you recall something to me, which in my haste to relate my exploits, I had forgotten; it is that there was with her Majesty the Queen of England, a gentleman who, when I pronounced your name, uttered a cry of surprise and joy; he said he was a friend of yours—asked your address and is coming to see you."

"What is his name?"

"I did not dare ask, sir; he spoke elegantly, although I thought from his accent he was an Englishman."

"Ah!" said Athos, leaning down his head as if he remembered who it could be. Then, when he raised it again, he was struck by the presence of a man who was standing at the open door, and was gazing at him with a compassionate air.

"Lord Winter!" exclaimed the count.

"Athos, my friend!"

And the two gentlemen were for an instant locked in each

other's arms; then Athos, looking into his friend's face, and taking him by both hands, said:

"What ails you, my lord? you appear us unhappy as I am happy!"

"Yes, truly, dear friend; and I may even say that the sight of you increases my dismay."

And Winter glancing around him, Raoul quickly understood that the two friends wished to be alone, and he therefore left the room unaffectedly.

"Come, now that we are alone," said Athos, "let us talk of yourself."

"Whilst we are alone let us speak of ourselves," replied Winter. "My lady's son is here."

Athos, who was again struck by this name, which seemed to pursue him like an echo, hesitated for a moment, then, slightly knitting his brow, he calmly said:

"I know it; Grimaud met him between Béthune and Arras, and then came here to warn me of his presence."

"Does Grimaud know him, then?"

"No; but he was present at the death-bed of a man who knew him."

"The headsman of Béthune!" exclaimed Winter.

"You know about that?" cried Athos, astonished.

"He has just left me," replied Winter, "after telling me all. Ah! my friend! what a horrible scene! Why did we not crush the child with the mother?"

"What need you fear?" said Athos, recovering from the instinctive fear he had first experienced, by the aid of reason; "are we not able to defend ourselves? Is this young man an assassin by profession—a murderer in cold blood? He has killed the executioner of Béthune in an impulse of passion, but now his fury is assuaged."

Winter smiled sorrowfully, and shook his head.

"Do you not then know the race?" said he.

"Pooh!" said Athos, trying to smile in his turn. "It must have lost its ferocity in the second generation. Besides, my friend, Providence has warned us that we may be on our guard. All we can do is to wait. Let us wait; and, as I said before, let us speak of yourself. What brings you to Paris?"

"Affairs of importance which you shall know later. But what is this that I hear from the Queen of England? D'Artagnan is with Mazarin! Pardon my frankness, dear friend. I neither hate nor blame the Cardinal, and your opinions will be held ever sacred by me; do you happen to belong to this man?"

"M. d'Artagnan," replied Athos, "is in the service; he is a soldier and obeys the constituted authority: M. d'Artagnan is not rich, and has need of his pay as lieutenant to enable him to live. Millionaires like yourself, my lord, are rare in France."

"Alas!" said Winter, "I am at this moment as poor as he is, if not poorer; but to return to our subject."

"Well, then, you wish to know if I am of Mazarin's party. No."

"I am obliged to you, Count, for this pleasing intelligence. You make me young and happy again by it. Ah! so you are not a Mazarinist? Delightful! Indeed, you could not belong to him. But pardon me, are you married?"

"Ah! as to that, no," replied Athos, laughing.

"Because that young man—so handsome, so elegant, so polished——"

"He is a child that I have adopted, and who does not even know who was his father."

"Very well—you are always the same, Athos, great and generous. Are you still friends with Porthos and Aramis?"

"And add d'Artagnan, too, my lord. We still remain four friends devoted to each other; but when it becomes a question of serving the Cardinal, or of fighting, of being Mazarinists or Frondists, then we are only two."

"Is Aramis with d'Artagnan?" asked Lord Winter.

"No," said Athos: "Aramis does me the honor to share my opinion."

"Could you put me in communication with your witty and agreeable friend? Is he changed?"

"He has become a priest, that is all."

"You alarm me; his profession must have made him renounce any great undertakings."

"On the contrary," said Athos, smiling, "he has never been so much a Musketeer as since he became a priest, and you will find him a true soldier."

"Could you engage to bring him to me to-morrow morning at ten o'clock, on the Louvre Bridge?"

"Oh, ho!" exclaimed Athos, smiling, "you have a duel in prospect."

"Yes, Count, and a splendid duel, too; one in which I hope you will take a hand."

"Where are we to go to, my lord?"

"To the Queen of England, who has desired me to present you to her."

"This is an enigma," said Athos; "but it matters not; from the moment that you have guessed the key, I ask no further. Will your lordship do me the honor to sup with me?"

"Thanks, Count, no," replied Winter. "I own to you that that young man's visit has taken away my appetite, and will probably deprive me of sleep. What undertaking can have brought him to Paris? It was not to meet me that he came, for he was ignorant of my journey. This young man terrifies me, my lord; for there lies in him a sanguinary predisposition."

"What occupies him in England?"

"He is one of Cromwell's most enthusiastic disciples."

"But what has attached him to this cause? His father and mother were Catholics, I believe."

"His hatred of the King, who deprived him of his estates, and forbade him to bear the name of Winter."

"And what is his name now?"

"Mordaunt."

"A Puritan, yet, disguised as a monk, he travels alone in France."

"Do you say as a monk?"

"It was thus, and by mere accident—may God pardon me if I blaspheme!—that he heard the confession of the executioner of Béthune."

"Then I understand it all; he has been sent by Cromwell to Mazarin, and the Queen guessed rightly; we have been forestalled. Everything is clear to me now. Farewell, Count, till to-morrow."

"But the night is dark," said Athos, perceiving that Lord Winter seemed more uneasy than he wished to show; "and you have no servant."

"I have Tony, a good but simple youth."

"Halloa there, Grimaud, Olivain, and Blaisois, call the viscount here, and take muskets with you."

Blaisois was the tall youth, half-groom, half-peasant, whom we saw at Bragelonne, whom Athos had christened by the name of his province.

"Viscount," said Athos to Raoul as he entered, "you will escort my lord as far as his hotel, and permit no one to approach him."

"Oh! Count," said Winter, "for whom do you take me?"

"For a stranger who does not know Paris," said Athos, "and to whom the viscount will show the way."

Winter shook him by the hand.

"Grimaud," said Athos, "put yourself at the head of the troop, and beware of the monk."

Grimaud shuddered, and nodding, awaited the departure, regarding the butt of his musket with silent eloquence. Then, obeying the orders given him by Athos, he headed the little procession, bearing the torch in one hand and the musket in the other, until it reached the door of Winter's inn, when, striking on the door with his fist, he bowed to my lord without saying a word.

The same order was pursued in returning; nor did Grimaud's searching glance discover anything of a suspicious appearance, save a dark shadow in ambuscade at the corner of the Quai. He fancied also that in going he had already observed

the street watcher who had attracted his attention. He pushed
on towards him, but before he could reach it, the shadow had
disappeared into an alley, in which Grimaud deemed it scarcely
prudent to pursue it.

The next day, on awakening, the count perceived Raoul by
his bedside. The young man was already dressed, and was
reading a book.

"Already up, Raoul!" exclaimed the count.

"Yes, sir," replied Raoul with a slight hesitation. "I did
not sleep well."

"You, Raoul, not sleep well! then you must have something
on your mind!" said Athos. .

"Sir, you will, perhaps, think that I am in a great hurry to
leave you, when I have only just arrived, but—I have the
wish to go and pass a day at Blois. You look at me, and are
going to laugh at me."

"No; on the contrary, I am not inclined to laugh," said
Athos, suppressing a sigh. "You wish to see Blois again;
go where you like, Raoul."

"Sir," said Raoul, as he turned to leave the room, "I have
thought of one thing, and that is about the Duchess of Chevreuse, so kind to me, and to whom I owe my introduction to
the prince."

"And you ought to thank her, Raoul. Well, try Luynes
Mansion, Raoul, and ask if the duchess can receive you. I am
glad to see that you pay attention to social usages. You must
take Grimaud and Olivain."

Raoul went out, and when Athos heard his young, joyous
voice calling to Grimaud and Olivain, he sighed.

"It is very soon to leave me," he thought, "but he follows
the common lot. Nature has made us thus; she looks ahead.
He certainly likes that girl, but will he love me less because
he loves others?"

Everything was ready at ten o'clock for their journey, and
as Athos was seeing Raoul mount, a groom rode up from the
Duchess de Chevreuse. He was charged to tell the Count
de la Fère that she had learnt the return of her youthful
protégé, and also the manner in which he had conducted himself on the field, and she added that she should be very glad to
offer him her congratulations.

"Tell her grace," replied Athos, "that the viscount has just
mounted his horse to proceed to her residence."

Then, with renewed instructions to Grimaud, Athos signified to Raoul that he could set out, and ended by reflecting that
it was, perhaps, better that Raoul should be away from Paris
at that moment.

CHAPTER XL.

ANOTHER QUEEN IN NEED.

ATHOS had not failed to send early to Aramis, and had given his letter to Blaisois, the only serving-man whom he had left. Blaisois found Bazin donning his beadle's gown, his services being required that day at Church.

Athos had desired Blaisois to try and speak to Aramis himself. Blaisois, a tall, simple youth, who understood nothing but what he was desired, asked, therefore, for the Abbé d'Herblay, and in spite of Bazin's assurances that his master was not at home, he persisted in such a manner as to put Bazin into a passion. Blaisois seeing Bazin in a clerical guise, was little discomposed at his denials, and wanted to pass at all risks, believing, too, that he with whom he had to do was endowed with the virtues of his cloth—namely, patience and Christian charity.

But Bazin, still the servant of a Musketeer, when once the blood mounted to his fat cheeks, seized a broomstick and began thumping Blaisois, saying:

"You insulted the Church; my friend, you have insulted the Church!"

At this moment Aramis, aroused by this unusual disturbance, cautiously opened the door of his room; and Blaisois, looking reproachfully at the Cerberus, drew the letter from his pocket, and presented it to Aramis.

"From the Count de la Fère," said Aramis. "All right." And he retired into his room without even asking the cause of so much noise.

At ten o'clock, Athos, with his habitual exactitude, was waiting on the Pont du Louvre, and was almost immediately joined by Lord Winter.

They waited ten minutes, and then his lordship began to fear that Aramis was not coming to join them.

"Patience," said Athos, whose eyes were fixed in the direction of the Rue du Bac, "patience; I see a priest giving a cuff to a man, and a bow to a woman—that must be Aramis."

It was he, in truth; having run against a young storekeeper who was gaping at the crows, and who had splashed him, Aramis with one blow of his fist had sent him ten paces.

At this moment one of his penitents passed, and as she was young and pretty, Aramis took off his cap to her, with his most gracious smile.

A most affectionate greeting, as one can well believe, took place between him and Lord Winter.

"Where are we going?" inquired Aramis; "are we going to

fight there, 'faith? I carry no sword this morning, and cannot return home to procure one."

"No," said Lord Winter, "we are going to pay a visit to the Queen of England."

"Oh, very well," replied Aramis; then, bending his face down to Athos' ear, "what is the object of this visit?" continued he.

"I'faith, I know not; some evidence required from us, perhaps."

"May it not be about that cursed affair?" asked Aramis, "in which case I do not greatly care to go, for it will be to pocket some reproofs; and since I am used to give it to so many, I do not like to receive it myself."

"If it were so," answered Athos, "we should not be taken there by Lord Winter, for he would come in for his share; he was one of us."

"Truly—yes, let us go."

On arriving at the Louvre, Lord Winter entered first; indeed, there was but one porter to receive them at the gate.

It was impossible, in daylight, for the impoverished state of the habitation, which avaricious charity had conceded to an unfortunate Queen, to pass unnoticed by Athos, Aramis, and even the Englishman.

"Mazarin is better lodged," said Aramis.

"Mazarin is almost King," answered Athos; "and Mdme. Henrietta is hardly yet a Queen."

The Queen appeared to be impatiently expecting them, for at the first slight noise which she heard in the hall leading to her room, she came herself to the door to receive the courtiers of the days of misfortune.

"Enter and be welcome, gentlemen," she said.

The gentlemen entered and remained standing, but at a motion from the Queen, they seated themselves. Athos was calm and grave, but Aramis was furious; the sight of such royal misery exasperated him, and his eyes examined every new trace of poverty which presented itself.

"You are admiring the luxury I enjoy?" said the Queen, glancing sadly around her.

"Madam," replied Aramis, "I must ask your pardon, but I know not how to hide my indignation at seeing how a daughter of Henry IV. is treated at the court of France."

"M. Aramis is not a military officer?" asked the Queen of Lord Winter.

"That gentleman is the Abbé d'Herblay," replied he.

Aramis blushed. "Madam," he said, "I am a priest, it is true, but I am so against my will; I never had a vocation for the bands; my cassock is fastened by one button only, and I am always ready to become a Musketeer again. This morning, being ignorant that I should have the honor of seeing your majesty, I encumbered myself with this dress, but you will find me no less a man devoted to your majesty's service, in whatever you see fit to command me."

"The Abbé d'Herblay," resumed Winter, "is one of those gallant Musketeers belonging to his majesty, King Louis XIII., of whom I have spoken to you, madam." Then, turning towards Athos, he continued: "And this gentleman is that noble Count de la Fère, whose high reputation is so well known to your majesty."

"Ah!" exclaimed the Queen, "a few years ago I had around me, gentlemen, treasures, and armies, and by the lifting of a finger all these were occupied in my service. To-day, look around you, and it may astonish you, that in order to accomplish a plan which is dearer to me than life, I have only Lord Winter, the friend of twenty years, and you, gentlemen, whom I see for the first time, and whom I know but as my countrymen."

"It is enough," said Athos, bowing low, "if the life of three men can purchase yours, madam."

"I thank you, gentlemen. But hear me," continued she, "I am not only the most miserable of queens, but the most unhappy of mothers, the most despairing of wives. My children —two of them at least—the Duke of York and the Princess Elizabeth, are far away from me, exposed to the arts of the ambitious and the blows of our foes; my husband, the King, is leading in England so wretched an existence, that it is no exaggeration to say that he seeks death, as a thing to be desired. Hold! gentlemen, there is a letter conveyed to me by Lord Winter. Read it."

Obeying the Queen, Athos read aloud the letter, which we have already seen, in which King Charles demanded whether the hospitality of France would be accorded to him.

"Well," said the Queen, "it has been refused."

The two friends exchanged a smile of contempt.

"And now," said Athos, "what is to be done? I have the honor to inquire from your majesty, what you desire d'Herblay and myself to do in your service. We are ready."

"Ah! sir, you have a noble heart!" exclaimed the Queen, with a burst of gratitude; whilst Lord Winter turned to her with a glance which said, "Did I not answer for them to you?"

"But you, sir?" said the Queen to Aramis.

"I, madam," replied he, "follow M. de la Fère wherever he leads, even were it to death, without demanding wherefore; but when it concerns your majesty's service, then," added he, looking at the Queen with all the grace of his former days, "I precede the count."

"Well, then, gentlemen," said the Queen, "since it is thus, and since you are willing to devote yourselves to the service of a poor princess whom the whole world has abandoned, this is what is required to be done for me. The King is alone with a few gentlemen, whom he fears to lose every day; surrounded by the Scotch, whom he distrusts, although he be himself a Scotchman. Since Lord Winter left him I am distracted, sirs. I ask much, too much perhaps, for I have no title to ask it. Go to England, join the King, be his friends, his protectors, march to battle at his side, and be near him in the interior of his house, where conspiracies, more dangerous than the perils of war, increase every day. And in exchange for the sacrifice that you make, gentlemen, I promise—not to reward you—I believe that word would offend you—but to love you as a sister, to prefer you next to my husband and my children, to every one. I swear it before Heaven."

And the Queen raised her eyes solemnly upwards.

"Madam," said Athos, "when must we set out? we are yours, body and soul."

"Oh, sirs," said the Queen, moved to tears, "this is the first time for five years that I have felt anything like joy or hope. God—who can read my heart, all the gratitude I feel—will reward you! Save my husband! Save the King, and although you care not for the price which is placed upon a good action in this world, leave me the hope that we shall meet again, when I may be able to thank you myself. In the meantime I remain here. Have you any counsel to give me? From this moment, I become your friend, and since you are engaged in my affairs, I ought to occupy myself in yours."

"Madam," replied Athos, "I have only to ask your majesty's prayers."

"And I," said Aramis, "I am alone in the world, and have only your majesty to serve."

The Queen held out her hand, which they kissed, and having two letters prepared for the King—one from herself, and one written by the Princess Henrietta—she gave one to Athos and the other to Aramis, that, should they be separated by chance, they might make themselves known to the King; after which they withdrew.

At the foot of the staircase Winter stopped.

"Not to arouse suspicions, gentlemen," said he, "go your way, and I will go mine, and this evening at nine o'clock we will assemble again at the gate St. Denis. We will travel on horseback as far as our horses can go, and afterwards we can take the post. Once more, let me thank you, my good friends, thank you in my own name, and in the Queen's.

The three gentlemen then shook hands, Lord Winter leaving Athos and Aramis together.

"Well," said Aramis, when they were alone, "what do you think of this business, my dear Count?"

"Bad," replied Athos, "very bad."

"But you received it with enthusiasm!"

"As I shall ever receive the defense of a great principle, my dear d'Herblay. Monarchs are only strong by the aid of the aristocracy, but aristocracy cannot exist without monarchs. Let us, then, support monarchy in order to support ourselves."

"We shall be murdered there," said Aramis. "I hate the English—they are coarse, like all people who drink beer."

"Would it be better to remain here?" said Athos, "and take a turn in the Bastille, or in Vincennes, for having favored the escape of Beaufort? I'faith, Aramis, believe me there is little left to regret. We avoid imprisonment, and we take the part of heroes—the choice is easy."

"It is true; but in everything, friend, one must always return to the same question, a stupid one I admit, but very necessary; have you any money?"

"Something like a hundred pistoles, that my farmer sent me the day before I left Bragelonne; but out of that sum, I ought to leave fifty for Raoul—a young man must live respectably. I have then, about fifty pistoles. And you?"

"As for me, I am quite sure that after turning out all my pockets and emptying my drawers, I shall not find ten louis at home. Fortunately, Lord Winter is rich."

"Lord Winter is ruined for the moment, for Cromwell sequestrates all his resources."

"Now is the time when Baron Porthos would be useful!"

"Now it is that I regret d'Artagnan."

"Let us entice them away."

"This secret, Aramis, does not belong to us; take my advice, then, and put no one into our confidence. And, moreover, in taking such a step, we should appear to be doubtful of ourselves. Let us regret to ourselves for our own sakes, but not speak of it."

"You are right; but what are you going to do till this evening? I have two things to postpone."

"And what are they?"

"First, a thrust with the Coadjutor, whom I met last night at Mdme. de Rambouillet's; he is a turbulent fellow who will ruin our party. I am convinced that if I gave him a box on the ear, such as I gave this morning to the little citizen who splashed me, it would change the appearance of things."

"And I, my dear Aramis," quietly replied Athos, "I think it would only change de Retz's appearance. Take my advice, leave things as they are; besides, you are neither of you now your own masters; he belongs to the Fronde, and you to the Queen of England. But now we must part. I have one or two visits to make, and a letter to write. Call for me at eight o'clock, or shall I wait supper for you at seven?"

"That will do very well," said Aramis. "I have twenty visits to make, and as many letters to write."

They then separated. Athos went to pay a visit to Mdme.

de Vendôme, left his name at Mdme. de Chevreuse's, and wrote the following letter to d'Artagnan:

"DEAR FRIEND,—I am about to set off with Aramis on important business. I wished to make my farewell to you, but time did not allow me. Remember that I write to you now to repeat how much affection I have for you.

"Raoul is gone to Blois, and is ignorant of my departure; watch over him in my absence as much as you possibly can, and if by chance you receive no news of me three months hence, tell him to open a packet which he will find addressed to him in my bronze casket at Blois, and of which I send you the key.

"Embrace Porthos for Aramis and myself. Adieu, perhaps farewell."

At the hour agreed upon, Aramis arrived; he was dressed as an officer, and had the old sword at his side which he had drawn so often, and which he was more than ever ready to draw.

"By-the-bye," he said, "I think that we are decidedly wrong to depart thus, without leaving a line for Porthos and d'Artagnan."

"The thing is done, dear friend," said Athos; "I foresaw that, and have embraced them both for you and myself."

"You are a wonderful man, my dear Count," said Aramis, "you think of everything."

"Well, have you made up your mind to this journey?"

"Quite; and now that I reflect about it, I am glad to leave Paris at this moment."

"And so am I," replied Athos; "my only regret is not having seen d'Artagnan; but that rascal is so cunning, he might have guessed our project."

When supper was over Blaisois entered. "Sir," said he, "here is M. d'Artagnan's answer."

"But I did not tell you there was an answer, stupid!" said Athos.

"And I set off without waiting for one, but he called me back and gave me this;" and he presented a little bag made of leather, round and ringing.

Athos opened it, and began by drawing from it a little note, written in these terms:

"MY DEAR COUNT,—When one travels—and especially for three months—one has never enough money. Now, recalling our former time of distress, I send you the half of my purse; it is money to obtain which I made Mazarin sweat. Don't make a bad use of it, I entreat you.

"As to what you say about not seeing you again, I believe not a word of it; with your heart and your sword one might pass through everything. Godspeed, then, and not farewell.

"It is unnecessary to say that from the day I saw Raoul I loved him; nevertheless, believe that I heartily pray to God that I may not become his father, however much I might be proud of such a son. YOURS, D'ARTAGNAN.

"P. S.—Be it well understood that the fifty louis which I send are equally for Aramis as for you, and for you as for Aramis."

Athos smiled, and his fine eyes were dimmed by tears. D'Artagnan, who had loved him so tenderly, loved him still, Mazarinist though he was.

"There are the fifty louis, i'faith," said Aramis, emptying the purse on the table, "all bearing the effigy of Louis XIII. Well, what shall you do with this money, Count; shall you keep it, or send it back?"

"I shall keep it, Aramis; and even had I no need of it, I should still keep it. What is offered from a generous heart should be accepted generously. Take twenty-five of them, Aramis, and give me the remaining twenty-five."

"All right; I am glad to see that you are of my opinion. Then, now shall we start?"

"When you like; but have you no groom?"

"No! that idiot Bazin had the folly to make himself verger, as you know, and therefore cannot leave Nôtre Dame."

"Very well, take Blaisois, with whom I know not what to do since I have Grimaud."

"Willingly," said Aramis.

At this moment Grimaud appeared at the door. "Ready," said he, with his usual curtness.

"Let us go then," said Athos.

The two friends mounted, as did their servants. At the corner of the Quai they encountered Bazin, who was running breathlessly.

"Oh, sir!" exclaimed he, "thank Heaven I have arrived in time. M. Porthos has just been to your house, and has left this for you, saying that the thing was important, and ought to be given to you before you left."

"Good," said Aramis, taking a purse which Bazin presented to him. "What is this?"

"Wait, your reverence, there is a letter."

"You know that I have already told you that if you ever call me anything but Chevalier I will break your bones. Give me the letter."

"How can you read?" asked Athos; "it is as dark as in an oven."

"Wait," said Bazin, striking a light, and lighting a twisted waxlight, with which he lighted the church candles. By this light Aramis read the following epistle:

"MY DEAR D'HERBLAY,—I learn from d'Artagnan, who has embraced me on the part of the Count de la Fère and yourself, that you are setting out on a journey which may perhaps last two or three months. As I know that you do not like to ask money of your friend, I offer to you. Here are two hundred pistoles, of which you can dispose, and return to me when an opportunity occurs. Do not fear that you put me to inconvenience; if I want money, I can send for some from one of my châteaux; at Bracieux alone I have twenty thousand francs in gold. So, if I do not send you more, it is because I fear you would not accept a large sum.

"I address you, because you know, that although I esteem him from my heart, I am a little awed by Count de la Fère; but it is understood, that what I offer to you, I offer to him at the same time.

"I am, as I trust you do not doubt, your devoted

"Du Vallon de Bracieux de Pierrefonds."

"Well," said Aramis, "what do you say to that?"

"I say, my dear d'Herblay, that it is almost sacrilege to distrust Providence when one has such friends, and therefore we will divide the pistoles from Porthos, as we divided the louis sent by d'Artagnan."

The division being made by the light of Bazin's taper, the two friends continued their road, and a quarter of an hour later they had joined Winter at the Porte St. Denis.

CHAPTER XLI.

IT IS PROVED THAT FIRST IMPULSES ARE BEST.

THE three gentlemen took the road to Picardy—a road well known to them, and recalling to Athos and Aramis. some of the most picturesque adventures of their youth.

At last, after traveling two days and one night, they arrived at Boulogne towards the evening, favored by magnificent weather.

"Gentlemen," said Winter, on reaching the gate of the town, "let us do here as at Paris; let us separate to avoid suspicion. I know an inn, little frequented, but of which the host is entirely devoted to me. I will go there, where I expect to find letters, and you go to the first tavern in the town, to L'Epée du Grand Henri for instance, refresh yourselves, and in two hours be upon the jetty—our boat is waiting for us."

The matter being thus decided, the two friends found, about two hundred paces further, the tavern indicated to them. The horses were fed, but not unsaddled; the grooms up—for it was already late—and their two masters, impatient to return, appointed a place of meeting with them on the jetty, and desired them on no account to exchange a word with anyone. It is needless to say that this caution concerned Blaisois alone; it was long since it had become a useless one to Grimaud.

Athos and Aramis walked down towards the port. From their dress, covered with dust, and from a certain easy manner by which a man accustomed to travel is always recognized, the two friends excited the attention of a few walkers. There was more especially one upon whom their arrival had produced a decided impression. This man, whom they had observed from the first for the same reason as they had themselves been remarked by others, walked in a melancholy way up and down the jetty. From the moment he perceived them he did not cease to look at them, and seemed to burn with the wish to speak to them.

On reaching the jetty, Athos and Aramis stopped to look at a smack fastened to a stake, and ready rigged as if waiting to start.

"That is doubtless our boat," said Athos.

"Yes," replied Aramis, "and the sloop sailing about there must be that which is to take us to our destination; now," continued he, "if only Winter does not keep us waiting. It is not at all amusing here—there is not a single woman passing."

"Hush!" said Athos, "we are overheard."

In truth, the walker, who, during the observations of the two friends, had passed and repassed behind them several times, stopped at the name of Winter; but as his face betrayed no emotion at the mention of this name, it might have been by chance that he had stopped.

"Gentlemen," said the man, who was young and pale, bowing with much ease and politeness, "pardon my curiosity, but I see you come from Paris, or at least that you are strangers in Boulogne."

"We came from Paris, yes," replied Athos with the same courtesy; "what have we at your service?"

"Sir," said the young man, "will you be so good as to tell me if it be true that Cardinal Mazarin is no longer Minister?"

"That is a strange question," said Aramis.

"He is and he is not," replied Athos; "that is to say, he is dismissed by one half of France; and that, by means of intrigues and promises, he makes the other half retain him; you will perceive that this may last a long time."

"However, sir," said the stranger, "he has neither fled, nor is in prison?"

"No, sir, not at this moment at least."

"Sirs, accept my thanks for your politeness," said the young man, retreating.

"What do you think of that questioner?" asked Aramis.

"I think he is either a clown who is dull, or a spy wishing for information."

"But if he be a spy——"

"What do you think a spy would be about here? We are

not living in the time of Cardinal Richelieu, who would have closed the ports on a bare suspicion."

"It matters not; you were wrong to reply to him as you did," continued Aramis, following with his eyes the man disappearing behind the cliffs.

"And you," said Athos, "you forget that you committed a very different kind of imprudence in pronouncing Lord Winter's name. Did you not see that at that name the young man stopped?"

"More reason, then, when he spoke to you, for sending him about his business."

"A quarrel?" asked Athos.

"And since when have you become afraid of a quarrel?"

"I am always afraid of a quarrel when I am expected at any place, and that such a quarrel might possibly prevent my reaching it. Besides, let me own something to you. I am anxious to see that young man nearer."

"And wherefore?"

"Aramis, you will certainly laugh at me—you will say that I am always repeating the same thing—you will call me the most timorous of visionaries; but to whom do you see a resemblance in that young man?"

"In beauty, or on the contrary?" asked Aramis, laughing.

"In ugliness, and as far as a man can resemble a woman!"

"Ah! egad!" cried Aramis, "you have made me think. No, in truth, you are no visionary, my dear friend, and now that I think of it—you—yes, i'faith, quite right—that delicate and compressed mouth, those eyes which seem always at the command of the intellect, and never of the heart! Yes, it is one of My lady's spawn!"

"You laugh, Aramis."

"From habit, that is all; for I swear to you, I should like no better than yourself to meet that viper in my path."

"Ah! here is Winter coming," said Athos.

"Good, one thing now is only wanting, and that is that our grooms should keep us waiting."

"No," said Athos, "I see them about twenty paces behind my lord. I recognize Grimaud by his long legs and stiff gait. Tony carries our muskets."

"Then we shall embark to-night?" asked Aramis, glancing towards the west, where the sun had left but one golden cloud, which, dipping into the ocean, appeared by degrees to be extinguished.

"Probably so," said Athos.

"The deuce!" resumed Aramis; "I have little fancy for the sea by day, but still less at night; the sounds of the winds and waves, the frightful motion of the vessel—I confess that I prefer to be in the convent of Noisy."

Athos smiled sadly, for it was evident that he was thinking

of other things as he listened to his friend, and he moved toward Winter.

"What ails our friend?" said Aramis. "He resembles one of Dante's damned souls whose neck Satan has dislocated, and who always look at their heels. What the devil makes him stare thus behind him?"

When Winter perceived them, he advanced toward them with surprising rapidity.

"What is the matter, my lord?" said Athos; "and what puts you out of breath thus?"

"Nothing," replied Winter, "nothing; and yet in passing the heights it seemed to me——" and he again turned around.

Athos glanced at Aramis.

"But let us go," continued Winter; "let us be off; the boat must be waiting for us, and there is our sloop at anchor. Do you see it there? I wish I were on board already," and he looked back again.

"He has seen him," said Athos, in a low tone to Aramis.

They had now reached the ladder which led to the boat. Winter made the grooms who carried the arms, and the porters with the luggage, descend first, and was about to follow them.

At this moment, Athos perceived a man walking on the sea shore parallel to the jetty, and hastening his steps as if to reach the other side of the port, scarcely twenty steps from the place of embarking. He fancied in the darkness that he recognized the young man who had questioned him. Athos now descended the ladder in his turn, without losing sight of the young man. The latter, to make a short cut, had appeared on a sluice.

"He certainly bodes us no good," said Athos; "but let us embark; once out at sea, let him come."

And Athos sprang into the boat, which was immediately pushed off, and which soon distanced the shore under the efforts of four strong rowers.

But the young man had begun to follow or rather to advance before the boat. She was obliged to advance between the point of the jetty, surmounted by a beacon just lighted, and a rock which jutted out. They saw him in the distance climbing the rock, in order to look down upon the boat as she passed.

"Ay, but," said Aramis, that young man is decidedly a spy."

"Which is the young man?" asked Winter, turning round.

"He who followed us, and spoke to us, awaits us there; see!"

Winter turned, and followed the direction of Aramis's fingers. The beacon bathed its light upon the little strait through which they were about to pass, and the rock where the young man stood with bare head and crossed arms.

"It is he!" exclaimed Winter, seizing the arm of Athos; "it is he! I thought I recognized him, and I was not mistaken."

"Who—him?" asked Aramis.

"My lady's son," replied Athos.

"The monk!" exclaimed Grimaud.

The young man heard the words and bent so forward over the rock that one might have supposed he was about to precipitate himself from it.

"Yes, it is I, my uncle. I, the son of My lady; I, the monk; I, the secretary and friend of Cromwell; and I know you, both you and your companions."

There were in that boat three men, unquestionably brave, and whose courage no man would have dared to dispute; nevertheless, at that voice, that accent, and those gestures, they felt a shudder of terror run through their veins. As for Grimaud, his hair stood on end, and drops of sweat ran from his brow.

"Ah!" exclaimed Aramis, "that is the nephew, the monk, and the son of My lady, as he says himself."

"Alas! yes," murmured Winter.

"Then wait," said Aramis; and with the terrible coolness which on important occasions he showed, he took one of the muskets from Tony, leveled and aimed it at the young man, who stood, like the accusing angel, upon the rock.

"Fire!" cried Grimaud, unconsciously.

Athos threw himself on the gun muzzle, and arrested the shot which was about to be fired.

"The devil take you," said Aramis, "I had him so fair at the point of my gun, I should have sent a ball into his breast."

"It is enough to kill the mother," said Athos, hoarsely.

"The mother was a wretch, who struck at us all, and at those dear to us."

"Yes, but the son has done us no harm."

Grimaud, who had risen to watch the effect of the shot, fell back hopeless, wringing his hands.

The young man burst into a laugh.

"Ah, it is certainly you," he cried, "and I know you now."

His mocking laugh and threatening words passed over their heads, carried on by the breeze, until lost in the depths of the horizon. Aramis shuddered.

"Be calm!" exclaimed Athos, "for Heaven's sake; have we ceased to be men?"

"No," said Aramis, "but that being is a fiend; and ask the uncle whether I was wrong to rid him of his nephew."

Winter only replied by a groan.

"It was all over with him," continued Aramis; "ah, I much fear that, with your wisdom, you have made me commit a great folly."

At this moment they were hailed by a voice from the sloop, and a few seconds later, men, servants, and baggage were on deck. The captain had been only awaiting his passengers, and hardly had they put foot on board ere her head was turned toward Hastings where they were to disembark. At this instant the three friends turned, in spite of themselves, a last look at the rock, upon the menacing figure which pursued them and stood out boldly. Then a voice reached them once more, sending out this threat: "We'll meet again, in England."

CHAPTER XLII.

THE TE DEUM FOR THE VICTORY OF LENS.

THE bustle observed by Henrietta Maria, for which she had vainly sought to discover a reason, was occasioned by the battle of Lens, announced by the prince's messenger, the Duc de Châtillon, who had taken such a noble part in the engagement; he was, besides, charged to hang twenty-five flags, taken from the Lorraine party, as well as from the Spaniards, within the vaulted roof of Nôtre Dame Cathedral.

On the following Sunday a "Te Deum" would be sung at Nôtre Dame in honor of the victory.

The following Sunday, then, the Parisians arose with joy; at that period a "Te Deum" was a grand affair; this kind of ceremony had not then been made an abuse of, and it produced a great effect. At eight o'clock in the morning, the Queen's guards, commanded by Guitaut, under whom was his nephew Comminges, marched, preceded by drums and trumpets, to file off from the Palais Royal as far as Nôtre Dame, a manœuvre which the Parisians witnessed tranquilly, delighted as they were with military music and brilliant uniforms.

Friquet had put on his Sunday clothes, under the pretext of having a gumboil which he had managed to procure momentarily, by introducing an infinite number of kernels into one side of his mouth, and had procured a whole holiday from Bazin. On leaving Bazin, Friquet started off to the Royal Palace, where he arrived at the moment of the turning out of the regiment of guards, and as he had only gone there for the enjoyment of seeing it and hearing the music, he took his place at their head, beating the drum on two slates, and passing from that exercise to that of the trumpet, which he counterfeited naturally with his mouth in a manner which had more than once called forth the praises of amateurs of imitative harmony.

This amusement lasted from the Barrière des Sergens to the place of Nôtre Dame; and Friquet found in it true enjoyment; but when at last the regiment separated, penetrated to the heart of the city, and placed itself at the extremity of the Rue St. Christophe, near the Rue Cocatrix, in which Broussel lived, then Friquet remembered that he had not had breakfast;

and after thinking to which side he had best turn his steps in order to accomplish this important act of the day, he reflected deeply, and decided that it should be Counsellor Broussel who should bear the cost of his repast.

In consequence he took a start, arrived breathlessly at the counsellor's door, and knocked violently.

His mother, the counsellor's old servant, opened it.

"What dost thou here, good-for-nothing?" she said, "and why are you not at Nôtre Dame?"

"I have been there, mother," said Friquet, "but I saw things happen of which Master Broussel ought to be warned, and so with M. Bazin's permission—you know, mother, M. Bazin, the verger?—I came to speak to M. Broussel."

"And what have you to say, boy, to M. Broussel?"

"I wish to tell him," replied Friquet, screaming with all his might, "that there is a whole regiment of guards coming this way. And, as I hear everywhere that at the court they are ill-disposed to him, I wish to warn him, that he may be on his guard."

Broussel heard the scream of the young oddity; and, enchanted with this excess of zeal, came down to the first floor, for he was, in truth, working in his room on the second.

"Well!" said he, "friend—what matters the regiment of guards to us, and art thou not mad to make such disturbance? Knowest thou not that it is the custom of these soldiers to act thus, and that it is usual for the regiment to form themselves into a hedge where the King passes?"

Friquet counterfeited surprise—and turning his new cap round his fingers, said:

"It is not astonishing for you to know it, M. Broussel, who know everything;—but me, by the holy truth, I do not know it, and I thought I would give you good advice:—you must not be angry with me for that, M. Broussel."

"On the contrary, my boy; on the contrary, I am pleased with your zeal. Dame Nanette, see for those apricots which Mdme. de Longueville sent to us yesterday from Noisy, and give half-a-dozen of them to your son, with a crust of new bread."

Oh, thank you, sir, thank you, M. Broussel," said Friquet; "I am so fond of apricots!"

Broussel then proceeded to his wife's room, and asked for breakfast; it was nine o'clock. The counsellor placed himself at the window; the street was completely deserted; but in the distance was heard, like the noise of the tide rushing in, the deep hum of the populous waves which increased around Nôtre Dame.

The noise redoubled, when d'Artagnan, with a company of Musketeers, placed himself at the gates of Nôtre Dame to secure the service of the church. He had told Porthos to profit by this opportunity to see the ceremony; and Porthos, in full dress, mounted his finest horse, doing the part of an honorary Musketeer, as d'Artagnan had so often done formerly. The sergeant of this company, an old veteran of the Spanish wars, had recognized Porthos, his old companion, and very soon all those who served under him had been placed in possession of heroic deeds concerning this honor to the Musketeers of Tréville. Porthos had not only been well received by the company, but he was looked upon with great admiration.

At ten o'clock the guns of the Louvre announced the departure of the King, and at last the King appeared with the Queen in a gilded chariot. Ten other carriages followed, containing the ladies of honor, the officers of the royal household, and all the court.

Just as the court took place in the cathedral, a carriage, bearing the arms of Comminges, quitted the line of court carriages, and proceeded slowly to the end of the Rue St. Christophe, now entirely deserted. When it arrived there, four guards and a police-officer, who accompanied it, mounted into the heavy machine, and closed the shutters; then, with a judicious admittance of the light, the policeman began to watch the length of the Rue Cocatrix, as if he was waiting for some one.

All the world was occupied with the ceremony, so that neither the chariot, nor the precautions taken by those who were within it, had been observed. Friquet, whose eye, always on the alert, could alone have discovered them, had gone to devour his apricots under the entablature of a house in the square of Nôtre Dame.

The ceremony ended, and the King remounted his carriage. Hardly had the police-officer observed Comminges at the end of the Rue Cocatrix, than he said one word to the coachman, who at once put his vehicle into motion, and drove up before Broussel's door. Comminges knocked at the door at the same moment, and Friquet was waiting behind Comminges until the door should be opened.

"What do you here, rascal?" asked Comminges.

"I want to go into Master Broussel's house, captain," replied Friquet, in that coaxing tone which boys know so well how to assume when necessary.

"And on what floor does he live?" asked Comminges.

"In the whole house," said Friquet; "the house belongs to him; he occupies the second floor when he works, and descends to the first floor to take his meals; he must be at dinner now—it is noon."

"Good," said Comminges.

At this moment the door was opened, and having questioned the servant, the officer learnt that Master Broussel was at home and at dinner.

Broussel was seated at the table with his family, having his wife opposite to him, his two daughters by his side, and his son Louvières, whom we have already seen when the accident happened to the counsellor—an accident from which he had quite recovered—at the bottom of the table. The worthy man, restored to perfect health, was tasting the fine fruit which Mdme. de Longueville had sent to him.

At the sight of the officer, Broussel was somewhat moved; but seeing him bow politely, he rose and bowed also. Still, in spite of this reciprocal politeness, the countenances of the women betrayed some uneasiness; Louvières became very pale, and waited impatiently for the officer to explain himself.

"Sir," said Comminges, "I am the bearer of an order from the King."

"Very well, sir," replied Broussel; "what is the order?" And he held out his hand.

"I am commissioned to seize your person, sir," said Comminges, in the same tone, and with the same politeness; "and if you will believe me, you had better spare yourself the trouble of reading that long letter, and follow me."

A thunderbolt falling in the midst of these good people, so peacefully assembled there, would not have produced a more appalling effect. It was a terrible thing at that period to be imprisoned by the enmity of the King.

"Impossible!" cried a shrill voice from the bottom of the room.

Comminges turned and saw Dame Nanette, her eyes flashing with anger and a broom in her hand.

"My good Nanette, be quiet, I beseech you," said Broussel. But Dame Nanette sprang to the window, threw it open, and in such a piercing voice that it might have been heard in the square of Nôtre Dame, "Help!" she screamed; "my master is being arrested! the Counsellor Broussel is arrested! help!"

Comminges seized the servant around the waist, and would have dragged her from her post; but at that instant a treble voice proceeding from below was heard screeching:

"Murder! fire! assassins! Master Broussel is being killed; Master Broussel is being strangled!"

It was Friquet's voice; and Dame Nanette, feeling herself supported, recommenced with all her strength to make a chorus.

Many curious faces had already appeared at the windows, and the people, attracted to the end of the street, began to run; first men, then groups, and then a crowd of people; hearing cries, and seeing a coach, they could not understand it; but Friquet sprang from the house on to the top of the carriage.

"They want to arrest Master Broussel," he cried; "the guards are in the carriage, and the officer is upstairs!"

The crowd began to murmur, and approached the horses. The two guards who had remained in the lane, mounted to the aid of Comminges; those who were in the coach opened the doors and presented arms.

"Don't you see them?" cried Friquet, "don't you see?—there they are!"

The coachman turned round and gave Friquet a cut with his whip, which made him scream with pain.

"Ah! devil's coachman!" cried Friquet, "you're meddling too;—wait!"

And regaining his perch, he overwhelmed the coachman with every projectile he could lay hands on.

The tumult now began to increase; the street was not able to contain the spectators, who assembled from every direction; the crowd invaded the space which the dreaded pikes of the guards kept clear, between them and the carriage. The soldiers, pushed back by these living walls, were about to be crushed against the nuts of the wheels and the panels of the carriage. The calls which the police-officer repeated twenty times, of "In the King's name," were powerless against the formidable multitude, and seemed on the contrary to exasperate it still more; when, at the cries, "In the name of the King," an officer ran up, and seeing the uniforms much ill-treated, he sprang into the scuffle, sword in hand, and brought unexpected help to the guards. This gentleman was young, scarcely sixteen years of age, perfectly pale with anger. He sprang on foot as the other guards, placed his back against the shaft of the carriage, making a rampart of his horse, drew his pistols from their holsters, and fastened them to his belt, and began to fight with the back sword, like a man accustomed to the handling of his weapon.

During ten minutes he alone kept the crowd at bay; at last Comminges appeared, pushing Broussel before him.

"Let us break the carriage!" cried the people.

"In the King's name!" cried Comminges.

"The first who advances is a dead man!" cried Raoul, for it was in fact he, who, feeling himself pressed and almost crushed by a kind of giant, pricked him with the point of his sword, and sent him groaning back.

Comminges, so to speak, threw Broussel into the carriage, and sprang in after him. At this moment a shot was fired, and a ball passed through the hat of Comminges, and broke the arm of one of the guards. Comminges looked up, and saw among the smoke a threatening face, appearing at the window of the second floor.

"Very well, sir," said Comminges, "you shall hear of me again."

"And you of me, too, sir," said Louvières, Broussel's son-in-law; "and we shall see who can speak the loudest."

Friquet and Nanette continued to shout; the cries, the noise of the shot, and the intoxicating smell of powder, produced their effect.

"Down with the officer! down with him!" was the cry.

"One step nearer," said Comminges, putting down the sashes

that the interior of the carriage might be well seen, and placing his sword on his prisoner's breast, "one step nearer, and I kill the prisoner; my orders are to bring him off alive or dead. I will take him dead, that's all."

A terrible scream was heard, and the wife and daughters of Broussel held up their hands in supplication to the people; the latter knew that this officer, who was so pale, but who appeared so determined, would keep his word; they continued to threaten, but they began to disperse.

"Drive to the palace," said Comminges to the coachman, more dead than alive.

The man whipped his animals, which cleared a way through the crowd; but on arriving on the Quai, they were obliged to stop; the carriage was upset, the horses were carried off, stifled, mangled by the crowd. Raoul, on foot, for he had not had time to mount his horse again, tired, like the guards, of distributing blows with the flat of his sword, had recourse to its point. But this last and dreaded resource served only to exasperate the multitude. From time to time a shot from a musket, or the blade of a rapier, flashed among the crowd; the projectiles continued to rain from the windows, and some shots were heard, the echo of which, though they were probably fired in the air, made all hearts vibrate. Voices, which are heard but on days of revolution, were distinguished; faces were seen that only appeared on days of bloodshed. Cries of "Death!—death to the guards!—into the Seine with the officer!" were heard above all the noise, deafening as it was. Raoul, his hat ground into powder, and his face bleeding, felt not only his strength, but also his reason going; a red mist covered his sight, and through this mist he saw a hundred threatening arms stretched over him, ready to seize upon him when he fell. The guards were unable to help any one, for each was occupied with his personal preservation. All was over; carriages, horses, guards, and perhaps even the prisoner, were about to be torn to shreds, when all at once a voice well known to Raoul was heard, and suddenly a large sword glistened in the air; at the same time the crowd opened—upset, trodden down—and an officer of the Musketeers, striking and cutting right and left, rushed up to Raoul, and took him in his arms, just as he was about to fall.

"God's-blood," cried the officer, "have they killed him? Woe to them if it be so."

And he turned round, so stern with anger, strength, and threat, that the most excited rebels hustled back against one another, in order to escape, and some of them even rolled into the Seine.

"M. d'Artagnan!" murmured Raoul.

"Yes, in person, and fortunately it seems for you, my young friend. Come on—here—you others," he continued, rising in his stirrups and raising his sword, and addressing those Musketeers who had not been able to follow his rapid pace, "come, sweep away all that trash for me, level muskets, present arms, take aim——"

At this command the mountains of populace thinned so suddenly that d'Artagnan could not suppress a burst of Homeric laughter.

"Thank you, d'Artagnan," said Comminges, showing half of his body through the window of the broken vehicle, "thanks, my young friend; your name?—that I may mention it to the Queen."

Raoul was about to reply, when d'Artagnan bent down to his ear.

"Hold your tongue," said he, "and let me answer. Do not lose time, Comminges," he continued; "get out of the carriage, if you can, and make another draw up; be quick, or in five minutes all the mob will be back with swords and muskets, you will be killed, and your prisoner freed. Hold—there is a carriage coming down there."

Then, bending again to Raoul, he whispered, "Above all things, don't tell your name."

"That's right. I will go," said Comminges; "and if they come back, fire!"

"Not at all—not at all," replied d'Artagnan; "let no one move. On the contrary, one shot at this moment would be paid for dearly to-morrow."

Comminges took his four guards and as many Musketeers, and ran to the carriage, from which he made the people inside dismount, and brought them to the vehicle which had upset. But when it was necessary to convey the prisoner from one carriage to the other, the people, catching sight of him whom they called their liberator, uttered every imaginable cry, and knotted once more against the vehicle.

"Start off!" said d'Artagnan. "There are ten men to accompany you. I will keep twenty to hold in the mob; go, and lose not a moment. Ten men for M. de Comminges!"

As the carriage started off the cries were redoubled, and more than ten thousand were hurried on the Quai, and encumbered the Pont-Neuf and the adjacent streets. A few shots were fired, and a Musketeer wounded.

"Forward!" cried d'Artagnan, driven to extremities, biting his moustache, and then he charged with his twenty men, and dispersed them in fear.

"Ah! sir," said Raoul, "allow me to thank you. I too, sir, was almost dead when you arrived."

"Wait—wait, young man, and do not fatigue yourself with speaking. We can talk of it afterwards."

Then, seeing that the Musketeers had cleared the Quai from the Pont-Neuf to the Quai St. Michael, and that they were returned, he waved his sword for them to double their speed. The Musketeers trotted up, and at the same time the ten men, whom d'Artagnan had given to Comminges, appeared.

"Halloa!" cried d'Artagnan; "has something fresh happened?"

"Eh, sir!" replied the sergeant, "their vehicle has broken down a second time—there's a curse on it."

"They are bad managers," said d'Artagnan, shrugging his shoulders. "When a carriage is chosen, it ought to be strong. The carriage in which a Broussel is to be arrested ought to be able to bear ten thousand men."

"What are your commands, my lieutenant?"

"Take the detachment to quarters."

"But you will be left alone!"

"Certainly. Do you suppose I have need of an escort? Go."

The Musketeers set off, and d'Artagnan was left alone with Raoul.

"Now," he said, "are you in pain?"

"Yes, my head is heavy and burning."

"What's the matter with this head?" said d'Artagnan, raising the battered hat. "Ah! ah! a bruise."

"Yes, I think I received a flower-pot on the head."

"Brutes!" said d'Artagnan. "But were you not on horseback?—you have spurs."

"Yes, but I got down to defend M. de Comminges, and my horse was taken away. Here it is, I see."

At this very moment Friquet passed, mounted on Raoul's horse, waving his parti-colored cap, and crying, "Broussel! Broussel!"

"Halloa! stop, rascal!" cried d'Artagnan. "Bring hither that horse."

Friquet heard perfectly, but he pretended not to do so, and tried to continue his road. D'Artagnan felt inclined for an instant to pursue Master Friquet, but not wishing to leave Raoul alone, he contented himself with taking a pistol from the holster, and cocking it.

Friquet had a quick eye and a fine ear. He saw d'Artagnan's movement; heard the sound of the click, and stopped at once.

"Ah! it is you, your honor," he said, advancing towards d'Artagnan; "and I am truly pleased to meet you."

D'Artagnan looked attentively at Friquet, and recognized the boy.

"Ah, 'tis you, rascal!" said he, "come here. So you have changed trades; you are no longer a choir-boy, or a tavern-boy; but a horse-thief."

"Ah, your honor, how can you say so!" exclaimed Friquet. "I was seeking the gentleman to whom this horse belongs—an officer, brave and handsome as a Cæsar,"—then, pretending to see Raoul for the first time,—

"Ah! but if I mistake not," continued he, "here he is; you won't forget the boy, sir?"

Raoul put his hand in his pocket.

"What are you about?" asked d'Artagnan.

"To give ten francs to this honest fellow," replied Raoul, taking a pistole from his pocket.

"Ten kicks!" said d'Artagnan; "be off, you little rascal, and forget not that I have your address."

Friquet, who did not expect to be let off so cheaply, made but one bound, and disappeared. Raoul mounted his horse and both leisurely took their way to the Rue Tiqetonne.

D'Artagnan shielded the youth as if he were his own son. They arrived without accident at the Buck Hotel.

The handsome Madeleine announced to d'Artagnan that Planchet had returned, bringing Mousqueton with him, who had heroically borne the extraction of the ball, and was as well as his state would permit.

D'Artagnan desired Planchet to be summoned, but he had disappeared.

"Then bring some wine," said d'Artagnan. "You are much pleased with yourself," said he to Raoul, when they were alone, "are you not?"

"Well, yes," replied Raoul; "it seems to me that I did my duty. I defended the King."

"And who told you to defend the King?"

"The Count de la Fère himself."

"Yes, the King; but to-day you have not fought for the King, you have fought for Mazarin; it is not the same thing."

"But you yourself?"

"Oh, for me, it is another matter. I obey my captain's orders. As for you, your captain is the prince. Understand that rightly; you have no other. But has one ever seen such a wild fellow?" continued he, "making himself a Mazarinist, and helping to arrest Broussel! Breathe not a word of that, or the Count de la Fère will be furious."

"You think that the count will be angry with me?"

"Do I think it? I am sure of it; were it not for that I should thank you, for you have worked for us. However, I scold you instead of him, and in his place; the storm will blow over more easily, believe me. And, moreover, my dear child," continued d'Artagnan, "I am making use of the privilege conceded to me by your guardian."

"I do not understand you, sir," said Raoul.

D'Artagnan rose, and taking a letter from his writing-desk, presented it to Raoul. The face of the latter became serious when he had cast his eyes on the paper.

"Oh," he said, raising his fine eyes to d'Artagnan, moist with tears, "the count has then left Paris without seeing me?"

"He left four days ago," said d'Artagnan.

"But his letter seems to intimate that he is about to incur danger, perhaps of death."

"He—he—incur danger of death!—no—be not anxious; he is traveling on business, and will return ere long. I hope you have no repugnance to accept me as a guardian in the interim?"

"No, no, M. d'Artagnan," said Raoul, "you are such a brave gentleman, and the Count de la Fère has so much affection for you!"

"S'death! love me too; I will not torment you much, but only on condition that you become a Frondist, my young friend, and a hearty Frondist, too."

"Well, sir, I will obey you, although I do not understand you."

"It is unnecessary for you to understand; hold," continued d'Artagnan, turning towards the door, which had just opened, "here is M. du Vallon, who comes with his coat torn."

"Yes, but in exchange," said Porthos, covered with perspiration, and soiled with dust, "in exchange, I have torn many skins. Those wretches wanted to take away my sword! Deuce take 'em, what a popular commotion!" continued the giant, in his quiet manner; "but I knocked down more than twenty with the hilt of Balizarde; a drop of wine, d'Artagnan."

"Oh, I'll answer for you," said the Gascon, filling Porthos' glass to the brim, "but when you have drunk, give me your opinion.

"Here is M. de Bragelonne, who determined, at all risks, to aid the arrest of Broussel, and whom I had great difficulty to prevent defending M. de Comminges."

"The devil!" said Porthos; "and what would the guardian have said to that?"

"Do you hear?" interrupted d'Artagnan; "be a Frondist, my friend, belong to the Fronde, and remember that I fill the count's place in everything;" and he jingled his money.

"Will you come?" said he to Porthos.

"Where to?" asked Porthos, filling a second glass with wine.

"To present our respects to the Cardinal."

Porthos swallowed the second glass with the same ease with which he had drunk the first, took his beaver, and followed d'Artagnan. As for Raoul, he remained bewildered with what he had seen, having been forbidden by d'Artagnan to leave the room until the tumult was over.

CHAPTER XLIII.

ROCHEFORT AT WORK.

D'ARTAGNAN had calculated that in not going at once to the Palais Royal he would give time to Comminges to arrive there before him, and consequently to make the Cardinal acquainted with the eminent services which he, d'Artagnan, and his friend, had rendered to the Queen's party in the morning.

They were indeed admirably received by Mazarin, who paid them numerous compliments, and announced that they were more than half on their way to obtain what they desired, namely, d'Artagnan his captaincy, and Porthos his barony.

Whilst the two friends were with the Cardinal, the Queen sent for him. Mazarin, thinking that it would be the means of increasing the zeal of his two defenders if he procured them personal thanks from the Queen, motioned to them to follow him. D'Artagnan and Porthos pointed to their dusty and torn dresses, but the Cardinal shook his head.

"Those costumes," he said, "are of more worth than most of those which you will see on the Queen's courtiers; they are the costumes of battle."

D'Artagnan and Porthos obeyed. The court of Anne of Austria was full of gaiety and animation; for, after having gained a victory over the Spaniard, it had just gained another over the people. Broussel had been conducted out of Paris without resistance, and was at this time in the prison of St. Germain; and Blancmesnil, who was arrested at the same time, but whose arrest had been made without difficulty or noise, was safe in the Castle of Vincennes.

Comminges was near the Queen, who was questioning him upon the details of his expedition, and everyone was listening to his account when d'Artagnan and Porthos were perceived at the door behind the Cardinal.

"Hey, madam," said Comminges, hastening to d'Artagnan, "here is one who can tell you better than myself, for he is my protector. Without him I should probably, at this moment, be caught in the nets at St. Cloud, for it was a question of nothing less than throwing me into the river. Speak, d'Artagnan, speak."

D'Artagnan had been a hundred times in the same room with the Queen since he had become lieutenant of the Musketeers, but her majesty had never once spoken to him.

"Well, sir," at last said Anne of Austria, "you are silent, after rendering such a service?"

"Madam," replied d'Artagnan, "I have nought to say, save that my life is ever at your majesty's service; and that I shall only be happy the day that I lose it for you."

"I know that, sir; I have known that," said the Queen, "a long time; therefore I am delighted to be able thus publicly to mark my gratitude and my esteem."

"Permit me, madam," said d'Artagnan, "to reserve a portion for my friend; like myself"—(he laid an emphasis on these words)—"a Musketeer of the company of Tréville, and he has done wonders."

"His name?" asked the Queen.

"In the regiment," said d'Artagnan, "it was Porthos" (the Queen started), but his true name is the Chevalier du Vallon."

"De Bracieux de Pierrefonds," added Porthos.

"These names are too numerous for me to remember them all, and I will content myself with the first," said the Queen, graciously; Porthos bowed. At this moment the Coadjutor was announced; a cry of surprise rang through the royal assemblage. Although the Coadjutor had preached that same morning, it was well known that he leant much to the side of the Fronde; and Mazarin, in requesting the Archbishop of Paris to make his nephew preach, had evidently had the intention of administering to M. de Retz one of those Italian kicks which he so much enjoyed giving.

The fact was, in leaving Nôtre Dame the Coadjutor had learnt the event of the day. Although almost engaged to the leaders of the Fronde, he had not gone so far but that retreat was possible, should the court offer him the advantages for which he was ambitious, and to which the Coadjutorship was but a stepping stone. M. de Retz wished to be archbishop in his uncle's place, and cardinal, like Mazarin; and the popular party could with difficulty accord to him favors entirely royal. He, therefore, hastened to the palace to congratulate the Queen on the battle of Lens, determined beforehand to act with or against the court, according as his congratulations were well or ill received.

The Coadjutor had, perhaps, in his own person, as much wit as all those together who were assembled at the court to laugh at him. His speech, therefore, was so well turned that in spite of the great wish felt by the courtiers to laugh, they could find no point upon which to vent their ridicule. He concluded by saying that he placed his feeble influence at her majesty's command.

During the whole time that he was speaking, the Queen appeared to be well pleased with the Coadjutor's harangue; but terminating as it did with such a phrase, the only one which could be caught at by the jokers, Anne turned round, and directed a glance towards her favorites, which announced that she delivered up the Coadjutor to their tender mercies. Immediately the wits of the court plunged into satire. Nogent-Beautin, the fool of the court, exclaimed that the Queen was very happy to have the succor of religion at such a moment. This caused a universal burst of laughter. The Count de Vil-

leroy said that he did not know how any fear could be entertained for a moment when the court had to defend itself
against the Parliament and the citizens of Paris, his holiness
the Coadjutor, who by a signal could raise an army of curates,
church porters and vergers and so on.

During this storm, Gondy, who had it in his power to make
it fatal to the jesters, remained calm and stern. The Queen
at last asked him if he had anything to add to the fine dis-
course which he had just made to her.

"Yes, madam," replied the Coadjutor; "I have to beg you to
reflect twice ere you cause a civil war in the kingdom."

The Queen turned her back, and the laughs recommenced.

The Coadjutor bowed and left the palace, casting upon the
Cardinal such a glance as is understood best between mortal
foes.

"Oh!" muttered Gondy, as he left the threshold of the palace;
"ungrateful court! faithless court! cowardly court! I will
teach you how to laugh to-morrow—but in another manner."

But whilst they were indulging in extravagant joy at the
Palais Royal, to increase the hilarity of the Queen, Mazarin, a
man of sense, and whose fear, moreover, gave him foresight,
lost no time in making idle and dangerous jokes; he went out
after the Coadjutor, settled his account, locked up his gold, and
had confidential workmen to contrive hiding-places in his walls.

At a quarter of six o'clock, Gondy, having finished his business, returned to the archiepiscopal palace.

At six o'clock the Curate of St. Merri was announced.

The Coadjutor glanced rapidly behind, and saw that he was
followed by another man. It was Planchet.

"Your holiness," said the curate, "here is a person disposed
to serve the cause of the people."

"Most undoubtedly," said Planchet. "I am a Frondist from
my heart. You see in me, such as I am, my lord, a person sen-
tenced to be hung."

"And on what account?"

"I rescued from the hands of Mazarin's police a noble lord,
whom they were conducting again to the Bastille, where he
had been for five years."

"Will you name him?"

"Oh, you know him well, my lord:—it is Count de Rochefort."

"Ah! really, yes," said the Coadjutor, "I have heard this
affair mentioned. You raised the whole district, they told me?"

"Very nearly," replied Planchet, with a self-satisfied air.

"And your business is——"

"That of a grocer in the Rue des Lombards."

"Explain to me how it happens that, following so peaceful a
business, you had such warlike inclinations."

"Why does my lord, belonging to the church, now receive

me in the dress of an officer with a sword at his side, and spurs to his boots?"

"Not badly answered, i'faith," said Gondy, laughing; "but I have, you must know, always had, in spite of my bands, war-like inclinations."

"Well, my lord, before I became a grocer, I myself was three years sergeant in the Piedmontese regiment, and before I became sergeant I was for eighteen months servant of M. d'Artagnan."

"Lieutenant in the Musketeers?" asked Gondy.

"Himself, my lord."

"But he is said to be a furious Mazarinist."

"Pooh!" said Planchet.

"What do you mean by pooh-poohing?"

"Nothing, my lord; M. d'Artagnan belongs to the service; he makes it his business to defend the Cardinal, who pays him, as much as we make it ours—we citizens—to attack him, whom he robs."

"You are an intelligent fellow, my friend; can we count upon you?"

"You may count upon me, my lord, provided you want to make a total upset in the city."

" 'Tis that exactly. How many men, think you, you could collect together to-night?"

"Two hundred muskets, and five hundred halberds."

"Let there be only one man in every district who can do as much, and by to-morrow we shall have a tolerably strong army. Are you disposed to obey Count de Rochefort?"

"I would follow him into hell; and that is not saying a little, as I believe him quite capable of descending there."

"Bravo!"

"By what sign to-morrow shall we be able to distinguish friends from foes?"

"Every Frondist must put a knot of straw in his hat."

"Good! Give the word."

"Do you want money?"

"Money never comes amiss at any time, my lord; if one has it not, one must do without it; with it matters go on much better, and more rapidly."

Gondy went to a box and drew forth a bag.

"Here are five hundred pistoles," he said; "and if the action goes off well you may reckon upon a similar sum to-morrow."

"I will give a faithful account of the sum to your lordship," said Planchet, putting the bag under his arm.

"That is right: I recommend the Cardinal to your attention."

"Make your mind easy, he is in good hands."

Planchet went out, and ten minutes later the Curate of St. Sulpice was announced. As soon as the door of Gondy's study was opened, a man rushed in; it was Count de Rochefort.

"It is you, then, my dear Count," cried Gondy, offering his hand.

"You have decided at last, my lord?" said Rochefort.

"I have ever been so," said Gondy.

"Let us speak no more on that subject; you tell me so; I believe you. Well, we are going to give a ball to Mazarin."

"I hope so."

"And when will the dance begin?"

"The invitations are given for this evening," said the Coadjutor, "but the violins will only begin to play to-morrow morning."

"You may reckon upon me, and upon fifty soldiers which the Chevalier d'Humières has promised to me, whenever I might need them."

"Upon fifty soldiers?"

"Yes, he is making recruits, and he will lend them to me; if any are missing when the fête is over, I shall replace them."

"Good, my dear Rochefort; but that is not all. What have you done with M. de Beaufort?"

"He is in Vendôme, where he waits until I write to him to return to Paris."

"Write to him—now's the time."

"You are sure of your enterprise?"

"Yes, but he must hurry himself. I answer for his consent. How soon can he be here?"

"In five days."

"Let him come, and he will find a change, I will answer for it. Therefore, go and collect your fifty men, and hold yourself in readiness."

"Is there any signal for rallying?"

"A knot of straw in the hat."

"Very good. Ah! M. Mazarin," said Rochefort, leading off his curate, who had not found an opportunity of uttering a single word during the foregoing dialogue, "you will see whether I am too old to be a man of action."

CHAPTER XLIV.

THE KING OF THE BEGGARS.

IT was half-past nine o'clock, and the Coadjutor took half an hour to go from the Archbishop's palace to the tower of St. Jaques-de-la-Boucherie. He remarked that a light burnt in one of the highest windows of the tower. "Good," said he, "our syndic is at his post."

He knocked, and the door was opened. The vicar himself awaited him, conducted him to the top of the tower, and when they pointed to a little door, placed the light which he had brought with him in a corner of the wall, that the Coadjutor might be able to find it on his return, and went down again. Although the key was in the door, the Coadjutor knocked.

"Come in," said a voice, that of a mendicant, whom he found lying on a kind of truckle bed. He rose on the entrance of the Coadjutor, and at that moment ten o'clock struck.

"Well," said Gondy, "have you kept your word with me?"

"Not quite," replied the beggar.

"How is that?"

"You asked me for five hundred men, did you not? Well, I shall have ten thousand for you."

"You are not boasting?"

"Do you wish for a proof?"

"Yes."

There were three candles alight—each of which burnt before a window—one looking upon the city, the other upon the Palais Royal, and the third upon the Rue St. Denis.

The man went silently to each of the candles, and blew them out one after the other.

"What are you doing?" asked the Coadjutor.

"I have given the signal."

"For what?"

"For the barricades. When you leave this, you will see my men at their work. Only take care not to break your legs in stumbling over some chain, nor to fall into some hole."

"Good! there is your money,—the same sum as that which you have received already. Now remember that you are a general, and do not go and drink."

"For twenty years I have tasted nothing but water."

The man took the bag from the hands of the Coadjutor, who heard the sound of his fingers counting and handling the gold pieces.

"Ah! ah!" said the Coadjutor, "you are avaricious, my good fellow."

The beggar sighed, and threw down the bag.

"Must I always be the same," said he, "and shall I never succeed in overcoming the old leaven? Oh, misery, oh, vanity!"

"You take it, however."

"Yes, but I make a vow in your presence, to employ all that remains to me in pious works."

"Come, be candid," said the Coadjutor, "you have not all your life followed the trade which you do now?"

"No, my lord. I have pursued it for six years only."

"And, previously, where were you?"

"In the Bastille."

"And before you went to the Bastille?"

"I will tell you, my lord, on the day when you are willing to hear my confession."

"Good! at whatever hour of the day, or of the night on which you present yourself, remember that I shall be ready to give you absolution."

"Thank you, my lord," said the mendicant in a hoarse voice, "But I am not yet ready to receive it."

"Very well. Adieu."

"Adieu, your holiness," said the mendicant, opening the door, and bending low before the prelate.

CHAPTER XLV.

THE RIOT.

It was about eleven o'clock at night. Gondy had not walked a hundred steps ere he perceived the strange change which had been made in the streets of Paris.

The whole city seemed peopled with fantastic beings; silent shadows were seen unpaving the streets, and others dragging and upsetting great wagons, whilst others again dug ditches large enough to engulf whole regiments of horsemen. These active beings flitted here and there like so many demons completing some unknown labor—these were the beggars preparing the barricades for the morrow.

Gondy gazed on these men of darkness, these nocturnal laborers, with a kind of fear: he asked himself if, after having called forth these foul creatures from their dens, he should have the power of making them retire again. He felt almost inclined to cross himself when one of these beings happened to approach him. He reached the Rue St. Honore, and went up it towards the Rue de la Ferronière: there the aspect changed; here it was the tradesmen who were running from shop to shop: their doors seemed closed like their shutters; but they were only pushed to in such a manner as to open and allow the men, who seemed fearful of showing what they carried, to enter, closing immediately. These men were shop-keepers, who had arms to lend to those who had none.

The work of revolt continued the whole night. The next morning, on awaking, Paris seemed to be startled at her own appearance. It was like a besieged town. Armed men, shouldering muskets, watched over the barricades with menacing looks; words of command, patrols, arrests, executions even, were encountered at every step. Those bearing plumed hats and gold swords were stopped and made to cry, "Long live Broussel!" "Down with Mazarin!" and whoever refused to comply with this ceremony was hooted at, spat upon, and even beaten. They had not yet begun to slay, but it was well felt that the inclination to do so was not wanting.

The barricades had been pushed as far as the Palais Royal, and the astonishment of Mazarin and Anne of Austria was great when it was announced to them that the city, which the previous evening they had left tranquil, had awakened so feverish and in such commotion; nor would either the one or the other believe the reports which were brought to them, and declared that they would rather rely on the evidence of their own eyes and ears. Then a window was opened, and when they saw and heard, they were convinced.

Mazarin shrugged his shoulders, and pretended to despise the populace much; but he turned visibly pale, and ran to his closet trembling all over, locked up his gold jewels in his caskets, and put his finest diamonds on his fingers. As for the Queen, furious, and left to her own guidance, she sent for Marshal de la Meilleraie, and desired him to take as many men as he pleased, and to go and see what was the meaning of this pleasantry.

We have already said that Mazarin was in his closet, putting his little affairs in order. He called for d'Artagnan, but in the midst of such tumult he little expected to see him, d'Artagnan not being on service. In about ten minutes d'Artagnan appeared at the door, followed by his inseparable, Porthos.

"Ah, come—come in, M. d'Artagnan," cried the Cardinal, "and be welcome, as well as your friend. But what is going on then, in this cursed Paris?"

"What is going on, my lord? nothing good," replied d'Artagnan, shaking his head; "the town is in open revolt; and just now, as I was crossing the Rue Montorgueil with M. du Vallon, who is here, and is your humble servant, they wanted, in spite of my uniform, or, perhaps, because of my uniform, to make us cheer 'Long live Broussel!' and must I tell you, my lord, what they wished us to cheer as well?"

"Speak, speak!"

"'Down with Mazarin!' I'faith, the big word is out now."

Mazarin smiled, but became very pale.

"And did you cheer?" he asked.

"I'faith, no," said d'Artagnan, "I was not in voice; M. du Vallon has a cold, and did not cry either. Then, my lord——"

"Then what?" asked Mazarin.

"Look at my hat and cloak."

And d'Artagnan displayed four gun-shot holes in his cloak and two in his beaver. As for Porthos' coat, a blow from a halberd had laid it open on the flank, and the pistol-shot had cut his feather in two.

"Diavolo!" said the Cardinal, pensively, gazing at the two friends with lively admiration; "I should have cheered, I think!"

At this moment the tumult was heard nearer.

Mazarin wiped his forehead and looked around him. He had a great desire to go to the window, but he dared not. "See what is going on, M. d'Artagnan," said he.

D'Artagnan went to the window, with his habitual composure. "Oh, oh!" said he, "what is that? Marshal de la Meilleraie returning without a hat—Fontailles with his arm in a sling—wounded guards—horses bleeding—eh, then, what are the sentinels about? they are aiming—they are going to fire!"

"They have received orders to fire on the people, if the people approach the Palais Royal!" exclaimed Mazarin.

"But if they fire, all is lost!" cried d'Artagnan.

"We have the gates."

"The gates! to hold for five minutes; the gates, they will be torn down, bent, ground to powder! S'death, don't fire!" screamed d'Artagnan, throwing open the window.

In spite of this recommendation, which, owing to the noise, could not have been heard, two or three musket-shots resounded, which were succeeded by a terrible discharge. The balls might be heard peppering the façade of the Palais Royal, and one of them, passing under d'Artagnan's arm, entered and broke a mirror, in which Porthos was complacently admiring himself.

"Alack, alack," cried the Cardinal; "a Venetian glass!"

"Oh, my lord," said d'Artagnan, quietly shutting the window, "it is not worth while weeping yet, for probably an hour hence there will not be one of your mirrors remaining in the Palais Royal, whether they be Venetian or Parisian."

"But what do you advise, then?" asked Mazarin, trembling.

"Eh, egad, to give up Broussel, as they demand! What the devil do you want with a member of the Parliament? He is of no use for anything."

"And you, M. du Vallon, is that your advice? what would you do?"

"I should give up Broussel."

"Come, come with me, gentlemen!" exclaimed Mazarin. "I will go and discuss the matter with the Queen."

He stopped at the end of the corridor, and said:

"I can count upon you, gentlemen, can I not?"

"We do not give ourselves twice over," said d'Artagnan; "we have given ourselves to you—command, we shall obey."

"Very well, then," said Mazarin; "enter this closet and wait there."

And turning off, he entered the drawing-room by another door.

CHAPTER XLVI.

THE RIOT BECOMES A REVOLUTION.

THE closet into which d'Artagnan and Porthos had been ushered was separated from the drawing-room where the Queen was, by tapestried curtains only, and this thin partition enabled them to hear all that passed in the adjoining room, while the aperture between the two hangings, small as it was, permitted them to see.

The Queen was standing in the room, pale with anger; her self-control, however, was so great that it might have been supposed that she was calm. Comminges, Villequier, and Guitaut were behind her, and the women again were behind the men. The Chancellor Sèguier, who, twenty years previously, had persecuted her so violently, was before her, relating how his carriage had been broken, how he had been pursued, and had rushed into the Hotel O——, that the hotel was immediately invested, pillaged, and devastated; happily, he had time to reach a closet hidden behind tapestry, in which he was secreted by an old woman together with his brother, the Bishop of Meaux. Fortunately, however, he had not been taken; the people, believing that he had escaped by some back entrance, had retired, and left him to retreat at liberty. Then, disguised in the clothes of the Marquis d'O——, he had left the hotel, stumbling over the bodies of an officer and those of two guards who were killed whilst defending the street door.

During the recital Mazarin entered and glided noiselessly up to the Queen to listen.

"Well," said the Queen, when the chancellor had finished speaking; "what do you think of it all?"

"I think that matters look very gloomy, madam."

"But what step would you propose to me?"

"Madam," said the chancellor, hesitating, "it would be to release Broussel."

The Queen, although already pale, became visibly paler, and her face was contracted.

"Release Broussel!" she cried, "never!"

At this moment steps were heard in the ante-room, and, without any announcement, the Marshal de la Meilleraie appeared at the door.

"Ah, there you are, marshal," cried Anne of Austria, joyfully. "I trust you have brought this rabble to reason."

"Madam," replied the marshal, "I have left three men on the Pont Neuf, four at the Halle, six at the corner of the Rue de l'Arbre-Sec, and two at the door of your palace—fifteen in all. I have brought away ten or twelve wounded. I know not where I have left my hat, and in all probability I should have been left beside my hat, had the Coadjutor not arrived in time to rescue me."

"Ah, indeed!" said the Queen, "it would have astonished me if that low cur, with his distorted legs, had not been mixed up with it."

"Madam," said La Meilleraie, "do not say too much against him before me, for the service he rendered me is still fresh."

"Very good," said the Queen, "be as grateful as you like, it does not implicate me; you are here safe and sound, that is all I wish for, therefore you are not only welcome, but welcome back."

"Yes, madam; but I only come back on one condition—that I would transmit to your majesty the will of the people."

"The will!" exclaimed the Queen, frowning. "Oh! oh! M. Marshal, you must indeed have found yourself in great peril to have undertaken so strange a commission!"

The irony with which these words were uttered did not escape the marshal.

"Pardon, madam," he said, "I am not a lawyer, I am a mere soldier, and probably, therefore, I do not quite comprehend the value of certain words; I ought to have said the wishes, and not the will, of the people. As for what you do me the honor to say, I presume that you mean that I felt fear."

The Queen smiled.

"Well, then, madam, yes, I did feel fear; and though I have seen twelve pitched battles, and I know not how many fights and skirmishes, I own that, for the third time in my life, I was afraid. Yes; and I would rather face your majesty, however threatening your smile, than face those hell-demons who accompanied me hither, and who sprang from I know not where."

"Bravo," said d'Artagnan, in a whisper to Porthos; "well answered."

"Well," said the Queen, biting her lips, whilst her courtiers looked at each other with surprise, "what is the desire of my people?"

"That Broussel should be given up to them, madam."

"Never!" said the Queen, "never!"

Mazarin sprang forward.

"Madam," said he, "if I dared in my turn advise——"

"Would it be to give up Broussel, sir? If so, you can spare yourself the trouble."

"No," said Mazarin; "although, perhaps, that is as good counsel as any other."

"Then what may it be?"

"To call for the Coadjutor."

"And hold, madam," suggested Comminges, who was near a window, out of which he could see; "hold, the moment is a happy one, for there he is now, giving his blessing in the square of the Palais Royal."

The Queen sprang to the window.

"It is true," she said; "the arch-hypocrite! see!"

"I see," said Mazarin, "that everybody kneels before him, although he be but Coadjutor, whilst I, were I in his place, though I be Cardinal, should be torn to pieces. I persist, then, madam, in my wish (he laid an emphasis on the word) that your majesty should receive the Coadjutor."

"And wherefore say you not, like the rest, your will?" replied the Queen, in a low voice.

Mazarin bowed.

"Marshal," said the Queen, after a moment's reflection, "go and find the Coadjutor, and bring him to me."

"And what shall I say to the people?"

"That they must have patience," said Anne, "as I have."

The marshal bowed and went out; and, during his absence, Anne of Austria approached Comminges, and conversed with him in a subdued tone, while Mazarin glanced uneasily at the corner occupied by d'Artagnan and Porthos. Ere long the door opened, and the marshal entered, followed by the Coadjutor.

"There, madam," he said, "is Gondy, who hastens to obey your majesty's summons."

The Queen advanced a few steps to meet him, and then stopped, cold, severe, and unmoved, and her lower lip scornfully projected. Gondy bowed respectfully.

"Well, sir," said the Queen, "what is your opinion of this riot?"

"That it is no longer a riot, madam," he replied, "but a revolt."

"The revolt is in those who think that my people can revolt," cried Anne, unable to dissimulate before the Coadjutor, whom she looked upon—and perhaps with reason—as the promoter of the tumult. "Revolt! thus is it called by those who have wished for this demonstration, and who are, perhaps, the cause of it; but wait, wait! the King's authority will put it all to rights."

"Was it to tell me that, madam," coldly replied Gondy, "that your majesty admitted me to the honor of entering your presence?"

"No, my dear Coadjutor," said Mazarin; "it was to ask your advice in the unhappy dilemma in which we find ourselves."

The Coadjutor bowed.

"Your majesty wishes then——"

"You to say what you would do in her place," Mazarin hastened to reply.

The Coadjutor looked at the Queen, who replied by a sign in the affirmative.

"Were I in her majesty's place," said Gondy, coldly, "I should not hesitate, I should release Broussel."

"And if I do not give him up, what think you will be the result?" exclaimed the Queen.

"I believe that not a stone in Paris will remain unturned," said the marshal.

"It was not your opinion that I asked," said the Queen, sharply, without turning round.

"If it is I whom your majesty interrogates," replied the Coadjutor, in the same calm manner, "I reply that I hold the marshal's opinion in every respect."

The color mounted to the Queen's face: her fine blue eyes seemed to start out of her head, and her carmine lips, compared by all the poets of the day to a pomegranate in flower, were white, and trembling with anger. Mazarin himself, who was well accustomed to the domestic outbreaks of this disturbed household, was alarmed.

"Give up Broussel!" she cried; "a good counsel, indeed. Upon my word! one can easily see that it comes from a priest."

Gondy remained firm; and the abuse of the day seemed to glide over his head as the sarcasms of the evening before had done; but hatred and revenge were accumulating in the depth of his heart, silently, and drop by drop.

"Madam," he said, "you should appear to have reflected, and publicly acknowledge an error,—which constitutes the strength of a strong government,—release Broussel from prison, and give him back to the people."

"Oh!" cried Anne, "to humble myself thus! Am I, or am I not, the Queen? This screaming mob, are they, or are they not, my subjects? Have I friends? Have I guards? Ah! by Nôtre Dame! as Queen Catherine used to say," continued she, excited by her own words, "rather than give up this infamous Broussel to them, I will strangle him with my own hands."

And she sprang towards Gondy, whom assuredly at that moment she hated more than Broussel, with outstretched arms. The Coadjutor remained immovable, and not a muscle of his face was discomposed: only his glance flashed like a sword, in returning the furious looks of the Queen.

"He were a dead man," cried the Gascon, "if there were still a Vitry at the court, and if Vitry entered at this moment; but for my part, before he could reach the good prelate, I would kill Vitry at once; the Cardinal would be infinitely pleased with me."

"Hush!" said Porthos, "and listen."

"Madam," cried the Cardinal, seizing hold of Anne, and drawing her back; "madam, what are you about?"

Then he added in Spanish, "Anne, are you mad? You a Queen and quarreling thus like a saleslady! And do you not perceive that in the person of this priest is represented the whole people of Paris, and that it is dangerous to insult him at this moment, and that if this priest wished it, in an hour you would be without a crown? Come, then, on another occasion you can be firm and strong; but to-day is not the proper time;

to-day, you must flatter and caress, or you will be but an ordinary person."

The rough appeal, marked by the eloquence which characterized Mazarin when he spoke in Italian or Spanish, and which he lost entirely in speaking French, was uttered with such impenetrable expression that Gondy, clever physiognomist as he was, had no suspicion of its being more than a simple warning to be more subdued.

The Queen, on her part, thus chided, softened immediately, and sat down, and in an almost weeping voice, letting her arms fall by her sides, said:

"Pardon me, sir, and attribute this violence to what I suffer. A woman, and, consequently, subject to the weaknesses of my sex, I am alarmed at the idea of civil war; a Queen—and accustomed to be obeyed—I am excited at the first opposition."

"Madam," replied Gondy, bowing, "your majesty is mistaken in qualifying your sincere advice as opposition. Your majesty has none but submissive and respectful subjects. It is not the Queen with whom the people are displeased; they ask for Broussel, and are only too happy, if you release him to them, to live under your government."

Mazarin, who at the words "It is not the Queen with whom the people are displeased," had pricked up his ears, thought that the Coadjutor was about to speak of the cries, "Down with Mazarin!" and pleased with Gondy's suppression of this fact, he said, with his sweetest voice, and his most gracious expression:

"Madam, believe the Coadjutor, who is one of the most able politicians that we have; the first vacant Cardinal's hat seems to belong to his noble head."

"Ah! how much you have need of me, cunning rogue," thought Gondy.

"And what will he promise us?" said d'Artagnan. "Plague, if he is giving away hats like that, Porthos, let us look out, and each ask a regiment to-morrow. Zounds, let the civil war last but one year, and I will have a Constable's sword gilt for me?"

"And for me?" said Porthos.

"For you! I will give you the truncheon of the Marshal de la Meilleraie, who does not seem to be much in favor just now."

"And so, sir," said the Queen, "you are seriously afraid of a public tumult?"

"Seriously," said Gondy, astonished at not having further advanced; "I fear that when the torrent has broken down its embankment it will cause fearful destruction."

"And I," said the Queen, "think that in such a case new embankments must be raised to oppose it. Go—I will reflect."

Gondy looked at Mazarin, astonished, and Mazarin approached

the Queen to speak to her, but at this moment a frightful crash
was heard. One of the gates began to yield.

"Oh! madam," cried Mazarin, "you have lost us all; the
King, yourself, and me."

At this cry from the soul of the frightened Cardinal, Anne
became alarmed in her turn.

"It is too late!" said Mazarin, tearing his hair, "too late!"

The gate had given way, and shouts were heard from the
mob. D'Artagnan put his hand to his sword, motioning to Porthos to follow his example.

"Save the Queen!" cried Mazarin to the Coadjutor.

Gondy sprang to the window and threw it open; he recognized
Louvières at the head of a troop of about three or four thousand men.

"Not a step further," he shouted, "the Queen is signing!"

"What are you saying?" asked the Queen.

"The truth, madam," said Mazarin, placing a pen and a paper
before her; "you must;" then he added, "Sign, Anne, I implore
you; I command you."

The Queen fell into a chair, took the pen and signed.

The people, kept back by Louvières, had not made another
step forward; but the awful murmuring, which indicates an
angry people, continued.

The Queen had written, "The keeper of the prison of St.
Germain will release Counsellor Broussel;" and she had
signed it.

The Coadjutor, whose eyes devoured her slightest movements, seized the paper immediately the signature had been af-
fixed to it, returned to the window, and waved it in his hand.

"This is the order," he said.

All Paris seemed to shout with joy; and then the air resounded with shouts of "Long live Broussel!" "Long live the
Coadjutor!"

"Long live the Queen!" cried de Gondy; but the cries which
replied to him were poor and few; and perhaps he had but
uttered it to make Anne of Austria sensible of her weakness.

"And now that you have obtained what you want, go," said
she, "M. de Gondy."

"Whenever her majesty has need of me," replied the Coadjutor, bowing, "her majesty knows that I am at her command."

"Ah, cursed priest!" cried Anne, when he had retired, stretching out her arm to the scarcely closed door, "one day I will
make you drink the remains of the gall which you have poured
out on me to-day.

Mazarin wished to approach her. "Leave me!" she exclaimed;
"you are not a man!" and she went out of the room.

"It is you who are not a woman," muttered Mazarin.

Then, after a moment of reverie, he remembered where he
had left d'Artagnan and Porthos, and that they must have

overheard everything. He knit his brows and went direct to the tapestry, which he pushed aside. The closet was empty.

At the Queen's last word, d'Artagnan had dragged Porthos into the gallery. Thither Mazarin went in his turn, and found the two friends walking up and down.

"Why did you leave the closet, M. d'Artagnan?" asked the Cardinal.

"Because," replied d'Artagnan, "the Queen desired every one to leave, and I thought that this command was intended for us as well as for the rest."

"And you have been here since——"

"About a quarter of an hour," said d'Artagnan, motioning to Porthos not to contradict him.

Mazarin saw the sign, and remained convinced that d'Artagnan had seen and heard everything; but he was pleased with his falsehood.

"Decidedly, M. d'Artagnan, you are the man I have been seeking—and you may reckon upon me, as may your friend, too."

Then, bowing to the friends, with his most gracious smile, he re-entered his closet more calmly, for on the departure of Gondy, the uproar had ceased as if by enchantment.

CHAPTER XLVII.

MISFORTUNE REFRESHES THE MEMORY.

THE next morning, when Broussel made his entrance into Paris in a large carriage, having his son at his side, and Friquet behind the vehicle, the people threw themselves in his way, and cries of "Long live Broussel!" "Long live our father!" resounded from all parts, and were death to Mazarin's ears; and the Cardinal's spies brought bad news from every direction, which greatly agitated the minister, but was calmly received by the Queen. The latter seemed to be maturing in her mind some great stroke—a fact which increased the uneasiness of the Cardinal, who knew the proud princess, and who dreaded much the determination of Anne of Austria.

The Coadjutor returned to Parliament more a monarch than the King, Queen, and Cardinal were, all three together. By his advice, a decree from Parliament had summoned the citizens to lay down their arms, and to demolish the barricades. They now knew that it required but one hour to take up arms again, and only one night to reconstruct barricades.

D'Artagnan profited by a moment of calm to send away Raoul, whom he had had great difficulty in keeping shut up during the riot, and who wished positively to strike a blow for one party or the other. Raoul had offered some opposition at first;

but d'Artagnan made use of Count de la Fère's name, and, after paying a visit to Mdme. de Chevreuse, Raoul started to rejoin the army.

Rochefort alone was dissatisfied with the termination of affairs. He had written to the Duke de Beaufort to come, and the duke was about to arrive, and he would find Paris tranquil. He went to the Coadjutor to consult with him whether it were not better to send to the duke to stop on the road, but Gondy reflected for a moment, and then said:

"Let him continue his journey."

"But all is not then over?" asked Rochefort.

"Good, my dear Count; we have only just begun."

"What induces you to think so?"

"The knowledge that I have of the Queen's heart; she will not rest beaten."

"Come, let us see what you know."

"I know that she has written to the prince to return in haste from the army."

"Ah, ha!" said Rochefort, "you are right. We must let Beaufort come."

In fact, the evening after this conversation, the report was circulated that the Prince Condé had arrived. It was a very simple and natural circumstance, and yet it created a great sensation.

That night was secretly agitated, and on the morrow the grey and black cloaks, the patrols of armed shop-people, and the bands of mendicants had reappeared.

The Queen had passed the night in conference alone with the prince, who had entered her oratory at midnight, and did not leave till five o'clock in the morning.

At five o'clock Anne went to the Cardinal's house. If she had not yet taken any repose, he at least was already up. Six days had already passed out of the ten he had asked from Mordaunt; he was therefore occupied in correcting his reply to Cromwell, when someone knocked gently at the door of communication with the Queen's apartments. Anne of Austria alone was permitted to enter by that door. The Cardinal therefore rose to open it.

The Queen was in a morning gown, but it became her still, for Anne of Austria enjoyed the privilege of remaining ever beautiful; nevertheless, this morning she looked handsomer than usual for her eyes had all the sparkle which inward satisfaction added to her expression.

"What is the matter, madam?" said Mazarin uneasily. "You have quite a proud look."

"Yes, Giulio," she said, "proud and happy; for I have found the means of stifling this hydra."

"You are a great politician, my Queen," said Mazarin; "let us see the means." And he hid what he had written by sliding the letter under a sheet of white paper.

"You know," said the Queen, "that they want to take the King away from me."

"Alas! yes, and to hang me!"

"They shall not have the King."

"Nor hang me."

"Listen. I want to carry off my son from them—with yourself and myself. I wish that this event, which, on the day it is known, will completely change the aspect of affairs, should be accomplished without the knowledge of any others but yourself, myself and a third person, M. le Prince, who has just left me."

"He will aid this project which is his own."

"And Paris?"

"He will starve it out and force it to surrender at discretion."

"The plan is wanting not in grandeur, but—have we money?"

"A little," said Mazarin, trembling lest Anne should ask to draw upon his purse.

"Have we troops?"

"Five or six thousand men."

"Have we courage?"

"Much."

"Then the thing is easy. Oh! do think of it, Giulio! Paris, this odious Paris, awaking one morning without Queen or King, surrounded, besieged, famished—having, as an only resource, its stupid Parliament, and their bandy-legged Coadjutor."

"Charming! charming!" said Mazarin. "I see the effect, but it will be war—civil war—furious, burning, and implacable."

"Oh! yes, yes. War," said Anne of Austria. "Yes, I will reduce this rebellious city to ashes. I will extinguish the fire by blood! I will perpetuate the crime and the punishment by making a frightful example. Paris! I hate it! I detest it!"

"Very fine, Anne; but take care. It is dangerous to go to war with a whole nation. Look at your brother monarch, Charles I. He is badly off—very badly."

"We are in France, and I am Spanish."

"So much the worse; I would much rather you were French, and myself also; they would hate us both less."

"Nevertheless you consent?"

"Yes, if the thing be possible."

"You torment me, Giulio, with your fears; and what are you afraid of, then?"

Mazarin's face, smiling as it was, became clouded.

"Anne," said he, "you are but a woman, and as a woman you may insult man at your ease, knowing that you can do it with impunity; you accuse me of fear; I have not so much as you have, since I do not flee as you do. Against whom do they cry out? is it against you, or against myself? Whom would they hang—yourself or me? Well, I can weather the storm; I, whom, notwithstanding, you tax with fear, not with bravado, that is not my way, but I am firm. Imitate me; make less noise, and do more. You cry very loud, you end by doing nothing; you talk of fleeing——"

Mazarin shrugged his shoulders, and taking the Queen's hand, led her to the window.

"Look!" he said.

"Well?" said the Queen, blinded by her obstinacy.

"Well, what do you see from this window? Your doors are guarded, the air-holes of your cellars are guarded, and I could say to you, as that good La Ramée said to me of Beaufort, you must be either bird or mouse to get out."

"He did get out, however."

"Do you think of escaping in the same way?"

"I am a prisoner, then?"

"Rather!" said Mazarin, "I have been proving it to you this last hour."

And he quietly resumed his despatch at the place where he had been interrupted.

Anne, trembling with anger, and red with humiliation, left the room, shutting the door violently after her. Mazarin did not even turn around. When once more in her own apartment, Anne fell into a chair and wept; then, suddenly struck with an idea:

"I am saved!" she exclaimed, rising; "oh, yes! yes! I know a man who will find the means of taking me from Paris; a man whom I have too long forgotten." Then, falling into a reverie, she added, however, with an expression of joy, "Ungrateful woman that I am, for twenty years I have forgotten this man, whom I ought to have made Marshal of France. My mother-in-law expended gold, caresses, and dignities on Concini, who ruined her; the King made Vitry Marshal of France for an assassination; while I have left in obscurity, in poverty, that noble d'Artagnan, who saved me!"

And running to a table, upon which were placed paper and ink, she began to write.

CHAPTER XLVIII.

THE INTERVIEW WITH THE QUEEN.

It had been d'Artagnan's practice, ever since the riots, to sleep in the same room as Porthos, and on this eventful morning he was still there, sleeping, and dreaming that a large yellow cloud had overspread the sky, and was raining gold pieces into his hat, whilst he held it under a spout. As for Porthos, he dreamed that the panels of his carriage were not spacious enough to contain the armorial bearings which he had ordered to be painted upon them. They were both aroused at seven o'clock by the entrance of an unliveried servant, who had brought a letter to d'Artagnan.

"From whom is it?" asked the Gascon.

"From the Queen," replied the servant.

"Ho!" said Porthos, raising himself in his bed, "what does she say?"

D'Artagnan requested the servant to wait in the next room, and when the door was closed, he sprang up from his bed, and read rapidly, whilst Porthos looked at him with starting eyes, not daring to ask a single question.

"Friend Porthos," said d'Artagnan, handing the letter to him, "this time, at least, you are sure of your title of baron, and I of my captaincy. There, read and judge."

Porthos took the letter, and with a trembling voice read the following words:

"The Queen wishes to speak to M. d'Artagnan, who must follow the bearer."

"Well!" exclaimed Porthos, "I see nothing in that very extraordinary."

"But I see much that is extraordinary in it," replied d'Artagnan. "It is evident, by their sending for me, that matters are becoming complicated. Just reflect a little what an agitation the Queen's mind must be in, for her to have remembered me after twenty years."

"It is true," said Porthos.

"Sharpen your sword, baron, load your pistols, and give some corn to the horses, for, I will answer for it, something new will happen before to-morrow."

"But stop; do you think it can be a trap that they are laying for us?" suggested Porthos, incessantly thinking how his greatness must be irksome to other people.

"If it is a snare," replied d'Artagnan, "I shall scent it out, be assured. If Mazarin be an Italian, I am a Gascon."

And d'Artagnan dressed himself in an instant.

Whilst Porthos, still in bed, was hooking on his cloak for him, a second knock at the door was heard.

"Come in!" cried d'Artagnan, and another servant entered.

"From his Eminence, Cardinal Mazarin," he said, presenting a letter.

D'Artagnan glanced at Porthos, and said:

"It is arranged capitally; his Eminence expects me in half an hour."

"Good."

"My friend," said d'Artagnan, turning to the servant, "tell his Eminence that in half an hour I shall be at his command."

"It is very fortunate," resumed the Gascon, when the valet had retired, "that he did not meet the other one."

"Do you not think that they have sent for you, both for the same thing?"

"I do not think it, I am certain of it."

"Quick, quick, d'Artagnan. Remember that the Queen awaits you; and after the Queen, the Cardinal; and after the Cardinal, myself."

D'Artagnan summoned Anne of Austria's servant, and answered that he was ready to follow him.

The servant conducted him, and d'Artagnan was ushered into the oratory. Emotion, for which he could not account, made the lieutenant's heart beat; he had no longer the assurance of youth, and experience taught him all the importance of past events. Formerly, he would have approached the Queen, as a young man, who bends before a woman; but now it was a different thing; he answered her summons as an humble soldier obeys an illustrious general.

The silence of the oratory was at last disturbed by a slight, rustling sound, and d'Artagnan started when he perceived the tapestry raised by a white hand, which, by its form, its color, and its beauty, he recognized as that royal hand, which had one day been presented to him to kiss. The Queen entered.

"It is you, M. d'Artagnan," she said, fixing a gaze full of melancholy interest on the countenance of the officer, "and I know you well. Look at me well in your turn. I am the Queen; do you recognize me?"

"No, madam," replied d'Artagnan.

"But are you no longer aware," continued Anne, giving that sweet expression to her voice which she could do at will, "that in former days the Queen had once need of a young, brave, and devoted cavalier; that she found this cavalier; and that, although he might have thought that she had forgotten him, she had kept a place for him in the depths of her heart?"

"No, madam, I was ignorant of that," said the Musketeer.

"So much the worse, sir," said Anne of Austria, "so much the worse, at least for the Queen; for to-day she has need of the same courage, and of the same devotion."

"What!" exclaimed d'Artagnan, "does the Queen, surrounded as she is by such devoted servants, such wise counsellors, men, in short, so great by their merit or their position, does she deign to cast her eyes on an obscure soldier?"

Anne understood this covert reproach, and was more moved than irritated by it. She had many a time felt humiliated by the self-sacrifice and disinterestedness shown by the Gascon gentleman, and she had allowed herself to be exceeded in generosity.

"All that you tell me of those by whom I am surrounded, M. d'Artagnan, is doubtless true," said the Queen, "but I have confidence in you alone. I know that you belong to the Cardinal; but belong to me as well, and I will take upon myself the making of your fortune. Come, will you do to-day what formerly the gentleman whom you do not know did for the Queen?"

"I will do everything which your majesty commands," replied d'Artagnan.

The Queen reflected for a moment, and then, seeing the cautious demeanor of the Musketeer,—

"Perhaps you like repose?" she said.

"I do not know, for I have never tested it, madam."

"Have you any friends?"

"I had three, two of whom have left Paris, to go I know not whither. One alone is left to me, but he is one of those known, I believe, to the cavalier, of whom your majesty did me the honor to speak to me."

"Very good," said the Queen, "you and your friend are worth an army."

"What am I to do, madam?"

"Return at five o'clock, and I will tell you: but do not breathe to a living soul, sir, the appointment which I give you."

"No, madam."

"Swear it."

"Madam, I have never been false to my word; when I say no, I mean no."

The Queen, although astonished at this language, to which she was not accustomed from her courtiers, argued from it a happy omen of the zeal with which d'Artagnan would serve her in the accomplishment of her project. It was one of the Gascon's artifices to hide his deep cunning occasionally under an appearance of rough loyalty.

"Has the Queen any further commands for me now?" asked d'Artagnan.

"No, sir," replied Anne of Austria, "and you may retire until the time that I mentioned to you."

D'Artagnan bowed and went out.

"The devil!" he exclaimed, when the door was shut, "they seem to have a great need of me here."

Then, as the half hour had already glided by, he crossed th gallery, and knocked at the Cardinal's door.

"I come for your commands, my lord," he said.

And according to his custom, d'Artagnan glanced rapidly round him, and remarked that Mazarin had a sealed letter before him.

"You come from the Queen?" said Mazarin, looking fixedly at d'Artagnan.

"I! my lord, who told you that?"

"Nobody, but I know it."

"I regret, infinitely, to tell you, my lord, that you are mistaken," replied the Gascon impudently, strong in the promise made to Anne of Austria.

"I opened the door of the ante-room myself, and I saw you enter at the end of the corridor."

"I know not, it must have been a mistake."

"How so?"

"Because I was shown up the private stairs."

Mazarin was aware that it was not easy to make d'Artagnan reveal anything which he was desirous of hiding, so he therefore gave up, for the time, the discovery of the mystery which the Gascon made.

"Let us speak of my affairs," said Mazarin, "since you will tell me nought of yours. Are you fond of traveling?"

"My life has been passed on the high roads," said the soldier, bowing.

"Would anything retain you particularly in Paris?"

"Nothing but superior orders would retain me in Paris."

"Very well. Here is a letter which must be taken to its address."

"To its address, my lord? But it has none."

"I regret to say," resumed Mazarin, "that it is a double envelope."

"I understand; and I am only to take off the first when I have reached a certain place?"

"Just so—take it and go. You have a friend, M. du Vallon, whom I like much; let him accompany you."

"The devil!" said d'Artagnan to himself. "He knows that we overheard his conversation yesterday, and he wants to get us away from Paris."

"Do you hesitate?" asked Mazarin.

"No, my lord, and I will set out at once. There is one thing only which I must request, that your Eminence will at once go to the Queen and merely say these words: 'I am going to send M. d'Artagnan away, and I wish him to set out directly.' "

"'Tis clear," said Mazarin, "that you have seen the Queen."

"I had the honor of saying to your Eminence that there had been some mistake."

"Very well; I will go. Wait here for me," and looking attentively around him, to see if he had forgotten any keys in his closets, Mazarin went out. Ten minutes elapsed ere he returned, pale, and evidently thoughtful. He seated himself at his desk, and d'Artagnan proceeded to examine his face, as he had examined the letter he held; but the envelope which covered his countenance was almost as impenetrable as that which covered the letter.

"Eh! eh!" thought the Gascon; "he looks displeased. Can it be with me? He meditates. Is it about sending me to the Bastille? All very fine, my lord; but at the very first hint you give of such a thing, I will strangle you, and become Frondist. I should be carried in triumph like M. Broussel, and Athos would proclaim me the French Brutus. It would be funny!"

The Gascon, with his swift imagination, had already seen the advantage to be derived from his situation; Mazarin gave, however, no order of the kind, but, on the contrary, began to speak softly.

"You are right," he said, "my dear M. d'Artagnan, and you

cannot set out yet. I beg you to return to me that despatch."

D'Artagnan obeyed, and Mazarin made sure that the seal was intact.

"I shall want you this evening," he said. "Return in two hours."

"My lord," said d'Artagnan, "I have an appointment in two hours, which I cannot miss."

"Do not be uneasy," said Mazarin; "it is the same."

"Good," thought d'Artagnan; "I fancied it was so."

"Return, then, at five o'clock, and bring our worthy M. du Vallon with you. Only, leave him in the ante-room, as I wish to speak to you alone."

D'Artagnan bowed, and thought, "Both at the same hour; both commands alike; both at the Palace. I guess. Ah! Gondy would pay a hundred thousand francs for such a secret!"

"You are thinking," said Mazarin, uneasily.

"Yes; I was wondering whether we ought to come armed or not."

"Armed to the teeth!" replied Mazarin.

"Very well, my lord, it shall be so."

The Musketeer bowed and hastened away to carry reassuring words to his comrade which would fill him with delight.

CHAPTER XLIX.

THE FLIGHT.

When d'Artagnan returned to the Palais Royal at five o'clock, it presented, in spite of the excitement which reigned in the town, a spectacle of the greatest rejoicing. Nor was that surprising. The Queen had restored Broussel and Blancmesnil to the people, and had therefore nothing to fear, since the people had nothing more to ask for. The return also of the conqueror of Lens was the pretext for giving a grand banquet. The princes and princesses were invited, and their carriages had crowded the court since noon; and after dinner the Queen was to form her pole of quadrille. Anne of Austria had never appeared more brilliant than on that day—radiant with grace and wit. Mazarin disappeared as they rose from table. He found d'Artagnan waiting for him already at his post in the ante-room. The Cardinal advanced to him with a smile, and taking him by the hand, led him into his study.

"My dear *Monsow* d'Artagnan," said the minister, sitting down, "I am about to give you the greatest proof of confidence that a minister can give to an officer."

"I hope," said d'Artagnan bowing, "that you give it, my

lord, without hesitation, and with the conviction that I am worthy of it."

"More worthy than everyone, my dear friend; therefore I apply to you. You are about to leave this evening," continued Mazarin. "My dear d'Artagnan, the welfare of the state is reposed in your hand." He paused.

"The Queen has resolved to make a little excursion with the King to St. Germain."

"Ah! ah!" said d'Artagnan, "that is to say, the Queen wishes to leave Paris."

"A woman's fancy—you understand."

"Yes, I understand perfectly," said d'Artagnan.

"It was for this that she summoned you this morning, and that she told you to return at five o'clock."

"Was it worth while to wish me to swear this morning that I would mention the appointment to no one?" muttered d'Artagnan. "Oh, women! women! whether queens or not, they are always the same."

"Do you disapprove of this journey, my dear M. d'Artagnan?" asked Mazarin, anxiously.

"I, my lord?" said d'Artagnan; "and why?"

"Because you shrug your shoulders."

"It is a way I have of speaking to myself, I neither approve nor disapprove, my lord; I merely await your commands."

"Good; it is you, therefore, that I have looked upon to escort the King and the Queen to St. Germain."

"You double deceiver!" said d'Artagnan to himself.

"You see, therefore," continued Mazarin, perceiving d'Artagnan's composure, "that, as I have told you, the welfare of the state is placed in your hands."

"Yes, my lord, and I feel the whole responsibility of such a charge, and accept."

"Do you think the thing possible?"

"Everything is."

"Should you be attacked on the road what would you do?"

"I shall pass through those who attack me."

"And suppose you cannot pass through them?"

"So much the worse for them. I must pass over them."

"And you will place the King and Queen safe and sound at St. Germain?"

"Yes, on my life."

"You are a hero, my dear friend," said Mazarin, gazing at the Musketeer with admiration.

D'Artagnan smiled.

"As for me?" asked Mazarin, after a moment's silence.

"How about you, my lord?"

"If I wish to leave?"

"That would be more difficult."

"Why so?"

"Your Eminence might be recognized.

"Even under this disguise?" asked Mazarin, raising a cloak which covered the arm-chair, upon which lay a complete dress for an officer, of pearl-grey and red, entirely embroidered with silver.

"If your Eminence is disguised, it will be more easy."

"Ah!" said Mazarin, breathing more freely.

"But it will be necessary for your Eminence to do what the other day you declared you should have done in our place, shout, 'Down with Mazarin!' "

"I will."

"In French—in good French, my lord—take care of your accent; they killed six thousand Angevines in Sicily, because they pronounced Italian badly. Take care that the French do not take their revenge on you for the Sicilian vespers."

"I will do my best."

"The streets are full of armed men," continued d'Artagnan.

"Are you sure that no one is aware of the Queen's project?"

"This would give a fine opportunity for a traitor, my lord; the chances in an attack would give an excuse for everything."

Mazarin shuddered; but he reflected that a man who had an intention to betray would not warn first.

"And, therefore," added he quietly, "I have not confidence in everyone; the proof of which is, that I have fixed upon you to escort me. I have my plan:—with the Queen, I double her risk,—after the Queen, her departure would double mine—then, the court once safe, I might be forgotten; the great are often ungrateful."

"Very true," said d'Artagnan, fixing his eyes, in spite of himself, on the Queen's diamond which Mazarin wore on his finger. Mazarin followed the direction of his eyes and gently turned the bezel of the ring inside.

"I wish," he said with a cunning smile, "to prevent them from being ungrateful to me."

"It is but Christian charity," replied d'Artagnan, "not to lead one's neighbors into temptation."

"It is exactly for that reason," said Mazarin, "that I wish to start *before* them."

D'Artagnan smiled—he was quite the man to understand the astute Italian. Mazarin saw the smile, and profited by the sympathy.

"You will begin, therefore, by taking me first out of Paris, will you not, my dear M. d'Artagnan?"

"A difficult commission, my lord," replied d'Artagnan, resuming his serious manner.

"But," said Mazarin, "you did not make so many difficulties with regard to the King and the Queen."

"The King and the Queen are my King and Queen, my lord," replied the Musketeer, "my life is theirs, and I ought to give it for them. They ask it; and I have nothing to say."

"That is true," murmured Mazarin, in a low tone, "but as thy

life is not mine, I suppose I must buy it, must I not?" and
sighing deeply, he began to turn the setting of his ring outside
again. D'Artagnan smiled. These two men met at one point,
and that was, cunning; had they been actuated alike by courage,
the one would have done great things for the other.

"But also," said Mazarin, "you must understand that if I
ask this service from you it is with the intention of being grateful."

"Is it still only in intention, my lord?" asked d'Artagnan.

"Stay," said Mazarin, drawing the ring from his finger, "my
dear M. d'Artagnan, here is a diamond which belonged to you
formerly, it is but fair that it should be returned to you;
take it, I pray."

D'Artagnan spared Mazarin the trouble of insisting, and after
looking to see if the stone were the same, and assuring himself
of the purity of its water, he took it, and passed it on to his
finger with indescribable pleasure.

"I valued it much," said Mazarin, giving a last look at it;
"nevertheless, I give it to you with great pleasure."

"And I, my lord," said d'Artagnan, "accept it as it is given.
Come, let us speak of your little affairs. You wish to leave
before everybody, and at what hour?"

"At ten o'clock, and the Queen at midnight."

"Then it is possible. I can get you out of Paris and leave
you beyond the bar, and can return for her."

"Capital, but how will you get me out of Paris?"

"Oh! as to that, you must leave it to me."

"I give you full power, therefore take as large an escort as
you like."

D'Artagnan shook his head.

"It seems to me, however," said Mazarin, "the safest
method."

"Yes, for you, my lord, but not for the Queen; you must
leave it to me, and give me the entire direction of the undertaking."

"Nevertheless——"

"Or find some one else," continued d'Artagnan, turning his
back.

"Oh!" muttered Mazarin; "I do believe he is walking off
with the diamond!"

"M. d'Artagnan, my dear M. d'Artagnan," he called out in a
coaxing voice, "will you answer for everything?"

"I will answer for nothing,—I will do my best."

"Well, then, let us go; I must trust to you."

"It is very lucky you do," said d'Artagnan to himself.

"You will be here at half-past nine?"

"And I shall find your Eminence ready?'

"Certainly, quite ready."

"Well, then, it is a settled thing, and now, my lord, will you

obtain for me an audience with the Queen? I wish to receive
her majesty's commands from her own lips."

"She desired me to give them to you."

"She may have forgotten something. It is indispensable,
my lord."

Mazarin hesitated for one instant, whilst d'Artagnan remained firm in determination.

"Come, then," said the Premier; "I will conduct you to her,
but remember, not one word of our conversation."

"What has passed between us concerns us alone, my lord,"
replied d'Artagnan.

"Swear to be mute."

"I never swear, my lord, I say yes or no, and, as I am a
gentleman, I keep my word."

"Come then, I see that I must trust unreservedly to you."

"Believe me, my lord, it will be your best plan."

"Come," said Mazarin, conducting d'Artagnan into the
Queen's oratory, and desiring him to wait there. He did not
wait long, for in five minutes the Queen entered in full gala
costume. Thus dressed she scarcely appeared thirty-five years
of age, and was still handsome.

"It is you, M. d'Artagnan," she said, smiling graciously,
"I thank you for having insisted on seeing me."

"I ought to ask your majesty's pardon; but I wish to receive your commands from your own mouth."

"Will you accept the commission which I have entrusted to
you?"

"With gratitude."

"Very well, be here at midnight."

"I will not fail."

"M. d'Artagnan," continued the Queen, "I know your disinterestedness too well to speak of my gratitude at this moment;
but I swear to you that I shall not forget this second service
as I forgot the first."

"Your majesty is free to forget or to remember as it pleases
you; and I know not to what you allude," said d'Artagnan,
bowing.

"Go, sir," said the Queen, with her most bewitching smile,
"go and return at midnight."

And d'Artagnan retired, but as he passed out he glanced
at the curtain through which the Queen had entered, and at
the bottom of the tapestry he noticed the tip of a velvet
slipper.

"Good," thought he; "Mazarin has been listening to discover
whether I had betrayed him. In truth, that Italian puppet does
not deserve the services of an honest man."

D'Artagnan was not less exact to his appointment, and at
half-past nine o'clock he entered the ante-room.

He found the Cardinal dressed as an officer, and he looked
very well in that costume, which, as we have already said, he

wore jauntily, only he was very pale, and trembled a little.
"Quite alone?" he asked.
"Yes, my lord."
"And that worthy M. du Vallon, are we to enjoy his society?"
"Certainly, my lord, he is waiting in his carriage at the gate
of the garden of the Palais Royal."
"Oh, we start in his carriage then? And with no other escort
but you two?"
"Is it not enough? One of us would suffice."
"Really, my dear M. d'Artagnan," said the Cardinal, "your
coolness startles me."
"I should have thought, on the contrary, that it ought to
have inspired you with confidence."
"Let us go," said Mazarin, "since everything must be ready;
do you wish it?"
"My lord, there is time to draw back," said d'Artagnan,
"and your Eminence is perfectly free."
"Not at all," said Mazarin, "let us be off."
And they both descended the private stair, Mazarin leaning
on d'Artagnan, but his arm the Musketeer felt trembling upon
his own. At last, after crossing the courts, they entered the
garden and reached the private gate. Mazarin attempted to open
it with a key which he took from his pocket, but his hand
trembled so much that he could not find the keyhole.
"Give it to me," said d'Artagnan, who, when the gate was
opened, deposited the key in his pocket, reckoning upon returning by that means.
The steps were already down, and the door open. Mousqueton held open the door, and Porthos was inside the carriage.
"Mount, my lord," said d'Artagnan to Mazarin, who sprang
into the carriage without waiting for the second bidding.
D'Artagnan followed him; and Mousqueton, having closed the
door, mounted behind the carriage with many groans. He
had made some difficulties about going, under pretext that he
still suffered from his wounds, but d'Artagnan had said to him:
"Remain if you like, my dear Mouston, but I warn you that
Paris will be burnt down to-night;" upon which Mousqueton
had declared, without asking anything further, that he was
ready to follow his master and M. d'Artagnan to the end of
the world.
The carriage started at a measured pace, without betraying
in the least that it contained people in a hurry. The Cardinal
wiped his forehead with his handkerchief, and looked around
him. On his left was Porthos, whilst d'Artagnan was on his
right; each guarded a door, and served as a rampart to him
on either side. Before him, on the front seat, lay two pairs
of pistols—one before Porthos, and the other before d'Artagnan.
About a hundred paces from the Palais Royal a patrol stopped
the carriage.

"Who goes?" asked the captain.

"Mazarin!" replied d'Artagnan, bursting into a laugh. The Cardinal's hair stood on end. But the joke appeared excellent to the citizens, who, seeing the conveyance without escort and unarmed, would never have believed in the reality of so great an imprudence.

"A good journey to ye!" they cried, allowing it to pass.

"Hem!" said d'Artagnan, "what does my lord think of that reply?"

"Man of talent!" cried Mazarin.

"In truth," said Porthos, "I understand; but now——"

About the middle of the Rue des Petits-Champs they were stopped by a second patrol.

"Who goes there?" inquired the captain of the patrol.

"Keep back, my lord," said d'Artagnan. And Mazarin buried himself so far behind the two friends that he disappeared, completely hidden between them.

"Who goes there?" cried the same voice, impatiently, whilst d'Artagnan perceived that they had rushed to the horses' heads. But, putting his head half out of the carriage, "Why! Planchet," said he.

The chief approached, and it was indeed Planchet; d'Artagnan had recognized the voice of his old servant.

"How, sir!" said Planchet, "is it you?"

"Oh, dear, yes, my good friend, our worthy Porthos has just received a sword wound, and I am taking him to his country house at St. Cloud."

"Oh! really," said Planchet.

"Porthos," said d'Artagnan, "if you can still speak, say a word, my dear Porthos, to this good Planchet."

"Planchet, my friend," groaned Porthos, in a melancholy voice, "I am very ill; should you meet a doctor, you will do me a favor by sending him to me."

"Oh! good Heaven!" said Planchet, "what a misfortune; and how did it happen?"

"I will tell you all about it by and by," replied Mousqueton. Porthos uttered a deep groan.

"Make way for us, Planchet," said d'Artagnan in a whisper to him, "or he will not arrive alive; the lungs are perforated, my friend."

Planchet shook his head with the air of a man who says: "In that case, things look ill." Then he exclaimed, turning to his men, "Let them pass, they are friends."

The carriage resumed its course, and Mazarin, who had held his breath, ventured to breathe again.

"Bricconi!" muttered he.

A few steps in advance of the gate of St. Honoré, they met a third troop; this latter party was composed of ill-looking fellows, who resembled bandits more than anything else; they were the men of the beggar of St. Eustache.

"Attention, Porthos!" cried d'Artagnan. Porthos placed his hand on his pistols.

"What is it?" asked Mazarin.

"My lord, I think we are in bad company."

A man advanced to the door with a kind of scythe in his hand.

"Stay, rascal!" said d'Artagnan, "do you not know his highness the prince's carriage?"

"Prince or not," said the man, "open; we are here to guard the gate, and no one whom we do not know shall pass."

"What is to be done?" said Porthos.

"By Heaven, to pass," replied d'Artagnan.

"But how?" asked Mazarin.

"Through or over; coachman, gallop on."

"Not a step further," said the man, who appeared to be the captain, "or I will hamstring your horses."

"*Pest!*" said Porthos, "it would be a pity; animals which cost me a hundred pistoles each."

"I will pay you two hundred for them," said Mazarin.

"Yes, but when once they are hamstrung, our necks will be strung next."

"If one of them comes to my side," asked Porthos, "must I kill him?"

"Yes, by a blow of your fist, if you can; we will not fire but at the last extremity."

"I can do it," said Porthos.

"Come and open then," cried d'Artagnan to the man with the scythe, taking one of the pistols up by the muzzle, and preparing to strike by the butt. And as the man approached, d'Artagnan, in order to have more freedom for his actions, leant half out of the door; his eyes were fixed upon those of the beggar which were lighted up by a lantern. Doubtless he recognized d'Artagnan, for he became deadly pale; doubtless, the Musketeer knew him, for his hair stood up on his head.

"M. d'Artagnan!" he cried, falling back a step, "M. d'Artagnan! let him pass."

D'Artagnan was, perhaps, about to reply, when a blow similar to that of a mallet falling on the head of an ox was heard; it was Porthos who had just knocked down his man.

D'Artagnan turned round and saw the unfortunate man writhing about four steps off.

"S'death!" cried he to the coachman. "Spur your horses! whip! get on!"

The coachman bestowed a heavy blow of the whip upon his horses; the noble animals reared, then cries of men who were knocked down were heard; then a double concussion was felt, and two of the wheels had passed over a round and flexible body. There was a moment's silence; the carriage had cleared the gate.

"To Cours-la-Reine!" cried d'Artagnan to the coachman;

then turning to Mazarin, he said, "Now, my lord, you can say five *paters* and five *aves* to thank Heaven for your deliverance. You are safe! you are free!"

Mazarin replied only by a groan; he could not believe in such a miracle. Five minutes later the carriage stopped, having reached Cours-la-Reine.

"Is my lord pleased with his escort?" asked d'Artagnan.

"Enchanted," said Mazarin, venturing his head out of one of the windows; "and now do as much for the Queen."

"It will be less difficult," replied d'Artagnan, springing to the ground. "M. du Vallon, I commend his Eminence to your care."

"Be quite at ease," said Porthos, holding out his hand, which d'Artagnan took and shook in his.

"Oh!" said Porthos.

D'Artagnan looked with surprise at his friend.

"What is the matter, then?" he asked.

"I think I have sprained the wrist," said Porthos.

"The devil! why do you strike like a blacksmith?"

"It was necessary—my man was going to fire a pistol at me; but you—how did you get rid of yours?"

"Oh! mine," replied d'Artagnan, "was not a man, but a ghost, and I conjured it away!"

Without further explanation, d'Artagnan took the pistols which were upon the front seat, and placed them in his belt, wrapped himself in his cloak, and, not wishing to enter by the same gate as that by which they had left, he took his way towards the Richelieu gate.

CHAPTER L.

THE COADJUTOR'S CARRIAGE.

D'ARTAGNAN was approached to be examined; and when it was discovered by his plumed hat and his laced coat that he was an officer of the Musketeers, he was surrounded, with an intention to make him cry "Down with Mazarin!" Their first demonstration did not fail to make him uneasy at first; but when he knew what was wanted, he shouted in such a hasty voice that even the most exacting were satisfied. He walked down the Rue Richelieu, meditating how he should carry off the Queen in her turn—for to take her in a carriage bearing the arms of France was not to be thought of—when he perceived an equipage standing at the door of Mdme. de Guéménée's residence.

He was struck by a sudden idea.

"Ah, by Jove!" he exclaimed; "This would be fair play."

And approaching the carriage, he examined the arms on the

panels, and the livery of the coachman on his box. The scrutiny was so much the more easy, the coachman being asleep with the reins in his hands.

"It is, in truth, the Coadjutor's carriage," said d'Artagnan; "upon my honor I begin to think that Heaven is prospering us."

He mounted noiselessly into the chariot, and pulled the silk cord which was attached to the coachman's little finger.

"To the Royal Palace," he called out.

The coachman awoke with a start, and drove off in the direction he was desired, never doubting but that the order had come from his master. The porter at the palace was about to close the gates, but seeing such a handsome equipage, he fancied that it was some visit of importance, and the carriage was allowed to pass, and to stop under the porch. It was then only that the coachman perceived that the grooms were not behind the vehicle; he fancied his master had sent them on, and without leaving the reins he sprang from his box to open the door. D'Artagnan sprang in his turn to the ground, and just at that moment when the coachman, alarmed at not seeing his master, fell back a step, he seized him by his collar with the left, whilst with the right he clapped a pistol to his throat.

"Try to utter one single word," muttered d'Artagnan, "and you are a dead man."

The coachman perceived at once, by the expression in the countenance of the man who thus addressed him, that he had fallen into a trap, and he remained with his mouth wide open and his eyes immoderately starting.

Two Musketeers were pacing the court, whom d'Artagnan called by their names.

"M. de Bellière," said he to one of them, "do me the favor to take the reins from the hands of this worthy man, to mount upon the box, and to drive to the door of the private stair, and to wait for me there; it is on an affair of importance in the service of the King."

The Musketeer, who knew that his lieutenant was incapable of jesting on duty, obeyed without saying a word, although he thought the order strange. Then turning toward the second Musketeer, d'Artagnan said:

"M. du Verger, help me to lodge this man in a place of safety."

The Musketeer, thinking that his lieutenant had just arrested some prince in disguise, bowed, and drawing his sword signified that he was ready. D'Artagnan mounted the staircase, followed by his prisoner, who in his turn was followed by the soldier, and entered Mazarin's ante-room. Bernouin was waiting there, impatient for news of his master.

"Well, sir?" he said.

"Everything goes on capitally, my dear M. Bernouin, but here is a man whom I must beg you to put in a safe place, with shutters secured by padlocks and a door which can be locked."

"We have that, sir," replied Bernouin; and the poor coachman was conducted to a closet, the windows of which were barred, and which looked very much like a prison.

"And now, my good friend," said d'Artagnan to him, "I must invite you to deprive yourself, for my sake, of your hat and cloak."

The coachman, as we can well understand, made no resistance; in fact, he was so astonished at what had happened to him that he stammered and reeled like a drunken man. D'Artagnan deposited his clothes under the arm of one of the valets.

"And now, M. du Verger," he said, "shut yourself up with this man until M. Bernouin returns to open the door. Your office will be tolerably long and not very amusing, I know; but," added he seriously, "you understand, it is in the King's service."

"Command me, lieutenant," replied the Musketeer, who saw that the business was a serious one.

"By-the-bye," continued d'Artagnan, "should this man attempt to flee or call out, run your sword through his body."

The Musketeer signified by a nod that the commands should be obeyed to the letter, and d'Artagnan went out, followed by Bernouin; midnight struck.

"Lead me into the Queen's oratory," said d'Artagnan, "announce to her I am here, and put this parcel, with a well-loaded musket, under the seat of the carriage which is waiting at the foot of the private stair."

Bernouin conducted d'Artagnan to the oratory, where he sat down pensively. Everything had gone on as usual at the Palace. As we said before, at ten o'clock almost all the guests were dispersed; those who were to fly with the court had the word of command, and they were each severely desired to be from twelve o'clock to one at Cours-la-Reine.

At ten o'clock Anne of Austria had visited the King's room, before she returned to her own apartments. She gave her orders, spoke of a banquet which the Marquis de Villequier was to give to her on the day after the morrow, indicated the persons whom she should admit to the honor of being at it, announced another visit on the following day to Val-de-Grace, where she intended to pay her devotions, and gave her commands to her senior valet to accompany her. When the ladies had finished their supper, the Queen feigned extreme fatigue, and passed into her bedroom. Mdme. de Motteville, who was on especial duty that evening, followed to aid and undress her. The Queen then began to read, and, after conversing with her affectionately for a few minutes, dismissed her.

A few minutes after twelve o'clock Bernouin knocked at the Queen's bedroom door, having come by the Cardinal's secret corridor. Anne of Austria opened the door herself. She was in negligé, wrapped in a long dressing gown.

"It is you, Bernouin," she said. "Is M. d'Artagnan there?"

"Yes, madam, in your oratory; he is waiting till your majesty be ready."

"I am. Go and tell Laporte to wake and dress the King, and then pass on to the Marshal de Villeroy and summon him to me."

Bernouin bowed and retired.

The Queen entered her oratory, which was lighted by a single lamp of Venetian crystal. She saw d'Artagnan, who stood expecting her.

"Are you ready?"

"I am."

"And his Eminence, the Cardinal?"

"Has got off without any accident. He is awaiting your majesty at Cours-la-Reine."

"But in what carriage do we start?"

"I have provided for everything—a carriage is waiting below for your majesty."

"Let us go to the King."

D'Artagnan bowed, and followed the Queen. The young Louis was already dressed with the exception of his shoes and doublet; he had allowed himself to be dressed in great astonishment, overwhelming with questions Laporte, who replied only in these words: "Sire, it is by the Queen's commands."

The bed was open, and the sheets were so worn that holes could be seen in some places—another evidence of the stinginess of Mazarin.

The Queen entered, and d'Artagnan remained at the door. As soon as the child perceived the Queen he escaped from Laporte, and ran to meet her. Anne then motioned to d'Artagnan to approach, and he obeyed.

"My son," said Anne of Austria, pointing to the Musketeer, calm, standing uncovered, "here is M. d'Artagnan, who is as brave as one of those ancient heroes of whom you like so much to hear from my women. Remember his name well, and look at him well, that his face may not be forgotten, for this evening he is going to render us a great service."

The King looked at the officer with his large-formed eye, and repeated:

"M. d'Artagnan."

"That is it, my son."

The young King slowly raised his little hand, and held it out to the Musketeer; the latter bent his knee, and kissed it.

"M. d'Artagnan," repeated Louis; "very well, madam."

At this moment they were startled by a noise as if a tumult were approaching.

"What is that?" exclaimed the Queen.

"Oh, oh!" replied d'Artagnan, straining both at the same time his quick ear, and his intelligent glance, "it is the sound of the people rising."

"We must flee," said the Queen.

"Your majesty has given me the control of this business; we should wait and see what they want. I will answer for everything."

Nothing is so speedily catching as confidence. The Queen, full of strength and courage, was quickly alive to these two virtues in others.

"Do as you like," she said, "I rely upon you."

"Will your majesty permit me to give orders in your name in this whole business?"

"Command, sir."

"What do the people want again?" asked the King.

"We are about to learn, sire," replied d'Artagnan, as he rapidly left the room.

The riot continued to increase, and seemed to surround the Palais Royal entirely. Cries were heard, from the interior of which they could not comprehend the sense. It was evident that there was clamor and sedition.

The King, half-dressed, the Queen and Laporte remained each in the same state, and almost in the same place where they were listening and waiting. Comminges, who was on guard that night at the Palais Royal, ran in. He had about two hundred men in the courtyards and stables and he placed them at the Queen's disposal.

"Well," asked Anne of Austria, when d'Artagnan reappeared, "what is it?"

"It is, madam, a report that the Queen has left the Palace, carrying off the King, and the people ask to have proof to the contrary, or threaten to demolish the Palace."

"Oh, this time it is too much," exclaimed the Queen, "and I will prove to them that I have not left!"

D'Artagnan saw from the expression of the Queen's face that she was about to issue some violent command. He approached her, and said, in a low voice:

"Has your majesty still confidence in me?"

This voice startled her. "Yes, sir," she replied, "every confidence—speak."

"Let your majesty dismiss M. de Comminges, and desire him to shut himself up with his men, in the guard-house and in the stables."

Comminges glanced at d'Artagnan, with the envious look with which every courtier sees a new favorite spring up; then bowing he took his leave.

"Come," said d'Artagnan to himself, "that is one more enemy for me there."

"And now," said the Queen, addressing d'Artagnan, "what

is to be done? for you hear that, instead of becoming calmer, the noise increases."

"Madam," said d'Artagnan, "the people want to see the King, and they must see him."

"How! they must see him! where, on the balcony?"

"Not at all, madam, but here, sleeping in his bed."

"Oh, your majesty," exclaimed Laporte, "M. d'Artagnan is right!"

The Queen became thoughtful, and smiled, for to a woman, duplicity is no stranger.

"Without doubt," she murmured.

"M. Laporte," said d'Artagnan, "go and announce to the people through the grating that they are going to be satisfied, and that in five minutes they shall not only see the King, but they shall see him in bed; and that the King sleeps, and that the Queen begs that they will keep silence, so as not to awaken him."

"But not everyone, a deputation of two or four people!"

"Everyone, madam."

"But reflect, they will keep us here till daybreak."

"It shall take but a quarter of an hour. I answer for everything, madam; believe me, I know the people—they are like a great child, who only wants humoring. Before the sleeping King they will be mute, gentle, and timid as lambs."

"Go, Laporte," said the Queen.

The Queen looked with surprise at this strange man, whose brilliant courage made him the equal of the bravest, and who was, by his fine and ready intelligence, the equal of all.

"Well?" asked the Queen, as Laporte entered.

"Madam," he replied, "M. d'Artagnan's prediction has been accomplished; they were calmed as if by enchantment. The doors are about to be opened, and in five minutes they will be here."

"Laporte," said the Queen, "suppose you put one of your sons in the King's place; we might be off during the time."

"If your majesty desires it," said Laporte, "my sons, like myself, are at the Queen's service."

"Not at all," said d'Artagnan; "for should one of them know his majesty, and find out the substitute, all would be lost."

"You are right, sir—always right," said Anne of Austria. "Laporte, place the King in bed."

Laporte placed the King, dressed as he was, in the bed, and then covered him as far as the shoulders with the sheet. The Queen bent over him, and kissed his brow.

"Pretend to sleep, Louis," said she.

"Yes," said the King, "but I wish not to be touched by one of those men."

"Sire, I am here," said d'Artagnan, "and I give you my word that if a single man has the audacity, his life shall pay for it."

"And now what is to be done?" asked the Queen, "for I hear them."

"M. Laporte, go to them, and again recommend silence. Madam, wait at the door, whilst I shall be at the head of the King's bed, ready to die for him."

Laporte went out; the Queen remained standing near the hangings, whilst d'Artagnan glided behind the curtains.

Then the heavy and collected tramp of a multitude was heard, and the Queen herself raised the tapestry hangings, and put her finger on her lips.

On seeing the Queen, the men stopped short, respectfully.

"Enter, gentlemen; enter," said the Queen.

There was then amongst that crowd a moment's hesitation, which looked like shame. They had expected resistance—they had expected to be thwarted—to have to force the gates, and to overturn the guards. The gates had opened of themselves, and the King, ostensibly at least, had no other guard at his bed-head, but his mother. The foremost of them stammered, and attempted to fall back.

"Enter then, gentlemen," said Laporte, "since the Queen permits you to do so."

Then one, more bold than the rest, ventured to pass the door, and to advance on tip-toe. This example was imitated by the rest, until the room filled silently, as if these men had been the most humble and devoted courtiers. Far beyond the door, the heads of those who were not able to enter could be seen, all rising on the tips of their feet.

D'Artagnan saw it all through an opening that he had made in the curtain, and in the first man who had entered he had recognized Planchet.

"Sir," said the Queen to him, thinking that he was the leader of the band, "you wish to see the King, and therefore I determined to show him to you myself. Approach, and look at him, and say if we have the appearance of people who wish to escape."

"No, certainly," replied Planchet, rather astonished at the unexpected honor conferred upon him.

"You will say, then, to my good and faithful Parisians," continued Anne, with a smile, the expression of which did not deceive d'Artagnan, "that you have seen the King in bed and asleep, and the Queen also ready to retire."

"I shall tell them, madam, and those who accompany me will say the same thing, but——"

"But what?" asked Anne of Austria.

"May your majesty pardon me," said Planchet, "but is it really the King who is lying there?"

Anne of Austria started. "If," she said, "there is one among you who knows the King, let him approach, and say whether it is really his majesty lying there."

A man, wrapped in a cloak, in the folds of which his face

was hidden, approached, and leaned over the bed and looked.

For one second d'Artagnan thought the man had some evil design and he put his hand to his sword; but in the movement made by the man in stooping, a portion of his face was uncovered, and d'Artagnan recognized the Coadjutor.

"It is certainly the King," said the man, rising again. "God bless his majesty!"

"Yes," repeated the leader in a whisper, "God bless his majesty!" and all these men who had entered furious, passed from anger to pity, and blessed the royal infant in their turn.

"Now," said Planchet, "let us thank the Queen. My friends, retire."

They all bowed, and retired by degrees, as noiselessly as they had entered. Planchet, who had been the first to enter, was the last to leave. The Queen stopped him.

"What is your name, my friend?" she said.

Planchet, much surprised at the inquiry, turned back.

"Yes," continued the Queen, "I think myself as much honored to have received you this evening as if you had been a prince, and I wish to know your name."

"Yes," thought Planchet, "to treat me as a prince. No, thank you."

D'Artagnan trembled lest Planchet should say his name, and the Queen, knowing his name, would discover that Planchet had belonged to him.

"Madam," replied Planchet, respectfully, "I am called Dulaurier, at your service."

"Thank you, M. Dulaurier," said the Queen, "and what is your business?"

"Madam, I am a clothier in the Rue Bourdonnais."

"That is all that I wished to know," said the Queen. "Much obliged to you, M. Dulaurier. You will hear from me."

"Come, come," thought d'Artagnan, emerging from behind the curtain, "decidedly M. Planchet is no fool, and it is evident he has been brought up in a good school."

The different actors in this strange scene remained facing one another, without uttering a single word; the Queen standing near the door, d'Artagnan half out of his hiding place, the King raised on his elbow, ready to fall down on his bed again, at the slightest sound which should indicate the return of the multitude; but instead of approaching, the noise became more and more distant, and finished by dying away entirely.

The Queen breathed more freely. D'Artagnan wiped his damp forehead, and the King slid off his bed, saying—"Let us go."

At this moment Laporte reappeared.

"Well?" asked the Queen.

"Well, madam!" replied the valet; "I followed them as far as the gates. They announced to all their comrades that they had seen the King, and that the Queen had spoken to them; and, in fact, they have gone off quite proud and happy."

"Oh, the miserable wretches!" murmured the Queen, "they shall pay dearly for their boldness, and it is I who promise it to them."

Then turning to d'Artagnan, she said:

"Sir, you have given me this evening the best advice that I have ever received. Continue, and say what we must do now."

"M. Laporte," said d'Artagnan, "finish dressing his majesty."

"We may go then?" asked the Queen.

"When your majesty pleases. You have only to descend by the private stairs, and you will find me at the door."

"Go, sir," said the Queen; "I will follow you."

D'Artagnan went down, and found the carriage at its post, and the Musketeer on the box. D'Artagnan took out the parcel, which he had desired Bernouin to place under the seat. It may be remembered that it was the hat and cloak belonging to Gondy's coachman.

He placed the cloak on his shoulders, and the hat on his head, whilst the Musketeer got off the box.

"Sir," said d'Artagnan, "you will go and release your companion, who is guarding the coachman. You must mount your horse, and proceed to Rue Tiquetonne, Hotel de la Chevrette, whence you will take my horse, and that of M. du Vallon, which you must saddle and equip as if for war, and then you will leave Paris, bringing them with you to Cours-la-Reine. If, when you arrive, you find no one, go on to St. Germain. In the King's service."

The Musketeer touched his cap, and went away to execute the orders he had received.

D'Artagnan mounted on the box, having a pair of pistols in his belt, a musket under his feet, and a naked sword behind him.

The Queen appeared, and was followed by the King and the Duke d'Anjou, his brother.

"Monsieur the Coadjutor's carriage!" she exclaimed, falling back.

"Yes, madam," said d'Artagnan; "but get in fearlessly, for I drive you."

The Queen uttered a cry of surprise, and entered the carriage, and the King and his brother took their places at her side.

"Come, Laporte," said the Queen.

"How, madam!" said the valet, "in the same carriage as your majesties!"

"It is not a matter of royal etiquette this evening but of the King's safety. Get in, Laporte."

Laporte obeyed.

"Pull down the blinds," said d'Artagnan.

"But will that not excite suspicion, sir?" asked the Queen.

"Your majesty's mind may be quite at ease," replied the officer. "I have my answer ready."

The blinds were pulled down, and they started at a gallop by the Rue Richelieu. On reaching the gate, the captain of the post advanced at the head of some ten men, holding a lantern in his hand.

D'Artagnan signed to them to draw near.

"Don't you recognize the carriage?" he asked the sergeant.

"No," replied the latter.

"Look at the arms."

The sergeant put the lantern near the panel.

"They are those of the Coadjutor," he said.

"Hush; he is enjoying a drive with Mdme. de Guéménée."

The sergeant began to laugh.

"Open the gate," he cried, "I know who it is!" Then, putting his face to the lowered blinds, he said:

"I wish you joy, my lord!"

"Impudent fellow," cried d'Artagnan, "you will get me turned off."

The gate groaned on its hinges, and d'Artagnan, seeing the gate cleared, whipped on his horses, who started at a canter and five minutes later they had joined the Cardinal.

"Mousqueton!" exclaimed d'Artagnan, "draw up the blinds of his majesty's carriage."

"It is he!" cried Porthos.

"As a coachman!" exclaimed Mazarin.

"And with the Coadjutor's carriage!" said the Queen.

"Corpo di Dio! Monsou d'Artagnan," said Mazarin, "you are worth your weight in gold."

CHAPTER LI.

WHAT D'ARTAGNAN AND PORTHOS EARNED BY THE SALE OF STRAW.

MAZARIN was desirous of setting out instantly for St. Germain; but the Queen declared that she should wait for the people whom she had appointed to meet her. However, she offered the Cardinal, Laporte's place, which he accepted, and went from one carriage to the other.

The first carriage which arrived after the Queen's, was that of the Prince de Condé, who, with the princess and dowager princess, was in it. Both these ladies had been awakened in the middle of the night, and did not know what it was all about. The second contained the Duke and Duchess of Orleans, etc.

Carriages now arrived in crowds; the two Musketeers arrived in their turn, holding the horses of d'Artagnan and Porthos. These two instantly mounted, the coachman of the latter replacing d'Artagnan on the coach-box of the royal coach. Mousqueton took the place of the coachman, and drove standing, for reasons known to himself, like the Phantom of antiquity.

The Queen, though occupied by a thousand details, tried to catch the Gascon's eye; but he, with his wonted prudence, had mingled with the crowd.

"Let us be the vanguard," said he to Porthos, "and find out good quarters at St. Germain; nobody will think of us, and for my part, I am much fatigued."

"As for me," replied Porthos, "I'm falling asleep, considering that we have not had any fighting; truly, the Parisians are dull."

"Or rather, we are very smart," said d'Artagnan. "And your wrist—how is it?"

"Better—but do you think that we've got them this time? You, your promotion—and I, my title."

"I'faith! yes—I should expect so—besides, if they forget, I shall take the liberty of reminding them."

"The Queen's voice! She is speaking," said Porthos; "I think she wants to ride on horseback."

"Oh, she would like it—she would—but—the Cardinal won't allow it."

"Gentlemen," he said, addressing the two Musketeers, "accompany the royal carriage; we are going on to seek for lodgings."

"Let us depart, gentlemen," said the Queen.

And the royal carriage drove on, followed by the other coaches and about fifty horsemen.

They reached St. Germain without any accident; on descending the footstep, the Queen found the prince awaiting her, bareheaded, to offer her his hand.

"What an alarum for the Parisians!" said the Queen.

"It is war," were the emphatic words of the prince.

"Well, then, let it be war! Have we not on our side the conqueror of Rocroy, of Nordlingen, of Lens?"

The prince bowed low.

It was then nine o'clock in the morning. The Queen walked first into the château; everyone followed her. About two hundred persons had accompanied her in her flight.

"Gentlemen," said the Queen, laughing, "pray take up your abode in the château; it is large, and there will be no want of room for you all; but, as we never thought of coming here, I am informed that there are, in all, only three beds here, one for the King, one for me——"

"And one for the Cardinal," muttered the prince.

"Am I—am I then to sleep on the floor?" asked Gaston d'Orleans, with a forced smile.

"No, my prince," replied Mazarin, "for the third bed is intended for your highness."

"But your Eminence?" replied the prince.

"I"—answered Mazarin— "I shall not sleep at all! I shall have work to do."

"Well, for my part, I shall not go to bed," said d'Artagnan; "come, Porthos."

Porthos followed the lieutenant with that profound confidence which he had in the wisdom of his friend. They walked from one end of the château to the other, Porthos looking with wondering eyes at d'Artagnan, who was counting on his fingers, "Four hundred at a pistole each, four hundred pistoles."

"Yes," interposed Porthos, "four hundred pistoles; but who is to make four hundred pistoles?"

"A pistole is not enough," said d'Artagnan, " 'tis worth a louis."

" What is worth a louis?"

"Four hundred, at a louis each, make four hundred louis."

"Four hundred!" exclaimed Porthos.

"Listen!" cried d'Artagnan.

But, as there were all descriptions of people about, who were in wonder at the arrival of the court, which they were watching, he whispered in his friend's ear.

"I understand;" answered Porthos, "I understand you perfectly, on my honor; two hundred louis, each of us, would be making a pretty thing of it; but what will the people say?"

"Let them say what they will; besides, how will they know it's us?"

"But who will distribute these things?" asked Porthos.

"I, and Mousqueton there."

"But he wears my livery; my livery will be known," replied Porthos.

"He can turn his coat inside out."

"You are always in the right, my dear friend," cried Porthos; "but where the devil do you discover all the notions you put into practice?"

D'Artagnan smiled. The two friends turned down the first street they came to. Porthos knocked at the door of a house to the right, whilst d'Artagnan knocked at the door of a house to the left.

"Some straw," they said.

"Sir, we don't keep any," was the reply of the people who opened the doors; "but ask, please, at the hay-dealer's."

"Where is the hay-dealer's?"

"At the last large gateway in the street."

"Are there any other people in St. Germain who sell straw?"

"Yes; there's the landlord of the Lamb, and Gros-Louis, the farmer—they live in the Rue des Ursulines."

"Very well."

D'Artagnan went instantly to the hay-dealer, and bargained with him for a hundred and fifty trusses of straw, which he had, at the rate of three pistoles each. He went afterwards to the innkeeper, and bought from him two hundred trusses at the same price. Finally, Farmer Louis sold them eighty trusses, making in all four hundred and thirty.

There was no more to be had in St. Germain. This foraging did not occupy more than half an hour. Mousqueton, duly instructed, was put at the head of this sudden and new business. He was cautioned not to let a bit of straw out of his hands under a louis a truss, and they entrusted to him straw to the amount of four hundred and thirty louis. D'Artagnan, taking with him three trusses of straw, returned to the château, where everybody, freezing with cold, and falling asleep, envied the King, the Queen, and the Duke of Orleans, on their camp-beds. The lieutenant's entrance produced a burst of laughter in the great drawing-room; but he did not appear to notice that he was the object of general attention, and began to arrange his straw bed with so much cleverness, nicety, and gaiety, that the mouths of all these sleepy creatures, who could not go to sleep, began to water.

"Straw!" they all cried out, "straw! where is any to be found?"

"I can show you," answered the Gascon.

And he conducted them to Mousqueton, who distributed lavishly the trusses at a louis a piece. It was thought rather dear, but people wanted to go to sleep, and who would not give even two or three gold coins for some hours of sound sleep?

Mousqueton, who knew nothing of what was going on in the château, wondered that the idea had not occurred to him sooner. D'Artagnan put the gold in his hat, and, in going back, settled the reckoning with Porthos; each of them had cleared two hundred and fifteen louis.

Porthos, however, found that he had no straw left for himself. He returned to Mousqueton, but the steward had sold the last wisp. He then repaired to d'Artagnan, who, thanks to his three trusses of straw, was in the act of making up and tasting, by anticipation, the luxury of a bed so soft, so well stuffed at the head, so well covered at the foot, that it would have excited the envy of the King himself, if his majesty had not been fast asleep in his own. D'Artagnan could, on no account, consent to pull his bed to pieces again for Porthos, but for a consideration of four louis that the latter paid him for it, he consented that Porthos should share his couch with him. He laid his sword at the head, his pistols by his side, stretched his cloak over his feet, placed his felt hat on the top of his cloak, and extended himself luxuriously on the straw, which rustled under him. He was already enjoying the sweet dreams engendered by the possession of two hundred and nineteen louis, made in a quarter of an hour, when a voice was heard at the door of the hall, which made him stir.

"M. d'Artagnan!" it cried.

"Here!" cried Porthos, "here!"

Porthos foresaw that if d'Artagnan was called away he should remain sole possessor of the bed. An officer approached.

"I am come to fetch you, M. d'Artagnan, to his Eminence."

"Tell my lord that I am going to sleep, and I advise him, as a friend, to do the same."

"His Eminence is not gone to bed, and will not go to bed, and wants you instantly."

"The devil take Mazarin, who does not know when to sleep at the proper time. What does he want with me? Is it to make me a captain? In that case I forgive him."

And the Musketeer arose, grumbling, took his sword, hat, pistols and cloak, and followed the officer, whilst Porthos, alone, and sole possessor of the bed, endeavored to follow the good example of falling asleep, which his predecessor had set him.

"M. d'Artagnan," said the Cardinal, on perceiving him, "I have not forgotten with what zeal you have served me. I am going to prove to you that I have not."

"Good," thought the Gascon, "this begins well."

"M. d'Artagnan," he resumed, "do you wish to become a captain?"

"Yes, my lord."

"And your friend still wishes to be made a baron?"

"At this moment, my lord, he's dreaming that he is one."

"Then," said Mazarin, taking from his portfolio the letter which he had already shown d'Artagnan, "take this despatch, and carry it to England."

D'Artagnan looked at the envelope, there was no address on it.

"Am I not to know to whom to present it?"

"You will know when you reach London; at London you may tear off the outer envelope."

"And what are my instructions?"

"To obey, in every particular, him to whom this letter is addressed. You must set out for Boulogne. At the 'Royal Arms of England' you will find a young gentleman, named Mordaunt."

"Yes, my lord; and what am I to do with this young gentleman?"

"To follow wherever he leads you."

D'Artagnan looked at the Cardinal with a stupefied air.

"There are your instructions," said Mazarin; "go!"

"Go! 'tis easy to say so, but that requires money, and I haven't any."

"Ah!" replied Mazarin, "so you've no money?"

"None, my lord."

"But the diamond I gave you yesterday?"

"I wish to keep it in remembrance of your Eminence."

Mazarin sighed.

" 'Tis very dear living in England, my lord, especially as envoy extraordinary."

"Zounds!" replied Mazarin, "the people there are very sober, and their habits, since the revolution, simple; but no matter."

He opened a drawer, and took out a purse.

"What do you say to a thousand crowns?"

D'Artagnan pouted out his lower lip in a most extraordinary manner.

"I reply, my lord, 'tis but little, as I certainly shall not go alone."

"I suppose not. M. du Vallon, that worthy gentleman, for, with the exception of yourself, M. d'Artagnan, there's not a man in France, that I esteem and love so much as him——"

"Then, my lord," replied d'Artagnan, pointing to the purse which Mazarin still held, "if you love and esteem him so much, you—understand me?"

"Be it so! on his account I add two hundred crowns."

"Scoundrel!" muttered d'Artagnan; "but on our return," he said aloud, "may we, that is, my friend and I, depend on having, he his barony, and I my promotion?"

"On the honor of Mazarin."

"I should like another sort of oath better," said d'Artagnan to himself; then aloud, "May I not offer my duty to her majesty the Queen?"

"Her majesty is asleep, and you must set off directly," replied Mazarin, "go, pray, sir——"

"One word more, my lord; if there's any fighting where I'm going, ought I to fight?"

"You are to obey the commands of the personage to whom I have addressed the enclosed letter."

" 'Tis well," said d'Artagnan, holding out his hand to receive the money. "I offer my best respects and services to you, my lord."

D'Artagnan then, returning to the officer, said:

"Sir, have the kindness also to awaken M. du Vallon, and to say 'tis by his Eminence's orders, and that I shall wait for him in the stables."

The officer went off with an eagerness that showed the Gascon that he had some personal interest in the matter.

Porthos was snoring most musically, when some one touched him on the shoulder.

"I come from the Cardinal," said the officer.

"Heigho!" said Porthos, opening his large eyes; "what do you say?"

"I say that his Eminence has ordered you to go to England, and that M. d'Artagnan is waiting for you in the stables."

Porthos sighed heavily, arose, took his hat, his pistols, and his cloak, and departed, casting a look of regret on the bed where he had hoped to sleep so well.

Scarcely had he turned his back than the officer laid himself down in it, and he had not crossed the threshold before his successor, in his turn, snored immoderately. It was very natural, being the only man in the whole assemblage, except the King, the Queen, and the Duke of Orleans, who slept gratis.

CHAPTER LII.

IN WHICH WE HEAR OF ARAMIS.

D'ARTAGNAN went straight to the stables; day had just dawned. He found his horse and that of Porthos fastened to the manger, but to an empty manger. He took pity on these poor animals, and went to a corner of the stable, where he saw a little straw, but in doing so he struck his foot against a round body, which uttered a cry, and arose on its knees, rubbing its eyes. It was Mousqueton, who, having no straw to lie upon himself, had helped himself to that of the horses.

"Mousqueton," cried d'Artagnan, "let us be off! Let us set off."

Mousqueton, recognizing the voice of his master's friend, got up suddenly, and in doing so, let fall some louis which he had appropriated to himself illegally during the night.

"Ho! ho!" exclaimed d'Artagnan, picking up a louis and displaying it; "here's a louis that smells of straw a little."

Mousqueton blushed so confusedly that the Gascon began to laugh at him, and said:

"Porthos would be angry, my dear M. Mouston, but I pardon you, only let us remember that this gold must serve us as a joke, so be gay, come along."

Mousqueton instantly assumed a most jovial countenance, saddled the horses quickly, and mounted his own without making faces over it.

Whilst this went on, Porthos arrived with a very cross look on his face, and was astonished to find the lieutenant resigned, and Mousqueton almost merry.

"Ah, that's it," he cried, "you have your promotion, and I my barony."

"We are going to fetch our brevets," said d'Artagnan, "and when we come back, Master Mazarin will sign them."

"And where are we going?" asked Porthos.

"To Paris first; I have affairs to settle."

And they both set out for Paris.

In the place of the Palais Royal d'Artagnan saw a sergeant who was drilling six or seven hundred citizens. It was Planchet, who brought into play profitably the recollections of the regiment. He recognized his old master, and, staring at him with wondering eyes, stood still. The first row, seeing their sergeant stop, stopped, and soon to the very last.

"These citizens are awfully ridiculous," observed d'Artagnan to Porthos, and went on his way.

Five minutes afterwards he entered the hotel of La Chevrette, where pretty Madeleine, the hostess, came to him.

"My dear Mistress Turquaine," said the Gascon, "if you happen to have any money, lock it up quickly—if you happen to have any jewels, hide them directly—if you happen to have any debtors, make them pay you, or have any creditors, don't pay them."

"Why, prythee?" asked Madeleine.

"Because Paris is going to be reduced to dust and ashes like Babylon, of which you have heard speak."

"And you are going to leave at such a time?"

"This very instant."

"And where are you going?"

"Ah, if you could tell me that, you'd be doing me a service."

"Ah, goodness gracious!"

"Have you any letters for me?" inquired d'Artagnan, wishing to signify to the hostess that her lamentations were superfluous, and that therefore she had better spare him the demonstrations of her grief.

"There's one just arrived."

"From Athos;" and he read as follows:

" 'Dear d'Artagnan, dear du Vallon—My good friends, perhaps this may be the last time that you ever hear from me. Let God, our courage, and the remembrance of our friendship, support you, nevertheless. I entrust to you certain papers which are at Blois, and in two months and a half, if you do not hear of us, take possession of them.

"Embrace, with all your heart, the viscount, for your devoted friend,   " 'Athos.'

"I believe, by Heaven," said d'Artagnan, "that I shall embrace him, since he's upon our road; and if he is so unfortunate as to lose our dear Athos, from this very day he becomes my son."

"And I," said Porthos, "shall make him my sole heir."

"Let us see, what more does Athos say?"

" 'Should you meet on your journey one, Mordaunt, distrust him—in a letter I cannot say more.' "

"M. Mordaunt!" exclaimed the Gascon, surprised.

"M. Mordaunt! 'tis well," said Porthos; "we shall remember that; but look, there's a postscript."

" 'We conceal the place where we are, dear friend, knowing

your brotherly affection, and that you would come and die with us were we to reveal it.'"

"Confound it," interrupted Porthos, with an explosion of passion which sent Mousqueton to the other end of the room; "are they in danger of death?"

D'Artagnan continued:

"'Athos bequeaths to you Raoul, and I bequeath to you my revenge. If by any good luck you lay your hand on a fellow, named Mordaunt, tell Porthos to take him into a corner, and to wring his neck. I dare not say more in a letter.'"

"If that is all, Aramis, it is easily done," said Porthos.

"On the contrary," observed d'Artagnan, with a vexed look; "it would be impossible. This is the same Mordaunt, whóm we are going to join at Boulogne, and with whom we cross to England."

"Well, suppose instead of joining this Mordaunt, we were to go and join our friends?" said Porthos, with a gesture fit to frighten a whole army.

"I did think of it, but this letter has neither date nor postmark."

"True," said Porthos. And he began to wander about the room like a man beside himself, gesticulating, and half drawing his sword out of the scabbard.

As to d'Artagnan, he remained standing like a man in consternation, with the deepest affliction depicted on his face.

"Ah, 'tis not right; Athos insults us, he wishes to die alone; that's bad."

Mousqueton, witnessing this despair, melted into tears, in a corner of the room.

"Stop—an idea!" cried Porthos; "indeed, my dear d'Artagnan, I don't know how you manage, but you are always full of ideas; let us go and embrace Raoul."

"Woe to that man who should happeɲ to contradict my master at this moment," said Mousqueton to himself; "I wouldn't give a farthing for his skin."

They set out. On arriving at St. Denis, the friends found a vast concourse of people. It was the Duke de Beaufort who was coming from the Vendômois, and whom the Coadjutor was showing to the Parisians, intoxicated with joy. With the duke's aid, they considered themselves already as invincible.

"Is it true," said the guard to the two cavaliers, "that the Duke de Beaufort has arrived in Paris?"

"Nothing more certain; and the best proof of it is," said d'Artagnan, "that he has despatched us to meet the Duke de Vendômee, his father, who is coming in his turn."

"Long live de Beaufort!" cried the guards, and they drew back respectfully to let the two friends pass. Once past the barriers, these two knew neither fatigue nor fear. Their horses flew, and they never ceased speaking of Athos and Aramis.

The camp had entered Saint Omer; the friends made a little

round, and went to the camp, and gave the army an exact account of the flight of the King and Queen. They found Raoul near his tent, reclining upon a truss of hay, of which his horse stole some mouthfuls; the young man's eyes were red, and he seemed dejected. Marshal de Grammont and the Duke de Guiche had returned to Paris, and he was quite lonely. As soon as he saw the two cavaliers, he ran to them with open arms.

"Oh is it you, dear friends? Do you come here to fetch me? Shall you take me away with you? Do you bring me tidings of my guardian?"

"Have you not received any?" said d'Artagnan to the youth.

"Alas! sir, no, and I do not know what has become of him; so that I am really so unhappy as to weep."

In fact, tears rolled down his cheeks.

Porthos turned aside, in order not to show on his good, round face what was passing in his mind.

"Deuce take it," cried d'Artagnan, more moved than he had been for a long time; "don't despair, my friend, if you have not received any letters from the count, we have received one."

"Oh, really!" cried Raoul.

"And a comforting one, too," added d'Artagnan, seeing the delight that his intelligence gave the young man.

"Have you got it?" asked Raoul.

"Yes, that is, I had it," replied the Gascon, making believe to try and find it. "Wait, it ought to be there, in my pocket; it speaks of his return, does it not, Porthos?"

"Yes," replied Porthos, laughing.

"Eh! I read it a little while since. Can I have lost it? Ah! confound it! my pocket has a hole in it."

"Oh, yes, M. Raoul!" said Mousqueton; "the letter was very consoling. These gentlemen read it to me, and I wept for joy."

"But then, at any rate, you know where he is, M. d'Artagnan?" asked Raoul, somewhat comforted.

"Ah! that's the point!" replied the Gascon. "Undoubtedly I know it, but it is a mystery."

"Not to me, I hope?"

"No, not to you, so I am going to tell you where he is."

Porthos looked at d'Artagnan with his large, wondering eyes.

"Where the devil shall I say that he is, so that he cannot try to rejoin him?" thought d'Artagnan.

"Well, where is he, sir?" asked Raoul, in a soft and coaxing voice.

"He is at Constantinople."

"Among the Turks!" exclaimed Raoul, alarmed. "Good heavens! how can you tell me that?"

"Does that alarm you?" cried d'Artagnan. "Pooh! what are the Turks to such a man as the Count de la Fère and the Abbé d'Herblay?"

"Ah, his friend is with him!" said Raoul; "that consoles me a little."

"What wit our devilish d'Artagnan has!" thought Porthos, astonished at his friend's deceptiveness.

"Now," said d'Artagnan, wishing to change the conversation, "here are fifty pistoles that the count has sent you by the same courier. I suppose you are out of money, and that they will be welcome."

"I have still twenty pistoles, sir."

"Well, take them; that makes seventy."

"And if you wish for more——" said Porthos, putting his hand to his pocket.

"Thank you, sir," replied Raoul, blushing; "thank you a thousand times."

At this moment Olivain appeared. "By the way," said d'Artagnan, loud enough for the servant to hear him, "are you satisfied with Olivain?"

"Yes, in some respects, pretty well."

"What fault do you find with the fellow?"

"He is a glutton."

"Oh, sir," cried Olivain, reappearing at this accusation.

"And somewhat of a thief, more especially a great coward."

"Oh, oh, sir! you really vilify me!" cried Olivain.

"The deuce!" cried d'Artagnan. "Pray learn, Olivain, that people like us are not to be served by cowards. You rob your master; you eat his sweetmeats and drink his wine; but, by Jove! don't be a coward, or I shall cut off your ears. Look at M. Mouston, see the honorable wounds he has received, and look how his habitual valor has given dignity to his countenance."

Mousqueton was in the third Heaven, and would have embraced d'Artagnan had he dared; meanwhile, he resolved to sacrifice his life to him on the next occasion that presented itself.

"Send away that fellow, Raoul," said the Gascon; "for if he's a coward he will disgrace thee some day."

"Master says I am a coward," cried Olivain, "because he wanted the other day to fight a cornet in Grammont's regiment, and I refused to accompany him."

"Olivain, a lackey ought never to disobey," said d'Artagnan, sternly; then, taking him aside, he whispered to him, "You did right; your master was wrong; here's a crown; but should he ever be insulted, and you do not let yourself be cut in quarters for him, I will cut out your tongue. Remember that well."

Olivain bowed, and slipped the crown into his pocket.

"And now, Raoul," said the Gascon, "M. du Vallon and I are going away as ambassadors, where, I know not; but should you want anything, write to Mdme. Turquaine, at

Nanny-goat, Rue Tiquetonne, and draw upon her money as on a banker, but with economy."

And having, meantime, embraced his ward, he passed him into the robust arms of Porthos, who lifted him up from the ground and held him a moment suspended, near the noble heart of the formidable giant.

"Come," said d'Artagnan, "let us be off."

And they set out for Boulogne, where, towards evening, they arrived, their horses covered with foam and heat.

At ten steps from the place where they halted was a young man in black, who seemed waiting for some one, and who, from the moment he saw them enter the town, never took his eyes off them.

D'Artagnan approached him, and seeing him stare so fixedly, said:

"Well, friend! I don't like people who scan me!"

"Sir," said the young man, "do you not come from Paris, if you please?"

D'Artagnan thought it was some gossip who wanted news from the capital.

"Yes," he said in a softened tone.

"Are you not to lodge at the 'Arms of England?' and are you not charged with a mission from his Eminence, Cardinal Mazarin?"

"Yes, sir."

"In that case I am the man you have to deal with. I am M. Mordaunt."

"Ah!" thought d'Artagnan, "the man I am warned against by Athos."

"Ah!" thought Porthos, "the man Aramis wants me to strangle."

"Well, gentlemen," resumed Mordaunt, "we must set off without delay; to-day is the last day granted me by the Cardinal. My ship is ready, and had you not come, I must have set off without you, for General Cromwell expects my return, impatiently."

"So!" thought the lieutenant, " 'tis to General Cromwell that our despatches are addressed."

"Have you no letter to him?" asked the young man.

"I have one, the seal of which I was not to break till I reached London; but since you tell me to whom it is addressed, 'tis useless to wait till then."

D'Artagnan tore open the envelope of the letter. It was directed to "Mr. Oliver Cromwell, General of the army of the English nation."

"Ah!" said d'Artagnan, "a singular commission."

"Who is Oliver Cromwell?" asked Porthos.

"Formerly a brewer," replied the Gascon.

"Perhaps Mazarin wishes to make a corner in beer, as we have in straw," said Porthos.

"Come, come, gentlemen," said Mordaunt impatiently, "let us depart."

"What!" cried Porthos, "without supper? Cannot M. Cromwell wait a little?"

"Yes, but how about me?" answered Mordaunt.

"Oh! as to you, that is not my concern, and I shall sup either with or without your permission."

"The young man's dull eyes kindled a little, but he restrained himself.

"Just as you please, gentlemen, provided we set sail," he said.

"The name of your ship?" inquired d'Artagnan.

"The *Standard.*"

"Very well; in half an hour we shall be on board." And the friends, spurring on their horses, rode to the hotel, the "Arms of England," where they supped with hearty appetite, and then at once proceeded to the port.

There they found a brig ready to set sail, upon the deck of which they recognized Mordaunt, walking up and down impatiently.

"It is singular," said d'Artagnan, whilst the boat was taking them to the *Standard,* "it is astonishing how that young man resembles some one whom I have known, but whom I cannot name."

A few minutes later they were on board; but the embarkation of the horses was a longer matter than that of the men, and it was eight o'clock before they raised the anchor.

CHAPTER LIII.

The foresworn Scot
Sold his master for a groat.

AND now our readers must leave the *Standard* to sail peaceably, not to London, where d'Artagnan and Porthos believed they were going, but to Durham, whither Mordaunt had been ordered to repair by the letter he had received during his sojourn at Boulogne, and accompany us to the Royalist camp, on this side of the Tyne, near Newcastle.

There, placed between two rivers on the borders of Scotland, but still on English soil, were the tents of a little army extended. It was midnight. Some Highlanders were carelessly keeping watch. The moon, which was partially obscured by two heavy clouds, now and then lit up the muskets of the sentinels, or silvered the walls, roofs, and spires of the town which Charles I. had just surrendered to the Parliamentary troops, whilst Oxford and Newark still held out for him, in the hopes of coming to some arrangement.

At one of the extremities of the camp, near an immense tent, in which the Scottish officers were holding a kind of council, presided over by Lord Leven, lay their commander, a man attired as a cavalier, sleeping on the turf, his right hand extended over his sword.

About fifty paces off, another young man, also apparelled as a cavalier, was talking to a Scotch sentinel, and, though a foreigner, he seemed to understand, without much difficulty, the answers given him in broad Perthshire dialect.

As the town clock of Newcastle struck one the sleeper awoke, and, with all the gestures of a man rousing himself out of a deep sleep, he looked attentively about him. Perceiving that he was alone, he rose, and making a little circuit, passed close to the young man who was speaking to the sentinel. The former had, no doubt, finished his questions, for a moment after he said good-night, and carelessly followed the same path taken by the first cavalier.

In the shadow of a tent the former was awaiting him.

"Well, friend," said he, in as pure French as has ever been uttered between Rouen and Tours, "there is not a moment to lose; we must let the King know immediately."

"Why, what is the matter?"

"It is too long to tell you; besides, you wish to hear it all directly, and the least word dropped here might ruin all. We must go and find Lord Winter."

They both set off to the other end of the camp, but as it did not cover more than a surface of five hundred feet, they quickly arrived at the tent they were looking for.

"Tony, is your master sleeping?" said one of the two cavaliers, to a servant who was lying in the outer compartment, which served as a kind of ante-room.

"No, my lord Count," answered the servant, "I think not; or at least, he was pacing up and down for more than two hours after he left the King, and the sound of his footsteps has only ceased during the last ten minutes; however, you may look and see," added the lackey, raising the curtained entrance of the tent.

As he had said, Lord Winter was seated near an aperture, arranged as a window to let in the night air, his eyes mechanically following the course of the moon, hidden, as we before observed, by heavy black clouds. The two friends approached Winter, who, leaning his head on his hands, was gazing at the heavens; he did not hear them enter, and remained in the same attitude till he felt a hand placed on his shoulder.

He turned round, recognized Athos and Aramis, and held out his hand to them.

"Have you observed," said he to them, "what a blood-red color the moon is to-night?"

"In a position so precarious as ours, we must examine the

earth, and not the heavens. Have you studied our Scotch troops, and have you confidence in them?"

"The Scotch?" inquired Winter. "What Scotch?"

"Ours! Egad!" exclaimed Athos. "Those in whom the King confides, Lord Leven's Highlanders."

"No," said Winter, then he paused; "but tell me can you not perceive the roseate tint which covers the heavens?"

"Not the least in the world," said Aramis and Athos at once.

"Tell me," continued Winter, possessed by the same idea, "is there not a tradition in France that Henry IV., the evening before the day he was assassinated, when he was playing at chess with M. de Bassompierre, saw spots of blood on the chessboard?"

"Yes," said Athos, "the Marshal often told me so himself."

"Then it was so," murmured Winter, "and the next day Henry IV. was killed."

"But what has this vision of Henry IV. to do with you, my lord?" inquired Aramis.

"Nothing; and, indeed, I am mad to amuse you with such things, when your coming to my tent at such an hour announces that you are the bearers of important news."

"Yes, my lord," said Athos. "I wish to speak to the King; I have something important to reveal to him."

"Cannot that be put off till to-morrow?"

"He must know it this moment; and, perhaps it is already too late."

"Come, then," said Lord Winter.

Lord Winter's tent was pitched by the side of the royal one; a kind of corridor communicating, guarded, not by a sentinel, but by a confidential servant, through whom in any case of urgency Charles could communicate instantly with his faithful subject.

"These gentlemen are with me," said Winter.

The lackey bowed and let them pass. As he had said, on a camp-bed, dressed in his black doublet, booted, unbelted, with his felt hat beside him, lay the King, overcome by sleep and fatigue. They advanced, and Athos, who was first to enter, gazed a moment in silence on that pale and noble face, encircled by his long and matty dark hair, the blue veins showing through his transparent skin; his eyes seemingly swollen by tears.

Athos sighed deeply; the sigh awoke the King—so lightly did he sleep.

He opened his eyes.

"Ah!" said he, raising himself on his elbow, "is it you, Count de la Fère?"

"Yes, sire," replied Athos.

"You were watching me while I slept, and you come to bring me some news?"

"Alas! sire," answered Athos, "your majesty has guessed rightly."

"Then it is bad news?"

"Yes, sire."

"Never mind! the messenger is welcome, and you never come here without giving me pleasure. You, whose devotion recognizes neither country nor misfortune; you, who are sent to me by Henrietta; whatever news you bring, speak out."

"Sire, Cromwell has arrived this night at Newcastle."

"Ah!" exclaimed the King, "to fight?"

"No, sire, but to purchase your majesty, who owes four hundred thousand pounds to the Scottish Army."

"For unpaid wages—yes, I know it. For the last year my faithful Highlanders have fought for honor alone."

Athos smiled.

"Well, sire! although honor is a fine thing, they are tired of fighting for it, and to-night they have sold you for two hundred thousand pounds—that is to say, the half of what is owing to them."

"Impossible!" cried the King; "the Scotch sell their King for two hundred thousand pounds? and who is the Judas who has concluded this infamous bargain?"

"Lord Leven."

The King sighed deeply, as if his heart would break, and then buried his face in his hands.

"Oh! the Scotch," he exclaimed; "the Scotch that I called 'my faithful,' to whom I trusted myself, when I could have fled to Oxford—the Scotch!—my own countrymen—the Scotch! my brothers! But are you well assured of it, sir?"

"Lying behind the tent of Lord Leven, I raised the canvas, and saw and heard all!"

"And when is this to be consummated?"

"To-day; this morning; so your majesty must perceive there is no time to lose!"

"To do what? since you say I am sold."

"To cross the Tyne, reach Scotland, and join Lord Montrose, who will not sell you."

"And what shall I wage in Scotland? a war of partizans, unworthy of a king."

"Robert Bruce's example will absolve you, sire."

"No! no, I have fought too long; they have sold me, they shall give me up, and the eternal shame of their treason shall fall on their heads."

"Sire," said Athos, "perhaps a king should act thus, but not a husband and a father. I have come in the name of your wife and daughter and two other children you have still in London, and I say to you, 'Live, sire, God wills it!'"

The King raised himself, buckled on his belt, and passing his handkerchief over his moist forehead, said:

"Well, what is to be done?"

"Sire, have you in the army even one regiment on which you may rely?"

"Winter," said the·King, "do you believe in the fidelity of yours?"

"Sire, they are but men, and men are become both weak and wicked. I will not answer for them. I would confide my life to them, but I should hesitate ere I confided to them your majesty's."

"Well!" said Athos, "since you have not a regiment, we three devoted men must be enough. Let your majesty mount and place yourself in the midst of us, and we will cross the Tyne, reach Scotland, and you are saved."

"As you all wish, then. Winter, give all the necessary orders."

Winter left the tent; in the meantime the King finished dressing. The first rays of daybreak penetrated through the apertures of the tent as Winter re-entered it.

"All is ready, sire," said he.

"For us also?" inquired Athos.

"Grimaud and Blaisois are holding your horses, ready saddled."

"In that case," exclaimed Athos, "let us not lose an instant in setting off!"

"Come," added the King.

"Sire," said Aramis, "will not your majesty acquaint some of your friends of this?"

"My friends!" answered Charles, sadly, "I have but three; one of twenty years, who has never forgotten me, and two of a week's standing, whom I shall never forget. Come, gentlemen, come."

The King quitted his tent, and found his horse ready, waiting for him. It was a chestnut that the King had ridden for three years, and of which he was very fond. It neighed with delight at seeing him.

"Ah!" said the King, "I was unjust; here is a creature that loves me. You, at least, will be faithful to me, Arthur."

The horse, as if it had understood those words, bent its red nostrils towards the King's face, and parting its lips, displayed all its white teeth as if with pleasure.

"Yes, yes," said the King, caressing it with his hand, "yes, my Arthur, you are a good creature."

After this little scene, Charles threw himself into the saddle, and, turning to Athos, Aramis, and Winter, said:

"Now, gentlemen, I am at your service."

But Athos was standing with his eyes fixed on a black line which bordered the banks of the Tyne, and seemed to extend double the length of the camp.

"What is that line?" cried Athos, as vision was still rather obscured by the uncertain daybreak. "What is that line? I did not perceive it yesterday."

"It must be the fog rising from the river," said the King.

"Sire, it is something more opaque than the fog."

"Indeed," said Winter. "It appears to me like a bar of red color."

"It is the enemy, who have made a sortie from Newcastle, and are surrounding us!" exclaimed Athos.

"The enemy!" cried the King.

"Yes, the enemy. It is too late. Stop a moment; does not that sunbeam yonder, just by the side of the town, glitter on Cromwell's guard, the Ironsides?"

"Ah!" said the King, "we shall soon prove whether my Highlanders have betrayed me or not."

"What are you going to do?" asked Athos.

"To give them the order to charge, and trample over these miserable rebels."

And the King, putting spurs to his horse, set off to the tent of Lord Leven.

"Follow him," said Athos.

"Come!" exclaimed Aramis.

"Is the King wounded?" cried Lord Winter, "I see spots of blood on the ground;" and he set off to follow the two friends.

He was stopped by Athos.

"Go and call out your regiment," said he, "I can foresee that we shall have need of it directly."

Winter turned his horse, and the two friends rode on. It had taken but two minutes for the King to reach the tent of the Scotch commander; he dismounted and entered.

"The King!" they exclaimed, as they all rose in bewilderment.

Charles was indeed in the midst of them; his hat on his head, his brows bent, striking his boot with his riding whip.

"Yes, gentlemen, the King, in person, come to ask an account of all that has happened."

"What is it, sire?" exclaimed Lord Leven.

"My lord," said the King angrily, "General Cromwell has arrived at Newcastle; you knew it, and I have not been informed of it; the enemy have left the town, and are now closing the passages of the Tyne against us; our sentinels have seen this movement, and I have been left unacquainted with it. By an infamous treaty, you have sold me for two hundred thousand pounds to the Parliament. Of this treaty at least I have been warned. This is the matter, gentlemen, answer and exculpate yourselves, for I stand here to accuse you."

"Sire," said Lord Leven, with hesitation, "sire, your majesty has been deceived by a false report."

"My own eyes have seen the enemy extend itself between myself and Scotland. With my own ears almost, I have heard the clauses of the treaty debated."

The Scotch chieftains looked at each other in their turn with frowning brows.

"Sire," faltered Lord Leven, crushed down by shame; "sire, we are ready to give you every proof of our fidelity."

"I ask but one," said the King; "put the army in battle array, and charge the enemy."

"That cannot be, sire," said the earl. "There is a truce between us and the English army."

"But if there were, the English army has broken it in leaving the town, contrary to the agreement which kept it there. Now, I tell you, you must pass with me through this army across to Scotland, and if you refuse, you may choose between two names which the contempt of all honest men will brand you with, you are either cowards or traitors!"

The eyes of the Scotch flashed fire; and, as often happens on such occasions, from shame they passed to extreme effrontery, and two chieftains of clans advanced towards the King.

"Ay," said they, "we have promised to deliver Scotland and England from him who for the last five-and-twenty years has sucked the blood and gold of Scotland and England. We have promised, and we will keep our promise. Charles Stuart you are our prisoner."

And both extended their hands as if to seize the King; but before they could touch him with the tips of their fingers, both had fallen—one dead and the other stunned.

Aramis had passed his sword through the body of the first, and Athos had knocked down the other with the butt-end of his pistol.

Then, as Lord Leven and the other chieftains retired, alarmed at this unexpected succor, which seemed to fall from Heaven for him whom they believed already their prisoner, Athos and Aramis dragged the King from the perjured assembly, into which he had so imprudently ventured, and throwing themselves on horseback, all three returned at full gallop to the royal tent.

On their road they perceived Lord Winter marching at the head of his regiment. The King motioned him to accompany them.

CHAPTER LIV.

THE AVENGER.

THEY all four entered the tent; they had no plan ready, and had to think of one.

The King threw himself into an arm-chair. "I am lost;" said he.

"No, sire," replied Athos; "you are only betrayed."

The King sighed deeply.

"Betrayed! yes—betrayed by the Scotch, amongst whom I

was born; whom I have always loved better than the English. Oh, traitors that ye are!"

"Sire," said Athos, "this is not a moment for recrimination, but a time to show yourself a King and a gentleman. Up, sire, up! for you have here at least three men who will not betray you. Ah! if we had been five!" murmured Athos, thinking of d'Artagnan and Porthos.

"What are you saying?" inquired Charles, rising.

"I said, sire, there is more than one thing open. Lord Winter answered for his regiment, or at least very nearly so—we will not split hairs about words—let him place himself at the head of his men, we will place ourselves at the side of your majesty and let us cut through Cromwell's army and reach Scotland."

"There is another method," said Aramis. "Let one of us put on the dress and mount the King's horse. Whilst they pursue him the King might escape."

"It is good advice," said Athos, "and if the King will do either of us the honor, we shall be truly grateful to him."

"What do you think of this counsel, Winter?" asked the King, looking with admiration at these two men, whose chief idea seemed to be how they could take on their own shoulders all the dangers which threatened him.

"I think that the only chance of saving your majesty has just been proposed by M. d'Herblay. I humbly entreat your majesty to choose quickly, for we have not a moment to lose."

"But if I accept, it is death, or at least imprisonment, for him who takes my place."

"It is the glory of having saved his King!" cried Winter.

The King looked at his old friend with tears in his eyes, undid the order of the Saint-Esprit which he wore, to honor the two Frenchmen who were with him, and passed it round Winter's neck, who received, on his knees, this striking proof of his sovereign's confidence and friendship.

"It is right," said Athos; "he has served your majesty longer than we have."

The King overheard these words, and turned round, with tears in his eyes.

"Wait a moment, sirs," said he; "I have an order for each of you also."

He turned to a closet where his own orders were locked up, and took out two ribbons of the Order of the Garter.

"These cannot be for us?" said Athos.

"Why not, sir?" asked Charles.

"Such are for royalty, and we are but nobles."

"Speak not of crowned heads. I shall not find amongst them such great hearts as yours. No, no, you do yourselves injustice; but I am here to do justice to you. On your knees, Count."

Athos knelt down, and the King passed the ribbon from left

to right as usual, and said: "I make you a knight. Be brave, faithful and loyal. You are brave, faithful, and loyal. I knight you, Count."

Then, turning to Aramis, he said:

"It is now your turn, Chevalier."

The same ceremony recommenced, with the same words, whilst Winter unlaced his buff outcoat that he might disguise himself like a king. Charles, having ended with Aramis the same as Athos, embraced them both.

"Sire," said Winter, who in this trying emergency felt all his strength and energy fire up, "we are ready."

The King looked at the three gentlemen. "Then we must fly!" said he.

"Fly through an army, sire?" said Athos.

"Then I shall die sword in hand," said Charles. "If ever I am King again!"

"Sire, you have already honored us more than nobles could ever aspire to, therefore gratitude is on our side. But we must not lose time; we have already wasted too much."

The King again shook hands with all three, exchanged hats with Winter, and went out.

Winter's regiment had ranged on some high ground above the camp. The King, followed by the three friends, turned his steps that way. The Scotch camp seemed as if at last awakened; the soldiers had come out of their tents, and taken up their station in battle array.

"Do you see that?" said the King. "Perhaps they are penitent, and preparing to march."

"If they are penitent," said Athos, "let them follow us."

"Well!" said the King, "what shall we do?"

"Let us examine the enemy's army."

At the same instant the eyes of the little group were fixed on the same line which at daybreak they had mistaken for fog, and which the morning sun now plainly showed was an army in order of battle. The air was soft and clear, as it always is at this hour of the morning. The regiments, the standards, and even the colors of the horses and uniforms were now clearly distinct.

On the summit of a rising ground, a little in advance of the enemy, appeared a short and heavy-looking man; this man was surrounded by officers. He turned a spy-glass towards the little group amongst which the King stood.

"Does this man know your majesty personally?" inquired Aramis.

Charles smiled.

"That man is Cromwell!" said he.

"Ah!" said Athos, "how much time we have lost."

"Now," said the King, "give the word, let us start."

"Will you not give it, sire?" asked Athos.

"No; I make you my lieutenant-general," said the King.

"Listen, then, Lord Winter. Proceed, sire, I beg. What we are going to say does not concern your majesty."

The King, smiling, turned a few steps back.

"This is what I propose to do," said Athos. "We will divide our regiment into two squadrons. You will put yourself at the head of the first; we and his majesty at the head of the second. If no obstacles occur, we will both charge together, force the enemy's line, and throw ourselves into the Tyne, which we must cross, either by fording or swimming; if, on the contrary, any repulse should take place, you and your men must fight to the last man, whilst we and the King proceed on our road. Once arrived at the brink of the river, should we even find them three ranks deep, as long as you and your regiment do your duty, we will look to the rest."

"To horse!" said Lord Winter.

"To horse!" re-echoed Athos; "all is arranged and decided."

"Now, gentlemen," cried the King, "forward! and rally to the old war cry of France—Montjoye and St. Denis. The war cry of England is too often in the mouths of those traitors."

The Scotch army stood motionless and silent with shame on viewing these preparations.

Some of the chieftains left the ranks, and broke their swords in two.

"There," said the King, "that consoles me; they are not all traitors."

At this moment Winter's voice was raised with the cry of "Forward!"

The first squadron moved off; the second followed it, and descended from the platform. A regiment of cuirassiers, nearly equal as to numbers, issued from behind the hill, and came full gallop towards it.

The King pointed this out.

"Sire," said Athos, "we foresaw this, and if Lord Winter's men do their duty, we are saved instead of lost."

At this moment they heard, above all the galloping and neighing of the horses, Winter's voice crying out:

"Sword in hand!"

At these words every sword was drawn, and glittered in the air like lightning.

"Now, gentlemen," said the King in his turn, excited by this sight, and the sound of it, "come, gentlemen, sword in hand!"

But Aramis and Athos were the only ones to obey this command and the King's example.

"We are betrayed," said the King, in a low voice.

"Wait a moment," said Athos, "perhaps they do not recognize your majesty's voice, and await the order of the captain."

"Have they not heard that of their colonel? But look! look!" cried the King, drawing up his horse with a sudden jerk, which threw it back on its haunches, and seizing the bridle of Athos' horse.

"Ah, cowards! ah, traitors!" cried out Lord Winter, whose voice they heard, whilst his men, quitting their ranks, dispersed all over the plain.

About a dozen men were ranged around him and awaited the charge of Cromwell's guards.

"Let us go and die with them!" said the King.

"Let us go," said Athos and Aramis.

"All faithful hearts with me!" cried out Winter.

This voice was heard by the two friends who set off at full gallop.

"No quarter," shouted a voice in French, answering to that of Winter, which made them tremble.

It was a roundhead mounted on a magnificent black horse, who was charging at the head of the English regiment, of which in his ardor he was ten steps in advance.

" 'Tis he!" murmured Winter, his eyes glazed, and letting his sword fall to his side.

"The King! the King!" cried out several voices, deceived by the blue ribbon, and the chestnut horse of Winter; "take him alive."

"No! it is not the King!" exclaimed the horseman. "Lord Winter, you are not the King; you are my uncle."

At the same moment, Mordaunt, for it was he, cocked his pistol at Winter, the fire flashed, and the ball entered the heart of the old cavalier, who, with one bound on his saddle, fell back into the arms of Athos, murmuring, "He is revenged."

"Think of my mother!" shouted Mordaunt, as his horse plunged and darted off at full gallop.

"Wretch!" exclaimed Aramis, raising his pistol, as he passed by him; but the fire flashed in the pan, and did not go off.

At this moment the whole regiment came up, and fell upon the few men who had held out, surrounding the two Frenchmen. Athos, after making sure that Lord Winter was really dead, let fall the corpse, and said:

"Come, Aramis, now for the honor of France," and the two Englishmen, who were nearest them, fell mortally wounded.

At the same moment a fearful "hurrah!" rent the air and thirty blades glittered above their heads.

Suddenly a man sprang out of the English ranks, fell upon Athos, entwining his muscular arms around him, and tearing his sword from him, said in his ear:

"Silence! yield yourself—you yield to me; do you not?"

A giant had seized also Aramis' two wrists, who struggled in vain to release himself from this formidable grasp.

"D'Ar——" exclaimed Athos, whilst the Gascon covered his mouth with his hand.

"I yield myself prisoner," said Aramis, giving up his sword to Porthos.

"Fire! fire!" cried out Mordaunt, returning to the group of friends.

"And wherefore fire?" said the colonel; everyone has yielded."

"It is the son of My lady," said Athos to d'Artagnan, "I recognize him."

"It is the monk," whispered Porthos to Aramis.

"I know it."

And now the ranks began to open. D'Artagnan held the bridle of Athos' horse, and Porthos that of Aramis. Both of them attempted to lead his prisoner off the battlefield.

This movement revealed the spot where Winter's body had fallen. Mordaunt had found it out, and was gazing at it with an expression of hatred.

Athos, though now quite cool and collected, put his hand to his belt, where his loaded pistol still remained.

"What are you about?" said d'Artagnan.

"Let me kill him."

"We are all four lost, if, by the least gesture, you discover that you recognize him."

Then turning to the young man, he exclaimed:

"A fine prize! friend Mordaunt; we have, both myself and M. du Vallon, taken two knights of the Garter, nothing less.

"But," said Mordaunt, looking at Athos and Aramis with bloodshot eyes, "these are Frenchmen, I imagine."

"I'faith, I don't know. Are you French, sir?" said he to Athos.

"I am," replied the latter gravely.

"Very well, my dear sir! you are the prisoner of a fellow countryman."

"But the King—where is the King?" exclaimed Athos anxiously.

"Oh! we have got him."

"Yes," said Aramis, "through an infamous act of treason."

Porthos pressed his friend's hand, and said to him:

"Yes, sir, all is fair in war, stratagem as well as force. Look yonder!"

At this instant the squadron—that ought to have protected Charles' retreat—was advancing to meet the English regiments. The King, who was entirely surrounded, walked alone on foot. He appeared calm, but it was evidently not without a great effort. Drops of perspiration rolled down his face; and from time to time he put a handkerchief to his mouth, to wipe off the blood that flowed from it.

"Behold Nebuchadnezzar!" exclaimed an old Puritan trooper whose eyes flashed at the sight of one whom he called the tyrant.

"Do you call him Nebuchadnezzar?" said Mordaunt, with a terrible smile; "no, it is Charles the First, the good King Charles, who despoils his subjects to enrich himself."

Charles glanced a moment at the insolent creature who uttered this, but he did not recognize him. Nevertheless, the calm and religious dignity of his countenance abashed Mordaunt.

"Good morning, gentlemen," said the King to the two gentlemen who were held by d'Artagnan and Porthos. "The day has been unfortunate, but it is not your fault, thank God! But where is my old friend, Winter?"

The two gentlemen turned away their heads in silence.

"Look for him where Strafford rots," Mordaunt shrilly answered.

Charles shuddered. The demon had known how to wound him. The remembrance of Strafford was a source of lasting remorse to him—the shadow that haunted him by day and night. The King looked around him. He saw a corpse at his feet; it was Winter's. He uttered not a word nor shed a tear, but a deadly pallor spread over his face; he knelt down on the ground, raised Winter's head, and unfastening the order of the Saint-Esprit, placed it on his own breast.

"Lord Winter is killed, then?" inquired d'Artagnan, fixing his eyes on the corpse.

"Yes," said Athos, "by his own nephew."

"Come, he was the first of us to go; peace be to him! he was an honest man," said d'Artagnan.

"Charles Stuart," said the colonel of the English regiment, approaching the King, who had just put on the insignia of royalty, "do you yield yourself a prisoner?"

"Colonel Tomlinson," said Charles, "the King cannot yield! the man alone submits to force."

"Your sword."

The King drew his sword and broke it on his knee.

At this moment a horse without a rider, covered with foam, his nostrils extended, and his eyes all fire, galloped past, and recognizing his master, stopped and neighed with pleasure; it was Arthur.

The King smiled, patted it with his hand, and then jumped lightly into the saddle.

"Now, gentlemen," said he, "conduct me where you will."

Turning back again he said, "I thought I saw Winter move; if he still lives, by all you hold most sacred, do not abandon him."

"Never fret, King Charles," said Mordaunt, "my bullet pierced his heart."

"Do not breathe a word, nor make the least sign to me or Porthos," said d'Artagnan to Athos and Aramis, "that you recognize this man, for My lady is not dead; her soul lives in the body of this fiend."

The detachment moved towards the town with the royal captive; but on the road an aide-de-camp from Cromwell sent orders that Colonel Tomlinson should conduct him to Holdenby Castle.

At the same time couriers started in every direction over

England and Europe, to announce that Charles Stuart was now the prisoner of Oliver Cromwell, while the Scotch looked on with sheathed claymores and grounded muskets.

CHAPTER LV.

OLIVER CROMWELL.

"HAVE you been to the general?" said Mordaunt to d'Artagnan and Porthos; "you know he sent for you after the action."

"We went first to put our prisoners in safety," replied d'Artagnan. "Do you know, sir, these gentlemen are each of them worth fifteen hundred pounds?"

"Oh! be assured," said Mordaunt, looking at them with an expression he in vain endeavored to soften, "my soldiers will guard them—and guard them well, I promise you."

"I shall take better care of them myself," answered d'Artagnan; "besides, all they require is a good room, with sentinels, from which their parole is enough that they will not attempt to escape. I will go and see about that, and then we shall have the honor of presenting ourselves to your general, and receiving his commands for his Eminence."

"You are thinking of starting home soon, then?" inquired Mordaunt.

"Our mission is ended, and there is nothing more to retain us now but the good pleasure of the great man to whom we have been sent."

The young man bit his lips, and whispered to his sergeant:

"You will follow these men, and not lose sight of them; when you have discovered where they lodge, come and await me at the town gate."

The sergeant nodded that he should be obeyed.

Instead of following the mass of prisoners taken into the town, Mordaunt turned his steps towards the rising ground whence Cromwell had witnessed the battle, and on which he had just had his tent pitched.

Cromwell had given orders that no one was to enter it; but the sentinel, who knew that Mordaunt was one of his confidential friends, thought the order did not extend to him. Mordaunt, therefore, raised the canvas flap, and saw Cromwell seated before a table, his head buried in his hands; his back was turned to him.

Whether he heard Mordaunt or not as he entered, Cromwell did not move. Mordaunt remained standing near the door. At last, after a few moments, Cromwell raised his head, and, as if he divined that someone was there, he turned slowly around.

"I said I wished to be alone!" he exclaimed, on seeing the young man.

"They thought this order did not concern me, sir; nevertheless, if you wish it, I am ready to go."

"Ah! it is you, Mordaunt!" said Cromwell, the cloud passing away by force of will, "since you are here, it is well, you may remain."

"I come to congratulate you on the capture of Charles Stuart. You are now master of England."

"I was much more really so two hours ago."

"How so, general?"

"Because England had need of me to take the tyrant, and now the tyrant is taken. Have you seen him?"

"Yes, sir," said Mordaunt.

"What is his bearing?"

Mordaunt hesitated; but he seemed as if compelled to speak the truth.

"Calm and dignified," said he.

"What did he say?"

"Some parting words to his friends."

"His friends!" muttered Cromwell. "Yes, *he* has friends!" Then he added aloud, "Did he make any resistance?"

"No, sir; with the exception of two or three, everyone deserted him; he had no means of resistance."

"To whom did he give up his sword?"

"He did not give it up—he broke it."

"He did well; but, instead of breaking it, he might have used it to more advantage. I heard that the colonel of the regiment that escorted Charles was killed," said Cromwell, staring very fixedly at Mordaunt.

"Yes, sir; by me. It was Lord Winter."

"Your uncle!" exclaimed Cromwell.

"My uncle," answered Mordaunt; "but traitors to England are not of my family."

Cromwell observed the young man a moment in silence, and then added:

"Mordaunt, you are a dreadful servant of the Lord. And the Frenchmen, how did they behave?"

"Like brave men."

"Yes, yes," murmured Cromwell; "the French fight well and if my glass was good, they were foremost in the fight."

"They were," replied Mordaunt.

"After you, however," said Cromwell.

"It was the fault of their horses, not theirs."

Another pause.

"And the Scotch?"

"They kept their word, and never stirred," said Mordaunt.

"Scoundrels!"

"Their officers wish to see you, sir."

"I have no time for them. Have they been paid?"

"Yes, to-night."

"Let them set off and return to their mountains, and there hide their shame, if their mountains are high enough. I have nothing more to do with them, or they with me. And now, go, Mordaunt."

"Before I go," said Mordaunt, "I have some questions and a favor to ask you, sir."

"A favor from me?"

Mordaunt bowed.

"I come to you, my leader, my head, my father, and I ask you, master, are you content with me?"

Cromwell looked at him with astonishment. The young man remained immovable.

"Yes," said Cromwell; "you have done, since I knew you, not only your duty, but more than your duty; you have been a faithful friend, a keen negotiator, and a good soldier."

"Do you remember, sir, it was my idea, this Scotch treaty, for giving up the King?"

"Yes, the idea was yours. I had not such a contempt for men before that."

"Was I not a good ambassador in France?"

"Yes, for Mazarin has granted what I desired."

"Have I not always fought for your glory and interests?"

"Too ardently, perhaps; it is what I have just reproached you for; but what is the meaning of all these questions?"

"To tell you, my lord, that the moment has now arrived when, with a single word, you may recompense all these services."

"Oh!" said Oliver, with slight scorn, "I forgot that every service merits some reward, and that up to this moment you have served me for nothing."

"Sir, you can give me in a moment all that I look for."

"What is it? Have they offered you money? Do you wish a grade? or a county government?"

"Sir, will you grant me my request?"

"Let us hear what it is first."

"Sir, when you have told me to obey an order, have I ever inquired what it is first? I cannot tell you."

"But a request made so formally——"

"Ah! do not fear, sir," said Mordaunt with apparent simplicity, "it will not ruin you."

"Well, then," said Cromwell, "I promise as far as lies in my power to grant your request. Proceed."

"Sir, two prisoners were taken this morning; will you let me have them?"

"For their ransom? Have they, then, offered a large one?" inquired Cromwell.

"On the contrary, I think they are poor, sir."

"They must be friends of yours, then?"

"Yes, sir," replied Mordaunt, "they are friends, dear friends of mine, and I would lay down my life for them."

"Very well, Mordaunt," said Cromwell, pleased at having his opinion of the young man raised once more, "I will give them to you; I will not even ask who they are; do as you like with them."

"Thank you, sir!" exclaimed Mordaunt, "thank you; my life is always at your service, and should I lose it I should still owe you something! thank you; you have indeed, repaid me munificently for my service."

And he threw himself at the feet of Cromwell; and in spite of the efforts of the Puritan general, who did not like this almost kingly homage, he took his hand and kissed it.

"What!" said Cromwell, arresting him for a moment as he rose, "is there nothing more you wish? neither gold nor rank?"

"You have given me all you can give me, and from to-day your debt is paid."

And Mordaunt darted out of the general's tent, his heart beating, and his eyes sparkling with joy.

Cromwell gazed a moment after him.

"He has killed his uncle!" he murmured. "Alas! what are my servants? Perhaps those who ask nothing or seem to ask nothing, have asked more in the eyes of Heaven than those who tax the country, and steal the bread of the poor. Nobody serves me for nothing! Charles, who is my prisoner, may still have friends; but I have none!"

And with a deep sigh he again sank into the reverie which had been interrupted by Mordaunt.

CHAPTER LVI.

LORD HAVE MERCY.

WHILST Mordaunt was making his way to Cromwell's tent, d'Artagnan and Porthos had brought their prisoners to the house assigned to them as their dwelling at Newcastle.

The two friends made the prisoners enter the house first, whilst they stood at the door, desiring Mousqueton to take all the four horses to the stable.

"Why don't we go in with them?" asked Porthos.

"We must first see what the sergeant wishes us to do," replied d'Artagnan, and he then asked the sergeant his wishes.

"We have had orders," answered the man, "to help you in taking care of your prisoners."

There could be no fault found with this arrangement; on the contrary, it seemed to be a delicate attention to be received gratefully. D'Artagnan, therefore, thanked the man, and gave him a crown piece, to drink to General Cromwell's health.

The sergeant answered that Puritans never drank, and put the crown piece into his pocket.

"Ah!" said Porthos, "what a fearful day, my dear d'Artagnan!"

"What! a fearful day, when we have to-day found our friends?"

"Yes; but under what circumstances?"

"'Tis true that our position is an awkward one; but let us go in and see more clearly what is to be done."

"Things look very bad," replied Porthos; "I understand now why Aramis advised me to strangle that horrible Mordaunt."

"Silence!" cried the Gascon; "do not utter that name."

"But," argued Porthos, "I speak French, and they are all English."

D'Artagnan looked at Porthos with that air of wonder which a sensible man cannot help feeling at stupidity in every degree.

But, as Porthos on his side could not comprehend his astonishment, he merely pushed him indoors, saying: "Let us go in."

They found Athos in profound despondency. Aramis looked first at Porthos and then at d'Artagnan, without speaking, but the latter understood his meaning look.

"You want to know how we came here; 'tis easily guessed. Mazarin sent us with a letter to General Cromwell."

"D'Artagnan! how came you to fall into company with Mordaunt, whom I bade you distrust?" asked Athos.

"Mazarin again. Cromwell had sent him to Mazarin. Mazarin sent us to Cromwell. There has been a fate in it."

"Yes, you are right, d'Artagnan; a fate which will separate and ruin us; so, my dear Aramis, say no more about it, and let us prepare to submit to our destiny."

"Zounds! let us speak about things, on the contrary, for we always agreed to keep on the same side; and here we are engaged in conflicting parties."

"Yes," added Athos, "I now ask you, d'Artagnan, what side you are on? Ah! behold for what end the wretched Mazarin has made use of you. Do you know in what crime you are to-day concerned? In the capture of a King, his degradation, his death."

"Oh! oh!" cried Porthos, "do you think so?"

"You are exaggerating, Athos; we are not so far gone as that."

"Good heavens! we are on the very eve of it. I say why is the King taken prisoner? Those who wish to respect him as a master, would not buy him as a slave."

"I don't say to the contrary," said d'Artagnan. "But what's that to us? I am here, because I am a soldier, and have to obey orders; I have taken an oath to obey, and I do obey; but you, who have taken no oath, why are you here, and what cause do you serve?"

"That most sacred in the world," said Athos; "the cause of misfortune, and religion, and royalty. A friend, a wife, and a daughter have done us the honor to call us to their aid. We have served them to the best of our poor means, and God will recompense the will, and forgive the want of power; you may see matters differently, d'Artagnan, and think otherwise. I do not attempt to argue with you, but I blame you."

"Pshaw!" cried d'Artagnan; "what matters it to me, after all, if Cromwell, who's an Englishman, revolts against his King, who is a Scotchman? I am myself a Frenchman, I have nothing to do with these things—why make me responsible for them?"

"Why you? Because you, d'Artagnan, a man sprung from the ancient nobility of France, bearing a good name, wearing a sword, have helped to give up a King to beersellers, storekeepers, and wagoners. Ah! d'Artagnan! perhaps you have done your duty as a soldier, but, as a gentleman, I say that you are very culpable."

D'Artagnan was chewing the stalk of a flower, unable to reply, and very uncomfortable, for Aramis was eyeing him, too.

"And you, Porthos, you, a gentleman in manners, in tastes, in courage, are as much to blame as d'Artagnan."

Porthos colored and hanging his head, said:

"Yes, yes, my dear Count, I feel that you are right."

Athos rose.

"Come," he said, stretching out his hand to d'Artagnan, "come, don't be sullen, my dear son, for I have said all this to you, if not in the tone, at least with the feelings of a father. It would have been easier for me merely to have thanked you for preserving my life, and not to have uttered a word of all this."

"Doubtless, doubtless, Athos. But this is it: you have sentiments, the devil knows what, such as every one can't have. Who could suppose that a sensible man could leave his house, France, his ward—a charming youth, for we saw him in the camp—to fly to the aid of a rotten, worm-eaten royalty, which is going to crumble one of these days like an old cask? The sentiments you speak are certainly fine, so fine that they are superhuman."

"However that may be, d'Artagnan," replied Athos, without falling into the snare which his Gascon friend had prepared for him by an appeal to his parental love, "whatsoever may be, you know, in the bottom of your heart, that it is true; but I am coming to dispute with my superiors. D'Artagnan, I am your prisoner, treat me as such."

D'Artagnan said nothing; but, after having gnawed the flower-stalk, he began to bite his nails. At last, he resumed:

"Do you imagine that they mean to kill you? And where-

fore should they do so? What interest have they in your
death? Moreover, you are *our* prisoner."

"Fool!" cried Aramis, "knowest thou not, then, Mordaunt?
I have merely exchanged with him one look, but that look
convinced me that we were doomed."

"The truth is, I am very sorry that I did not strangle him
as you advised me to do," said Porthos.

"Stop," cried Athos, extending his hand to one of the grated
windows by which the room was lighted; "you will soon know
what to expect, for here he is."

In fact, looking at the place to which Athos pointed, d'Artagnan saw a horseman coming towards the house full gallop.

It was Mordaunt.

D'Artagnan rushed out of the room.

Porthos wanted to follow him.

"Stay," said d'Artagnan, "and do not come till you hear me
beat with my fingers upon the door as on a drum."

When Mordaunt arrived opposite the house he saw d'Artagnan upon the threshold, and the soldiers lying on the grass,
here and there, with their arms.

"Halloa!" he cried, "are the prisoners still there?"

"Yes, sir," answered the sergeant, saluting.

" 'Tis well; order four men to conduct them to my lodging."

Four men stepped out to do so.

"What do you want, sir?" asked d'Artagnan.

"Sir," replied Mordaunt, "I have ordered the two prisoners
that we captured this morning to be conducted to my lodging."

"Wherefore, sir? Excuse curiosity, but I wish to be en-
lightened on the subject."

"Because these prisoners, sir, are at my disposal, and I choose
to dispose of them as I like."

"Allow me—allow me," said d'Artagnan, "to observe you are
in error. The prisoners belong to those who took them, and
not to those who only saw them taken. You might have taken
Lord Winter—who, 'tis said, is your uncle—prisoner, but you
preferred killing him; 'tis well—we, that is, M. du Vallon and
I, could have killed our prisoners—we preferred keeping them."

Mordaunt's very lips were white with rage.

D'Artagnan now saw that affairs were growing worse, and
he beat the guard's march upon the door. At the first beat
Porthos rushed out, and stood on the other side of the door,
filling it up from sill to top.

This movement was observed by Mordaunt.

"Sir!" he thus addressed d'Artagnan, "your resistance is
useless, these prisoners have just been given me by my illustrious patron, Oliver Cromwell."

These words struck d'Artagnan like a thunderbolt. The blood
mounted to his temples, his eyes became dim; he saw from what
source the ferocious hopes of the young man arose. He put
his hand to the hilt of his sword.

As to Porthos, he looked inquiringly at d'Artagnan if he should also draw.

This look of Porthos' made the Gascon regret that he had summoned the brute force of his friend to aid him in an affair which seemed to require chiefly cunning.

"Violence," he said to himself, "would spoil all; d'Artagnan, my friend, prove to this young serpent that you are not only stronger, but more subtle than he is."

"Oh!" he said, making a low bow, "why did you not begin by saying that, M. Mordaunt? What! are you sent by General Oliver Cromwell, the most illustrious captain of his age?"

"I have this instant left him," replied Mordaunt, alighting, in order to give his horse to a soldier to hold.

"Why did you not say so at once, my dear sir! all England is with Cromwell; and since you ask for my prisoners, I bend, sir, to your wishes. They are yours, take them."

Mordaunt, delighted, advanced; Porthos looked at d'Artagnan with open mouthed astonishment. But d'Artagnan trod on his foot, and Porthos began to understand that this was all acting.

Mordaunt put his foot on the first step of the door, and, with his hat in his hand, prepared to pass by the two friends, motioning to the four men to follow him.

"But pardon me," said d'Artagnan, stopping the roundhead short, "since the illustrious general has given my prisoners into your hands, he has of course confirmed that act in writing."

Mordaunt retreated, casting a terrible glance at d'Artagnan which was answered by the most amicable and friendly mien that could be imagined.

"Speak out, sir," said Mordaunt.

"M. du Vallon, yonder, is rich, and has forty thousand francs yearly, so he does not care about money. I do not speak for him, but for myself—I'm not rich. In Gascony 'tis no dishonor, sir, nobody is rich; and Henry IV., of glorious memory, who was the King of the Gascons, never had a penny in his pocket."

"Go on, sir. I see where you wish to come to, and if it is what ·I think that stops you, I can obviate that difficulty."

"Ah, I knew well," said the Gascon, "that you are a man of talent. Well, here's the case; here's where the shoe pinches. I am an officer of fortune, nothing else; I have nothing but what my sword brings me in—that is to say, more blows than bank notes. Now, on taking prisoners this morning two Frenchmen, who seemed to me of high birth—in short, two knights of the Garter—I said to myself, 'my fortune is made.' "

Mordaunt, completely deceived by the wordy civility of d'Artagnan, smiled like a man who understands perfectly the reasons given him, and said:

"I shall have the order signed directly, sir, and with, it two thousand pistoles; meanwhile, let me take these men away."

"No," replied d'Artagnan; "what signifies a delay of half an hour? I am a man of order, sir; let us do things in order."

"Mark," replied Mordaunt, "I could compel you; I command here."

"Come, come," replied d'Artagnan, "I see that although we have had the honor of traveling in your company, you do not know us. We are gentlemen; able to kill you and your eight men; though two only. For Heaven's sake don't be obstinate, for when others are obstinate, I am obstinate likewise, and then I become ferocious and headstrong; and there's my friend, who is even more headstrong and ferocious than I am; besides, we are sent here by Cardinal Mazarin, and at this moment represent both the King and the Cardinal, and are therefore, as ambassadors, able to act with impunity, a thing that General Oliver Cromwell, who is assuredly as great a politician as general, is quite a man to understand. Ask him then, for the written order. What will that cost you, my dear M. Mordaunt?"

"Yes, the written order," said Porthos, who now began to comprehend what d'Artagnan was aiming at, "nothing but that will satisfy us."

However anxious Mordaunt was to have recourse to violence, he quite understood the reasons that d'Artagnan gave him; and, besides, completely ignorant of the friendship which existed between the four Frenchmen, all his uneasiness disappeared when he heard of the plausible motive of the ransom. He decided, therefore, not only to fetch the order, but the two thousand pistoles at which he estimated the prisoners. He therefore mounted his horse, and disappeared.

"Good!" thought d'Artagnan; "a quarter of an hour to go to the tent, a quarter of an hour to return;" then turning, without the least change of countenance, to Porthos, he said, looking him full in the face, "Friend Porthos, listen; first, not a syllable to either of our friends about the service we are going to render them."

"Very well; I understand."

"Go to the stable; you will find Mousqueton there. Saddle your horses, put your pistols in your saddle-bags, take out the horses, and lead them to the street below this, so that there will be nothing to do but to mount them; all the rest is my business."

Porthos made no remark, but obeyed, with the sublime confidence that he had in his friend. He then proceeded, with his usual calm gait, to the stable, and went into the very midst of the soldiery, who, Frenchman though he was, could not help admiring his height and powerful limbs.

At the corner of the street he met Mousqueton and took him with him.

D'Artagnan, meantime, went into the house, whistling a tune which he had begun before Porthos went away. "My dear Athos, I have reflected on your arguments, and am convinced. I am sorry to have had anything to do with this matter. As you say, Mazarin is a knave. I have resolved to flee with you; not a word; be ready; your swords are in the corner; do not forget them, they are, in many circumstances, very useful; there's Porthos' purse, too."

He put it into his pocket. The two friends were stupefied.

"Well—pray, is there anything to be surprised at?" he said. "I was blind; Athos made me see clearly; that's all. Come here."

The two friends went near him.

"Do you see that street? There stand the horses. Go out by the door, turn to the right, jump into your saddles, all will be right; don't be uneasy at anything except mistaking the signal. That will be the signal when I call out, 'Lord have mercy!' "

"But give us your word that you will come too, d'Artagnan," said Athos.

"I swear I will, by Heaven!"

" 'Tis settled," said Aramis, "at the shout, we go out, upset all that stands in our way, run to our horses, jump into our saddles, spur them—is that all?"

"Exactly."

"See Aramis, as I have told you, d'Artagnan is the best of us all," said Athos.

"Very true," replied the Gascon, "but I always run away from compliments. Don't forget the signal." And he went out whistling.

The soldiers were playing or sleeping; two of them were singing in a corner, out of tune, the psalm—"By the rivers of Babylon."

D'Artagnan called the sergeant. "My dear friend, General Cromwell has sent M. Mordaunt to fetch me. Guard the prisoners well, I beg of you."

The sergeant made a sign, as much as to say he did not understand French, and d'Artagnan tried to make him comprehend by signs and gestures. Then he went into the stable; he found the five horses and his own, among others, saddled. He gave his instructions, and Porthos and Mousqueton went to their post according to his directions.

Then d'Artagnan, being alone, struck a light and lighted a small bit of tinder, mounted his horse, and stopped at the door, in the midst of the soldiers. There, caressing, as he pretended, the animal with his hand, he put this bit of tinder, while burning, into his ear.

It was necessary to be as good a horseman as he was to risk such a scheme; for hardly had the animal felt the burning tinder than he uttered a cry of pain, and reared and jumped as if he had been mad.

The soldiers, whom he nearly trampled upon, ran away from him.

"Help! help!" cried d'Artagnan; "stop, my horse has the blind staggers."

In an instant blood came from the horse's eyes, and he was white with foam.

"Help! help!" cried d'Artagnan. "What! will you let me be killed? Lord have mercy!"

Scarcely had he uttered this cry than the door opened, and Athos and Aramis rushed out. The coast, owing to the Gascon's stratagem, was clear.

"The prisoners are escaping!" yelled the sergeant.

"Stop! stop!" cried d'Artagnan, giving rein to his famous steed, who, darting forth, overturned several men.

"Stop! stop!" cried the soldiers, and ran for their arms.

But the prisoners were on their saddles, and lost no time, hastening to the nearest gate.

In the middle of the street they saw Grimaud and Blaisois coming to find their master. With one wave of his hand, Athos made Grimaud, who followed the little troop, understand everything, and they passed on like a whirlwind, d'Artagnan still directing them from behind with his voice.

They passed through the gate like apparitions, without the guards thinking of detaining them, and reached the open country.

All this while the soldiers were calling out, "Stop! Stop!" and the sergeant, who began to see that he was the victim of an artifice, was almost in a frenzy of despair; whilst all this was going on, a cavalier in full gallop was seen approaching. It was Mordaunt with the order in his hand.

"The prisoners!" he exclaimed, jumping off his horse.

The sergeant had not the courage to reply; he showed him the open door and the empty room. Mordaunt darted to the steps, understood all, uttered a scream as if his entrails were torn out, and fell fainting on the stone steps.

CHAPTER LVII.

UNDER THE MOST TRYING CIRCUMSTANCES NOBLE NATURES NEVER LOSE COURAGE, NOR GOOD STOMACHS, APPETITE.

THE little troop, without looking behind them, or exchanging a single word, fled at a rapid gallop, crossing on foot a little stream, and leaving Durham on their left. At last they came in sight of a small wood, and spurring their horses afresh, they rode in the direction of it.

As soon as they had disappeared behind a green curtain sufficiently thick to conceal them from the sight of any who might be in pursuit of them, they drew up to hold a council together. The two grooms held the horses, that they might take rest without being unsaddled, and Grimaud was posted as sentinel.

"Come, first of all," said Athos to d'Artagnan, "my friend,

that I may shake hands with you—you, our rescuer; you, the true hero among us all."

"Athos is right, and you win my admiration," said Aramis, in his turn pressing his hand; "to what are you not equal? with superior intelligence, and an infallible eye; an arm of iron, and an enterprising mind."

"Now," said the Gascon, "that is all well, I accept for Porthos and myself, everything, thanks and embracing we have plenty of time to lose."

The two friends, recalled by d'Artagnan to what was also due to Porthos, pressed his hand in their turn.

"And now," said Athos, "it is not our plan to run by hazard, and like madmen; but we must arrange some plan. What shall we do?"

"We are going to reach the nearest sea-port, unite our little resources, hire a vessel, and return to France. As for me, I will give my last *sou* for it. Life is the greatest treasure, and speaking candidly, ours is only held by a thread."

"What do you say to this, du Vallon?"

"I," said Porthos, "I am entirely of d'Artagnan's opinion; England is a measly place."

A glance was exchanged between Athos and Aramis.

"Go, then, my friends," said the former, sighing.

"How, go then?" exclaimed d'Artagnan. "Let us go, you mean."

"No, my friend," said Athos, "you must leave us. You can, and you ought, to return to France; your mission is accomplished, but ours is not."

"Your mission is not accomplished!" exclaimed d'Artagnan, looking in astonishment at Athos.

"No, my good fellow," replied Athos, in his gentle, but decided voice, "we came here to defend King Charles; we have but ill defended him; it remains for us to save him."

"To save the King?" said d'Artagnan, looking at Aramis as he had looked at Athos.

Aramis contented himself by making a sign with his head.

D'Artagnan's countenance took an expression of the deepest compassion; he began to think he had to do with two madmen.

"You cannot be speaking seriously, Athos?" said he; "the King is surrounded by an army, which is conducting him to London. This army is commanded by a butcher, or the son of a butcher—it matters little—Colonel Harrison. His majesty, I can assure you, is about to be tried on his arrival in London; I have heard enough from the lips of Mr. Oliver Cromwell to know what to expect."

A second look was exchanged between Athos and Aramis.

"And when his trial is ended, there will be no delay in putting the sentence into execution," continued d'Artagnan.

"And to what penalty do you think the King willl be condemned?" asked Athos.

"To the penalty of death, I much fear; they have gone too far for him to pardon them, and there is nothing left to them but one thing, and that is to kill him."

"There is the more reason why we must not abandon the august head so threatened."

"Athos, you are becoming mad."

"Well, you know beforehand that you must perish!" said d'Artagnan.

"We fear so, and our only regret is, to die so far from you both."

"What will you do in a foreign land, an enemy's country?"

"I have traveled in England when young; I speak English like an Englishman; and Aramis, too, knows something of the language. Ah! if we had you, my friends! With you, d'Artagnan, with you, Porthos—all four, and reunited for the first time in twenty years—we would dare, not only England, but the three kingdoms together!"

"And did you promise the Queen," resumed d'Artagnan, petulantly, "to storm the Tower of London, kill a hundred thousand soldiers, to fight victoriously against the wishes of a nation and the ambition of a man, and that man Cromwell? Do not exaggerate your duty. In Heaven's name, my dear Athos, do not make a useless sacrifice. When I see you merely, you look like a reasonable being; when you speak, I seem to have to do with a madman. Come, Porthos, join me; say, frankly what do you think of this business?"

"Nothing good," replied Porthos.

"Come," continued d'Artagnan, irritated, that instead of listening to him, Athos seemed to be attending to his own thoughts, "you have never found yourself the worse for my advice. Well, then, believe me, Athos, your mission is ended, and ended nobly; return to France with us."

"Friend," said Athos, "our resolution is unchangeable."

"Then you have some other motive unknown to us?"

Athos smiled, and d'Artagnan struck his heels in anger, and muttered the most convincing reasons that he could discover; but to all these reasons Athos contented himself by replying with a calm, sweet smile, and Aramis by nodding his head.

"Very well," cried d'Artagnan at last, furious; "very well, since you wish it, let us leave our bones in this beggarly land, where it is always cold; where the fine weather comes after a fog, and a fog after a rain, and the rain after the deluge; where the sun represents the moon, and the moon a cream cheese; in truth, whether we die here or elsewhere, matters little, since we must die."

"But your future career, d'Artagnan?—your ambition, Porthos?"

"Our future, our ambition!" replied d'Artagnan, with feverish volubility; "need we think of that since we are to save the King? The King saved, we shall assemble our friends together; we will head the Puritans; re-conquer England; we shall re-enter London and place him securely on his throne——"

"And he will make us dukes and peers," said Porthos, whose eyes sparkled with joy at this imaginary prospect.

"Or he will forget us," added d'Artagnan sagely.

"Well! then," said Athos, offering his hand to d'Artagnan.

" 'Tis settled," replied d'Artagnan. "I find England a charming country, and I stay, but only on condition that I am not forced to learn English."

"Well, then, now," said Athos, triumphantly, "I swear to you, my friend, by the God who hears us, I believe that there is a power watching over us, and we shall all four meet in France."

"So be it!" said d'Artagnan, "but I—I confess I have quite a contrary conviction."

"But which in the meantime saves the country," added Athos.

"Well, now that everything is decided," cried Porthos, rubbing his hands, "suppose we think of dinner! It seems to me that in the most critical positions of our lives we have always dined."

"Oh! yes, speak of dinner in a country where for a feast they eat boiled mutton, and where as a treat they drink beer. What the devil did you come to such a country for, Athos? But, I forgot," added the Gascon, smiling, "pardon, I forgot you are no longer Athos; but never mind, let us hear your plan for dinner, Porthos."

"My plan!"

"Yes; have you a plan?"

"No! I am hungry, that is all."

"If that is all, I am hungry, too; but it is not everything to be hungry; one must find something to eat, unless we browse on the grass, like our horses——"

"But," suggested d'Artagnan, "have we not our friend Mousqueton, he who managed for us so well at Chantilly, Porthos?"

"Indeed," said Porthos, "we have Mousqueton, but since he has been steward, he has become very dull; never mind, let us call him," and to make sure that he would reply agreeably, "Here! *Mouston,*" called Porthos.

Mousqueton appeared, with a piteous face.

"What is the matter, my dear M. Mouston?" asked d'Artagnan. "Are you ill?"

"Sir, I am very hungry!" replied Mousqueton.

"Well, it is just for that reason that we have called you, my good M. Mouston. Could you not procure us a few of those nice little rabbits and some of those delicious partridges, of which you used to make fricassees at the hotel ——? Faith, I do not remember the name of the hotel."

"At the hotel of ——," said Porthos, "by my faith, nor do I remember it either."

"It does not matter; and a few of those bottles of old Burgundy wine, which cured your master so quickly of his sprain!"

"Alas! sir," said Mousqueton, "I much fear that what you ask for are very rare things in this frightful country, and I think we should do better to go and seek hospitality from the owner of a little house that we see at the extremity of the wood."

"What! is there a house in the neighborhood?" asked d'Artagnan.

"Yes, sir!" replied Mousqueton.

"Well, let us, as you say, go and ask a dinner from the master of the house. What is your opinion, gentlemen, and does not M. Mouston's suggestion appear to you full of sense?"

"Oh! oh!" said Aramis, "suppose the master is a roundhead."

"So much the better," replied d'Artagnan; "we will inform him of the capture of the King, and in honor of the news he will kill for us his white hens."

"But if he should be a cavalier?" said Porthos.

"In that case, we will put on an air of mourning, and we will pluck his black fowls."

"You are very happy," said Athos, laughing in spite of himself at the sally of the irresistible Gascon; "f r you see the bright side of everything."

"What would you have?" said d'Artagnan. "I come from a land where there isn't a cloud in the sky."

"It is not like this, then," said Porthos, stretching out his hand to assure himself whether the freshness which he had just felt on his cheek was not really caused by a drop of rain.

"Come, come," said d'Artagnan, "more reason why we should start on a journey; halloa, Grimaud!"

Grimaud appeared.

"Well, Grimaud, my friend, have you seen anything?" asked the Gascon.

"Nothing," replied Grimaud.

"Those idiots!" cried Porthos, "they have not even pursued us. Oh! if we had been in their place!"

"Yes, they are wrong," said d'Artagnan. "I would willingly have said two words to Mordaunt in this little Thebes. See what a nice place for bringing down a man properly."

"I think, decidedly, gentlemen," observed Aramis, "that the son is not so sharp as his mother."

"Stop!" replied Athos, "wait awhile, we have scarcely left him two hours ago; he does not know yet in what direction we came, nor where we are. We may say that he is not equal to his mother when we put foot in France, if we are not poisoned or killed before then."

"Meanwhile, let us dine," suggested Porthos.

And the four friends, guided by Mousqueton, took up the way

towards the house, already almost restored to their former gaiety; for they were now, as Athos had said, all four united and of one mind.

CHAPTER LVIII.

RESPECT TO FALLEN MAJESTY.

As our fugitives approached the house, they found the ground cut up, as if a considerable body of horsemen had preceded them. Before the door, the traces were yet more apparent; these horsemen, whoever they might be, had halted there.

"Egad!" cried d'Artagnan, "it is quite clear that the King and his escort have been here."

He pushed open the door, and found the first room empty and deserted.

"Well!" cried Porthos.

"I can see nobody," said d'Artagnan. "Aha, blood!"

At this word the three friends leapt from their horses, and entered. D'Artagnan had already opened the door of the inner room, and, from the expression of his face, it was clear that he there beheld some extraordinary object.

The three friends drew near and discovered a young man stretched on the ground, and bathed in a pool of blood. It was evident that he had attempted to regain his bed, but had not had the strength to do so.

The wounded man heaved a sigh. D'Artagnan took some water in the hollow of his hand, and threw it upon his face. The man opened his eyes, made an effort to raise his head, and fell back again. The wound was in the top of his skull, and the blood was flowing copiously.

Aramis dipped a cloth in some water, and applied it to the gash. Again the wounded man opened his eyes and looked in astonishment at these strangers, who appeared to pity him.

"You are among friends," said Athos, in English; "so cheer up, and tell us, if you have the strength to do so, what has happened."

"The King," muttered the wounded man, "the King is a prisoner."

"Make your mind easy," resumed Athos, "we are all faithful servants of his majesty."

"Is what you tell me true?" asked the wounded man.

"On our honor as gentlemen."

"Then I may tell you all. I am the brother of Parry, his majesty's valet."

Athos and Aramis remembered that this was the name by which Winter had called the man whom they had found in the passage of the King's tent.

"We know him," said Athos; "he never left the King."

"Yes, that is he; well, he thought of me, when he saw that the King was taken, and as they were passing before the house here, he begged in the King's name that they would stop, as the King was hungry. They brought him into this room, and placed sentinels at the doors and windows. Parry knew this room, as he had often been to see me when the King was at Newcastle. He knew that there was a trap door communicating with the cellar, from which one could get into the orchard. He made me a sign, which I understood, but the King's guards must have noticed it, and put themselves on their guard. I went out, as if to fetch wood, passed through the subterranean passage into the cellar, and while Parry was gently bolting the door, pushed up the board, and beckoned to the King to follow me. Alas! he would not. But Parry clasped his hands and implored him, and at last he agreed. I went on first, quite delighted. The King was a few steps behind me, when suddenly I saw something rise up in front of me, like a huge shadow. I wanted to cry out to warn the King, but at the same moment I felt a blow as if the house was falling on my head, and fell insensible. When I came to myself again, I was stretched in the same place. I dragged myself as far as the yard. The King and his escort were gone."

"And now what can we do for you?" asked Athos.

"Help me to get onto the bed; that will ease me."

They helped him onto the bed, and, calling Grimaud to dress his wound, returned to the outer room to consult, having no appetite.

"Now," said Aramis, "we know how the matter stands. The King and his escort have gone this way; we had better take the opposite direction, eh?"

"Yes," said Porthos; "if we follow the escort we shall find everything devoured, and die of hunger. What a confounded country this England is! This is the first time I shall have lost my dinner, and it's my best meal."

"What do you say about it, d'Artagnan?" said Athos.

"Just the contrary to Aramis."

"What! follow the escort?" cried Porthos, quite alarmed.

"No, but join them. They will never look for us among the Puritans!"

"A good idea," said Athos, "they will think we want to leave England, and will seek us in the ports. Meanwhile we shall reach London with the King, and, once there, it is not difficult to conceal one's self."

"I think I know what you want," replied Athos. "Winter took us to the house of a Spaniard, who, he said, had been naturalized in England by his new fellow-countrymen's guineas."

"Well, we must take every precaution."

"Yes, and among others, that of changing our clothes."

"Changing our clothes!" exclaimed Porthos. "I don't see why; we are very comfortable in those we have on."

"To prevent recognition," said d'Artagnan.

"But can you find your man?" said Aramis to Athos.

"Oh! to be sure, yes. He lives at the Bedford Tavern, Green Hall Street. Besides, I can find my way about the city with my eyes shut."

Athos was right. He went direct to the Bedford Tavern, and the host, who recognized him, was delighted to see him again with such worthy and numerous company.

Though it was scarcely daylight, our four travelers found the town in a great bustle, owing to the reported approach of Harrison and the King.

"Now," said d'Artagnan, "for the actual man. We must cut off our hair, that the populace may not insult us. As we no longer wear the sword of the gentleman, we may as well have the head of the Puritan. This, as you know, is the important point of distinction between the Covenanter and the Cavalier."

"We look hideous," said Athos.

"And smack of the Puritan to a frightful extent," said Aramis.

"My head feels quite cold," said Porthos.

"And as for me, I feel anxious to snuffle a sermon," said d'Artagnan.

"Now," said Athos, "that we cannot even recognize one another, and have, therefore, no fear of others recognizing us, let us go and see the King's entrance."

They had not been long in the crowd before loud cries announced the King's arrival. A carriage had been sent to meet him; and the gigantic Porthos, who stood a head above all the other heads, soon announced that he saw the royal equipage approaching. D'Artagnan raised himself on tip-toe, and as the carriage passed, saw Harrison at one window and Mordaunt at the other.

The next day, Athos, leaning out of his window, which looked upon the most populous part of the city, heard the Act of Parliament, which summoned the ex-king, Charles I., to the bar, publicly cried.

"The Parliament, indeed!" cried Athos. "Parliament can never have passed such an act as that."

"But," said Aramis, "if they dare to condemn their King, it can only be to exile or imprisonment."

D'Artagnan whistled a little air of incredulity.

"We shall see," said Athos, "for we shall go to the sittings, I presume."

"You will not have long to wait," said the landlord; "they begin to-morrow."

"So, then, they drew up the indictment before the King was taken?"

"Of course," said d'Artagnan; "they began the day he was sold."

"And you know," said Aramis, "that it was our friend Mordaunt who made, if not the bargain, at least the first overtures."

"And you know," added d'Artagnan, "that whenever I catch him, I kill him, this M. Mordaunt."

"And I, too!" exclaimed Porthos.

"And I, too!" added Aramis.

"Touching unanimity!" cried d'Artagnan; "which well becomes good citizens like us. Let us take a turn round the town, and imbibe a little fog."

"Yes," said Porthos, "it will be a change from the beer."

CHAPTER LIX.

THE TRIAL.

THE next morning King Charles I. was brought by a strong guard before the high court which was to judge him. All London crowded to the doors of the house. The throng was terrific; and it was not till after much pushing and some fighting that our four friends reached their destination. When they did so, they found the three lower rows of benches already occupied; but, as they were not anxious to be too conspicuous, all, with the exception of Porthos, who was anxious to display his red doublet, were quite satisfied with their places, the more so as chance had brought them to the centre of their row, so that they were exactly opposite the arm-chair prepared for the royal prisoner.

Towards eleven o'clock the King entered the hall, surrounded by guards, but wearing his head covered, and with a calm expression turned to every side with a look of complete assurance, as if he were there to preside at an assembly of submissive subjects, rather than to reply to the accusations of a rebel court.

The judges, being proud of having a monarch to humble, evidently prepared to employ the right they had arrogated to themselves, and sent an officer to inform the King that it was customary for the accused to uncover his head.

Charles, without replying a single word, turned his head in another direction, and pulled his felt hat over it. Then, when the officer was gone, he sat down in the arm-chair opposite the president, and lashed his boot with a little cane which he carried in his hand. Parry, who accompanied him, stood behind him.

D'Artagnan was looking at Athos, whose face betrayed all those emotions which the King, possessing more power over

himself, had chased from his own. This agitation, in one so
cool and calm as Athos, frightened him.

"I hope," he whispered to him, "that you will follow his
majesty's example and not get killed for your folly in this den."

"Set your mind at rest," replied Athos.

"Aha!" continued d'Artagnan, "it is clear that they are afraid
of something or other; for, look, the sentinels are being rein-
forced. They had only halberds before, and now they have
muskets. The halberds were for the audience in the area. The
muskets are for us."

"Thirty, forty, fifty, sixty-five men," said Porthos, counting
the reinforcements.

"Ah," said Aramis. "But you forget the officer."

D'Artagnan grew pale with rage. He had recognized Mordaunt, who, with bare sword, was marshalling the Musketeers
before the King, and opposite the benches.

"Do you think they have recognized us?" said d'Artagnan.
"In that case I should beat a retreat. I don't care to be shot
in a trap."

"No," said Aramis, "he has not seen us. He sees no one
but the King. How he stares at him,—the insolent dog! Does
he hate his majesty as much as he does us?"

"Oh," answered Athos, "we only carried off his mother, and
the King has spoiled him of his name and property."

"True," said Aramis; "but silence! the president is speaking
to the King."

"Stuart," Bradshaw was saying, "listen to the roll-call of
your judges, and address to the court any observations you
may have to make."

The King turned his head away, as if these words had not
been intended for him. Bradshaw waited, and, as there was
no reply, there was a moment of silence.

Out of the hundred and sixty-three members designated, there
were only seventy-three present, for the rest, fearful of taking
part in such an act, remained away.

The roll-call finished, the president ordered them to read the
act of accusation. Athos turned pale. A second time he was
disappointed in his expectation.

"I told you so, Athos," said d'Artagnan, shrugging his
shoulders. "Now pluck up your courage, and hear what this
gentleman in black is going to say about his sovereign, with
full licence and privilege."

Never had a more brutal accusation or meaner insults tar-
nished the kingly majesty.

At this moment the accuser concluded with these words:

"The present accusation is preferred by us in the name of
the English people."

At these words there was a murmur along the benches, and
a voice, stout and furious, thundered behind d'Artagnan.

"You lie," it cried, "and nine-tenths of the English people shudder at what you say."

This voice was Athos', as, standing up with outstretched arm, and quite out of his mind, he thus assailed the public accuser.

King, judges, spectators, all turned their eyes to the bench where the four friends were seated. Mordaunt did the same, and recognized the gentleman, around whom the three other Frenchmen were standing, pale and menacing. His eyes glittered with delight. He had discovered those to whose death he had devoted his life. A movement of fury called to his side some twenty of his musketeers, and, pointing to the bench where his enemies were,—"Fire on that row," he cried.

But, rapid as thought, d'Artagnan seized Athos by the middle of the body, and, followed by Porthos with Aramis, leapt down from the benches, rushed into the passages, and, flying down the staircase, was lost in the crowd without, while the muskets within were pointed on some three thousand spectators, whose piteous cries and noisy alarms stopped the impulse already given to bloodshed.

Mordaunt, pale, and trembling with anger, rushed from the hall, sword in hand, followed by six pikemen, pushing, inquiring, and panting in the crowd, and then, having found nothing, returned.

Quiet was at length restored.

"What have you to say in your defense?" asked Bradshaw of the King.

Then, rising with his head still covered, in the tone of a judge rather than a prisoner, Charles began.

"Before questioning me," he said, "reply to my question. I was free at Newcastle, and had there concluded a treaty with both houses. Instead of performing your part of this contract, as I performed mine, you bought me from the Scotch, not dear, I know, and that does honor to the economy of your government. But because you have paid the price of a slave, do you expect that I have ceased to be your King? No! To answer you would be to forget it. I shall only reply to you when you have satisfied me of your right to question me. To answer you would be to acknowledge you as my judges, and I only acknowledge you as my executioners." And in the midst of a death-like silence, Charles, calm, lofty, and with his head still covered, sat down again in his arm-chair.

"Why are not my Frenchmen here?" he murmured proudly, and turning his eyes to the benches where they had appeared for a moment; "they would have seen that their friend was worthy of their defense, while alive; and of their tears, when dead."

When the King reached the door, a long stream of people, who had been disappointed in not being able to get into the house, and to make amends, had collected to see him come out, stood on each side as he passed, many among them glaring on him with threatening looks.

"How many people," thought he, "and not one true friend." And as he uttered these words of doubt and depression within his mind, a voice near him said:

"Respect to fallen majesty."

The King turned quickly round, with tears in his eyes and heart. It was an old soldier of the guards, who could not see his King pass captive before him without rendering him this last homage. But the next moment the unfortunate man was nearly stunned with blows from the hilts of swords; and among those who set upon him the King recognized Captain Groslow.

"Alas!" said Charles, "that is a severe chastisement for a very slight fault."

He continued his way; but he had scarcely gone a hundred paces, when a dirty fellow, leaning between two soldiers, spit in the King's face. Loud roars of laughter and sullen murmurs rose together. The crowd opened and closed again, undulating like a stormy sea; and the King imagined that he saw shining in the midst of this living wave the bright eyes of Athos.

Charles wiped his face, and said, with a sad smile, "Poor wretch, for half-a-crown he would do as much to his own father."

The King was not wrong. Athos and his friends, again mingling with the throng, were taking a last look at the martyr King.

When the cowardly insulter had spat in the face of the captive monarch, Athos had grasped his dagger. But d'Artagnan stopped his hand, and in a hoarse voice cried, "Wait!"

Athos stopped. D'Artagnan, leaning on Athos, made a sign to Porthos and Aramis to keep near them, and then placed himself behind the man with the bare arms, who was still laughing at his own vile pleasantry, and receiving the congratulations of several others.

The man took his way towards the City. The four friends followed him. The man, who had the appearance of being a butcher, descended a little steep and isolated street, looking onto the river, with two of his friends. Arrived at the bank of the river, the three men perceived that they were followed, turned around, and looked insolently at the Frenchmen.

"Athos," said d'Artagnan, "will you interpret for me?"

At this, d'Artagnan walked straight up to the butcher, and touching him on the chest with the tip of his finger, said to Athos:

"Say this to him in English, 'You are a coward. You have insulted a defenseless man. You have sullied the face of your King. You must die.'"

Athos, pale as a ghost, repeated these words to the man, who seeing the unpleasant preparations that were making, fell into an attitude of defense. Aramis, at this movement, drew his sword.

"No," cried d'Artagnan, "no steel. Steel is for gentlemen."

And seizing the butcher by the throat,—

"Porthos," said he, "knock this fellow down for me with a single blow."

Porthos raised his terrible arm, which whistled through the air like a sling, and the heavy mass fell with a dull noise on the skull of the coward and broke it. The man dropped like an ox under the mallet. His companions, horror-struck, could neither move nor cry out.

"Tell them this, Athos," resumed d'Artagnan; " 'thus shall all die who forget that a fettered man wears a sacred head, and a captive King doubly his Lord's anointed.' "

The two men looked at the body of their companion, swimming in black blood; and then, recovering voice and legs together, ran shouting away.

"Justice is done," said Porthos, wiping his forehead.

"And now," said d'Artagnan to Athos, "do not have any doubts about me; I undertake everything that concerns the King."

CHAPTER LX.

WHITEHALL.

It was easy to foresee that the Parliament would condemn Charles to death. Political judgments are generally merely vain formalities, for the same passions which give rise to the accusations give rise also to the condemnation. Such is the terrible logic of revolutions.

Meanwhile, before our four friends could mature their plans, they determined to put every possible obstacle in the way of the execution of the sentence. To this end they resolved to get rid of the London executioner; for though, of course, another could be sent for from the nearest town, there would be still a delay of a day or two gained. D'Artagnan undertook this more than difficult task. The next thing was to warn Charles of the attempt about to be made to save him. Aramis undertook the perilous office. Bishop Juxon had received permission to visit Charles in his prison at Whitehall; Aramis resolved to persuade the bishop to let him enter with him. Lastly, Athos was to prepare, in every emergency, the means of leaving England.

The palace of Whitehall was guarded by three regiments of cavalry, and still more by the anxiety of Cromwell, who came and went, or sent his generals or his agents continually. Alone, in his usual room, lighted by two candles, the condemned monarch gazed sadly on the luxury of his past greatness, just as, at the last hour, one sees the image of life, milder and more brilliant than ever.

Parry had not quitted his master, and, since his condemnation, had not ceased to weep. Charles, leaning on a table, was gazing at a medallion of his wife and daughter; he was waiting first for Juxon, next for martyrdom.

"Alas!" he said to himself, "if I only had for a confessor one of those lights of the Church, whose soul has sounded all the mysteries of life, all the littleness of greatness, perhaps his voice would choke the voice that wails within my soul. But I shall have a priest of vulgar mind, whose career and fortune I have ruined by my misfortune. He will speak to me of God and of death, as he has spoken to many another dying man, not understanding that this one leaves his throne to a usurper and his children to starve."

And he raised the medallion to his lips.

It was a dull, foggy night. A neighboring church clock slowly struck the hour. The pale light of the two candles raised flickering phantoms in the lofty room. These phantoms were the ancestors of King Charles, standing out from their gilt frames. A profound melancholy had possessed itself of Charles. He buried his brow in his hands, and thought of all that was so dear to him, now to be left forever. He drew from his bosom the diamond cross which La Garretière had sent him by the hands of those generous Frenchmen, and kissed it, and remembered that she would not see it again till he was lying cold and mutilated in the tomb.

Suddenly the door opened, and an ecclesiastic, in episcopal robes, entered, followed by two guards, to whom the King waved an imperious gesture. The guards retired. The room resumed its obscurity.

"Juxon!" cried Charles, "Juxon, thank you, my last friend, you are come at a fitting moment."

The bishop looked anxiously at the man sobbing in the Inglenook.

"Come, Parry," said the King, "cease your tears."

"If it's Parry," said the bishop, "I have nothing to fear; so allow me to salute your majesty, and to tell him who I am, and for what I am come."

At this sight, and this voice, Charles was about to cry out, when Aramis placed his finger on his lips, and bowed low to the King of England.

"The chevalier!" murmured Charles.

"Yes, sire," interrupted Aramis, raising his voice, "Bishop Juxon, faithful chevalier of Christ, and obedient to your majesty's wishes."

Charles clasped his hands, amazed, stupefied to find that these foreigners, without other motive than that which their conscience imposed on them, thus combated the will of a people, and the destiny of a King.

"You!" he said, "you! how did you penetrate hither? If they recognize you, you are lost."

"Care not for me, sire; think only of yourself. You see, your friends are wakeful. I know not what we shall do yet, but four determined men can do much. Meanwhile, do not be surprised at anything that happens; prepare yourself for every emergency."

Charles shook his head.

"Do you know that I die to-morrow, at ten o'clock?"

"Something, your majesty, will happen, between now and then, to make the execution impossible."

At this moment, a strange noise, like the unloading of a cart, and followed by a shriek of pain, was heard beneath the window.

"What is this noise and this cry?" said Aramis, perplexed.

"I know not who can have uttered that cry," said the King, "but the noise is easily understood. Do you know that I am to be beheaded outside this window? Well, this wood, that you hear fall, is the posts and planks to build my scaffold. Some workmen must have been hurt in unloading them."

Aramis shuddered in spite of himself.

"You see," said the King, "that it is useless for you to resist. I am condemned; leave me to my death."

"My King," said Aramis, "they may well raise a scaffold, but at this hour, the headsman is removed by force or persuasion. The scaffold will be ready by to-morrow, but the headsman will be wanting, and they will put it off till the day after to-morrow."

"What then?" said the King.

"To-morrow night we shall rescue you."

"Oh! sir," cried Parry, "may you and yours be blessed!"

"I know nothing about it," continued Aramis, "but the sharpest, bravest, and most devoted of us four, said to me, when I left him, 'Knight, tell the King, that to-morrow, at ten o'clock at night, we shall carry him off.' He has said it, and will do it."

"You are really wonderful men," said the King; "take my hand, knight, it is that of a friend, who will love you to the last."

Aramis stooped to kiss the King's hand, but Charles clasped his and pressed it to his heart.

The King accompanied him to the door, where Aramis pronounced his benediction upon him, and, passing through the ante-rooms, filled with soldiers, jumped into his carriage, and drove to the bishop's palace. Juxon was waiting for him impatiently.

Aramis resumed his own attire, and left Juxon with the notification that he might again have recourse to him.

He had scarcely gone ten yards in the street, when he perceived that he was followed by a tall man, wrapped in a large cloak. He placed his hand on his dagger, and stopped. The man came straight towards him. It was Porthos.

"My dear friend," cried Aramis.

"You see, we had each our mission," said Porthos; "mine was to guard you, and I was doing so. Have you seen the King?"

"Yes, and all goes well."

"We are to meet our friends at the tavern, at eleven."

It was then striking half-past ten by St. Paul's.

Arrived at the hotel, it was not long before Athos entered. "All's well," he cried, as he entered; "I have hired a cutter, as narrow as a canoe, and as light as a swallow. It is waiting for us, opposite the Isle of Dogs, manned by a captain and four men, who, for the sum of fifty pounds sterling, will keep themselves at our call three successive nights. Once on board, we drop down the Thames, and, in two hours, are in the open sea. In case I am killed, the captain's name is Rogers, and the bark is called the 'Lightning.' A handkerchief, knotted at the four corners, is to be the token."

The next moment d'Artagnan entered.

"Empty your pockets," said he, "I want a hundred pounds, and as for my own——" and he emptied them inside out.

The sum was collected in a minute. D'Artagnan ran out, and returned directly after.

"There," said he, "it's done. Whew! but not without a deal of trouble, too."

"Has the executioner left London?" said Aramis.

"No, he is in the cellar, our landlord's. Mousqueton is sitting on the doorstep, and here's the key."

"Bravo!" said Aramis; "but how did you manage it?"

"Like everything else—with money; it cost me five hundred pounds. The Queen's famous diamond," answered d'Artagnan with a sigh.

"Ah! true," said Aramis, "I recognized it on your finger."

"You bought it back, then, from M. Essarts?" asked Porthos.

"Yes, but it was fated that I should not keep it."

"Well, so much for the executioner," said Athos; "but unfortunately, every executioner has his assistant, his man, or whatever you call him."

"And this one had his," said d'Artagnan; "but, as good luck would have it, just as I thought I should have two affairs to manage, my friend was brought home with a broken leg. In the excess of his zeal, he had accompanied the cart containing the scaffolding as far as the King's window, and one of the planks fell on his leg and broke it."

"Ah!" cried Aramis, "that accounts for the cry that I heard."

"Probably," said d'Artagnan; "but as he is a thoughtful

young man, he promised to send four expert workmen in his place to help those already at the scaffold, and wrote, the moment he was brought home, to Master Tom Lowe, a carpenter and friend of his, to go down to Whitehall, with three of his mates. Here's the letter he sent by a messenger for sixpence, who sold it to me for a guinea."

"And what on earth are you going to do with it?" asked Athos.

"Can't you guess, my dear Athos? You, who speak English like John Bull himself, are Master Tom Lowe, we, your three mates. Do you understand now?"

CHAPTER LXI.

THE WORKMEN.

Towards midnight Charles heard a great noise beneath his window. It arose from blows of the hammer and hatchet, clinking of pincers and shrieking of saws.

Lying dressed upon his bed, this noise awoke him with a start, and found a gloomy echo in his heart. He could not endure it, and sent Parry to ask the sentinel to beg the workmen to strike more gently, and not disturb the last slumber of one who had been their King. .The sentinel was unwilling to leave his post, but allowed Parry to pass.

Arriving at the window, Parry found an unfinished scaffold, over which they were nailing a covering of black serge. Raised to the height of twenty feet, so as to be on a level with the window, it had two lower stories. Parry, odious as was this sight to him, sought for those among some eight or ten workmen, who were making the most noise; and fixed on two men, who were loosening the last hooks of the iron balcony.

"My friends," said Parry, when he had mounted the scaffold and stood beside them, "would you work a little more quietly? The King wishes to get a sleep." One of the two, who was standing up, was of gigantic size, and was driving a pick with all his might into the wall, while the other, kneeling beside him was collecting the pieces of stone. The face of the first was lost to Parry in the darkness, but as the second turned round and placed his fingers on his lips, Parry started back in amazement.

"Very well," said the workman aloud in excellent English. "Tell your master that if he sleeps badly to-night, he will sleep sound to-morrow."

These blunt words, so terrible if taken literally, were received by the other workmen with a roar of laughter. But Parry withdrew, thinking he was dreaming.

"Sire," said he to the King, when he had returned, "do you

know who these workmen are who are making so much noise?"

"I! no, how would you have me know?"

Parry bent his head and whispered to the King, "It is the Count de la Fère and his friend."

"Raising my scaffold," cried the King, astonished.

"Yes, and at the same time making a hole in the wall."

The King clasped his hands, and raised his eyes to Heaven; then, leaping down from his bed, he went to the window, and pulling aside the curtain tried to distinguish the figures outside, but in vain.

Parry was not wrong. It was Athos whom he had recognized, and it was Porthos who was boring a breach through the wall.

This tunnel communicated with a low loft, the space between the floor of the King's room and the ceiling of the one below it. Their plan was to pass through the hole they were making into this loft, and cut out from below a piece of the flooring of the King's room, so as to form a kind of trap-door.

Through this the King was to escape the next night, and, hidden by the black covering of the scaffold, was to change his dress for a workman's, slip out with his deliverers, pass the sentinels, who would suspect nothing, and so reach the waiting vessel for him at Greenwich.

Day gilded the tops of the houses. The hole was finished, and Athos passed through it, carrying the clothes destined for the King, wrapped in a piece of black cloth, and the tools with which he was to open a communication with the King's room.

D'Artagnan returned to change his workman's clothes for his chestnut-colored suit, and Porthos to put on his red doublet. As for Aramis, he presented himself at the bishop's. Juxon consented the more readily to take him with him, as he would require an assistant priest, in case the King should wish to communicate. The bishop got into his carriage, and Aramis, more disguised by his pallor and sad countenance than by his deacon's dress, got in by his side. The carriage stopped at the palace door.

It was about nine o'clock in the morning. The King was already sanguine, but when he perceived Aramis his hope turned to joy.

"Oh! Juxon," said the King, seizing the bishop's two hands in his own, "promise that you will pray all your life for this gentleman, and for the other that you hear beneath your feet, and for two others again, who, wherever they may be, are vigilant, I am sure, for my salvation."

"Sire," replied Juxon, "you shall be obeyed."

Meanwhile, the miner underneath was heard working away incessantly, when suddenly an unexpectd noise resounded in the passage. Aramis seized the poker, and gave the signal to stop; the noise came nearer and nearer. It was that of a num-

ber of men steadily approaching. The four men stood motionless. All eyes were fixed on the door, which opened slowly, and
with a kind of solemnity.

A parliamentary officer, clothed in black, and with a gravity
that augured ill, entered, bowed to the King, and, unfolding a
parchment, read him the arrest which is usually made to
criminals before their execution.

"What is this?" said Aramis to Juxon.

Juxon replied with a sign which meant that he knew as little
as Aramis about it.

"Then it is for to-day?" asked the King.

"Was not your majesty warned that it was to take place this
morning?"

"Then I must die like a common criminal by the hand of the
London executioner?"

"The London executioner has disappeared, your majesty, but
a volunteer has offered his services instead. The execution
will therefore only be delayed long enough for you to arrange
your spiritual and temporal affairs."

A slight moisture on his brow was the only trace of emotion
that Charles evinced, as he learned these tidings. But Aramis
was livid. His heart ceased beating, he closed his eyes, and
leaned upon the table. Charles perceived it, and took his hand.

"Come, my friend," said he, "courage." Then he turned to
the officer. "Sir, I am ready. I have little to delay you. Firstly,
I wish to communicate, secondly, to embrace my children, and
bid them farewell for the last time. Will this be permitted
me?"

"Certainly," replied the officer, and left the room.

Aramis dug his nails into his flesh and groaned aloud.

"Oh, my Lord Bishop!" he cried, seizing Juxon's hands,
"where is God?"

"My son," replied the bishop with firmness, "you see Him
not, because the passions of the world conceal Him."

"Be seated, Juxon," said the King, falling upon his knees.
"I have now to confess to you. Remain, sir," he added to
Aramis, who had moved to leave the room, "Remain, Parry, I
have nothing to say that cannot be said before all."

Juxon sat down and the King, kneeling humbly before him,
began his confession.

CHAPTER LXII.

REMEMBER!

MEANWHILE, Athos, in his concealment, waited in vain the
signal to recommence his work. Two long hours he waited
in terrible inaction. A death-like silence reigned in the room
above. At last he determined to discover the cause of this

stillness. He crept from his hole, and stood, hidden by the black drapery, beneath the scaffold. Peeping out from the drapery, he could see the rows of halberdiers and Musketeers round the scaffold, and the first ranks of the populace, swaying and groaning like the sea.

"What's wrong?" he asked himself, trembling more than the cloth he was holding back. "The people are hurrying on, the soldiers under arms, and among the spectators I see d'Artagnan. What is he waiting for? What is he looking at? Good God! have they let the headsman escape?"

Suddenly the dull beating of muffled drums filled the square. The sound of heavy steps was heard above his head. The next moment the very planks of the scaffold creaked with the weight of an advancing procession, and the eager faces of the spectators confirmed what a last hope at the bottom of his heart had prevented him believing till then. At the same moment a well-known voice above him pronounced these words:

"Colonel, I wish to speak to the people."

Athos shuddered from head to foot. It was the King speaking on the scaffold. By his side stood a man wearing a mask, and carrying an ax in his hand, which he afterwards laid upon the block.

The sight of the mask excited a great amount of curiosity in the people, the foremost of whom strained their eyes to discover who it could be. But they could discern nothing but a man of middle height, dressed in black, apparently aged, for the end of a grey beard peeped out from the bottom of the mask which concealed his features.

The King's request had undoubtedly been acceded to by an affirmative sign, for, in firm, sonorous accents, which vibrated in the depths of Athos' heart, the King began his speech, explaining his conduct, and counselling them for the welfare of England.

He was interrupted by the clash of the ax grating on the block.

"Do not touch the ax," said the King, and resumed his speech.

At the end of his speech the King looked tenderly round upon the people. Then, unfastening the diamond ornament which the Queen had sent him, he placed it in the hands of the priest who accompanied Juxon. Then he drew from his breast a little cross set in diamonds, which, like the order, had been the gift of Henrietta Maria.

"Sir," said he to the priest, "I shall keep this cross in my hand till the last moment. You will take it from me when I am dead."

He then took his hat from his head, and threw it on the ground. One by one he undid the buttons of his doublet, took it off, and deposited it by the side of his hat. Then, as it was cold, he asked for his gown, which was brought to him.

All the preparations were made with a frightful calmness. One would have thought the King was going to bed, and not to his coffin.

"Will these be in your way?" he said to the executioner, raising his long locks; "if so they can be tied up."

Charles accompanied these words with a look designed to penetrate the mask of the unknown deathsman. His calm, noble gaze forced the man to turn away his head, and the King repeated his question.

"It will do," replied the man in a deep voice, "if you separate them across the neck."

"This block is very low; is there no other to be had?"

"It is the usual block," answered the man in the mask.

"Do you think you can behead me with a single blow?" asked the King.

"I hope to," was the reply. There was something so strange in these three words that everybody except the King, shuddered.

"I do not wish to be taken by surprise," added the King. "I shall kneel down to pray, do not strike then."

"When shall I strike?"

"When I shall lay my head on the block, and say 'Remember!' then strike stoutly."

"Gentlemen," said the King to those around him, "I leave you to brave the tempest, and go before you to a kingdom which knows no storms. Farewell."

Then he knelt down, made the sign of the cross, and lowering his face to the planks, as if he would have kissed them, said in a low tone, in French, "Count de la Fère, are you there?"

"Yes, your majesty," he answered, trembling.

"Faithful friend, noble heart," whispered the King, "I should not have been rescued. I have addressed my people, and I have spoken to God; last of all I speak to you. To maintain a cause which I believe sacred, I have lost the throne, and my children their inheritance. A million in gold remains: I buried it in the vaults of Newcastle Keep. You alone know that this money exists. Make use of it, then, whenever you think it will be most useful, for my eldest son's welfare. And now, farewell."

"Farewell, saintly, martyred majesty," lisped Athos, chilled with terror.

A moment's silence ensued, and then, in a full, sonorous voice, the King said, *"Remember!"*

He had scarcely uttered the word when a heavy blow shook the scaffold, and where Athos stood immovable a warm drop fell upon his brow. He reeled back with a shudder, and the same moment the drops became a black torrent.

Athos fell on his knees and remained some moments, as if bewildered or stunned. At last he arose, and taking his handkerchief, steeped it in the blood of the martyred King. Then, as the crowd gradually dispersed, he leapt do *i*n, crept from behind the drapery, gliding between two horses, mingled with the crowd, and was the first to arrive at the inn.

Having gained his room, he raised his hand to his forehead, and finding his fingers covered with the King's blood, fell down insensible.

CHAPTER LXIII.

THE MAN IN THE MASK.

THE snow was falling thick, and frozen. Aramis was the next to come in, and to discover Athos almost insensible. But at the first words he uttered, the count roused from the kind of lethargy into which he had sunk.

"Are you wounded?" cried Aramis.

"No, this is his blood. I was under the scaffold. I heard all. God preserve me from another such hour as I have just passed."

"Here is the order he gave me, and the cross I took from his hand; he desired they should be returned to the Queen."

"Then here's a handkerchief to wrap them in," replied Athos, drawing from his pocket the one he had steeped in the King's blood.

"Well, cheer up," said a loud voice from the staircase, which Porthos had just mounted. "We are all mortal, my poor friends."

"You are late, my dear Porthos."

"Yes, there were some pople on the way who delayed me. The wretches were dancing. I took one of them by the throat, and think I throttled him a little. Just then a patrol rode up. Luckily the man I had had most to do with for some minutes could not speak, so I took advantage of his silence to walk off."

"Have you seen d'Artagnan?"

"We got separated in the crowd, and I could not find him again."

"Oh!" said Athos, satirically, "I saw him. He was in the front row of the crowd, admirably placed for seeing; and, as on the whole, the sight was curious, he probably wished to stay to the end."

"Oh! Count de la Fère," said a calm voice, though hoarse with running, "is it you who slander the absent?"

This reproof stung Athos to the heart, but as the impression produced by seeing d'Artagnan foremost in a coarse, ferocious crowd had been very strong, he contented himself by replying:

"I do not calumniate you, my friend. They were anxious about you here, and I told them where you were."

So saying, he stretched out his hand, but the other pretended not to see it, and he let it drop again slowly by his side.

"Heigho! I am tired," sighed d'Artagnan, sitting down.

"Drink a glass of port," said Aramis, "it will refresh you."

"Yes, let us drink," said Athos, anxious to make it up by nobnobbing glasses with d'Artagnan, "let us drink and get away from this hateful country."

"You are in a hurry," said d'Artagnan.

"But what would you have us to do here, now that the King is dead?"

"Go, Count," replied d'Artagnan carelessly; "you see nothing to keep you a little longer in England. Well, for my part, I, a bloodthirsty ruffian, who can go and stand close to a scaffold, in order to have a better view of the King's execution, I remain."

Athos turned pale. Every reproach his friend made struck deeply into his heart.

"Hang it!" said Porthos, a little perplexed, "I suppose, as I came with you, I must leave with you. I can't leave you alone in this abominable country."

"Thanks, my worthy friend. So then I have a little adventure to propose to you when the count is gone. I want to find out who was the man in the mask, who so obligingly offered to cut the King's throat."

"A man in a mask!" cried Athos. "You did not let the executioner escape, then?"

"The executioner is still in the cellar, where, I presume, he has had a few words conversation with mine host's bottles. But you remind me. Mousqueton, let out your prisoner. All is over."

"But," said Athos, "who is the wretch who has dared to raise his hand against the King?"

"An amateur headsman," replied Aramis, "who, however, does not handle the ax amiss, as he hoped."

"Did you not see his face?" asked Athos.

"He wore a mask."

"But you, Aramis, who were close to him."

"I could see nothing but a grey beard under the bottom of the mask."

"Then it must be a man of some age."

"Oh!" said d'Artagnan, "that matters little. When one puts on a mask, it is not difficult to wear a beard under it."

"I am sorry I did not follow him," said Porthos.

"Well, my dear Porthos," said d'Artagnan, "that's the very thing which it came into my head to do."

Athos understood it all now.

"Forgive me, my friend," he said, offering his hand to d'Artagnan.

"Well," said d'Artagnan, "while I was looking on, the fancy took me to discover who this masked volunteer might be. Well, I looked about for Porthos, and as I did so, I saw near me a head which had been broken, but which, for better or worse, had been mended with black silk. 'Humph!' thought I, 'that looks like my cut; I fancy I must have mended that skull somewhere or other.' And in fact, it was that unfortunate Scotchman, Parry's brother, you know, on whom Groslow amused himself by trying his strength. Well, this man was making signs to another at my left, and turning round, I recognized the honest Grimaud. 'Hell ⌐!' said I to him. Grimaud turned round with a jerk, recognized me, and pointed to the man in the mask. 'Eh?' said he, which meant, 'Do you see him?' 'Aye!' I answered, and we perfectly understood one another. Well, everything finished you know how. The mob dispersed. I made a sign to Grimaud and the Scotchman, and we all three retired into a corner of the square. I saw the executioner return to the King's room, change his clothes, put on a black hat and a large cloak, and disappear. Five minutes later he came down the grand staircase."

"You followed him?" cried Athos.

"I should think so, but not without difficulty. Every minute he turned round, and thus obliged ·us to conceal ourselves. I might have gone up to him and killed him. But I am not selfish; and I thought it might console you all a little to have a share in the matter. So we followed him through the lowest streets in the city, and, in half an hour's time, he stopped before a small, lonely house. Grimaud drew out a pistol. 'Eh?' said he, showing it. I held back his arm. The man in the mask stopped before a low door, and drew out a key; but before he placed it in the lock, he turned round to see if he was not followed. Grimaud and I had got behind a tree, and the Scotchman having nowhere to hide himself, threw himself on his face in the road. Next moment the door opened, and the man disappeared. I placed the Scotchman at the door by which he entered, making a sign to follow the man wherever he might go, if he came out again. Then going round the house, I placed Grimaud at the other exit, and here I am. Our game is earthed. Now for the death!"

Athos threw himself into d'Artagnan's arms.

"Humph!" said Porthos, "Don't you think the executioner might be Master Cromwell himself, who, to make sure of the affair, undertook it himself?"

"Ah! just so. Cromwell is stout and short, and this man thin and lank, and rather tall than otherwise."

"Some condemned soldier, perhaps," suggested Athos, "whom they have pardoned at the price of this deed."

"No, no," continued d'Artagnan. "It is not the measured step of a foot-soldier, nor the easy gait of a horseman. If I am not mistaken, it was a gentleman's walk."

"A gentleman!" exclaimed Athos. "Impossible! It would be a disgrace to his whole family."

"Fine sport, by Jove!" cried Porthos, with a laugh that shook the windows. "Fine sport!"

"Swords!" cried Aramis, "swords! and let us not lose a moment."

The four friends resumed their own clothes, girded on their swords, ordered Mousqueton and Blaisois to pay the bill, and to arrange everything for immediate departure, and, wrapped in their large cloaks, left in search of their game.

The night was dark, the snow still falling, and the streets deserted. D'Artagnan led the way through the intricate windings and narrow alleys of the city, and ere long they had reached the house in question. For a moment d'Artagnan thought that Parry's brother had disappeared; but he was mistaken. The robust Scotchman, accustomed to the snows of his native hills, had stretched himself against a post, and like a fallen statue, insensible to the inclemencies of the weather, had allowed the snow to cover him. He rose, however, as they approached.

"Come," said Athos, "here's another good servant. Really, honest men are not so scarce as I thought."

"Don't be in a hurry to weave crowns for our Scotchman. I believe the fellow is here for his own hatred; for I have heard that these gentlemen, born beyond the Tweed, are very vindictive. I should not like to be Groslow, if he meets him."

"Well?" said Athos to the man in English.

"No one has come out," he replied.

"Then Porthos and Aramis, will you remain with this man, while we go round to Grimaud?"

Grimaud had made himself a kind of sentry-box out of a hollow willow, and as they drew near, he put his head out and gave a low whistle.

"Eh!" said Athos.

"Aye," replied Grimaud.

"Well, has anybody come out?"

"No, but a man has gone in."

"At the same time he pointed to a window, through the shutters of which a faint light streamed.

They turned round the house to fetch Porthos and Aramis, "Have you seen anything?" they asked.

"No, but we are going to," replied d'Artagnan, pointing to Grimaud, who had already climbed some five or six feet from the ground.

All four came up together. Grimaud continued to climb like a cat, and succeeded at last in catching hold of a hook which served to keep one of the shutters back when opened. Then resting his foot on a small ledge, he made a sign to show that he was all right.

"Well?" asked d'Artagnan.

Grimaud showed his closed hand, with two fingers spread out.

"Speak," said Athos; "we cannot see your signs. How many are they?"

"Two. One opposite to me, the other with his back to me."

"Good. And the man opposite to you is ——?"

"The man I saw go in."

"Short and stout. General Cromwell."

The four friends looked at one another.

"And the other?" asked Athos.

"Thin and lank."

"The executioner," said d'Artagnan and Aramis at the same time.

"I can see nothing but his back," resumed Grimaud. "But wait. He is moving; and if he has taken off his mask I shall be able to see. Ah!——"

And, as if struck in the heart, he let go the hook, and dropped with a groan.

"Did you see him?" they all asked.

"Yes," said Grimaud, with his hair standing on end.

"The thin and spare man, the executioner, it is he," murmured Grimaud, pale as death, and seizing his master's hand.

"Who? He?" asked Athos.

"Mordaunt!" replied Grimaud.

"D'Artagnan, Porthos, and Aramis uttered a cry of joy."

Athos stepped back, and passed his hand over his brow.

"Fatality!" he muttered.

CHAPTER LXIV.

CROMWELL'S PRIVATE HOUSE.

It was, indeed, Mordaunt, whom d'Artagnan followed, without knowing it. On entering the house he had taken off his mask and the false beard, and mounting a staircase, had opened a door, and in a room lighted by a single lamp, found himself face to face with a man seated behind a desk.

This man was Cromwell.

Cromwell had two or three of these retreats in London, unknown except to the most intimate of his friends. Now Mordaunt was among these.

"It is you, Mordaunt," he said. "You are late."

"General, I wished to see the ceremony to the end, which delayed me."

"Ah! I scarcely thought you were so curious as that."

"I am always curious to see the downfall of your honor's enemies, and that one was not among the least of them. But you, general, were you not at Whitehall?"

"No," said Cromwell. "I only know that there was a conspiracy to rescue the King."

"Ah, you knew that," said Mordaunt.

"It matters little. Four men, disguised as workmen, were

to get the King out of prison, and take him to Greenwich, where a cutter was waiting."

"And, knowing all that, your honor remained here, far from the city, calm and inactive?"

"Calm? yes," replied Cromwell. "But who told you I was inactive?"

"I thought your excellency considered the death of Charles I. as a misfortune necessary to the welfare of England?"

"Yes, his death; but it would have been better not on the scaffold."

"Why so?" asked Mordaunt.

Cromwell smiled. "Because it could have been said that I had had him condemned for the sake of justice, and had let him escape out of pity."

"But if he had escaped?"

"Impossible; my precautions were taken."

"And does your honor know the four men who undertook to rescue him?"

"The four Frenchmen, of whom two were sent by the Queen to her husband, and two by Mazarin to me."

"And do you think Mazarin commissioned them to act as they have done?"

"It is possible. But he will not avow it because they have failed."

"Your honor gave me two of these Frenchmen when they were only fighting for Charles I. Now that they are guilty of a conspiracy against England, will your honor give me all four of them?"

"Take them," said Cromwell.

Mordaunt bowed with a smile of triumphant ferocity.

"Where were you placed?"

Mordaunt tried for a moment to read in the General's face if this was simply a useless question, or whether he knew everything. But his piercing eye could not penetrate the sombre depths of Cromwell's.

"I was placed so as to hear and see everything," he answered.

It was now Cromwell's turn to look fixedly at Mordaunt, and Mordaunt's to make himself impenetrable.

"It appears," said Cromwell, "that this volunteer executioner did his duty very well. The blow, so they told me at least, was struck with a master's hand."

Mordaunt remembered that Cromwell had told him he had had no detailed account, and he was now quite convinced that the general had been present at the execution, hidden behind some curtain or screen.

"Perhaps it was some one in the trade?" said Cromwell.

"Do you think so, sir? It might have been some personal enemy of the King, who made a vow of vengeance, and accomplished it in this manner."

"Possibly."

"And if that were the case, would your honor condemn his action?"

"It is not for me to judge. It rests between him and God."

"But if your honor knew this man?"

"I neither know, nor wish to know him. Provided Charles is dead, it is the ax, not the man, we must thank."

"And yet, without the man, the King would have been rescued."

Cromwell smiled.

"They would have carried him to Greenwich," he said, "and put him on board a skiff, with five barrels of powder in the hold. Once out at sea, you are too good a politician not to understand the rest, Mordaunt."

"Yes, they would all have been blown up."

"Just so. The explosion would have done what the ax had failed to do. They would have said that the King had escaped human justice, and been overtaken by God's arm. You see now why I did not care to know your gentleman in a mask."

Mordaunt bowed humbly. "Sir," he said, "you are a profound thinker, and your plan was sublime."

"Say absurd, since it is become useless. The only sublime ideas in politics, are those which bear fruit. So, to-night, Mordaunt, go to Greenwich, and ask for the captain of the skiff 'Lightning.' Show him a white handkerchief knotted at the four corners, and tell the crew to disembark, and carry the powder back to the Arsenal, unless indeed——"

"Unless?"

"This skiff might be of use to you for your personal projects."

"Oh, my lord, my lord!"

"That title," said Cromwell, laughing, "is all very well here, but take care a word like that does not escape in public."

"But your honor will soon be called so generally."

"I hope so, at least," said Cromwell, rising and putting on his cloak.

"Then," said Mordaunt, "your honor gives me full power?"

"Certainly."

"Thank you, thank you."

Cromwell turned as he was going.

"Are you armed?" he asked.

"I have my sword."

"And no one waiting for you outside?"

"No."

"Then you had better come with me."

"Thank you, sir, but the way by the subterranean passage would take me too much time, and I have none to lose."

Cromwell placed his hand on a hidden handle, and opened a door so well concealed by the tapestry, that the most practiced eye could not have discovered it, and which closed after him with a spring. This door communicated with a subterranean passage, leading under the street to a grotto in the garden of a house about a hundred yards from that of the future Lord Protector.

It was just before this that Grimaud had perceived the two men seated together.

D'Artagnan was the first to recover from his surprise.

"Mordaunt," he cried, "thank Heaven!"

"Yes," said Porthos, "let us knock the door in, and fall upon him."

"No," replied d'Artagnan, "no noise. Now, Grimaud, you come here, climb up to the window again, and tell us if Mordaunt is alone, and whether he is preparing to go out or to go to bed. If he comes out, we shall catch him. If he stays in, we will break in the window. It is easier and less noisy than the door."

Grimaud began to scale the wall again.

"Keep guard at the other door, Athos and Aramis. Porthos and I will stay here."

The friends obeyed.

"He is alone," said Grimaud.

"We did not see his companion come out."

"He may have gone by the other door."

"What is he doing?"

"Putting on his cloak and gloves."

"He is ours," muttered d'Artagnan.

Porthos mechanically drew his dagger from the scabbard.

"Put it up again, my friend," said d'Artagnan. "We must proceed in an orderly manner."

"Hush!" said Grimaud, "he is coming out. He has put out the lamp. I can see nothing now."

"Get down then, get down."

Grimaud leapt down, and the snow deadened the noise of his fall.

"Now, go and tell Athos and Aramis to stand on each side of their door, and clap their hands if they catch him. We will do the same."

The next moment the door opened, and Mordaunt appeared on the threshold, face to face with d'Artagnan. Porthos clapped his hands, and the other two came running round. Mordaunt was livid, but he uttered no call for assistance. D'Artagnan quietly pushed him in again, and by the light of a lamp on the staircase made him ascend the steps backward one by one, keeping his eyes all the time on Mordaunt's hands, who, however, knowing that it was useless, attempted no resistance. At last they stood face to face in the very room where ten minutes before Mordaunt had been talking to Cromwell.

Porthos came up behind, and unhooking the lamp on the

staircase re-lit that in the room. Athos and Aramis entered last and locked the door after them.

"Oblige me by taking a seat," said d'Artagnan, pushing a chair towards Mordaunt, who sat down, pale but calm. Aramis, Porthos, and d'Artagnan drew their chairs near him. Athos alone kept away, and sat in the furthest corner of the room, as if determined to be merely a spectator of the proceedings. He seemed to be quite overcome. Porthos rubbed his hands in feverish impatience. Aramis bit his lips till the blood came. D'Artagnan alone was calm, at least in appearance.

"M. Mordaunt," he said, "since after running after one another so long, chance has at last brought us together, let us have a little light conversation, if you please.

CHAPTER LXV.

THE LIGHT CONVERSATION.

THOUGH Mordaunt had been so completely taken by surprise, and had mounted the stairs under the impression of utter confusion, when once seated he recovered himself, as it were, and prepared to seize any possible opportunity of escaping. His eye wandered to a long, stout sword on his flank, and he instinctively slipped it round within reach of his right hand.

D'Artagnan was waiting for a reply to his remark, and said nothing. Aramis muttered to himself, "We shall hear nothing but the usual commonplaces."

Porthos champed his moustache, muttering, "A good deal of ceremony here about crushing a viper." Athos shrank into his corner, pale and motionless as a bas-relief.

The silence, however, could not last forever. So d'Artagnan began:

"Sir," he said, with desperate politeness, "it seems to me that you change your costume almost as rapidly as I have seen the Italian mummers do, whom the Cardinal Mazarin brought over from Bergamo, and whom he doubtless took you to see, during your travels in France."

Mordaunt did not reply.

"Just now," d'Artagnan continued, "you are disguised—I mean to say, attired—as a murderer, and now——"

"And now I look very much like a man who is going to be murdered."

"Oh, sir," answered d'Artagnan, "how can you talk like that, when you are in the company of gentlemen, and have such an excellent sword at your side?"

"No sword is good enough to be of any use against four swords and four daggers."

"Well, that is scarcely the question. I had the honor of

asking you why you altered your costume. Surely the mask
and beard suited you very well, and as to the ax, I do not
think it would be out of keeping even at this moment."

"Because, remembering the scene at Armentières, I thought
I should find four axes for one, as I was to meet four executioners."

"Sir," replied d'Artagnan, in the calmest manner possible,
"you are very young; I shall therefore overlook your frivolous
remarks. What took place at Armentières, has no connection whatever with the present occasion. We could scarcely
have requested your mother to take a sword and fight with
us."

"Loho! It's only a duel then?" cried Mordaunt, as if disposed to reply at once to the provocation.

Porthos rose, always ready for this kind of exercise.

"Pardon me," said d'Artagnan. "Do not let us be in a hurry.
We will arrange the matter rather better. Confess, Monsieur
Mordaunt that you are anxious to kill some of us."

"Ah!" replied Mordaunt.

"Then, my dear sir, I am convinced that these gentlemen
return your kind wishes, and will be delighted to kill you also.
Of course they will do so as honorable gentlemen, and the best
proof I can furnish is this——"

So saying, he threw his hat on the ground, pushed back his
chair to the wall, and bowed to Mordaunt with true French
grace.

"At your service, sir," he continued. "My sword is shorter
than yours, it's true, but bah! I hope the arm will make up
for the sword."

"Halt!" cried Porthos, coming forward. "I begin, and that's
logic."

"Allow me, Porthos," said Aramis.

Athos did not move. You might have taken him for a statue.

"Gentlemen," said d'Artagnan, "you shall have your turn.
M. Mordaunt dislikes you sufficiently not to refuse you afterwards. You can see it in his eye. So pray keep your places,
like Athos, whose calmness is most laudable. Besides, we will
have no words about it. I have a particular business to settle
with this gentleman, and I shall and will begin."

Porthos and Aramis drew back disappointed; and, drawing
his sword, d'Artagnan turned to his adversary.

"Sir, I am waiting for you."

"And for my part, gentlemen, I admire you. You are disputing which shall fight me first, and you do not consult me
who am most concerned in the matter. I hate you all, but not
equally. I claim the right to choose my opponent. If you
refuse this right, you may kill me, for I shall not fight."

"It is but fair," said Porthos and Aramis, hoping he would
choose one of them.

"Well, then," said Mordaunt, "I choose for my adversary

the man who, not thinking himself worthy to be called Count de la Fère, calls himself Athos."

Athos sprang up, but after an instant of motionless silence, he said, to the astonishment of his friends, "M. Mordaunt, a duel between us is impossible. Give this honor to somebody else." And he sat down.

"Ah!" said Mordaunt with a sneer, "Here's one who shows the white feather."

"Zounds!" cried d'Artagnan, bounding towards him, "who says that Athos is afraid?"

"Let him go on, d'Artagnan," said Athos, with a smile of sadness and contempt.

"It is your decision, Athos?" resumed the Gascon.

"Yes, irrevocably."

"You hear, sir," said d'Artagnan, turning to Mordaunt, "choose one of us to replace the Count de la Fère."

"As long as I don't fight with him, it is the same to me with whom I fight. Put your names into a hat, and draw lots."

Aramis opened the chosen paper. It fell to d'Artagnan.

The Gascon uttered a cry of joy, and turning to Mordaunt,—

"I hope, sir," said he, "you have no objection to make."

"None whatever," replied the other, drawing his sword and resting the point on his boot.

The moment that d'Artagnan saw that his wish was accomplished, and his man would not escape him, he recovered his usual tranquility. He turned up his cuffs neatly, and rubbed the sole of his right boot on the floor, but did not fail, however, to remark that Mordaunt was looking about him in a singular manner.

"You are ready, sir?" he said at last.

"I was waiting for you, sir," said Mordaunt, raising his head and casting at his opponent a look impossible to describe.

"Well, then," said the Gascon, "take care of yourself, for I am not a bad hand at the rapier."

"Nor I either."

"So much the better. That sets my mind at rest. Defend yourself!"

"One minute," said the young man; "give me your word, gentlemen, that you will not attack me otherwise than one after the other."

"Is it to have the pleasure of insulting us that you say that, little serpent?"

"No, but to set my mind at rest, as you said just now."

"It is for something else than that, I imagine," muttered d'Artagnan, shaking his head doubtfully.

"On the honor of gentlemen," said Aramis and Porthos.

"In that case, gentlemen, have the kindness to retire into the corners, and leave us room. We shall want it."

"Yes, gentlemen," said d'Artagnan, "we must not leave this

person the slightest pretext for behaving badly, which, with all due respect, I fancy he is anxious to do."

This new show made no impression on Mordaunt. The space was cleared, the two lamps placed on Cromwell's desk, in order that the combatants might have as much light as possible; and the swords crossed.

D'Artagnan was too good a swordsman to trifle with his opponent. He made a rapid and brilliant feint which Mordaunt parried.

"Aha!" he cried, with a smile of satisfaction.

And without losing a minute, thinking he saw an opening, he thrust right in, and forced Mordaunt to parry a counter-quart so fine that the points of the weapons might have been held within a wedding ring.

This time it was Mordaunt who smiled.

"Ah, sir," said d'Artagnan, "you have a wicked smile. It must have been the devil who taught it to you."

Mordaunt replied by trying his opponent's weapon with an amount of strength which the Gascon was astonished to find in a form apparently so weak; but, thanks to a parry no less skillful than that which Mordaunt had just achieved, he succeeded in meeting his sword, which slid along his own without touching his breast.

Mordaunt rapidly sprang back a step.

"Ah, you lose ground, you are turning? Well, as you please. I even gain something by it, for I no longer see that wicked smile of yours. You have no idea what a false look you have, particularly when you are afraid. Look at my eyes and you will see what your looking-glass never showed you, a frank, and honorable countenance."

To this flow of words, not perhaps in the best taste, but characteristic of d'Artagnan, whose principal object was to divert his opponent's attention, Mordaunt did not reply, but, continuing to turn around, he succeeded in changing places with d'Artagnan.

He smiled more and more, and his smile began to make the Gascon anxious.

"Come, come," said d'Artagnan, "we must finish with this," and in his turn he pressed Mordaunt hard, who continued to lose ground, but evidently on purpose, and without letting his sword leave the line for a moment. However, as they were fighting in a room, and had not space to go on like that forever, Mordaunt's foot at last touched the wall, against which he rested his left hand.

"Ah! this time you cannot break away, my fine friend," exclaimed d'Artagnan. "Gentlemen, did you ever see a scorpion pinned to a wall? No. Well, then you shall see it now."

In a second d'Artagnan had made three terrible thrusts at Mordaunt, all of which touched but only pricked him. The three friends looked on panting and astonished. At last d'Ar-

tagnan, having got up too close, stepped back to prepare a
fourth thrust, but the moment when, after a fine, quick feint,
he was attacking as sharply as lightning, the wall seemed to
give way, Mordaunt disappeared through the opening, and d'Artagnan's sword, caught between the panels, shivered like glass.
D'Artagnan sprang back for the wall had closed again.

Mordaunt, while defending himself, had manœuvred so as
to reach the secret door by which Cromwell had left, had felt
for the handle with his left hand, turned it, and disappeared.

The Gascon uttered a furious imprecation, which was answered by a wild, menacing, blood-curdling laugh on the other
side of the iron panel.

"Help me, gentlemen," cried d'Artagnan, "We must break
in this door."

"He escapes us," growled Porthos, pushing his huge shoulder
against the hinges, but in vain. "S'blood, he escapes us."

"So much the better," muttered Athos.

"I thought as much," said d'Artagnan, wasting his strength
in useless efforts. "Zounds, I thought as much, when the
wretch kept moving around the room. I thought he was up to
some trick."

"It's a misfortune which his friend, the devil, sends us," said
Aramis.

"It's a piece of good fortune sent from Heaven," said Athos,
evidently pleased.

"Really!" said d'Artagnan, abandoning the attempt to burst
open the panel after several ineffectual attempts, "Athos, I
cannot imagine how you can talk to us in that way. You cannot understand the position we are in. In this kind of game,
not to kill, is to let one's self be killed. This wretched fellow
will be sending us a hundred Iron-sided beasts who will pick
us off like berries in this place. Come, come, we must be off.
If we stay here five minutes more, there's an end of us."

"Yes, you are right."

"But where shall we go?" asked Porthos.

"To the hotel, to be sure, to get our baggage and horses;
and from there, if it please God, to France, where, at least, I
understand the architecture of the houses."

So, suiting the action to the word, d'Artagnan thrust the remains of his sword into his scabbard, picked up his hat, and
ran down the stairs followed by the others.

CHAPTER LXVI.

THE LUGGER "LIGHTNING."

MORDAUNT glided through the subterranean passage, and going to the neighboring house, stopped to take breath.

"Good," said he, "a mere trifle. Scratches, that is all. Now to my work."

He walked on at a quick pace, till he reached a neighboring cavalry-barrack, where he happened to be known. Here he borrowed a horse, the best in the stables, and in a quarter of an hour was at Greenwich.

"'Tis well," said he, as he reached the river bank. "I am half an hour before them. Now," he added, rising in the stirrup, and looking about him, "which, I wonder, is the 'Lightning?'"

At this moment, as if to reply to his words, a man lying on a heap of cables rose and advanced a few steps towards him.

Mordaunt drew a handkerchief from his pocket, and tying a knot at each corner—the signal agreed upon—waved it in the air, and the man came up to him. He was wrapped in a large hooded cape, which concealed his form and partly his face.

"Do you wish to go on the water, sir?" said the sailor.

"Yes, just so. Along the Isle of Dogs."

"And perhaps you have a preference for one boat more than another. You would like one that sails rapidly——"

"As *lightning*," interrupted Mordaunt.

"Then mine is the boat you want, sir. I'm your man."

"I begin to think so, particularly if you have not forgotten a certain signal."

"Here it is, sir," and the sailor took from his coat a handkerchief, tied at each corner.

"Good; quite right!" cried Mordaunt, springing off his horse. "There is no time to lose; now have my horse taken to the nearest inn, and conduct me to your vessel."

"But," asked the sailor, "where are your companions? I thought there were four of you."

"Listen to me sir; I'm not the man you take me for; you are in Captain Rogers' post, are you not? under orders from General Cromwell? Mine, also, are from him!"

"Indeed, sir, I recognize you; you are Captain Mordaunt. Don't be afraid, you are with a friend. I am Captain Groslow. The general remembered that I had formerly been a naval officer, and he gave me the command of this expedition; has anything new occurred?"

"Nothing."

"I thought, perhaps, that the King's death——"

"It has only hastened their flight; in ten minutes they will, perhaps, be here. I am going to embark with you. I wish to aid in the deed of vengeance. All is ready, I suppose?"

"Yes."

"The cargo on board?"

"Yes—and we are carrying port wine to Antwerp, remember."

" 'Tis well. Look alive—they are coming."

They then went down to the Thames. A boat was fastened to the shore by a chain fixed to a stake. Groslow jumped in, followed by Mordaunt, and in five minutes they were quite away from that world of houses which then crowded the outskirts of London; and Mordaunt could discern the little vessel riding at anchor near the Isle of Dogs. When they reached the side of this lugger, Mordaunt, dexterous in his eager desire for vengeance, seized a rope, and climbed up the sides of the vessel with a coolness and agility very rare among landsmen. He went with Groslow to the captain's cabin of planks, for the chief apartment had been given up by Captain Rogers to the passengers, accommodated at the other end of the boat.

"They will have nothing to do with this side of the ship, then," said Mordaunt.

"That's a capital arrangement. Return to Greenwich, and bring them here. I shall hide in your cabin. You have a long boat?"

"That in which we came."

"It appeared light, and well-constructed. Fasten it astern with a painter; put the oars into it, so that it may follow in the track, and that there will be nothing to do except to cut adrift. Put a good supply of rum and biscuit in it for the seamen; should the night happen to be stormy, they will not be sorry to find something to console themselves with."

"All shall be done. Do you wish to see the powder magazine?"

"No; when you return, I will put the match myself, but be careful to conceal your face, so that you cannot be recognized by them."

"Never fear."

"There's ten o'clock striking, at Greenwich."

Groslow, then having given the sailor on duty an order to be on the watch with more than usual attention, went down into the long boat, and soon reached Greenwich. The wind was chilly, and the jetty was deserted as he approached it; but he had no sooner landed, than he heard a noise of horses galloping upon the paved road.

These horsemen were our friends, or rather a vanguard, composed of d'Artagnan and Athos. As soon as they arrived at the spot where Groslow stood, they stopped, as if guessing that he was the man they wanted. Athos alighted, and calmly opened the handkerchief tied at each corner, and unfolded it; whilst d'Artagnan, ever cautious, remained on horseback, one hand upon his pistol, leaning anxiously forward.

On seeing the appointed signal, Groslow, who had, at first, crept behind one of the cannon planted on that spot, walked straight up to the gentlemen. He was so well wrapt up in his cloak that it would have been impossible to have seen his face even if the night had not been so dark as to render any precaution superfluous; nevertheless, the keen glance of Athos perceived that it was not Rogers who stood before them.

"What do you want with us?" he asked of Groslow.

"I wish to inform you, my lord," replied Groslow, with an Irish accent, feigned of course, "that if you are looking for Captain Rogers you will not find him. He fell down this morning and broke his leg; but I am his cousin; he told me everything, and desired me to look out for, and to conduct you to any place named by the four gentlemen who should bring me a handkerchief tied at each corner, like that one which you hold, and one which I have in my pocket."

And he drew out the handkerchief.

"Was that all he said?" inquired Athos.

"No, my lord; he said you had engaged to pay seventy-five English pounds if I landed you safe and sound at Boulogne, or any other port you choose, in France."

"What do you think of all this?" said Athos, in a low tone to d'Artagnan."

"It seems a likely story to me. Besides, we can blow out his brains if he proves false," said the Gascon; "and you, Athos, you know something of everything, and can be our captain. I dare say you know how to navigate, should he fail us."

"My dear friend, you guess well; my father destined me for the navy, and I have some vague notions about navigation."

"You see!" cried d'Artagnan.

They then summoned their friends, who, with the servants, promptly joined them—leaving behind them Parry, who was to take their horses back to London; and they all proceeded instantly to the shore, and placed themselves in the boat, which, rowed by Groslow, began rapidly to clear the coast.

"At last!" exclaimed Porthos, "we are afloat."

"Alas!" said Athos, "we depart alone."

"Yes; but all four together, and without a scratch; which is a consolation."

"We are not yet arrived at our destination," observed the prudent d'Artagnan; "beware of stoppages."

"Ah! my friend!" cried Porthos; "like the crows, you always bring bad omens. Who could intercept us in such a night as this—pitch dark—when one does not see more than twenty yards before one?"

"Yes, but to-morrow morning——"

"To-morrow we shall be at Boulogne; however, I like to hear M. d'Artagnan confess that he's afraid."

"I not only confess it, but am proud of it," returned the Gascon; "I am not such a rhinoceros as you are. Oho! what's that?"

"The 'Lightning,' " answered the captain, "our lugger."

"Lo! we've arrived!" said Athos.

They went on board, and the captain instantly conducted them to the berth destined for them, a cabin which was to serve for all purposes, and for the whole party; he then tried to slip away under pretext of giving orders to some one.

"Stop a moment," cried d'Artagnan; "pray how many men have you on board, captain?"

"I don't understand," was the reply.

"Explain it, Athos."

Groslow, on the question being interpreted, answered:

"Three, without counting myself."

"Oh!" exclaimed d'Artagnan. "I begin to be more at my ease; however, whilst you settle yourselves, I shall make the round of the boat."

"As for me," said Porthos, "I will see to the supper."

"A very good deed, Porthos," replied the Gascon. "Athos, lend me Grimaud, who in the society of his friend Parry, has, perhaps, picked up a little English, and can act as my interpreter."

"Go, Grimaud," said Athos.

D'Artagnan, finding a lantern on the deck, took it up, and with a pistol in his hand, he said to the captain, in English, "Come" (being, with the usual English oath, the only English word he knew), and so saying, he descended to the lower deck,

This was divided into three compartments; one which was covered by the floor of that room in which Porthos, Athos, and Aramis were to pass the night; the second was to serve as the sleeping room for the servants; the third, under the prow of the ship, was underneath the temporary cabin in which Mordaunt was concealed.

"Oho!" cried d'Artagnan, as he went down the steps of the hatchway, preceded by the lantern; "what a number of barrels! one would think one was in the cave of the Forty Mines. What is there in them?" he added, putting his lantern on one of the bins.

The captain inclined to go upon deck again, but, controlling himself, he answered:

"Port wine."

"Ah! port wine! 'tis a comfort," said the Gascon, "that we shall not die of thirst; are they all full?"

Grimaud translated the question, and Groslow, who was wiping the perspiration from off his forehead, answered:

"Some full, others empty."

D'Artagnan rapped the barrels with his knuckles, and having ascertained that he spoke the truth, pushed his lantern, greatly to the captain's alarm, into the interstices between the barrels, and finding that there was nothing concealed in them, said:

"Come along," and he went towards the door of the second compartment.

"Stop!" said the Englishman. "I have the key of that door;" and he opened the door, with a trembling hand, into the second compartment, where Mousqueton and Blaisois were just going to supper.

Here there was evidently nothing to seek, or to reprehend and they passed rapidly to examine the third compartment.

This was the sailors' forecastle. Two or three hammocks hung up on the ceiling, a table and two benches, composed all the furniture. D'Artagnan pulled up two or three old sails, hung on the walls, and seeing nothing to suspect, regained, by the hatchway, the deck of the vessel.

"And this room?" he asked, pointing to the captain's cabin.

"That's my room," replied Groslow.

"Open the door."

The captain obeyed. D'Artagnan stretched out his arm, in which he held the lantern, put his head in at the half-opened door, and seeing that the cabin was nothing better than a shed, he said:

"Good! if there is an army on board, it is not here that it is hidden. Let us see what Porthos has found for supper." And thanking the captain, he regained the state cabin, where his friends were.

Porthos had found nothing; and fatigue had prevailed over hunger. He had fallen asleep, and was in a profound slumber when d'Artagnan returned. Athos and Aramis were beginning to close their eyes, which they half opened when their companion came in again.

"Well?" said Aramis.

"All is well; we may sleep tranquilly."

On this assurance the two friends fell asleep; and d'Artagnan, who was very weary, bade good-night to Grimaud, and laid himself down in his cloak, with a naked sword at his side, in such a manner that his body might barricade the passage, and that it should be impossible to enter the room without overturning him.

CHAPTER LXVII.

A NEW KIND OF PORT WINE.

IN ten minutes the masters slept, but not so the servants, hungry and uncomfortable.

"Grimaud," said Mousqueton to his companion, who had just come in after his round with d'Artagnan, "are you thirsty?"

"As thirsty as a Scotch!" was Grimaud's laconic reply.

He sat down and began to cast up the accounts of his party whose money he managed.

"Oh, law! I'm beginning to feel queer!" cried Blaisois.

"If that's the case," said Mousqueton, with a learned air, "take some nourishment."

"Do you call that nourishment?" asked Blaisois, pointing to the barley bread and the pot of beer.

"Blaisois," replied Mousqueton, "remember that bread is the true nourishment of a Frenchman, who is not always able to get that; ask Grimaud."

"Yes, but beer?" asked Blaisois, sharply; "is that their true drink?"

"As to that," answered Mousqueton, puzzled how to get out of the difficulty, "I must confess, that to me beer is as disagreeable as wine to the English."

"M. Mousqueton! what, do the English dislike wine?"

"They hate it."

"But I have seen them drink it."

"As a punishment; for example an English prince died one day because he was put into a butt of Malmsey. I heard the Chevalier d'Herblay say so."

"The fool!" cried Blaisois; "I wish I had been in his place."

"You can be," said Grimaud, writing down his figures.

"How?" asked Blaisois, "I can? Explain yourself."

Grimaud went on with his sum, and cast up the whole.

"Port!" he said, extending his hand in the direction of the first compartment examined by d'Artagnan and himself.

"How? those barrels I saw through the door?"

"Port!" replied Grimaud, who began a fresh sum.

"I have heard," said Blaisois, "that port is a very good wine."

"Excellent!" cried Mousqueton, smacking his lips.

"Supposing these Englishmen would sell us a bottle," said the honest Blaisois.

"Sell!" cried Mousqueton, about whom there was a remnant of his ancient maurauding character left. "One may well perceive, young man, that you are still inexperienced. Why buy when one can take?"

"To take?" answered Blaisois. "To covet one's neighbor's goods is forbidden, I believe."

"What a childish reason!" said Mousqueton, condescendingly; "yes, childish; I repeat the word. Where did you learn, pray, to consider the English as your neighbors?

"Had you been ten years engaged in war, as Grimaud and I have been, my dear Blaisois, you would know the difference that there is between the goods of others and the goods of your enemies. Now an Englishman is an enemy; as this port wine belongs to the English, therefore it belongs to us."

"And our masters?" asked Blaisois, stupefied by this harangue, delivered with an air of profound sagacity, "will they be of your opinion?"

Mousqueton smiled disdainfully.

"I suppose you think it necessary that I should disturb the repose of these illustrious lords to say, 'Gentlemen, your servant, Mousqueton, is thirsty.' What does M. de Bracieux care, think you, whether I am thirsty or not?"

"'Tis a very expensive wine," said Blaisois, shaking his head.

"Were it gold, M. Blaisois, our masters would not deny themselves this wine. Know that M. de Bracieux is rich enough to drink a ton of port wine, even if obliged to pay a pistole for every drop." His manner became more and more lofty every instant; then he arose, and after finishing off the beer at one draught, he advanced majestically to the door of the compartment where the wine was. "Ah! locked!" he exclaimed; "these devils of English, how suspicious they are!"

"Shut!" cried Blaisois; "ah, the deuce it is; unlucky, for I feel the sickness coming on more and more."

"Shut!" repeated Mousqueton.

"But," Blaisois ventured to say, "I have heard you relate, M. Mousqueton, that once on a time, at Chantilly, you fed your master and yourself with partridges which were snared, carps caught by a line, and wine drawn with a corkscrew."

"Perfectly true; but there was an air-hole in the cellar, and the wine was in bottles. I cannot throw the loop through this partition, nor move with a pack-thread a cask of wine which may, perhaps, weigh two hogsheads."

"No, but you can take off two or three boards of the partition," answered Blaisois, "and bore a hole in the cask with a gimlet."

Mousqueton opened his great, round eyes to the utmost, astonished to find in Blaisois qualities for which he did not give him credit.

"'Tis true," he said, "but where can I get a chisel to take the planks out or a gimlet to pierce a cask?"

"The tool-case!" said Grimaud, still balancing his accounts.

"Oh, yes!" said Mousqueton.

Grimaud, in fact, was not only the accountant, but the armorer of the party, and as he was a man full of forethought, his necessary case, carefully rolled up in his valise, contained every sort of tool for immediate use.

Mousqueton, therefore, was soon provided, and he began his task. In a few moments he had got out three pieces of board. He tried to pass his body through the aperture, but, not being like the frog in the fable, who thought he was larger than he really was, he found he must take out three or four more boards, before he could get through.

He sighed, and began to work again.

Grimaud had now finished his accounts. He arose, and stood near Mousqueton.

"I——" he said.

"What?" said Mousqueton.

"I pass——"

"True, you——" answered Mousqueton, casting a glance at the long, thin form; "you can pass, and easily, go in, then."

"Rinse the glasses," said Grimaud.

"Now," said Mousqueton, addressing Blaisois, "now you will see how we old campaigners drink when we are thirsty."

"My cloak," said Grimaud from the bottom of the hold, "stop up the hole with it."

"Why?" asked Blaisois.

"Simpleton!" exclaimed Mousqueton; "suppose any one came into the room."

"Ah, true!" cried Blaisois, with evident admiration; "but it will be dark in the hold."

"Grimaud always sees, dark or light—night as well as day," answered Mousqueton.

"Silence!" cried Grimaud, "some one is coming."

In fact, the door of the cabin was opened. Two men, wrapped in their cloaks, appeared.

"Oh, ho!" said they, "not in bed at a quarter past eleven. That's against all rules. In a quarter of an hour let every-one be in bed, and snoring."

These two men then went towards the compartment in which Grimaud was secreted; opened the door, entered, and shut it after them.

"Oh!" cried Blaisois; "he's lost!"

"Grimaud's a cunning fox," murmured Mousqueton.

They waited for ten minutes, during which time no noise was heard to indicate that Grimaud was discovered; and at the expiration of that anxious interval the two men returned, closed the door after them, and repeating their orders that the servants should go to bed, and extinguish the lights, disappeared.

At that very moment Grimaud drew back the cloak which hid the aperture, and came in with his face livid, his eyes staring wide open with terror, so that the pupil was contracted almost to nothing, with a large circle of white around it. He

held in his hand a tankard full of some substance or another;
and approaching the gleam of light shed by the lamp he uttered
this single monosyllable: "Oh!" with such an expression of
extreme terror that Mousqueton started, alarmed, and Blaisois
was near fainting from fright.

Both, however, cast an inquisitive glance into the tankard;
it was full of gunpowder.

Convinced that the ship was full of powder instead of having a cargo of wine, Grimaud hastened to awake d'Artagnan,
who had no sooner beheld him than he perceived that something extraordinary had taken place. Imposing silence, Grimaud put out the little night lamp, then knelt down, and poured
into the lieutenant's ear a recital melodramatic enough not to
require play of feature to give it force.

This was the pith of his story.

The first barrel that Grimaud had found on passing into the
cellar, he struck; it was empty. He passed on to another;
it was empty. He passed on to another; it was also empty;
but the third which he tried was, from the dull sound that it
gave out, evidently full. At this point, Grimaud stopped, and
was preparing to make a hole with his gimlet, when he found
a spigot, he therefore placed his tankard under it, and turned
the spout; something, whatever it was that the cask contained,
fell into the tankard.

Whilst he was thinking that he should first taste the liquor
which the tankard contained, before taking it to his companions, the door of the cellar opened, and a man with a lantern
in his hands, and enveloped in a cloak, came and stood just
before the barrel, behind which Grimaud, on hearing him come
in, instantly crept. This was Groslow. He was accompanied
by another man who carried in his hand something whitish,
long and flexible, rolled up, resembling a clothes-line.

"Have you the match?" asked the one who carried the lantern.

"Here it is," answered the other.

At the voice of this last speaker, Grimaud started, and felt
a shudder creeping through his very bones. He rose gently,
so that his head was just above the round of the barrel; and,
under the large hat, he recognized the pale face of Mordaunt.
"How long will this slow match burn?" asked this person.

"Nearly five minutes," replied the captain.

"Then tell the men to be in readiness; don't tell them why,
now; when the clock strikes a quarter after midnight collect
your men. Get down into the long boat."

"That is, when I have lighted the match?"

"I shall undertake that. I wish to be sure of my revenge;
are the oars in the canoe?"

"Everything is ready."

" 'Tis well."

Mordaunt knelt down and struck one end of the train in

the bunghole, in order that he might have nothing to do but set it on fire at the opposite end with the match.

"I understand it all perfectly, sir," replied Groslow; "but allow me to say, there is great danger in what you undertake; would it not be better to entrust one of the men to set fire to the train?"

"My dear Groslow," answered Mordaunt, "you know the proverb, 'if you want things done well, do them yourself!' I shall carry it out."

Grimaud had heard all this; had recognized the two mortal enemies of the Musketeers; had seen Mordaunt lay the train; then he felt, and felt again, the contents of the tankard that he held in his hand; and, instead of the liquid expected by Blaisois and Mousqueton, he felt beneath his fingers the grains of some coarse powder.

Mordaunt went away with the captain. At the door he stopped to listen.

"Do you hear how they sleep?" he said.

In fact, Porthos could he heard snoring through the partition.

" 'Tis God who gives them into our hands," answered Groslow.

"This time the devil himself shall not save them," rejoined Mordaunt.

And they went out together.

CHAPTER LXVIII.

CUT ADRIFT.

D'ARTAGNAN, as one may suppose, listened to all these details with a growing interest. He awoke Aramis, Athos, and Porthos; and then, stretching out his arms, and closing them again, the Gascon collected in one small circle the three heads of his friends, so near as almost to touch each other.

He then told them the bark was a mine; that they had Groslow for their captain, and Mordaunt acting under him as his lieutenant. Something more deathly than a shudder at this moment, shook the brave Musketeers. The name of Mordaunt seemed to exercise over them a mysterious and fatal influence to bring terror even at the very sound.

"What is to be done?" asked Athos.

D'Artagnan replied by going towards a porthole, just large enough to let a man through. He turned its lid gently on its hinges.

"There," he said, "is our road."

"The deuce—'tis very cold, my dear friend," said Aramis.

"Stay here, if you like, but I warn you, 'twill be rather too warm presently."

"But we cannot swim to the shore."

"The long boat is yonder, towed by the lugger; we can take possession of it, and cut the connection. Come, my friends."

"A moment's delay," said Athos; "our servants?"

"Here we are," they answered.

Meantime the three friends were standing motionless before the awful sight which d'Artagnan, in raising the shutters, had disclosed to them through the narrow opening of the window.

Those who have once beheld such a scene know that there is nothing more solemn, more striking than the raging sea, rolling, with its deafening roar, its dark billows, beneath the pale light of a wintry moon.

"Gracious Heaven! we are hesitating," cried d'Artagnan; "if we hesitate, what will the servants do?"

"I do not hesitate, you know," said Grimaud.

"Sir," interposed Blaisois, "I warn you that I cannot swim except in rivers."

"And I not at all," said Mousqueton.

But d'Artagnan had now slipped through the window.

"You have then decided, my friend?" said Athos.

"Yes," the Gascon answered; "Athos! you, who are a perfect being, bid the spirit to triumph over the body."

"Do you, Aramis, order the servants and Porthos to kill everyone who stands in your way."

And, after pressing the hands of Athos, d'Artagnan chose a moment when the ship tossed, so that he had only to plunge into the water up to his waist.

Athos followed him before the vessel rose again on the waves; the rope which tied the boat to the vessel was then seen plainly rising out of the sea.

D'Artagnan swam to it, and held it, suspending himself by this rope, his head alone out of the water.

In one second Athos joined him.

They then saw two other heads against the bend of the hull emerging—Aramis' and Grimaud's.

"I am uneasy about Blaisois," said Athos; "he can, he says, only swim in fresh water."

"When people can swim at all they can swim everywhere. To wherry."

"But Porthos? I do not see him."

"Porthos is coming; he swims like Leviathan."

Porthos, in fact, did not appear. Mousqueton and Blaisois had been appalled by the sight of the black gulf below them, and had shrunk back.

"Come along! I shall strangle you both if you don't get out," said Porthos, at last seizing Mousqueton by the throat.

"Forward! Blaisois."

A groan stifled by the grasp of Porthos, was all the reply of poor Blaisois, for the giant, taking him neck and heels, plunged him into the water head foremost, pushing him out by the window as if he had been a plank.

"Now, Mouston," he said, "I hope you don't mean to desert your master?"

"Ah, sir," replied Mousqueton, his eyes filling with tears, "why did you re-enter the army? We were so happy in the Château du Pierrefonds!"

And, without any other complaint, passive and obedient, either from true devotion to his master, or from the example set by Blaisois, Mousqueton went into the sea head foremost. A sublime action, at all events, for Mousqueton looked upon himself as dead. But Porthos was not a man to abandon an old servant; and when Mousqueton rose above the water, blinded, he found that he was supported by the large hand of Porthos, and that he could, without having occasion to move, advance towards the tow-line with the dignity of a sea-god.

In a few minutes, Porthos had rejoined his companions, who were already in the canoe; but when, after they had all got in, it came to his turn, there was great danger that in putting his huge leg over the edge of the boat he would have upset the little vessel. Athos was the last to enter.

"Are you all here?" he asked.

"Ah! have you your sword, Athos?" cried d'Artagnan.

"Yes."

"Cut the painter, then."

Athos drew a sharp poignard from his belt, and cut the cord. The lugger went on; the boat continued stationary, only tossed by the waves.

"We did it in high time, Athos!" said d'Artagnan, giving his hand to the count; "you are going to see something very funny."

CHAPTER LXIX.

FATALITY.

SCARCELY had d'Artagnan uttered these words than a whistle was heard resounding on the vessel, which now became dim in the fog and obscurity.

"That, you may be sure," said the Gascon, "that means something new."

They then, at the same instant, perceived a large lantern carried on a pole on the deck, defining the forms of shadows behind it.

Suddenly a terrible yell of despair was wafted through the space, and as if the shrieks of anguish had driven away the clouds, the veil which hid the moon was cleared away, and the grey sails and dark shrouds were outlined beneath the silvery gleam.

Shadows ran, bewildered, to and fro, on the deck, and mournful cries accompanied these delirious walkers. In the midst of these screams they saw standing on the rounded poop-deck, Mordaunt, with a torch in his hand.

The figures, apparently excited with terror, were Groslow, who, at the hour fixed by Mordaunt, had collected his men and the sailors. Groslow, after having listened at the door of the cabin to hear if the Musketeers were still asleep, had gone down into the cellar, convinced by the silence that they were all in a deep slumber. Then Mordaunt had opened the door, and run to the train; impetuous as a man who is excited by revenge and full of confidence—as are those whom God blinds—he had set fire to the slow-match.

All this while, Groslow and his men were assembled on deck.

"Haul in the painter, and draw the boat to us," said Groslow.

One of the sailors bestrode the side, seized the rope, and drew it; it came without any resistance.

"It is cut!" he cried, "no yaive!"

"What?" exclaimed Groslow, " 'tis impossible."

" 'Tis true, however," answered the sailor; "there's nothing in the wake of the ship, besides, here's the rope's end. Look yourself, sir!"

"What's the matter?" cried Mordaunt, who, coming up out of the hatchway, rushed to the stern, his torch in his hand.

"Only that our enemies have escaped—they have cut the rope, and gone off with our yaive."

Mordaunt bounded with one step to the cabin and kicked open the door.

"Empty!" he exclaimed, "the demons!"

"We must pursue them," said Groslow; "they can't be gone far, and we can sink them by running them down!"

"Yes, but the train," ejaculated Mordaunt; "I have lighted it."

"A thousand devils!" cried Groslow, rushing to the hatchway; "perhaps there is still time to put it out."

Mordaunt answered only by a dreadful laugh, threw his torch into the sea, and plunged. The instant that Groslow put his foot upon the steps of the hatchway the ship opened like the crater of a volcano; a burst of flame arose toward the skies with an explosion like that of a hundred cannon; the air itself burned, ignited by brands; then the frightful lightning disappeared, the embers sank down, one after another, into the abyss, where they were extinguished; and, except a slight vibration in the air, after a few minutes had elapsed, one would have thought that nothing had happened.

But the lugger had disappeared from the surface and Groslow and his three sailors were annihilated.

Our four friends saw all this; not a single detail of this fearful scene escaped them; at one moment, bathed as they were in a flood of brilliant light, which illumined the sea for the space of a league, they might each be seen, each in his own peculiar attitude and manner, expressing the awe, which, even in their hearts of bronze, they could not help feeling. Soon the torrent of flame fell all around them; then, at last, the volcano was extinguished and all was dark over the floating boat and the rolling ocean.

They were all silent and dejected.

"By Heaven!" at last said Aramis, "by this time, I think, all must be over."

"Here! my lords! save me! help!" cried a voice, whose mournful accents reaching the four friends, seemed to proceed from some sea spirit.

All looked around; Athos shuddered.

" 'Tis he! 'tis his voice!" he said.

All still remained silent; the eyes of all were still turned in the direction where the vessel had disappeared, endeavoring in vain to penetrate the darkness. After a minute or two they were able to distinguish a man who approached them, swimming vigorously.

Athos extended his arm towards him. "Yes, yes, I know him well," he said.

"He—again!" cried Porthos, who was breathing like a black—smith's bellows, "why, he's made of iron."

"God's mercy!" muttered Athos.

Aramis and d'Artagnan whispered to each other.

Mordaunt made several strokes more and raised his arm in a sign of distress above the waves. "Pity, pity me! gentlemen, in Heaven's name. I feel my strength failing me; I am dying."

The voice that implored aid was so piteous, that it awakened compassion in Athos.

"Poor wretch!" he exclaimed.

"Indeed," cried d'Artagnan, "people have only to complain to you. I believe he's swimming towards us. Does he think we are going to take him in? Row, Porthos, row." And setting the example, he ploughed his oar into the sea. Two strokes sent the boat on twenty fathoms further.

"Ah! ha!" said Porthos to Mordaunt, "I think we have you in a tight corner now, my hero! your only *port* now is below."

"Fie! Porthos!" murmured the Count de la Fère.

"Oh, pray! for mercy's sake don't fly from me. For pity's sake!" cried the young man, whose agonized breathing at times, when his head was under wave, made the icy waters bubble.

D'Artagnan, however, who had consulted with Aramis, spoke to the poor wretch. "Go away," he said, "your repentance is too recent to inspire confidence. See! the vessel in which you wished to fry us is still smoking; and your fix is a bed of roses compared to that in which you wished to place us, and in which you have placed M. Groslow and his companions."

"Sir!" replied Mordaunt, in a tone of deep despair, "my penitence is sincere. Gentlemen, I am young, scarcely twenty-three years old. I was drawn on by a very natural resentment to avenge my mother. You would have done what I did."

Mordaunt wanted now only two or three fathoms to reach the boat, for the approach of death seemed to give him supernatural strength.

"Alas!" he said, "am I to die! are you going to kill the son as you killed the mother? Surely, if I am culpable, and ask for pardon, I ought to be forgiven."

Then, as if his strength failed him, he seemed unable to sustain himself above the water, and a wave passed over his head, which drowned his voice.

"Oh! this tortures me!" Athos resumed, as Mordaunt reappeared.

"For my part," said d'Artagnan, "I say, this must come to an end. Murderer, as you were, of your uncle; executioner, as you were, of King Charles! Incendiary! I recommend you to sink forthwith to the bottom of the sea; and if you come another stroke nearer, I'll break your head with my oar."

"D'Artagnan! d'Artagnan!" cried Athos, "my son! I entreat you; the wretch is dying; and it is horrible to let a man die without extending a hand to save him. I cannot resist doing so; he must live."

"Zounds!" replied d'Artagnan, "why don't you give yourself up directly, feet and hands bound, to that wretch? Ah! Count de la Fère, you wish to perish by his hands? I, your son, as you call me; I will not!"

'Twas the first time that d'Artagnan had ever refused a request of Athos.

Aramis calmly drew his sword, which he had carried between his teeth as he swam.

"If he lays his hand on the boat's edge, I will cut it off, regicide as he is."

"And I," said Porthos. "Wait."

"What are you going to do?" asked Aramis.

"To throw myself in the water and strangle him."

"Oh, gentlemen!" cried Athos; "be men! be Christians. See! death is depicted on his face! Ah! do not bring on me the horrors of remorse! Grant me this poor wretch's life. I will bless you. I——"

"I am dying!" cried Mordaunt, "come to me! come to me!"

D'Artagnan began to be touched. The boat at this moment turned round, and the dying man was by that turn brought nearer to Athos.

"My lord la Fère!" he said; "I supplicate you!—pity me! I call on you! where are you? I see you no longer—I am dying —help me!—help me!"

"Here I am, sir!" said Athos, leaning, and stretching out his arm to Mordaunt with that air of dignity and nobleness of soul habitual to him; "here I am; take my hand, and jump into our boat."

Mordaunt made a last effort, rose, seized the hand thus extended to him, and grasped it with the vehemence of despair.

"That's right," said Athos, "put your other hand here."

And he offered him his shoulders as another stay and support, so that his head almost touched that of Mordaunt; and these two mortal enemies were in as close an embrace as if they had been brothers.

"Now, sir," said the count, "you are safe; calm yourself!"

"Ah! my mother!" cried Mordaunt, with an eye of fire and a look of hatred impossible to describe, "I can only offer thee one victim, but it shall, at any rate, be the one whom thou wouldst have chosen!"

And whilst d'Artagnan uttered a cry, whilst Porthos raised the oar, and Aramis sought a place to strike, a frightful shake given to the boat precipitated Athos into the sea, whilst Mordaunt, with a shout of triumph, grasped the neck of his victim, and, in order to paralyze his movements, intertwined his legs with his, like a serpent might have done around some object. In an instant, without uttering an exclamation, without a cry for help, Athos tried to sustain himself on the surface of the waters; but the weight dragged him down; he disappeared by degrees; soon nothing was to be seen except his long, floating hair; then everything disappeared, and the bubbling of the water, which, in its turn, was effaced, alone indicated the spot where these two men had sunk.

Mute with horror, the three friends had remained open-mouthed, their eyes dilated, their arms extended like statues, and motionless as they were, the beating of their hearts was audible. Porthos was the first who came to himself—he tore his hair.

"Oh!" he cried, "Athos! Athos! thou man of noble heart! Woe is me! I have let thee perish!"

At this instant, in the midst of a vast circle, illumined by the light of the moon, the same whirlpool which had been made by the sinking men was again obvious; and first were seen, rising above the waves, locks of hair; then a face, pale, and with open eyes, yet, nevertheless, those of death; then a body which, after having raised itself even to the waist above the sea, turned gently on its back, according to the caprice of the waves, and floated.

In the bosom of this corpse was plunged a poniard, the gold hilt of which shone in the moonbeams.

"Mordaunt! Mordaunt!" cried the three friends; " 'tis Mordaunt!"

"But Athos!" exclaimed d'Artagnan.

Suddenly the boat leaned on one side, beneath a new and

unexpected weight, and Grimaud uttered a shout of joy; everyone turned round, and beheld Athos, livid, his eyes dim, and his hands trembling, supporting himself on the edge of the boat. Eight vigorous arms bore him up immediately, and laid him in the bark, where, directly, Athos was warmed, reanimated, reviving with the caresses and cares of his friends, who were intoxicated with joy.

"You are not hurt?" asked d'Artagnan.

"No," replied Athos, "and he——"

"Oh, he! Now we may say, thank God! he is really dead. Look!" and d'Artagnan, obliging Athos to look in the direction that he pointed, showed him the body of Mordaunt floating on its back, and which, sometimes submerged, sometimes rising, seemed still to pursue the four friends with a look full of insult and mortal hatred.

At last he sank. Athos had followed him with a glance in which the deepest melancholy and pity were expressed.

"Bravo, Athos!" cried Aramis, with an emotion very rare in him.

"A capital blow you gave!" cried Porthos.

"I have a son," said Athos, "I wished to live."

"In short," said d'Artagnan, "this has been the will of God."

"It is not I who killed him," added Athos, in a soft, low tone, "it is destiny."

CHAPTER LXX.

HOW MOUSQUETON, AFTER NEARLY ROASTING, HAD A NARROW ESCAPE FROM BEING EATEN.

A DEEP silence reigned for a long time in the canoe after the fearful scene just described.

The moon, which had shone for a short time, disappeared behind the clouds; every object was again plunged in that obscurity so awful in deserts, and still more in that liquid desert, the ocean, and nothing was heard, save the whistling of the west wind driving along the tops of the crested billows.

Porthos was the first to speak.

"I have seen," he said, "many things, but nothing that ever agitated me so much as what I have just witnessed. Nevertheless, even in my present state of perturbation, I protest I feel happy. I have a hundred pounds' weight less upon my chest. I breathe more freely." In fact, Porthos breathed so loud as to do credit to the powerful play of his lungs.

"For my part," observed Aramis, "I cannot say the same as you do, Porthos. I am still terrified to such a degree that I scarcely believe my eyes. I look around the canoe, expect-

ing, every moment, to see that poor wretch holding in his hands
the poniard which was plunged into his heart."

"Oh, I am quite easy," replied Porthos. "The sword was
pointed at the sixth rib, and buried up to the hilt in his body. I
do not reproach you Athos, for what you have done; quite
the contrary; when one aims a blow, that is the way to strike.
So now, I breathe again, I am happy!"

"Don't be in haste to celebrate a victory, Porthos," interposed d'Artagnan; "never have we incurred a greater danger
than we are now encountering. A man may subdue a man;
he can't conquer an element. We are now on the sea, at night,
without any pilot, in a frail bark; should a blast of wind upset
the canoe, we are lost."

Mousqueton heaved a deep sigh.

"You are ungrateful, d'Artagnan," said Athos; "yes, ungrateful to Providence—to whom we owe our safety in a
miraculous manner. Let us sail before the wind, and, unless it
changes, we shall be drifted either to Calais or Boulogne. Should
our bark be upset, we are five of us good swimmers, and able
enough to turn it over again; or, if not, to hold on by it.
Now we are on the very road which all the vessels between
Dover and Calais take, 'tis impossible but that we should meet
with a fisherman who will pick us up."

"But should we not find any fisherman, and should the wind
shift to the north?"

"Then," said Athos, "it would be quite another thing; and
we should never see land until we were on the other side of
the Atlantic."

"Which implies that we may die of hunger," said Aramis.

" 'Tis more than probable," answered the Count de la Fère.

Mousqueton sighed again, more deeply than before.

"What is the matter? what ails you?" asked Porthos.

"I am cold, sir," said Mousqueton.

"Impossible! your body is covered with a coating of fat,
which preserves it from the cold air."

"Ah! sir, 'tis that very coating of fat which alarms me."

"How is that, Mouston?"

"Alas! your honor! in the library of the Château of Bracieux there's a number of books of travels. Amongst them
the voyages of Jean Mocquet in the time of Henry IV. In
these books, your honor, 'tis told how hungry voyagers, drifted
out to sea, have a bad habit of eating each other, and beginning by —— "

"By the fattest among them!" cried d'Artagnan, unable, in
spite of the gravity of the occasion, to help laughing.

"Yes, sir," answered Mousqueton; "but permit me to say, I
see nothing laughable in it. However," he added, turning to
Porthos, "I should not regret dying, sir, were I sure that by
doing so I might still be useful to you."

"Mouston," replied Porthos, much affected, "should we ever

see my castle of Pierrefonds again, you shall have as your own, and for your descendants, the vineyard which surmounts the farm."

"And you shall call it, Mouston," added Aramis, "the .vineyard of self-sacrifice, to transmit to latest ages the recollection of your devotion to your master."

One may readily conceive that during these jokes, which were intended chiefly to divert Athos from the scene which had just taken place, the servants, with the exception of Grimaud, were not at ease. Suddenly Mousqueton uttered a cry of delight, in taking from beneath one of the benches a bottle of wine; and, on looking more closely still in the same place, he discovered a dozen of similar bottles, some bread, and a piece of salted beef.

"Oh, sir!" he cried, passing the bottle to Porthos, "we are saved; the craft is provisioned."

This intelligence restored everyone, save Athos, to gaiety.

"Zounds!" exclaimed Porthos, " 'tis astonishing how empty violent agitation makes the stomach."

And he drank off one bottle at a draught, and ate a good third of the bread and salted meat.

"Now," said Athos, "sleep, or try to sleep, my friends, I will watch."

In a few moments, notwithstanding their wet clothes, the icy blast that blew, and the previous scene, these hardy adventurers, with their iron frames, fitted for every hardship, threw themselves down, intending to profit by the advice of Athos, who sat at the helm, pensive and wakeful, guiding the little bark in the way it was to go, his eyes fixed on the heavens, as if he sought to discern, not only the road to France, but the benign aspect of protecting Providence. After some hourse of repose, the sleepers were aroused by Athos.

Dawn had shed its light upon the blue ocean, and at the distance of a musket's shot from them was seen a dark mass, above which was displayed a triangular sail; then masters and servants joined in a fervent cry to the crew of that vessel, to hear them, and to save.

"A sail!" all cried together.

It was, in fact, a small craft from Dunkirk, sailing towards Boulogne.

A quarter of an hour afterwards, the boat of this craft took them on board the little vessel. Grimaud offered twenty guineas to the captain from his master, and, at nine o'clock in the morning, having a fair wind, our Frenchmen set foot on their native land.

"Egad! how strong one feels here!" said Porthos, almost burying his large feet in the sands. "Zounds! I could now defy a whole nation!"

"Be quiet, Porthos," said d'Artagnan, "we are observed."

"We are admired, i'faith," answered Porthos.

"These people who are looking at us, are only merchants," said Athos, "and are looking more at the cargo than at us."

"I shall not trust to that," said the lieutenant, "and I shall make for the sandhills as soon as possible."

The party followed him, and soon disappeared with him behind the hillocks of sand unobserved. Here, after a short conference, they proposed to separate.

"And why separate?" asked Athos.

"Because," answered the Gascon, "we were sent by Cardinal Mazarin to fight for Cromwell; instead of fighting for Cromwell, we have served Charles I., not the same thing at all. In returning with the Count de la Fère and M. d'Herblay, our crime would be confirmed. We have escaped Cromwell, Mordaunt, and the sea, but we should not escape from Mazarin."

"You forget," replied Athos, "that we consider ourselves as your prisoners, and not free from the engagement we entered into."

"Truly, Athos," interrupted d'Artagnan, "I am vexed that such a man as you are should talk nonsense which schoolboys would be ashamed of. Chevalier," he continued, addressing Aramis, who, leaning proudly on his sword, seemed to agree with his companion, "Chevalier, Porthos and I run no risks; besides, should any ill-luck happen to two of us, will it not be much better that the other two should be spared to assist those who may be apprehended? Besides, who knows whether, divided, we might not obtain a pardon—you from the Queen, we from Mazarin—which, were we all four together, would never be granted. Come, Athos and Aramis, go to the right, Porthos, come with me to the left; these gentlemen should file off towards Normandy, we will, by the nearest road, reach Paris."

He then gave his friends minute directions as to their route.

"Ah! my dear friend," cried Athos, "how I should admire the resources of your mind, did I not stop to adore those of your heart."

And he gave him his hand.

"Is the fox a genius, Athos?" asked the Gascon. "No! he knows how to crunch fowls, to dodge the huntsman, and to find his way home by day or by night, that's all. Well, is all said?"

"All."

"Then let's count our money, and divide it. Ah! hurrah! there's the sun! Good morrow, my friend, the sun, 'tis a long time since I saw you!"

"Come, come, d'Artagnan," said Athos, "do not affect to be strong-minded; there are tears in your eyes, let us always be open to each other, and sincere."

"What!" cried the Gascon, "do you think, Athos, we can take leave, calmly, of two friends, at a time not free from danger to you and Aramis?"

"No," answered Athos; "embrace me, my son."

"Zounds!" said Porthos, sobbing, "I believe I'm blubbering; but how foolish it is!"

They then embraced. At that moment, their fraternal bond of union was closer than ever, and, when they parted, each to take the route agreed on, they turned back, to utter to each other affectionate expressions which the echoes repeated.

At last they lost sight of each other, Porthos and d'Artagnan taking the road to Paris, followed by Mousqueton, who, after having been too cold all night, found himself, at the end of half an hour, too warm.

CHAPTER LXXI.

THE RETURN HOME.

DURING the six months that Athos and Aramis had been absent from France, the Parisians, finding themselves, one morning, without either a Queen or a King, were greatly annoyed at being thus deserted, and the absence of Mazarin, so much desired, did not compensate for that of the two august fugitives.

Parliament, which, supported by the citizens, declared that Cardinal Mazarin was the cause of all the discontents, denounced him as the enemy, both to the King and the state, and ordered him to retire from the court that very day, and from France within a week afterwards, and enjoining, in case of disobedience on his part, all the subjects of the King to pursue and take him.

Mazarin being thus put out of the protection of the law, preparations on both sides were commenced; the Queen, to attack Paris; the citizens, to defend it. The latter were occupied in breaking up the pavement, and stretching chains across the street, when, headed by the Coadjutor, appeared the Prince de Conti (the brother of the Prince de Condé) and the Duke de Longueville, his brother-in-law. This unexpected band of auxiliaries arrived at Paris on the tenth of January, and the Prince of Conti was named, but not until a stormy discussion, generalissimo of the army of the King, out of Paris.

As for the Duke de Beaufort, he arrived from Vendôme, according to the annals of the day, bringing with him his high bearing, and his long and beautiful hair, qualifications which ensured him the sovereignty of the market-places and their occupants.

It was just at this epoch that the four friends had landed at Dunkirk, and begun their route towards Paris. On reaching that capital, Athos and Aramis found it in arms. The sentinel at the gate refused even to let them pass, and called his sergeant.

The sergeant, with that air of importance which such people assume when they are clad with military dignity, said:

"Who are you, gentlemen? And where do you come from?"

"From London, going with a mission to the Queen of England."

"Where are your orders?"

"We have none; we quitted England ignorant of the state of politics here, having left Paris before the departure of the King."

"Oh!" said the sergeant with a cunning smile, "you are Mazarinists, sent as spies."

"My dear friend," here Athos spoke, "be assured, if we were Mazarinists, we should have all sorts of passports. In your situation distrust those who are well provided with every formality."

"Enter into the guard-room," said the sergeant; "we will lay your case before the commandant of the post."

The guard-room was filled with citizens and common people, some playing, some drinking, some talking. In a corner, almost hidden from view, were three gentlemen, who had preceded Athos and Aramis, and an officer was examining their passports. The first impulse of these three gentlemen, and of those who last entered, was to cast an inquiring glance to each other. Those first arrived wore long cloaks, in the drapery of which they were carefully enveloped; one of them, shorter than the rest, remained pertinaciously in the background.

When the sergeant, on entering the room, announced that, in all probability, he was bringing in two Mazarinists, it appeared to be the unanimous opinion of the officers on guard that they ought not to pass.

"Be it so," said Athos; "yet it is probable, on the contrary, that we shall enter, because we seem to have to do with sensible people. There seems to be only one thing to do, which is, to send our names to the Queen of England, and, if she answers for us, I presume we shall be allowed to enter."

On hearing these words, the shortest of the other three men seemed more attentive than ever to what was going on, and he wrapped his cloak around him more carefully than before.

"Merciful goodness!" whispered Aramis to Athos, "did you see the face of the shortest of those three gentlemen?"

"No."

At this instant the sergeant, who had been for his orders, returned, and, pointing to the three gentlemen in cloaks, said:

"The passports are right; let these three gentlemen pass."

The three gentlemen bowed, and hastened to take advantage of this permission.

Aramis looked after them, and, as the last of them passed close to him, he pressed the hand of Athos.

"What is the matter with you, my friend?" asked the latter.

"I have, doubtless, been dreaming; tell me, sir," he said to the sergeant, "do you know those three gentlemen just gone out?"

"Only by their passports; they are three Frondists, who are gone to rejoin the Duke de Longueville."

" 'Tis strange," said Aramis, almost involuntarily; "I fancied that I recognized Mazarin himself."

The sergeant burst out into a fit of laughter.

"He!" he cried; "he venture himself amongst us to be hung! Not so foolish as all that."

"Ah!" muttered Athos, "I may be mistaken; I haven't the unerring eye of d'Artagnan."

"Who is speaking of d'Artagnan?" asked an officer, who appeared at that moment upon the threshold of the room.

"What!" cried Aramis and Athos, "what! Planchet!"

"Planchet," added Grimaud, "Planchet, in a gilt gorget, indeed!"

"Ah, gentlemen!" cried Planchet, "so you are back again in Paris. Oh, how happy you make us! no doubt you are come to join the princes!"

"As you see, Planchet," said Aramis, whilst Athos smiled at the importance now assumed by the old comrade of Mousqueton in his new rank, in the City Militia.

"Ah! so!" said Aramis; "allow me to congratulate you, M. Planchet."

"Oh, the chevalier!" returned Planchet, bowing.

"Lieutenant?" asked Aramis.

"Lieutenant, with a promise of becoming a captain."

" 'Tis capital; and pray how did you acquire all these honors?"

"In the first place, gentlemen, you know that I was the means of M. de Rochefort's escape; so, I was very near being hung by Mazarin, and that made me more popular than ever."

"So, owing to your popularity——"

"No; thanks to something better. You know, gentlemen, that I served in the Piedmont regiment, and had the honor of being a sergeant? Well, one day, when no one could drill a mob of citizens, who began to march, some with the right foot, others with the left, I succeeded in making them all begin with the same foot, and I was made a lieutenant on the field."

"So, I presume," said Athos, "that you have a large number of the nobles with you?"

"Certainly. The Prince de Conti, the Duke de Longueville, de Beaufort, de Bouillon, and I don't know who else, for my part."

"And Viscount Raoul de Bragelonne?" inquired Athos, in a tremulous voice; "d'Artagnan told me that he had recommended him to your care, in parting."

"Yes, Count; nor have I lost sight of him for an instant since."

"Then," said Athos, in a tone of delight, "he is well? no accident has happened to him?"

"None, sir."

"And he lives?"

"Still, at the hotel of the Great Charlemagne."

"And passes his time?"

"Sometimes with the Queen of England, sometimes with Mdme. de Chevreuse. He and Count de Guiche are never asunder."

"Thanks, Planchet, thanks," cried Athos, extending his hand to the lieutenant.

"Oh, sir!" Planchet only touched the tips of the count's fingers. "Oh, sir! and now, gentlemen, what do you intend to do?"

"To re-enter Paris, if you will let us, my good Planchet."

"Let you, sir? I am nothing but your servant!" Then, turning to his men, "Allow these gentlemen to pass," he said; "they are friends of the Duke de Beaufort."

"Long live the duke!" cried all the sentinels.

"Farewell till we meet again," said Aramis, as they took leave of Planchet; "if anything happens to us, we shall refer to you."

"Sir," answered Planchet, "I am in all things your servant."

"That fellow is no fool," said Aramis, as he got on his horse.

"How should he be?" replied Athos, whilst mounting also, "seeing that he has been so long used to brush his master's hats?"

CHAPTER LXXII.

THE AMBASSADORS.

THE two friends rode rapidly down the Faubourg, but on arriving at the bottom were surprised to find that the streets of Paris had become rivers, and the open places lakes; after the great rains which fell in the month of January, the Seine had overflowed its banks, and the river had inundated half the capital. The two gentlemen were obliged, therefore, to get off their horses and take a boat, and in that manner they approached the Louvre.

Night had closed in, and Paris, seen thus, by the light of some lanterns, flickering on the pools of water, with boats laden with patrols and glittering arms, and watchword passing from post to post, Paris presented such an aspect as to seize strongly on the senses of Aramis—a man most susceptible of warlike impressions.

They reached the Queen's apartments, and were instantly

admitted to the presence of Henrietta Maria, who uttered a cry of joy on hearing of their arrival.

"Let them come in!" exclaimed the poor Queen.

"Let them come in!" reiterated the young princess, who had never left her mother's side, but essayed in vain to make her forget, by her filial affection, the absence of her two sons and her other daughter.

"Come in, gentlemen," repeated the princess, opening the door herself.

The Queen was seated in a fauteuil, and before her were standing two or three gentlemen, and, among them, the Duke de Châtillon, the brother of the nobleman who was killed eight or nine years previously in a duel, on account of Mdme. de Longueville, on the Place Royale. Two of these gentlemen had been noticed by Athos and Aramis in the guardhouse; and, when the two friends were announced, they started and exchanged some words in a low tone.

"Well, sirs!" cried the Queen, on perceiving the two friends; "you are come, faithful friends! but the royal couriers have been more expeditious than you; and here are Messrs. de Flamareus and de Châtillon, who bring me, from Queen Anne of Austria, the most recent intelligence."

Aramis and Athos were astonished by the calmness, even the gaiety, of the Queen's manner.

"Go on with your recital, sir," said the Queen, turning to the Duke de Châtillon. "You said that his majesty, King Charles, my august consort, had been condemned to death by a majority of his subjects!"

"Yes, madam," Châtillon stammered.

Athos and Aramis seemed more and more astonished.

"And that, being conducted to the scaffold," resumed the Queen, "—oh, my God! oh, my King!—and that being led to the scaffold, he had been saved by an indignant people?"

"Just so, madam," replied Châtillon, in so low a voice that though the two friends were listening eagerly, they could hardly hear this affirmation.

The Queen clapped her hands in enthusiastic gratitude, whilst her daughter threw her arms round her mother's neck, and kissed her, her own eyes streaming with tears.

"Now, madam, nothing remains to me except to proffer my respectful homage," said Châtillon, who felt confused and ashamed beneath the stern gaze of Athos.

"One moment, yes," answered the Queen. "One moment, I beg, for here are the Chevalier d'Herblay and Count de la Fère —just arrived from London—and they can give you, as eyewitnesses, such details as you can convey to the Queen, my royal sister. Speak, gentlemen, speak—I am listening—conceal nothing—gloss over nothing. Since his majesty still lives; since the honor of the throne is in safety, everything else is a matter of indifference to me."

Athos turned pale, and laid his hand on his heart.

"Well!" exclaimed the Queen, who remarked this movement and this paleness. "Speak, sir! I beg you to do so."

"I beg you to excuse me, madam. I wish to add nothing to the recital of these gentlemen until they perceive, themselves, that they have, perhaps, been mistaken."

"Mistaken!" cried the Queen, almost suffocated by emotion; "mistaken! What has happened, then!"

"Sir!" interposed de Flamareus to Athos, "if we are mistaken, the error has originated with the Queen. I do not suppose you will have the presumption to set it to rights; that would be to accuse her majesty, Queen Anne, of falsehood."

Athos sighed deeply.

"Or rather, sir," said Aramis, with his irritating politeness, "the error of that person with you when we met in the guardroom, for if the Count de la Fère and I are not mistaken, when we saw you there you had with you a third gentleman."

Châtillon and Flamareus started.

"Explain yourself, Count!" cried the Queen, whose anguish became greater every moment. "On your brow I read despair; your lips falter, ere you announce some terrible tidings; your hands tremble. Oh, my God! my God! what has happened!"

"Lord!" ejaculated the young princess, falling on her knees, "have mercy on us!"

A short altercation ensued in a low tone between the Duke de Châtillon and Aramis during which Athos, his hands on his heart, his head bent low, approached the Queen, and in a voice of deep sorrow, said:

"Madam! princes—who by nature are above other men—receive from Heaven courage to support greater misfortunes than those of lower rank, for their hearts are elevated as their fortunes. We ought not, therefore, I think, to act towards a Queen so illustrious as your majesty, as we should do toward a woman of our lowlier condition. Queen, destined as you are to endure every sorrow on this earth, hear the result of our mission."

Athos, kneeling down before the Queen, trembling and very cold, drew from his bosom, inclosed in the same case, the order set in diamonds, which the Queen had given to Lord Winter, and the wedding-ring which Charles I. before his death had placed in the hands of Aramis. Since the moment that he had first received these two things, Athos had never parted with them.

He opened the case, and offered them to the Queen, with silent and deep anguish.

The Queen stretched out her hand, seized the ring, pressed it convulsively to her lips, and without being able to breathe a sigh, to give vent to a sob, she extended her arms, became deadly pale, and fell senseless in the arms of her attendants and her daughter.

Athos kissed the hem of the robe of the widowed Queen, and rising, with a dignity that made a deep impression on those around:

"I, the Count de la Fère, a gentleman who has never deceived any human being, swear before God, and before this unhappy Queen, that all that was possible to save the King of England was done whilst we were on English ground. Now, Chevalier," he added, turning to Aramis, "let us go. We have still a word to say to these gentlemen."

And turning to Châtillon, he said, "Sir, be so good as not to go away without hearing something that I cannot say before the Queen."

Châtillon bowed in token of assent, and they all went out, stopping at the window of a gallery on the ground floor.

"Sir!" said Aramis, "you allowed yourself just now to treat us in a most extraordinary manner."

"Sir!" cried de Châtillon.

"What have you done with M. de Bruy? Has he, perchance, gone to change his face, which was too like that of M. de Mazarin? There are abundance of Italian masks at the Palais Royal, from harlequin even to pantaloon."

"Chevalier! Chevalier!" said Athos.

"Leave me alone," replied Aramis, impatiently. "I don't like things that stop half way."

"Finish then, sir," answered de Châtillon, with as much hauteur as Aramis.

"Gentlemen," resumed Aramis, "any one but the Count de la Fère and myself would have had you arrested—for we have friends in Paris—but we are contented with another course. Come and talk with us for five minutes, sword in hand, upon this deserted terrace."

"Willingly," replied de Châtillon.

"Duke," said Flamareus, "you forget that to-morrow you are to command an expedition of the greatest importance, projected by the prince, assented to by the Queen. Until to-morrow evening you are not at your own disposal."

"Let it be then, the day after to-morrow," said Aramis.

"To-morrow, rather," said de Châtillon, "and if you will take the trouble of coming so far as the gates of Charenton."

"Well, then, to-morrow. Pray, are you going to rejoin your Cardinal? Swear first, on your honor, not to inform him of our return."

De Châtillon looked at him. There was so much irony in his speech, that the duke had great difficulty in bridling his anger; but, at a word from Flamareus, he restrained himself, and contented himself with saying:

"You promise me, sir—that's agreed—that I shall find you to-morrow at Charenton?"

"Oh, sir, don't be afraid!" replied Aramis; and the two gentlemen shortly afterwards left the Louvre.

"For what reason is all this fume and fury?" asked Athos. "What have they done to you?"

"They did—did you not see their laugh when we swore that we had done our duty in England. Now, if they believed us, they laughed in order to insult us; if they did not believe us, they insulted us still more. However, I'm glad not to fight them until to-morrow. I hope to have something better to do to-night than to draw my sword."

"What have you to do?"

"Egad! to take Mazarin."

Athos curled his lip with disdain.

"These undertakings do not suit me, as you know, Aramis."

"Why?"

"Because they are taking people unawares."

"Really Athos, you would make a singular general. You would fight only by broad daylight; warn your foe before an attack; and never attempt anything by night, lest you should be accused of taking advantage of the darkness.

Athos smiled.

"Say, at once, you disapprove of my proposal."

"I think you ought to do nothing, since you exacted a promise from these gentlemen not to let Mazarin know that we were in France."

"I have entered into no engagement, and consider myself quite free. Come, come."

"Where?"

"Either to seek the Duke de Beaufort, or the Duke de Bouillon, and to tell them about this."

"Yes, but on one condition, that we begin by the Coadjutor. He is a priest, learned in cases of conscience, and we will tell him ours."

It was then agreed that they were to go first to M. de Bouillon, as his house came first; but first of all Athos begged that he might go to the Hôtel du Grand Charlemagne, to see Raoul.

They re-entered the boat which had brought them to the Louvre, and went thence to the Markets; and finding there Grimaud and Blaisois, they proceeded to the Rue Guénégand.

But Raoul was not at home. He had received a message from the prince, to whom he had hastened with Olivain the instant he had received it.

CHAPTER LXXIII.

THE THREE LIEUTENANTS.

At ten o'clock the next day the friends met again.

There were still no tidings of d'Artagnan or Porthos, whom they had expected. Raoul was gone to St. Cloud, in consequence of a message from the Prince de Condé, and had not returned; and Aramis had not been able to see Mdme. de Longueville, who was installed at the Hôtel de Ville, where she played the part of Queen, not having quite courage enough as Aramis remarked, to take up her abode at the Palais Royal or Tuileries.

"Well, then," said Athos, "now, then, what shall we do this evening?"

"You forget, my friend, that we have work cut out for us in the direction of Charenton; I hope to see de Châtillon, whom I've hated a long time, there."

"Why have you hated him?"

"Because he is the brother of Coligny."

"Ah, true! he who presumed to be a rival of yours, for which he was severely punished; that ought to satisfy you."

"Yes, but it does not; I am rancorous, the only point which shows me to be a churchman. Do you understand? Let us go, then, Aramis."

"If we go, there is no time to lose; the drum has beat; I saw cannon on the road; I saw the citizens in order of battle on the place of the Hôtel de Ville; certainly the fight will be in the direction of Charenton, as the Duke de Châtillon said."

"Poor creatures!" said Athos, "who are going to be killed, in order that M. de Bouillon should have his estate at Sedan restored to him, that the reversion of the Admiralty should be given to the Duke de Beaufort, and that the Coadjutor should be made a Cardinal."

"Come! come, dear Athos, you will not be so philosophical if your Raoul should happen to be in all this confusion."

"Perhaps you speak the truth, Aramis."

"Well, let us go, then, where the fighting is, for that is the most likely place to meet with d'Artagnan, Porthos, and Raoul. Stop, there are a fine body of citizens passing; quite attractive, by Jupiter! and their captain! see! in the true military style."

"What, ho!" said Grimaud.

"What?" asked Athos.

"Planchet, sir."

"Lieutenant yesterday," said Aramis, "a captain to-day, a colonel, doubtless, to-morrow; in a week the fellow will be a field-marshal of France."

"Ask him some questions about the fight," said Athos.

Planchet, prouder than ever of his new duties, deigned to explain to the two gentlemen that he was ordered to take up his position on the Place Royale, where two hundred men formed the rear of the army of Paris, and to march towards Charenton, when necessary.

"The day will be warm," said Planchet, in a warlike tone.

But the friends, not caring to mix themselves up with the citizens, set off towards Charenton, and passed the valley of Fecamp, darkened by the presence of armed troops.

CHAPTER LXXIV.

THE BATTLE OF CHARENTON.

As Athos and Aramis proceeded, and passed different companies on the road, they became aware that they were arriving near the field of battle.

"Ah! my friend!" cried Athos, suddenly, "where have you brought us? I fancy I perceive around us faces of different officers in the royal army; is it not Châtillon himself with his brigadiers?"

"Good day, sirs," said the duke, advancing; "you are puzzled by what you see here, but one word will explain everything. There is now a truce, and a conference. The prince, M. de Retz, the Duke de Beaufort, the Duke de Bouillon, are talking over public affairs. Now, one of two things must happen; either matters will be arranged, or they will not be arranged, in which last case I shall be relieved of my command, and we shall still meet again."

"This conference has not then been preconcerted?"

"No; 'tis the result of certain propositions made yesterday by Cardinal Mazarin to the Parisians."

"Where, then, are the plenipotentiaries?" asked Athos.

"At the house of de Chaulieu, who commands your troops at Charenton. I say your troops, for I presume that you gentlemen are Frondeurs?"

"We are for the King, and the princes," said Athos.

"We must understand each other," said the duke; "the King is with us, and his generals are, the Duke of Orleans and the Prince de Conti, although, I must add, 'tis almost impossible now to know what party one is on."

"Yes," answered Athos, "but his right place is in our ranks, with the Prince de Conti, de Beaufort, d'Elbeuf, and de Bouillon; but, my lord, supposing that the conferences are broken off, are you going to try to take Charenton?"

"Such are my orders."

"My lord, since you command the cavalry——"

"Pardon me, I am commander-in-chief."

"So much the better. There is a youth, of fifteen years of age, the Viscount de Bragelonne, attached to the Prince de Conti. Has he the honor of being known to you?" inquired Athos, diffident in allowing the sceptical Aramis to perceive how strong were his paternal feelings.

"Yes, surely, he came with the prince; a charming young man; he is one of your friends, then?"

"Yes," answered Athos, slightly agitated; "so much so, that I wish to see him, if possible."

"Quite possible, sir; do me the favor to accompany me, and I will conduct you to headquarters."

"Halloa, there!" cried Aramis, turning round, "what a noise behind us!"

"A stout cavalier coming towards us," said Châtillon; "I recognize the Coadjutor, by his Frondist hat."

"And I, the Duke de Beaufort, by his plume of white feathers."

"They are coming full gallop; the prince is with them; ah! he is leaving them."

"They are beating the rally!" cried Châtillon; "we must find out what's going on."

They saw the soldiers running to their arms; the trumpets sounded; the drum beat; the Duke de Beaufort drew his sword. On his side, the prince sounded a call, and all the officers of the royalist army, mingled momentarily with the Parisian troops, ran to him.

"Gentlemen," cried Châtillon, "the truce is broken, that's evident; they are going to fight; go, then, Charenton, for I shall begin in a short time; hark! there's a signal from the prince!"

The cornet of the troop had, in fact, just raised the standard of the prince.

"Farewell, till the next time!" cried Châtillon, and he set, full gallop.

Aramis and Athos turned also, and went to salute the Coadjutor, and Beaufort. As to Bouillon, he had such a fit of gout as obliged him to return to Paris in a litter; but his place was supplied by the Duke d'Elbeuf and his four sons, ranged around him like a staff. Meantime, between Charenton and the royal army, was left a long space, which seemed prepared to serve as a last resting-place for the dead.

"Gentlemen," cried the Coadjutor, tightening his sash, which he wore after the fashion of the ancient military prelates, over his Archiepiscopal simar, "there's the enemy approaching us, we shall, I hope, save them the half of their journey."

And, without caring whether he were followed or not, he set off; his regiment, which bore the name of the regiment of Corinth, from the name of his Archbishopric, darted after him, and began the fight. Beaufort sent his cavalry towards Etampes, and M. de Chaulieu, who defended the place, was ready to resist an assault, or, if the enemy were repulsed, to attempt a sortie.

The battle soon became general, and the Coadjutor performed miracles of valor. His proper vocation had always been the sword, and he was delighted whenever he could draw it from the scabbard, no matter for whom, or against whom.

Chaulieu, whose fire at one time repulsed the royal regiments, thought that the moment was come to pursue it; but it was reformed, and led again to the charge, by Châtillon, in person. This charge was so fierce, so skilfully conducted, that Chaulieu was almost surrounded. He commanded a retreat, which began, step by step, foot by foot; unhappily, in an instant, he fell, mortally wounded. De Châtillon saw him fall, and announced it, in a loud voice, to his men, which raised their spirits, and completely disheartened their enemies, so that every man thought only of his personal safety, and tried to regain the trenches, where the Coadjutor was trying to reform his disorganized regiment.

Suddenly, a squadron of cavalry came to an encounter with the royal troops who were entering into the intrenchments, mixed with the fugitives. Athos and Aramis charged at the head of their squadron; Aramis with his sword and pistol in his hands; Athos, with his sword in the scabbard, his pistol in his saddle-bags: calm and cool as if on parade, except that his noble and beautiful countenance became sad as he saw slaughtered, so many men who were sacrificed on one side to the obstinacy of royalty, on the other to the rancorous party feeling of the princes; Aramis, on the contrary, struck right and left, and was almost delirious with excitement. His bright eyes kindled, and his mouth, so finely formed, assumed a dark smile; every blow he aimed was sure, and his pistol finished the deed, and annihilated the wounded wretch who tried to rise again.

On the opposite side, two cavaliers, one covered with a gilt cuirass, the other wearing simply a buff doublet, from which fell the sleeves of a vest of blue velvet, charged in front. The cavalier in the gilt cuirass fell upon Aramis and hit him a blow that Aramis parried with his wonted skill.

"Ah! 'tis you, M. Châtillon," cried the chevalier, "welcome to you, I await you."

"I hope I have not made you wait too long, sir," said the duke; "at all events, here I am."

"M. de Châtillon," cried Aramis, taking from his saddle bags a second pistol, "I think if your pistols have been discharged, you are a dead man."

"Thank God, sir, they are not!"

And the duke, pointing his pistol at Aramis, fired. But Aramis instantly bent his head, and the ball passed without touching him.

"Oh! you've missed me," cried Aramis; "but I swear to Heaven, I will not miss you."

"If I give you time!" cried the duke, spurring on his horse, and rushing upon him with drawn sword.

Aramis awaited him with a terrible smile which was peculiar to him on such occasions; and Athos, who saw the duke advancing toward Aramis with the rapidity of lightning, was just going to cry out, "fire! fire! then!" when the shot was fired, de Châtillon opened his arms and fell back on his horse.

The ball had penetrated into his chest through the crank of his cuirass.

"I am a dead man," he said, and he fell from his horse to the ground.

"I told you this; I am now grieved I have kept my word; can I be of any use to you?"

Châtillon made a sign with his hand, and Aramis was about to dismount, when he received a violent shock in the side, 'twas a thrust from a sword, but his cuirass turned aside the blow.

He turned round and seized his new antagonist by the wrist, when he started back, exclaiming, "Raoul!"

"Raoul?" cried Athos.

The young man recognized at the same time the voice of his father and that of the Chevalier d'Herblay; several chevaliers in the Parisian forces rushed at that instant on Raoul, but Aramis protected him with his sword.

"My prisoner!" he cried.

At this crisis of the battle, the Prince, who had seconded de Châtillon in the second line, appeared in the midst of the fight; his eagle eye made him known, and his blows proclaimed the hero.

On seeing him, the regiment of Corinth, which the Coadjutor had not been able to reorganize in spite of his efforts, threw themselves into the midst of the Parisian forces, put them into confusion, and re-entered Charenton, flying. The Coadjutor, dragged along with his fugitive forces, passed near the group formed by Athos, Raoul, and Aramis. Aramis could not, in his jealousy, avoid being pleased at the Coadjutor's misfortune and was about to make some bon-mot, more witty than correct, when Athos stopped him.

The three cavaliers continued their road on a full gallop.

"What were you doing in the battle, my friend?" inquired Athos of the youth; "'twas not your right place, I think, as you were not equipped for an engagement."

"I had no intention of fighting to-day, sir; I was charged, indeed, with a mission for the Cardinal, and had set out for Rueil, when seeing M. de Châtillon charge, a wish possessed me to charge at his side. Two cavaliers from the Parisian troops told me that you were there."

"What! you knew we were there, and yet wished to kill your friend and the chevalier?"

"I did not recognize the chevalier in his armor, sir!" said Raoul, blushing; "though I might have known him by his skill and coolness in danger."

"Thank you for the compliment, my young friend," replied Aramis, "we can see from whom you learnt lessons of courtesy; you were going, then, to Rueil?"

"Yes; I have a despatch from the Prince to his Eminence."

"You must deliver it," said Athos.

"Give me the despatch, Raoul! you are the chevalier's prisoner."

Raoul gave it up reluctantly; Aramis instantly seized and read it.

"You," he said, "you, who are so trusting, read and reflect that there is something in this letter important for us to see."

Athos took the letter, frowning, but an idea that he should hear something in this letter about d'Artagnan, conquered his unwillingness to finish it.

"My lord, I shall send this evening to your Eminence in order to reinforce the troops of M. Comminges, the ten men demanded. They are good soldiers, fit to master the two rough adversaries whose skill and resolution your Eminence is fearful of."

"Oh!" cried Athos.

"Well," said Aramis, "what think you about these two enemies, when it requires, besides Comminges' troop, ten good soldiers to guard; are they not as like as two drops of water to d'Artagnan and Porthos?"

"We'll search Paris all to-day," said Athos, "and if we have no news this evening, we will return to the road to Picardy; and I feel no doubt that, thanks to d'Artagnan's ready invention, we shall then find some clue which will solve our doubts."

CHAPTER LXXV.

THE ROAD TO PICARDY.

In leaving Paris, Athos and Aramis well knew that they would be encountering great danger; but one can imagine how such men look at a question of personal risk.

They quitted Paris, beholding it abandoned to extreme want bordering on famine, agitated by fear, torn by faction. Parisians and Frondeurs though they were, the two friends expected to find the same misery, the same fears, the same intrigues in the enemy's camp; but what was their surprise, after passing St. Denis, to hear that, at St. Germain, people were singing and laughing, and leading a cheerful life. The two gentlemen travelled by by-ways, in order not to encounter Mazarinists, who were scattered about the Isle of France, and also to escape the Frondeurs, who were in possession of Normandy, and who would not have failed to conduct them to the Duke de Longueville, in order that he might tell whether they were friends or enemies. Having escaped these dangers, they returned by the main road to Boulogne, at Abbeville, and followed it step by step, examining every track.

Nevertheless, they were still in a state of uncertainty. Several inns were visited by them, several innkeepers questioned, with-

out a single clue being given, to guide their inquiries. When at Montreuil, Athos felt, upon the table, that something rough was touching his delicate fingers. He turned up the cloth, and found these hieroglyphics carved upon the wood with a knife:—
"Port . . . . D'Art . . . . 2nd February."
"This is capital," said Athos to Aramis; "we were to have slept here, but we cannot, we must push on." They rode forward, and reached Abbeville. There the great number of inns puzzled them; they could not go to all; how could they guess in which he whom they were seeking had stayed.

"Trust me," said Aramis; "do not expect to find anything in Abbeville. If we had only been looking for Porthos, Porthos would have fixed himself in one of the finest of the hotels, and we could easily have traced him. But d'Artagnan is devoid of such weaknesses. Porthos would have found it very difficult even to make him see that he was dying of hunger; he has gone on his road as inexorable as fate, and we must seek him somewhere else."

They continued their route; it had now become a weary and almost hopeless task; and had it not been for the threefold motives of honor, friendship, and gratitude, implanted in their hearts, these two travelers would have given up, many a time, their searches over the sands, their questions to the peasantry, and their inspection of faces.

They proceeded to Compiègne.

Athos began to despair. His noble nature felt that their ignorance was a reflection upon them. They had not looked well enough for their lost friends. They had not shown sufficient pertinacity in their inquiries. They were willing and ready to retrace their steps, when, in crossing the suburb which leads to the gates of the town, upon a white wall which was at the corner of a street turning round the rampart, Athos cast his eyes upon a drawing in black chalk, which represented, with the awkwardness of a first attempt, two cavaliers riding furiously, and carrying a roll of paper, on which were written these words,—"They are chasing us."

"Oh!" exclaimed Athos; "here it is as clear as day. Pursued as he was, d'Artagnan would not have tarried here five minutes had he been pressed very closely, which gives us hopes that he may have succeeded in escaping."

Athos shook his head.

"Had he escaped we should either have seen him or have heard him spoken of."

"You are right, Aramis; let us travel on."

To describe the impatience and uneasiness of these two gentlemen would be impossible. Anxiety took possession of the tender and constant heart of Athos; and impatience was the torment of the impulsive Aramis. They galloped on for two or three hours with the frenzy of two knights in pursuit. All at once, in a narrow pass, they perceived that the road was partially barricaded by an enormous stone. It had evidently been rolled across the path by some arm of gigantic power.

Aramis stopped.

"Oh!" he said, looking at the stone, "this is the work either of Ajax, or of Briareus, or of Porthos. Let us get down, Count, and examine this rock."

They both alighted. The stone had been brought with the evident intention of barricading the road; but some one, having perceived the obstacle, had partially turned it aside.

With the assistance of Blaisois and Grimaud, the friends succeeded in turning the stone over. Upon the side next the ground was written:

"Eight Light Dragoons are pursuing us. If we reach Compiègne, we shall stop at the Crowned Peacock, kept by a friend of ours."

"This is something positive," said Athos, "let us go to the Peacock."

"Yes," answered Aramis, "but if we are to get there, we must rest our horses, for they are almost broken-winded."

Aramis was right; they stopped at the first tavern, and made each horse swallow a double quantity of grain steeped in wine; they gave them three hours' rest, and then set off again. The men themselves were almost killed with fatigue, but hope supported them.

In six hours they reached Compiègne, and alighted at the Peacock. The host proved to be a worthy man, as bald as a Chinaman. They asked him if some time ago he had not received in his house two gentlemen who were pursued by Dragoons; without answering, he went out and brought in the blade of a rapier.

"Do you know that?" he asked.

Athos merely glanced at it.

"'Tis d'Artagnan's sword," he said.

"Does it belong to the shorter, or taller of the two?" asked the host.

"To the lesser."

"I see that you are the friends of these gentlemen. They were pursued by eight Light Horsemen, who rode into the court-yard before they had time to close the gate; but these men would not have succeeded in taking them prisoners, had they not been assisted by twenty soldiers of the Italian regiment in garrison in this town, so that your friends were overpowered by numbers."

"Arrested, were they?" asked Athos; "is it known why?"

"No, sir, they were carried off directly, and had not time to tell me why; but, as soon as they were gone, I found this broken blade of a sword, as I was helping in raising up two dead men, and five or six wounded ones."

"'Tis still a consolation that they were not wounded," said Aramis.

"Where were they taken?" asked Athos.

"Towards Louvres," was the reply.

The two friends, having agreed to leave Blaisois and Grimaud at Compiègne with the horses, resolved to take post horses; and having snatched a hasty dinner, they continued their journey to Louvres.

Here they found only one inn.

"Let us alight here," said Athos, "d'Artagnan will not have let slip an opportunity of drinking a glass of the famous liquor made here, and, at the same time, leaving some trace of himself."

They went into the town, and asked for two glasses of liquor, at the counter, as their friends must have done before them. The counter, as usual, was covered with a plate of pewter; upon this plate was written with the point of a large pin :—

" Rueil......D...... "

"They went to Rueil," cried Aramis.

"Let us go to Rueil," said Athos. "Had I been as great a friend of Jonah's as I am of d'Artagnan, I should have followed him even into the whale itself; and you would have done the same."

"Certainly, but you make me better than I am, dear Count. Had I been alone, I should scarcely have gone to Rueil without great caution."

They then set off for Rueil. Here the deputies of the Parliament had just arrived, in order to enter upon those famous conferences which were to last three weeks, and produced, eventually, a shameful peace.

The two friends mingled in the crowd, and fancied that every one was occupied with the same thought that tormented them.

But everyone was engrossed by articles and reforms.

They continued their inquiries, and at last met with a Light Dragoon, who had formed one of the guard which had escorted d'Artagnan to Rueil, by which they knew that they had entered that house.

Athos, therefore, perpetually recurred to his proposed interview with the Queen.

"I shall go," he said, "to the Queen."

"Well, then," answered Aramis, "Pray tell me a day or two beforehand, that I may take that opportunity of going to Paris."

"To whom?"

"Zounds! how do I know? perhaps to Mdme. de Longueville. She is all powerful yonder; she will help me. But send me word should you be arrested, for then I will return directly."

"Why do you not take your chance, and be arrested with me?"

"No, I thank you."

"Should we, by being arrested, be all four together again, we should not, I am sure, be twenty-four hours in prison without getting free."

"My friend, since I killed Châtillon, the adored of the ladies of St. Germain, I have too great a celebrity not to fear a prison doubly. The Queen is likely to follow Mazarin's counsels, and to have me tried. Do you think that she loves this Italian so much as they say she does?"

"She loved an Englishman passionately."

"Well, my friend, she is a woman."

"No, no, you are deceived—she is a Queen.

"Dear friend, I shall sacrifice myself and go and see Anne of Austria."

"Athos, I am going to raise an army."

"For what purpose?"

"To come back, and besiege Rueil."

"Where shall we meet again?"

"At the foot of the Cardinal's gallows."

The two friends parted, Aramis to return to Paris, Athos to take some measures preparatory to an interview with the Queen.

CHAPTER LXXVI.

THE GRATITUDE OF ANNE OF AUSTRIA.

ATHOS found much less difficulty than he had expected in obtaining an audience of Anne of Austria; it was granted, and was to take place, after her morning's 'levée,' at which, in accordance with the rights he derived from his birth, he was entitled to be present. A vast crowd filled the apartments of St. Germain.

When the hour appointed for the audience arrived, Athos was obliged to stay until the Queen, who was waited upon by a new deputation from Paris, had consulted with her minister as to the propriety and manner of receiving them. All were fully engrossed with the affairs of the day, and there could be few opportunities less favorable to make an appeal upon; but Athos was a man of inflexible temper, and insisted on his right of being admitted into the Queen's presence. Accordingly, at the close of the audience, she sent for him.

The name of the Count de la Fère was then announced to Anne. Often must she have heard that name, and felt that it had made her heart beat; nevertheless, she remained unmoved, and was contented to look steadfastly at this gentleman, with that set stare which can alone be permitted to a Queen.

"Do you come, then, to offer me your services?" she asked, after some moments' silence.

"Yes, madam," replied Athos, shocked at her not recognizing him. Athos had a noble heart, and made, therefore, but a poor courtier.

Anne frowned. Mazarin, who was sitting at a table, folding up papers, as if he had only been a secretary of state, looked up.

"Speak," said the Queen.

Mazarin turned again to his papers.

"Madam," resumed Athos, "two of my friends, named d'Artagnan and Porthos, sent to England by the Cardinal, have suddenly disappeared; ever since they set foot on the shores of France, no one knows what has become of them."

"Well?" said the Queen.

"I apply, therefore, first to the benevolence of your majesty, that I may know what has become of my friends, reserving to myself, if necessary, the right of appealing afterwards to your justice."

"Sir," repiled Anne, with a degree of haughtiness, which, to some, became impertinence, "is this the reason that you trouble me in the midst of so many absorbing concerns? An affair for the police! Well, sir, you ought to know that since we left Paris there no longer exists a police."

"I think that your majesty will have no need to apply to the police to know where my friends are, but that if you will deign to interrogate the Cardinal, he can reply without any further inquiry than into his own recollections."

"But God forgive me!" cried Anne, with that disdainful curl of the lip peculiar to her, "I think you can inquire yourself."

"Yes, madam, here I have a right to do so, for it concerns M. d'Artagnan; d'Artagnan," he repeated, in such a manner as to bow down the regal brow beneath the recollections of the weak and erring woman.

The Cardinal saw that it was now high time to come to the assistance of Anne.

"Sir," he said, "I can tell what is at present unknown to her majesty. These individuals are under arrest; they disobeyed orders."

"I beg of your majesty, then," said Athos, calm, and not replying to Mazarin, "to relieve of arrest Messrs. d'Artagnan and du Vallon.

"What you ask is an affair of discipline and police," said the Queen.

"M. d'Artagnan never made such an answer as that when the service of your majesty was concerned," said Athos, bowing with great dignity. He was going towards the door, when Mazarin stopped him.

"You have also been in England, sir?" he said, making a sign to the Queen, who was evidently going to issue a severe order.

"I was present at the last hours of Charles I. Poor King. Culpable, at the most, of weakness, how cruelly punished by his subjects! Thrones are at this time shaken, and it is to little purpose for devoted hearts to serve the interests of princes. This is the second time that M. d'Artagnan has been in England. He went the first time to save the honor of a great Queen; the second, to avert the death of a great King."

"My lord," said Anne to Mazarin, with an accent from which daily habits of dissimulation could not entirely chase the real expression, "see if we cannot do something for these gentlemen."

"I wish to do, madam, all that your majesty pleases."

"Do what M. de la Fère requests; that is your name, is it not, sir?"

"I have another name, madam; I am Athos."

"Madam," said Mazarin, with a smile, "you may be easy; your wishes shall be fulfilled."

"You hear, sir?" said the Queen.

"Yes, madam; I expected nothing less from the justice of your majesty. May I not, then, go and see my friends?"

"Yes, sir, you shall see them. But, by the way, you belong to the Fronde, do you not?"

"Madam, I serve the King."

"Yes, in your own way."

"My way is the way of all gentlemen; and I know only one," answered Athos, haughtily.

"Go, sir, then," said the Queen; "you have obtained what you wish, and we know all we wish to know."

Scarcely, however, had the tapestry closed behind Athos than she said to Mazarin:

"Cardinal, desire them to arrest that insolent fellow before he leaves the court."

"Your majesty," answered Mazarin, "desires me to do only what I was going to ask you to let me do. These bravos, who bring back to our epoch the traditions of the other reign, are troublesome; since there are two of them already there, let us add a third."

Athos was not completely the Queen's dupe, but he was not a man to run away merely on suspicion, above all, when distinctly told that he should see his friends again. He waited then, in the ante-chamber with impatience, till he should be conducted to them.

He walked to the window and was looking into the court when some one touched him softly on the shoulder.

"Ah! M. de Comminges," he said.

"Yes, Count, charged with a mission for which I beg of you to accept my excuses. Be so good as to give me up your sword, Count."

Athos smiled and opened the window.

"Aramis!" he cried.

A gentleman turned round. It was Aramis. He bowed with great friendship to the count.

"Aramis!" cried Athos, "I am arrested."

"Very well," replied Aramis, calmly.

"Sir," said Athos, turning to Comminges, and giving him politely his sword by the hilt; "there is my sword; have the kindness to keep it for me until I shall quit my prison. I prize it; it was given to my ancestors by King Francis I. In his time they armed gentlemen, they did not disarm them. Now, whither do you conduct me?"

"Into my room at first," replied Comminges, "the Queen will ultimately decide on the place of your domicile."

Athos followed Comminges without saying a single word.

CHAPTER LXXVII.

THE ROYALTY OF CARDINAL MAZARIN.

THE arrests produced no sensation, and were almost unknown, and scarcely interrupted the course of events. To the deputation it was formally announced that the Queen would receive it.

Accordingly it was admitted to the presence of Anne, who, silent and lofty as ever, listened to the speeches and complaints of the deputies; but when they had finished their harangues, not one of them could say, so calm had been her face, whether she had heard them or not. Whilst thus she was silent, Mazarin, who was present, and knew what the deputies asked, answered in these terms:

"Gentlemen," he said, "I shall join with you in supplicating the Queen to put an end to the miseries of her subjects. I have done all in my power to ameliorate them, and yet the belief of the public, you say, is that they proceed from me, an unhappy foreigner who has been unable to please the French. Alas! 'tis not for me, a private individual, to disunite a queen from her kingdom. Since you require my resignation, I shall retire."

"Then," said Aramis, in his neighbor's ears, "the conferences are over. There is nothing to do but to send M. Mazarin to the most distant frontier, and to take care that he does not return even by that, nor any other enrance, into France."

Anne dropped her head and fell into one of those reveries so habitual with her. Her recollection of Athos came into her mind. His fearless deportment; his words, so firm, yet so dignified; the shades which by one word he had evoked, recalled to her the past in all its intoxication of poetry and romance, youth, beauty, the éclat of love at twenty years of age, the bloody death of Buckingham, the only man whom she ever really loved, and the heroism of those obscure champions who had saved her from the double hatred of Richelieu and of the King.

Mazarin looked at her, and whilst she seemed herself alone and freed from that world of enemies who sought to spy into her secret thoughts, he read her thoughts in her countenance, as one sees in a transparent lake clouds pass—reflections, like thoughts, of the heavens.

"Must we, then," asked Anne of Austria, "yield to the storm, purchase a peace, and await patiently and piously for better times?"

Mazarin smiled sarcastically at this speech, which showed that she had taken the minister's proposal seriously.

Anne's head was bent down, and she did not see this smile; but finding that her question elicited no reply, she looked up. "Well, you do not answer, Cardinal; what do you think about it?"

"I am thinking, madam, of the allusion made by that insolent gentleman, whom you have caused to be arrested, to the Duke of Buckingham, whom you suffered to be assassinated; to the Duchess de Chevreuse, whom you suffered to be exiled; to Duke de Beaufort, exiled; but he made no allusion to me, because he is ignorant of the relation in which I stand to you."

Anne drew up, as she always did, when anything touched her pride. She blushed, and that she might not answer, clasped her beautiful hands till her sharp nails almost pierced them.

"That man has sagacity, honor, and wit, not to mention likewise that he is a man of undoubted resolution. You know something about him, do you not, madam? I shall tell him, therefore, and in doing so I shall confer a personal favor on him, how he is mistaken in regard to me. What is proposed to me would be, in fact, almost an abdication, and an abdication requires reflection."

"An abdication?" repeated Anne; "I thought, sir, that it was only Kings who abdicated?"

"Well," replied Mazarin, "and am I not almost a King; ruler, indeed, of France? Thrown over the foot of the royal bed, my simar, madam, is not unlike the mantle worn by a King."

This was one of the humiliations which Mazarin made Anne undergo more frequently than any other, and which bowed her head with shame. Queen Elizabeth and Catherine II. of Russia are the only two monarchs on record who were at once sovereigns and lovers. Anne of Austria looked with a sort of terror at the threatening aspect of the Cardinal; his physiognomy in such moments was not destitute of grandeur.

"Sir," she replied, "did I not say, and did you not hear me say to those people, that you should do as you pleased?"

"In that case," said Mazarin, "I think it must please me best to remain; not only on account of my own interest, but for your safety."

"Remain, then, sir; nothing can be more agreeable to me; only do not allow me to be insulted."

"I understand; you allude to the recollections perpetually revived by these three gentlemen. However, we hold them safe in prison; and they are just sufficiently culpable for us to keep them in prison as long as is convenient to us. One, only, is still not in our power, and braves us. But devil take him! we shall soon succeed in sending him to rejoin his companions. We have accomplished more difficult things than that. In the first place, I have, as a precaution, shut up, at Rueil, near me, under my own eyes, within reach of my hand, the two most intractable ones. To-day the third will be there also."

"As long as they are in prison, all will be well," said Anne; "but one of these days they will get out."

"Yes; if your majesty releases them."

"Ah!" exclaimed Anne, following the train of her own thoughts on such occasions; "one regrets Paris on account of the Bastille, sir, which is so strong and so secure."

"Madam, these conferences will bring us peace; when we have peace we shall regain Paris; with Paris the Bastille, and our three bullies shall rot therein."

Anne frowned slightly, when Mazarin, in taking leave, kissed her hand.

Mazarin, after this half humble, half gallant attention, went away. Anne followed him with her eyes, and as he withdrew, at every step he took, a disdainful smile was seen playing, then gradually burst upon her lips.

"I once," she said, "despised the love of a Cardinal who never said 'I shall do,' but 'I have done.' That man knew of retreats more secure than Rueil; darker, and more silent even than the Bastille. Oh, the degenerate world!"

CHAPTER LXXVIII.

PRECAUTIONS.

AFTER quitting Anne, Mazarin took the road to Rueil, where he usually resided; in those times of disturbance he went about with numerous followers, and often disguised himself. In the military dress he was indeed, as we have before stated, a very handsome man.

In the court of the old château of St. Germain, he entered his coach, and reached the Seine at Chalon. The prince had supplied him with fifty light horse, not so much by the way of a guard, as to show the deputies how readily the Queen's generals dispersed their troops, and to prove that they might be scattered about at pleasure. Athos, on horseback, without his sword, and kept in sight by Comminges, followed the Cardinal in silence. Grimaud, finding that his master had been arrested, fell back into the ranks, near Aramis, without saying a word, as if nothing had happened.

Grimaud had, indeed, during twenty-two years of service, seen his master extricate himself from so many difficulties, that nothing made him uneasy.

At the branching off of the road towards Paris, Aramis, who had followed in the Cardinal's suite, turned back. Mazarin went to the right hand, and Aramis could see the prisoner disappear at the turning of the avenue. Athos, at the same moment, moved by a similar impulse, looked back also. The two friends exchanged a simple inclination of the head, and Aramis put his finger to his hat, as if to bow; Athos, alone, comprehended by that signal that he had some project in his head.

Ten minutes afterwards, Mazarin entered the court of that château which his predecessor had built for him, at Rueil; as he alighted, Comminges approached him.

"My lord," he asked, "where does your Eminence wish Count de la Fère to be lodged?"

"Certainly in the pavilion of the orangery; in front of the pavilion where the guard is. I wish every respect shown to the count, although he is the prisoner of the Queen."

"My lord," answered Comminges, "he begs to be taken into the place where M. d'Artagnan is confined, that is, in the hunting lodge opposite the orangery."

Mazarin thought for an instant.

Comminges saw that he was undecided.

"'Tis a very strong post," he resumed; "and forty good men, tried soldiers, and consequently having nothing to do with Frondeurs, nor any interest in the Fronde."

"If we put these three men together, M. Comminges," said Mazarin, "we must double the guard, and we are not rich enough in defenders to commit such acts of prodigality."

Comminges smiled; Mazarin read, and construed that smile.

"You do not know these men, M. Comminges, but I know them, first, personally; also, by hearsay. I sent them to carry aid to King Charles, and they performed prodigies to save him; had it not been for an adverse destiny, that beloved monarch would, this day, have been among us."

"But, since they served your Eminence so well, why are they, my lord Cardinal, in prison?"

"In prison?" asked Mazarin; "and when has Rueil been a prison?"

"Ever since there were prisoners in it," answered Comminges.

"These gentlemen, Comminges, are not prisoners," returned Mazarin, with his ironical smile, "but guests; and guests so precious, that I have put a grating before each of their windows, and bolts to their doors, that they may not be weary of being my visitors. So much do I esteem them, that I am going to make the Count de la Fère a visit, that I may converse with him tête-a-tête; and that we may not be disturbed at our interview, you must conduct him, as I said before, into the pavilion of the orangery; that, you know, is my daily promenade."

Comminges bowed, and returned to impart to Athos the result of his request. Athos, who had been awaiting the Cardinal's decision, with outward composure, but secret uneasiness, then entreated that Comminges would do him one favor, which was to intimate to d'Artagnan that he was placed in the pavilion of the orangery, for the purpose of receiving a visit from the Cardinal, and that he should profit by the opportunity, in order to ask for some mitigation of their close imprisonment.

"Which cannot last," interrupted Comminges, "the Cardinal said so; there is no prison here."

"But there are oubliettes!" replied Athos, smiling.

"Oh! that's a different thing; yes, I know there are traditions of that sort," said Comminges; "it was in the time of the other Cardinal, who was a great nobleman; but our Mazarin—impossible! an Italian adventurer could not go to such lengths towards such men as us. Dungeons are employed as a means of kindly vengeance, and a low-born fellow, such as he is, dare not have recourse to them. No, no, be easy on that score. I shall, however, inform M. d'Artagnan of your arrival here."

Comminges then led the count to a room on the ground floor of a pavilion, at the end of the orangery. They passed through a court-yard, as they went, full of soldiers and courtiers. In the centre of this court, in the form of a horse-shoe, were the buildings occupied by Mazarin, and at each wing the pavilion (or smaller building) where d'Artagnan was, and that, level with the orangery, where Athos was to be. Behind each end of these two wings extended the park.

Athos, when he reached this appointed room, observed, through the gratings of his window, walls, and roofs; and was told, on inquiry, by Comminges, that he was looking on the back of the pavilion where d'Artagnan was confined.

"Yes, 'tis too true," said Comminges, "'tis almost a prison; but what a singular fancy this is of yours, Count—you, who are the very flower of our nobility—to go and spend your valor and loyalty amongst these upstarts, the Frondists!"

"Besides," said Athos, "what a charming thing it would have been to serve the Cardinal! Look at that wall—without a single window—which tells you fine things about Mazarin's gratitude!"

"Yes," replied de Comminges, "more especially if that could reveal how M. d'Artagnan for this last week has been swearing at him."

"Poor d'Artagnan," said Athos, with that charming melancholy which was one of the external traits of his character, "so brave and good, but terrible to the enemies of those whom he loves; you have two unruly prisoners there, sir."

"Unruly," Comminges smiled, "you wish to make me afraid, I suppose. When he came here, M. d'Artagnan provoked and braved all the soldiers and inferior officers, in order, I suppose, to have his sword back—that mood lasted some time—but now he's as gentle as a lamb, and sings Gascon songs which make one die with laughing."

"And du Vallon?" asked Athos.

"Ah, he's quite another sort, a formidable gentleman, indeed. The first day he broke all the doors in with a single push of his shoulder; and I expected to see him leave Rueil in the same way as Samson left Gaza. But his temper cooled down like his friend's; he not only gets used to his captivity, but jokes about it."

"So much the better," said Athos; and, on reflection, he felt convinced that this improvement in the spirits of the two captives proceeded from some plan formed by d'Artagnan for their escape.

CHAPTER LXXIX.

CAGED.

Now let us pass the orangery, to the hunting lodge. At the extremity of the court-yard, where, close to a portico formed of Ionic columns, there were dog-kennels, rose an oblong building, the pavilion of the orangery, a half-circle, enclosing the court of honors. It was in this summer-house, on the ground floor, that d'Artagnan and Porthos were confined, suffering the hours of a long imprisonment in a manner suitable to each different temperament.

D'Artagnan was walking about like a tiger, his eyes fixed, growling as he paced along by the bars of a window looking upon the yard of servants' offices.

Porthos was ruminating over an excellent dinner which had been served up to him.

The one seemed to be deprived of reason, yet he was meditating. The other seemed to meditate, yet he was sleeping. But his sleep was a nightmare which might be guessed by the incoherent manner in which he snored.

"Look," said d'Artagnan, "day is declining. It must be nearly four o'clock. We have been in this place nearly eighty-three hours."

"Hem!" muttered Porthos, with a kind of pretence of answering.

"Did you hear, eternal sleeper?" cried d'Artagnan, irritated that any one could doze during the day when he had the greatest difficulty in sleeping during the night.

" 'Tis your fault," answered Porthos. "I offered to you escape."

"By tearing down an iron bar and pushing in a door, Porthos. People like us cannot just go out as they like; besides, going out of this room is not everything."

"Well, then, let us kill the sentinel, and then we shall have arms."

"Yes; but before we can kill him—and hard to kill is a Swiss —he will howl, and the whole piquet will come, and we shall be taken like foxes—we, who are lions—and thrown into some dungeon, where we shall not even have the consolation of seeing this frightful grey sky of Rueil, which is no more like the sky of Tarbes than the moon to the sun. Lack-a-day! if we only had some one to instruct us about the physical and moral topography of this castle. Ah, when one thinks that for twenty years—during which time I did not know what to do with myself—it never occurred to me to come to study Rueil. And after all, 'tis impossible but that Aramis, or Athos, that wise gentleman, should discover our retreat, then, faith, it will be time to act."

"Yes, more especially as it is not very disagreeable here, with one exception; three days running they have brought us braised mutton!"

"If that occurs a fourth time I shall complain of it, so never mind."

"And then I feel the loss of my house; 'tis a long time since I visited my castles."

"Forget them for a time; we shall return to them, unless Mazarin razes them to the ground."

"Do you think that likely?"

"No; the other Cardinal would have done so; but this one is too low a fellow to risk it."

"You console me, d'Artagnan."

The two prisoners were at this point of their conversation when Comminges entered, preceded by a sergeant and by two men, who brought supper in a basket with two handles, filled with basins and plates.

"What!" exclaimed Porthos, "mutton again?"

"My dear M. de Comminges," said d'Artagnan, "you will find my friend, du Vallon, will go to the most fatal lengths if M. Mazarin continues to provide us with this sort of meat; mutton every day."

"I declare," said Porthos, "I shall eat nothing if they do not take it away."

"Take away the mutton," said Comminges; "I wish M. du Vallon to sup well, more especially as I have news to give him which will improve his appetite."

"Is Mazarin put to death?" asked Porthos.

"No; I am sorry to tell you he is perfectly well."

"So much the worse," said Porthos.

"Should you be very glad to hear that the Count de la Fère was well?" asked de Comminges.

D'Artagnan's small eyes were opened to the utmost.

"Glad!" he cried; "I should be more than glad! Happy! beyond measure!"

"Well, I am desired by him to give you his compliments, and to say that he is in good health."

"Then you have seen him?"

"Certainly, I have."

"Where? if it is not impertinent."

"Near here," replied de Comminges, smiling; "so near that if the windows which look on the orangery were not stopped up you might see the place where he is."

"He is wandering about the environs," thought d'Artagnan. Then he said aloud:

"You met him, I dare say, in the park, hunting, perhaps?"

"No; nearer, nearer still. Look behind this wall," said de Comminges, knocking against the wall.

"Behind this wall? What is there, then, behind this wall? I was brought here by night, so devil take me if I know where I am. The count is then in the château!"

"Yes."

"For what reason?"

"The same as yourself."

"Athos is, then, a prisoner?"

"You know well," replied de Comminges, "that there are no prisoners at Rueil, because there is no prison."

"Don't let us play upon words, sir. Athos has been arrested?"

"Yesterday, at St. Germain, as he came out from the presence of the Queen."

The arms of d'Artagnan fell powerless by his side. One might have supposed him thunderstruck; a paleness ran like a cloud over his dark skin, but disappeared immediately.

"A prisoner?" he reiterated.

"A prisoner," repeated Porthos, quite dejected.

Suddenly d'Artagnan looked up, and in his eyes there was a gleam which scarcely even Porthos observed; but it died away, and he remained more sorrowful than before.

"Come, come," said Comminges, who, since d'Artagnan, on the day of Broussel's arrest, had saved him from the hands of the Parisians, had entertained a real affection for him; "don't be downcast, I never thought of bringing you bad news. Laugh at the mischance which has befallen your friend and M. du Vallon, instead of being in the depths of despair about it."

But d'Artagnan was still in a desponding mood.

"And how did he look?" asked Porthos, who, perceiving

that d'Artagnan had allowed the conversation to drop, profited
by it to put in his word.

"Very well, indeed, sir," replied Comminges; "at first, like
you, he seemed distressed; but when he heard that the Cardinal was going to pay him a visit this very evening——"

"Ah!" cried d'Artagnan; "the Cardinal going to visit the
Count de la Fère?"

"Yes; and the count desired me to tell you that he should
take advantage of this visit to plead for you and for himself."

"Ah! the dear count!" said d'Artagnan.

"A fine thing, indeed!" grunted Porthos. "A great favor!
Zounds! The Count de la Fère, whose family is allied to the
Montmorencys and the Rohans, is well worthy of M. Maz-
arin's civilities."

"Never mind!" said d'Artagnan, in his calmest tone, and
looking, but in vain, at Porthos, to see if he comprehended all
the importance of this visit. "'Tis then, M. Mazarin's custom
to walk in his orangery?" he added.

"He shuts himself up there every evening, to ponder over
state affairs."

"It looks as if he would receive the count," observed d'Artagnan; "of course he will be attended?"

"A couple of guards——"

"He talks politics before troopers?"

"No, Swiss who know only German, and stay by the door."

"Let the Cardinal take care of going alone to visit the Count
de la Fère," said d'Artagnan; "for the count must be mad."

Comminges began to laugh. "Really, to hear you talk, one
would suppose you were cannibals. The count is an affable
man; besides, he is unarmed; at the first word from his Eminence the two soldiers about him would run to him."

"Now," said d'Artagnan; "I've one last favor to ask of you,
M. de Comminges."

"At your service, sir."

"You will see the count again?"

"To-morrow morning."

"Will you remember us to him, and ask him to solicit one
favor for me—that his Eminence should do me the honor to
give me a hearing; that is all I want."

"Oh!" muttered Porthos, shaking his head; "never should
I have thought this of *him!* How misfortune humbles a man!"

"That shall be done," answered de Comminges.

"Tell the count that I am well; that you found me sad, but
resigned."

"I am pleased, sir, to hear that."

"And the same, also, for M. du Vallon——"

"Not for me!" cried Porthos; "I'm not at all resigned."

He will be so, monsieur; I know him better than he knows
himself. Be silent, dear du Vallon, and resign yourself."

"Adieu, gentlemen," said Comminges; "sleep well!"

"We will try."

Comminges went away, d'Artagnan remaining apparently in the same attitude of humble resignation; but scarcely had he departed than he turned, and hugged Porthos with joy not to be doubted.

"Oh!" cried Porthos; "What's the matter now? Are you mad, my dear friend?"

"What's the matter?" returned d'Artagnan; "we are saved!"

"I don't see that at all," answered Porthos. "I think we are all taken prisoners, except Aramis, and that our chances of going out are lessened since we were entangled in Mazarin's trap."

"Which is far too strong for two of us, but not strong enough for three of us," returned d'Artagnan.

"I don't understand," said Porthos.

"Never mind; let's sit down to table, and take something to strengthen us for the night."

"What are we to do to-night?"

"Travel—perhaps."

"But——"

"Sit down, dear friend, at table. While we are eating, ideas flow easily. After supper, when they are perfected, I will communicate my plans to you."

So Porthos sat down to the table without another word, and ate with an appetite that did honor to the confidence which d'Artagnan's imagination had inspired him with.

CHAPTER LXXX.

THE STRONG ARM.

Supper was eaten in silence, but not in sadness; from time to time one of those sweet smiles which were habitual to him in his moments of good-humor illuminated the face of d'Artagnan. Not one of these smiles was lost on Porthos and at everyone he uttered an exclamation which betrayed to his friend that he had not lost sight of the idea which possessed his brain.

At dessert d'Artagnan reposed in his chair, crossed one leg over the other, and lounged about like a man perfectly at his ease.

"Well, you were saying you wished to leave this place."

"Ah, indeed! will is not wanting."

"To go away hence you would not mind, you added, knocking down a door or a wall."

" 'Tis true, I said so, and I say it again."

"At what o'clock did we see, pray, the two Swiss guards walk last night?"

"An hour after sunset."

"If they go out to-day, as they did yesterday, we shall have the honor, then, of seeing them in half-an-hour?"

"In a quarter of an hour, at most."

"Your arm is still strong enough, is it not, Porthos?"

Porthos unbuttoned his sleeve, raised his shirt, and looked complacently on his strong arm, as large as the leg of any ordinary man.

"Yes, indeed," he said; "pretty good."

"So that you could, without trouble, convert these tongs into a hoop, and the shovel into a corkscrew?"

"Certainly." And the giant took up these two articles, and, without any apparent effort, produced in them the metamorphosis requested by his companion.

"There!" he cried.

"Capital!" exclaimed the Gascon. "Really, Porthos, you are a gifted individual!"

"I have heard speak," said Porthos, "of a certain Milo of Crete, who performed wonderful feats, such as binding his forehead with a cord and bursting it; of killing an ox with a blow of his fist, and carrying it home on his shoulders, etc. I used to learn all these facts by heart yonder, down at Pierrefonds, and I have done all that he did except breaking a cord by the swelling of my temples."

"Because your strength is not in your head, Porthos," said his friend.

"No; it is in my arms and shoulders," answered Porthos, with simplicity.

"Well, my dear friend, let us go near the window, and try your strength in severing an iron bar."

Porthos approached the window, took a bar in his hands, clung to it, and bent it like a bow, so that the two ends came out of the socket of stone in which for thirty years they had been fixed.

"Well, friend, the Cardinal, although such a genius, could never have done that."

"Shall I take out any more of them?" asked Porthos.

"No; that is sufficient; a man can pass through that."

Porthos tried, and passed the trunk of his body through.

"Yes," he said.

"Now run your arm through this opening."

"Why?"

"You will know presently; run it through."

"I wish to know, however, that I may understand," said Porthos.

"You will know directly; see, the door of the guard-room opens. They are going to send into the court the two guards, who accompany Mazarin when he crosses into the orangery.

See, they are coming out, and have closed the door after them."

The two soldiers advanced on the side where the window was, rubbing their hands, for it was cold, it being the month of February.

At this moment the door of the guard-house was opened, and one of the soldiers was summoned away.

"Now," said d'Artagnan, "I am going to call this soldier and talk to him. Don't lose a word of what I am going to say to you, Porthos. Everything is in the execution."

"Good, the execution of a plot is my forte."

"I know it well. I depend on you. Look, I shall turn to the left; so that the soldier will be at your right, as soon as he mounts on the bench to talk to us."

"But supposing he doesn't mount?"

"He will; rely on it. As soon as you see him get up, stretch out your arm and seize him by his neck. Then raising him up, you must pull him into our room, taking care to squeeze, so tight that he can't cry out."

"Oh!" said Porthos. "Suppose I were to strangle him?"

"There would only be a Swiss the less in the world; but you will not do so, I hope. Lay him down here; we'll gag him, and tie him—no matter where—somewhere. So we shall get from him one uniform and a sword."

"Marvellous!" exclaimed Porthos; looking at the Gascon with the most profound admiration.

"Pooh!" replied d'Artagnan.

"Yes," said Porthos, recollecting himself, "but one uniform and one sword are not enough for two."

"Well; but there's his comrade."

"True;" said Porthos.

"Therefore, when I cough, stretch out your arm."

"Good!"

The two friends then placed themselves as they had agreed, Porthos being completely hidden in an angle of the window.

"Good evening, comrade," said d'Artagnan, in his most fascinating voice and manner.

"Goot efening, zir," answered the soldier, in a strong accent.

"'Tis not too warm for a walk?" resumed d'Artagnan.

"Not doo varm."

"And I think a glass of wine will not be disagreeable to you?"

"A class of vine will pe bery velcome."

"The fish bites! the fish bites!" whispered the Gascon to Porthos.

"I understand," said Porthos.

"A bottle, perhaps?"

"A whole pottle? Yah, zir."

"A whole one, if you will drink to my health."

"Mit bleasure," answered the soldier.

"Come then and take it, friend," said the Gascon.

"Mit all my heart. How convenient! dere's a pench here! One would dink it was blaced here on burbose."

"Get on it; that's it, friend."

And d'Artagnan coughed.

That instant the arm of Porthos fell. His hand of iron grasped, quick as lightning, and firm as a pair of pincers, the soldier's throat. He raised him, almost stifling him as he drew him through the aperture at the risk of flaying him as he pulled him through. He then laid him down on the floor, where d'Artagnan, after giving him just time enough to draw his breath, gagged him with his scarf; and the moment he had done so began to undress him with the promptitude and dexterity of a man who learned his business on the field of battle. Then the soldier, gagged and bound, was carried inside of the hearth, the fire of which had been previously extinguished by the two friends.

"Here's a sword and a dress," said Porthos.

"I take them," said d'Artagnan, "for myself. If you want another uniform and sword, you must play the same trick over again. Stop! I see the other soldier issue from the guard-room, and come towards us."

"I think," replied Porthos, "it would be imprudent to attempt the same manœuvre again; a failure would be ruinous. No; I will go down, seize the man unawares, and bring him to you ready gagged."

He did as he said. Porthos seized his opportunity, caught the next soldier by his neck, gagged him, and pushed him like a mummy through the bars into the room, and entered after him. Then they undressed him as they had done the first; laid him on their bed, and bound him with the straps which composed the bed, the bedstead being of oak. This operation proved as successful as the first.

"There," said d'Artagnan, " 'tis capital! Now let me try on the dress of yonder chap. Porthos, I doubt if you can wear it; but should it be too tight, never mind, you can wear the breastplate, and the hat with the red feathers."

It happened, however, that the second soldier was a Swiss of gigantic proportions, so, except that some of the seams split, his dress fitted Porthos perfectly.

They then dressed themselves.

" 'Tis done!" they both exclaimed at once. "As to you, comrades," they said to the men, "nothing will happen to you if you are discreet; but if you stir, you are dead men."

The soldiers were pliant; they had found the grasp of Porthos rather powerful, and that it was no joke to contend against it.

"Follow me," said d'Artagnan. "The man who lives to see, shall see."

And, slipping through the aperture, he alighted in the court.

CHAPTER LXXXI.

THE KEEN WIT.

SCARCELY had the two Frenchmen touched the ground than a door opened, and the voice of the valet-de-chambre called out, "Make ready!"

At the same moment the guard-house was opened, and a voice called out:

"La Bruyère and du Barthois! March!"

"It seems that I am named la Bruyère," said d'Artagnan.

"And I, du Barthois," added Porthos.

"Where are you?" asked the valet-de-chambre, whose eyes, dazzled by the light, could not clearly distinguish our heroes in the gloom.

"Here we are," said the Gascon.

These two newly-enlisted soldiers marched gravely after the valet-de-chambre, who opened the door of the vestibule; then another, which seemed to be that of a waiting-room, and showing the tools, he said:

"Your orders are very simple, don't allow anybody, except one person, to enter here. Do you hear? not a single creature! Obey that person completely. On your return you cannot make a mistake. You have only to wait here till I release you."

D'Artagnan was known to this valet-de-chambre, who was no other than Bernouin, and he had, during the last six or eight months, introduced the Gascon a dozen times to the Cardinal. The Gascon, therefore, instead of answering, growled out "Yah! Yah!" in the most German and the least Gascon accent possible.

As to Porthos, with whom d'Artagnan had insisted on a perfect silence, and who did not even now begin to comprehend the scheme of his friend, which was to follow Mazarin in his visit to Athos, he was mute. All that he was allowed to say, in case of emergencies, was the proverbial and solemn *Der Teufel!*

Bernouin went away and shut the door. When Porthos heard the key turn, he began to be alarmed, lest they should only have exchanged one prison for another.

"Porthos, my friend," said d'Artagnan, "don't distrust Providence! Let me consider. We have walked eight paces," whispered d'Artagnan, "and gone up six steps, so hereabouts is the pavilion called the orangery. Count de la Fère cannot be far off, only the doors are locked."

"A grand difficulty!" cried Porthos.

"Hush!" said d'Artagnan.

The sound of a light step was heard in the vestibule. The

hinges of the door creaked, and there appeared a cavalier, wrapped in a brown cloak, with a lantern in his hand, and a large beaver hat pulled down over his eyes.

Porthos stood with his face against the wall, but he could not render himself invisible; and the man in the cloak said to him, giving him his lantern:

"Light the lamp which hangs from the ceiling."

Then, addressing d'Artagnan,—

"You know the watchword?" he said.

"Yah!" replied the Gascon, determined to confine himself to this specimen of the German tongue.

"*Tedesco!*" answered the cavalier; "*va bene.*"

And advancing towards the door opposite to that by which he came in, he opened it and disappeared behind it, shutting it as he went.

"Now," asked Porthos, "what are we to do?"

"Now we shall make use of your shoulder, friend Porthos, if this door should be locked. Everything in its proper time, and all comes right to those who know how to wait patiently. But first barricade the first door well, and then we will follow yonder cavalier."

The two friends set to work and crowded the space before the door with all the furniture in the room, so as not only to make the passage impassable, but that the door could not open inwards.

"There!" said d'Artagnan, "we can't be overtaken. Come! forward!"

CHAPTER LXXXII.

MAZARIN'S DUNGEONS.

At first, on arriving at the door through which Mazarin had passed, d'Artagnan tried in vain to open it; but on the powerful shoulder of Porthos being applied to one of the panels, to press it, d'Artagnan introduced the point of his sword between the bolt and the staple of the lock. The bolt gave way and the door opened.

"As I told you, one can overcome women and doors, by gentleness."

"You're a great moralist," said Porthos.

They entered; behind a glass window, by the light of the Cardinal's lantern, placed on the floor in the midst of the gallery, they saw the orange and pomegranate trees in long lines, forming one great alley and two smaller side ones.

"No Cardinal!" said d'Artagnan, "but only his lamp; where the devil is he then?"

Exploring, however, one of the side wings of the gallery, he saw all at once, at his left, a tub containing an orange tree, which had been pushed out of its place, and in its place an open aperture. He also perceived in this hold the steps of a winding staircase.

He called Porthos to look at it.

"Had our object been money only," he said, "we should be rich directly. At the bottom of that staircase is, probably, the Cardinal's treasury, of which everyone speaks so much; and we should only have to descend—empty a chest—shut the Cardinal up in it—double-lock it—go away, carrying off as much gold as we could—put this orange tree over the place, and no one would ever ask us where our fortune came from, not even the Cardinal."

"It would be a happy hit for rogues to make, but it seems to be unworthy of two gentlemen," said Porthos.

"So I think; and, we said if we want gold—we want other things," replied the Gascon.

At the same moment, while d'Artagnan was leaning over the aperture to listen, a metallic chink, as if some one was moving a bag of gold, struck on his ear; he started; instantly afterwards a door opened, and a light played upon the staircase.

Mazarin had left his lamp in the gallery to make people believe that he was walking about, but he had with him a waxlight to explore with its aid his mysterious strong box.

" 'Faith!" he said, in Italian, as he was reascending the steps, and looking at a bag of reals, " 'faith, there's enough to pay five councillors of the Parliament, and two generals in Paris. I am a great captain—that I am! but I make war in my own style."

The two friends were crouching down, meantime, behind a tub in the side alley.

Mazarin came within three steps of d'Artagnan, and pushing a spring in the wall, the slab on which the orange tree was, turned, and the orange tree resumed its place.

Then the Cardinal put out the wax light, slipped it into his pocket, and taking up the lantern, "Now," he said, "for M. de la Fère."

"Very good," thought d'Artagnan, " 'tis our road likewise; we can go together."

All three set off on their walk, Mazarin taking the middle and the friends a side one.

The Cardinal reached a second door without perceiving that he was followed; the sand by which the alley was covered deadened the sound of footsteps.

He then turned to the left, down a corridor which had escaped the attention of the two friends; but as he opened the door, he stopped, as if in thought.

"Ah! Diavolo!" he exclaimed, "I forgot the recommendation of Comminges, who advised me to take a guard and place it at this door, in order not to put myself at the mercy of that fourheaded devil." And, with impatience, he turned to retrace his steps.

"Do not give yourself the trouble, my lord," said d'Artagnan, with his right foot forward, his beaver in his hand, a smile on his face; "we have followed your Eminence, step by step, and here we are."

"Yes, here we are," said Porthos.

And he made the same friendly salute as d'Artagnan.

Mazarin gazed at each of them with an affrighted stare, recognized them, and let drop his lantern, uttering a cry of terror. D'Artagnan picked it up; by good luck it had not been extinguished by the fall.

"Oh! what imprudence, my lord," said d'Artagnan; "'tis not good to go about here without a light. Your Eminence might knock against something or fall into some hole."

"M. d'Artagnan!" muttered Mazarin, not able to recover from his astonishment.

"Yes, my lord, it is I; I've the honor of presenting you M. du Vallon, that excellent friend of mine, in whom your Eminence had the kindness to interest yourself once."

And d'Artagnan held the lamp before the merry face of Porthos, who now began to comprehend the affair, and be very proud of the whole undertaking.

"You were going to visit M. de la Fère?" said d'Artagnan. "Don't let us disarrange your Eminence. Be so good as to show us the way, and we will follow you."

Mazarin was by degrees recovering his senses.

"Have you been long in the orangery?" he asked in a trembling voice, remembering the visit he had been paying to his treasury.

"We are just come, my lord."

Mazarin breathed again. His fears were now no longer for his hoards, but for himself. A sort of smile played on his lips.

"Come," he said, "you have taken me in a snare, gentlemen. I confess myself conquered. You wish to ask for your liberty, and I give it you."

"Oh, my lord!" answered d'Artagnan, "you are very good; as to our liberty, we have that; we want to ask something else of you."

"You have your liberty?" repeated Mazarin, in terror.

"Certainly; and on the other hand, my lord, you have lost it; and now 'tis the law of war, sir, you must buy it back again."

Mazarin felt a shiver all over him, a chill even to his heart's core. His piercing look was fixed in vain on the satirical face of the Gascon and on the unchanging countenance of Porthos. Both were in shadow, and even a sybil could not have read them.

"And how much will that cost me, Monsieur d'Artagnan?"

"Zounds, my lord, I don't know yet. We must ask the Count de la Fère the question. Will your Eminence deign to open the door which leads to the count's room, and in ten minutes it will be settled."

Mazarin started.

"My lord," said d'Artagnan, "your Eminence sees that we wish to act with all due forms of respect; but I must warn you that we have no time to lose; open the door then, my lord, and be so good as to remember, once for all, that on the slightest attempt to escape or the least cry for help, our position being a very critical one, you must not be angry with us if we go to extremities."

"Be assured," answered Mazarin, "that I shall attempt nothing; I give you my word of honor."

D'Artagnan made a sign to Porthos to redouble his watchfulness; then turning to Mazarin, said:

"Now, my lord, let us enter, if you please."

CHAPTER LXXXIII.

CONFERENCES.

MAZARIN opened the lock of a double door, on the threshold of which they found Athos ready to receive his illustrious guest; on seeing his friends he started with surprise.

"D'Artagnan! Porthos!" he exclaimed.

"My very self, dear friend."

"Me also," repeated Porthos.

"What means this?" asked the count.

"It means," replied Mazarin, trying to smile, and biting his lips in smiling, "that our parts are changed, and that instead of these gentlemen being my prisoners, I am theirs; but, gentlemen, I warn you, unless you kill me, your victory will be of short duration; people will come to the rescue."

"Ah! my lord," said the Gascon, "don't threaten! 'tis a bad example. We are so good and gentle to your Eminence. Come, let up, put aside all rancor and talk pleasantly."

"There's nothing I wish more," replied Mazarin. "But don't think yourselves in a better position than you are. In ensnaring me you have fallen into the trap yourselves. How are you to get away from here? remember the soldiers and sentinels who guard these doors. Now I am going to show to you how sincere I am."

"Good," thought d'Artagnan, "we must look about us; he's going to play us a trick."

"I offered you your liberty," continued the minister; "will you take it? Before an hour will have passed you will be discovered, arrested, obliged to kill me, which would be a crime unworthy of loyal gentlemen like you."

"He is right," thought Athos.

And, like every other reflection passing in a mind that entertained none but noble thoughts, this feeling was expressed in his eyes.

"We shall not," answered d'Artagnan, "have recourse to violence, except in the last extremity" (for he saw that Athos seemed to lean towards Mazarin).

"If, on the contrary," resumed Mazarin, "you accept your liberty——"

"Why you, my lord, might take it away from us five minutes afterwards; and from my knowledge of you, I believe you will take it away from us."

"No, on the faith of a Cardinal. You do not believe me?"

"My lord, I never believe Cardinals who are not priests."

"Well, on the faith of a minister."

"You are no longer a minister, my lord; you are a prisoner."

"Then, on the honor of a Mazarin, as I am, and ever shall be, I hope," said the Cardinal.

"Hem!" replied d'Artagnan. "I have heard speak of a Mazarin who had little religion when his oaths were in question. I fear he may have been an ancestor of your Eminence."

"M. d'Artagnan, you are a great wit, and I'm quite sorry to be on bad terms with you."

"My lord, let us make it up; one recourse always remains to us. That of dying together."

Mazarin shuddered.

"Listen," he said; "at the end of yonder corridor is a door, of which I have the key; it leads into the park. Go, and take this key with you; you are active, vigorous, and you have arms. At a hundred steps to the left, you will find the wall of the park; get over it, and in three jumps you will be on the road, and free."

"Ah! S'death, my lord," said d'Artagnan, "you have well said, but these are only words. Where is the key you spoke of?"

"Here it is."

"Ah! my lord! You will conduct us yourself, then, to that door?"

"Very willingly, if it be necessary to reassure you," answered Mazarin, who was delighted to get off so cheaply, and he led the way, in high spirits, to the corridor, and opened the door.

It led into the park, as the three fugitives perceived by the night breeze which rushed into the corridor, and blew the wind into their faces.

"The devil!" exclaimed the Gascon. " 'Tis a dreadful night, my lord. We don't know the localities, and shall never find the wall. Since your Eminence has come so far, a few steps farther conduct us, my lord, to the wall."

"Be it so," replied the Cardinal; and at a straight line he walked to the wall, at the foot of which they all four arrived at the same instant.

"Are you satisfied, gentlemen?" asked Mazarin.

"I think so; indeed, we should be hard to please if we were not. Deuce take it; three gentlemen escorted by a prince of the Church! Ah! my lord! you remarked that we were all vigorous, active, and armed. M. du Vallon and I are the only two who are armed. The count is not; and should we meet with any patrol, we must defend ourselves."

" 'Tis true."

"Where can we find a sword?" asked Porthos.

"My lord," said d'Artagnan, "will lend his—which is no use to him—to the Count de la Fère."

"Willingly," said the Cardinal; "I will even ask the count to keep it for my sake."

"I promise you, my lord, never to part with it," replied Athos.

"Well," remarked d'Artagnan, "this change of measures, how touching it is! have you not tears in your eyes, Porthos?"

"Yes," said Porthos; "but I do not know if it is that or the wind that makes me weep; I think it is the wind."

"Now climb up, Athos, quickly," said d'Artagnan. Athos, assisted by Porthos, who lifted him up like a feather, arrived at the top.

"Now jump down, Athos."

Athos jumped and disappeared on the other side of the wall.

"Porthos, whilst I get up, watch the Cardinal. No, I don't want your help. Watch the Cardinal. Lend me your back, but don't let the Cardinal go."

Porthos lent him his back, and d'Artagnan was soon on the summit of the wall, where he seated himself.

"Now, what?" asked Porthos.

"Now give me the Cardinal up here; if he makes any noise, stifle him."

Mazarin wished to call out, but Porthos held him tight, and passed him to d'Artagnan, who seized him by the neck and made him sit down by him; then, in a menacing tone, he said:

"Sir, jump directly down, close to M. de la Fère, or, on the honor of a gentleman, I'll kill you!

"*Monsou,*" cried Mazarin, "you are breaking your word to me!"

"I—did I promise you anything, my lord?"

Mazarin groaned.

"You are free," he said, "through me; your liberty was my ransom."

"Agreed; but the ransom of that immense treasure buried under the gallery—must not one speak of that a little, my lord?"

"Diavolo!" cried Mazarin, almost choked, and clasping his hands; "I am a ruined man!"

But, without listening to his grief, d'Artagnan slipped him gently down into the arms of Athos, who stood immovable at the bottom of the wall.

Porthos next made an effort, which shook the wall; and by the aid of his friend's hand, gained the summit.

"I did not understand at all," he said, "but I understand now; how funny it is!"

"You think so? so much the better; but, that it may be droll even to the end, let us not lose time." And he jumped off the wall.

Porthos did the same.

The Gascon then drew his sword, and marched as an avant-guard.

"My lord, which way do we go? think well of your reply; for should your Eminence be mistaken, there might be very grave results for all of us."

"Along the wall, sir," said Mazarin, "there will be no danger of losing yourselves."

The three friends hastened on, but in a short time were obliged to slacken their pace. The Cardinal could not keep up to them, though with every wish to do so.

Suddenly d'Artagnan touched something warm, and which moved.

"Stop! A horse!" he cried; "I have found a horse!"

"And I likewise," said Athos.

"I, too," said Porthos, who, faithful to instructions, still held the Cardinal's arm.

"There's luck, my lord! just as you were complaining of being tired, and obliged to walk."

But, as he spoke, a pistol was levelled at his breast, and these words were gravely pronounced:

"Hands off!"

"Grimaud!" he cried, "Grimaud! what are you about! were you sent by Heaven?"

"No, sir," said the honest servant; "it was M. Aramis who told me to take care of the horses."

"Is Aramis here?"

"Yes, sir; he has been here since yesterday."

"What are you doing?"

"On the watch——"

"What! Aramis here?" cried Athos.

"At the lesser gate of the castle; he's posted there."

"Are you a large party?"

"Sixty."

"Let him know."

"This moment, sir."

And, believing that no one could execute the commission better than he could, Grimaud set forth at full speed; whilst, enchanted at being all together again, the three friends awaited his return.

There was no one in the whole group in ill humor except Cardinal Mazarin.

CHAPTER LXXXIV.

WE BEGIN TO THINK THAT PORTHOS WILL BE A BARON AND D'ARTAGNAN A CAPTAIN.

AT the expiration of ten minutes Aramis arrived, accompanied by Grimaud, and eight or ten followers. He was much delighted, and threw himself into his friend's arms.

"You are then free, brothers! free without my aid!"

"Do not be unhappy, dear friend, on that account; if you have done nothing as yet, you will do something," replied Athos.

"I have well concerted my plans," pursued Aramis; "the Coadjutor gave me sixty men; twenty guard the walls of the park, twenty the road from Rueil to St. Germain, twenty are dispersed in the woods. I lay in ambuscade with my sixty men; I encircled the castle; the riding horses I entrusted to Grimaud, and I awaited your coming out, which I did not expect till to-morrow, and I hoped to free you without a skirmish. You are free to-night, without fighting; so much the better! How could you escape that scoundrel, Mazarin?"

" 'Tis thanks to him," said d'Artagnan, "that we made our escape, and——"

"Impossible!"

"Yes, indeed, 'tis owing to him that we are at liberty."

"Well!" exclaimed Aramis, "this will reconcile me to him; but I wish he were here that I might tell him that I did not believe him capable of so noble an act."

"My lord," said d'Artagnan, no longer able to contain himself, "allow me to introduce to you the Chevalier d'Herblay, who wishes—as you may have heard—to offer his congratulations to your Eminence."

And he retired, discovering Mazarin—who was in great confusion—to the astonished gaze of Aramis.

"Ho! Ho!" exclaimed the latter, "the Cardinal! a fine prize! halloo! halloo! friends! to horse! to horse!"

Several horsemen quickly ran to him.

"Zounds!" cried Aramis, "I may have done some good, then; my lord, deign to receive my most respectful homage! I will lay a wager that 'tis that Saint Christopher, Porthos, who per-

formed this feat! Oh, I forgot——" and he gave some orders
in a low voice to one of the horsemen.

"I think it will be wise to set off," said d'Artagnan.

"Yes; but I am expecting some one—a friend of Athos."

"A friend!" exclaimed the count.

"And here he is, galloping through the bushes."

"The count! the count!" cried a young voice, which made
Athos start.

"Raoul! Raoul!" he ejaculated.

For one moment the young man forgot his habitual respect;
he threw himself on his father's neck.

"Look, my lord Cardinal," said Aramis, "would it not have
been a pity to have separated those who love each other as
we love? Gentlemen," he continued, addressing the cavaliers,
who became more and more numerous every instant, "gentlemen, encircle his Eminence, that you may show him the
greater honor. He will, indeed, give us the favor of his company; you will, I hope, be grateful for it. Porthos, do not
lose sight of his Eminence."

Aramis then joined Athos and d'Artagnan, who were con-
sulting together.

"Come," said d'Artagnan, after a conference of five minutes'
duration, "let us begin our journey."

"Where are we to go?" asked Porthos.

"To your house, dear Porthos, at Pierrefonds; your fine
château is worthy of affording a princely hospitality to his
Eminence; it is also well situated; neither too near Paris,
nor too far from it. We can establish a communication between it and the capital with great facility. Come, my lord,
you shall there be treated like a prince, as you are."

"A fallen prince!" exclaimed Mazarin piteously.

"The chances of war," said Athos, "are many; but be assured
we shall not take an improper advantage of them."

"No; but we shall make use of them," interposed d'Artagnan.

The rest of the night was employed by these cavaliers in
traveling, with the wonderful rapidity of former days. Mazarin, continuing sombre and pensive, permitted himself to be
dragged along in this way, which was like a race of phantoms.
At dawn twelve leagues had been passed, without stopping;
half the escort were exhausted, and several horses fell down.

"Horses now-a-days are not what they were formerly," observed Porthos; "everything degenerates."

"We are four of us," said d'Artagnan; "we must relieve
each other in mounting guard over my lord, and each of us
must watch for three hours at a time. Athos is going to examine the castle, which it will be necessary to render impreg-
nable in case of a siege; Porthos will see to the provisions
and Aramis to the troops of the garrison. That is to say,

Athos will be chief engineer, Porthos surveyor in general, and Aramis governor of the fortress."

Meanwhile they gave up to Mazarin the handsomest room.

"Gentlemen," he said, when he was in his room, "you do not expect, I presume, to keep me here a long time incognito?"

"No, my lord," replied the Gascon; "on the contrary, we think of announcing very soon that we have you here."

"Then you will be besieged."

"We expect it."

"And what shall you do?"

"Defend ourselves. Were the late Cardinal Richelieu alive, he would tell you a certain story of the Bastion Saint Gervaise, which we four, with our four lackeys and twelve dead men, held out against a whole army."

"Such feats, sir, are done once, and are never repeated."

"However, now-a-days there's not need of so much heroism. To-morrow the army of Paris will be summoned; the day after it will be here! The field of battle, instead, therefore, of being at St. Denis, or at Charenton, will be near Compiègne, or Villars-Cotterets."

"The prince will beat you, as he has always done."

"'Tis possible, my lord; but before an engagement we shall move away your Eminence to another castle belonging to our friend du Vallon, who has three. We will not expose your Eminence to the chances of war."

"Come," answered Mazarin. "I see it will be necessary to capitulate. Tell me at once what you want, that I may see if an arrangement be possible. Speak, Count de la Fère!"

"My lord," replied Athos, "for myself I have nothing to ask; for France, were I to specify, I should have too much. I beg you excuse me, and propose to the chevalier."

And Athos, bowing retired, and remained leaning against the mantelpiece, merely as a spectator of the scene.

"Speak, then, chevalier!" said the Cardinal. "What do you want? Nothing ambiguous, if you please. Be short, clear, and precise."

"As for me," replied Aramis, "I have in my pocket that programme of the conditions which the deputation—of which I formed one—went yesterday to St. Germain to impose on you. Let us consider the debts and claims first. The demands in that programme must be granted."

"We were almost agreed as to those," replied Mazarin; "let us pass on to private and personal stipulations."

"You suppose, then, that there will be some?" asked Aramis, smiling.

"I do not suppose that you will all be so disinterested as M. de la Fère," replied the Cardinal, bowing to Athos.

"My lord! you are right! The count has a mind far above vulgar desires and human passions! He is a proud soul, he is a man by himself! You are right, he is worth us all, and we avow it to you!"

"Aramis!" said Athos, "are you jesting?"

"No, no, dear friend; I state only what we all know. You are right; it is not you alone this matter concerns, but my lord, and his unworthy servant, myself."

"Well, then, what do you require besides the general conditions before recited?"

"I require, my lord, that Normandy should be given to Mdme. de Longueville, with five hundred thousand francs, and full absolution. I require that his majesty should deign to be godfather to the child she has just borne; and that my lord, after having been present at the christening, should go to proffer his homage to our Holy Father the Pope."

"That is, that you wish me to lay aside my ministerial functions, to quit France, and be an exile."

"I, my lord," answered the Gascon, "differ from M. d'Herblay totally in the last point, though I agree with him in the first. Far from wishing my lord to quit Paris, I hope he will stay there and continue to be Prime Minister, as he is a great statesman. I shall try, also, to help him to put down the Fronde; but on one condition—that he sometimes remembers the King's faithful servants, and gives the first vacant company of Musketeers to some one I can mention to him. And you, M. du Vallon——"

"Yes, you, sir! Speak, if you please," said Mazarin.

"As to me," answered Porthos, "I wish my lord Cardinal, to do honor to my house, which has given him an asylum, would, in remembrance of this adventure, erect my estate into a barony, with a promise to confer that order on one of my friends, whenever his majesty next creates peers."

Mazarin bit his lip.

"All that," he said, "appears to me to be ill-connected, gentlemen; for if I satisfy some I shall displease others. If I stay in Paris, I cannot go to Rome; and if I become Pope I could not continue to be Prime Minister; and it is only by continuing Prime Minister that I can make M. d'Artagnan a captain and M. du Vallon a baron."

"True," said Aramis, "so, as I am in the minority, I give up my proposal."

"Well, then, gentlemen, take care of your own concerns, and let France settle matters as she will with me," resumed Mazarin.

"Ho! ho!" replied Aramis. "The Frondeurs will have a treaty, and your Eminence must sign it before us, promising, at the same time, to obtain the Queen's consent to it. Here is the treaty,—may it please your Eminence, read and sign it."

"I know it," answered Mazarin.

"Then sign it."

"But, suppose I refuse?"

"Then," said d'Artagnan, "your Eminence must expect the consequences of a refusal."

"Would you dare to touch a Cardinal?"

"You have dared, my lord, to imprison her majesty's Musketeers."

"The Queen will revenge me, gentlemen."

"I do not think so, although inclination might lead her to do so, but we shall take your Eminence to Paris, and the Parisians will defend us; therefore, sign this treaty, I beg of you."

"Suppose the Queen should refuse to ratify it?"

"Ah! nonsense!" cried d'Artagnan, "I can manage so that her majesty will receive me well; I know one method."

"What?"

"I shall take her majesty the letter in which you tell her that the finances are exhausted."

"And then?" asked Mazarin, turning pale.

"When I see her majesty embarrassed, I shall conduct her to Rueil, make her enter the orangery, and show her the spring which turns a tree-box."

"Enough, sir," muttered the Cardinal, "you have said enough; where is the treaty?"

"Here it is," said Aramis. "Sign, my lord," and he gave him a pen.

Mazarin arose, walked some moments, thoughtful, but not dejected.

"And when I have signed," he said, "what is to be my guarantee?"

"My word of honor, sir," said Athos.

Mazarin started, turned towards the Count de la Fère, and looking for an instant at his noble and honest countenance, took the pen.

"It is sufficient, Count," he said, and he signed the treaty.

"And now, M. d'Artagnan," he said, "prepare to set off for St. Germain, and to leave a letter from me to the Queen."

CHAPTER LXXXV.

SHOWS HOW WITH A THREAT AND A PEN MORE IS EFFECTED THAN BY A SWORD.

D'ARTAGNAN knew his part well; he was aware that opportunity has a forelock only for him who will take it, and he was not a man to let it go by him without seizing it. He soon arranged a prompt and certain manner of traveling, by sending relays of horses to Chantilly, so that he could be in Paris in five or six hours.

Nothing was known at St. Germain about Mazarin's disappearance, except by the Queen, who concealed, from her friends even, her uneasiness. She had heard all about the two soldiers who were found, bound and gagged. Bernouin, who knew more about the affair than anybody, had, in fact, gone to acquaint the Queen of the circumstances which had occurred. Anne had enforced the utmost secrecy, and had disclosed the event to no one except the Prince de Condé, who had sent five or six horsemen into the environs of St. Germain, with orders to bring any suspicious person who was going away from Rueil, in whatsoever direction it might be.

On entering the court of the palace, d'Artagnan encountered Bernouin, to whose instrumentality he owed a prompt introduction to the Queen's presence. He approached the sovereign with every mark of profound respect, and having fallen on his knees, presented to her the Cardinal's letter.

It was, however, merely a letter of introduction. The Queen read it, recognized the writing, and, since there were no details in it of what had occurred, asked for particulars. D'Artagnan related everything, with that simple and ingenuous air which he knew how to assume on some occasions. The Queen, as he went on, looked at him with increasing astonishment.

"How, sir!" she cried, as d'Artagnan finished, "you dare to tell me the details of your crime—to give me an account of your treason!"

"Your majesty, on your side," said d'Artagnan, "is as much mistaken as to our intentions as the Cardinal Mazarin has always been."

"You are in error, sir," answered the Queen. "I am so little mistaken, that in ten minutes you shall be arrested, and in an hour I shall set off to release my minister."

"I am sure your majesty will not commit such an act of imprudence; first, because it would be useless, and would produce the most serious results. Before he could be set free, the Cardinal would be dead; and, indeed, so convinced is he of this, that he entreated me, should I find your majesty disposed to act in this way, to do all I could to induce you to change your intentions."

"Well, then! I shall be content with only arresting you!"

"Madam, the possibility of my arrest has been foreseen, and should I not have returned to-morrow, at a certain hour the next day, the Cardinal will be brought to Paris, and delivered up to the Parliament."

"I think," returned Anne of Austria, fixing upon him a glance which, in any woman's face, would have expressed disdain, but in a Queen's, spread terror to those she looked upon, "I perceive that you dare to threaten the mother of your sovereign."

"Madam," replied d'Artagnan, "I threaten only because I am forced to do so. Believe me, madam, as true a thing as it is that a heart beats in this bosom—a heart devoted to you—believe that you have been the idol of our lives; that we have—as you well know—good Heaven!—risked our lives twenty times for your majesty. Have you then, madam, no compassion on your people, who love you, and yet who suffer—who love you, and who are yet famished—who have no other wish than to bless you, and who, nevertheless——no, I am wrong, your subjects, madam, will never curse you! Say one word to them! and all will be ended; peace succeeds to war, joy to tears, happiness to misfortune!"

Anne of Austria looked with wonderment on the warlike countenance of d'Artagnan, which betrayed a singular expression of deep feeling.

"Why did you not say all this before you acted?" she said.

"Because, madam, it was necessary to prove to your majesty one thing of which you doubted, that is, that we still possess amongst us some valor, and are worthy of some consideration at your hands."

"Then, in case of my refusal, this valor, should a struggle occur, will go even to the length of carrying me off in the midst of my court, to deliver me into the hands of the Fronde, as you have done my minister?"

"We have not thought about it, madam," answered d'Artagnan, with that Gascon effrontery which had in him the appearance of "naïveté;" "but if we four had so settled it, we should certainly have done so."

"I ought," muttered Anne to herself, "by this time to remember that these are men of iron mould."

"Alas! madam!" exclaimed d'Artagnan, "this proves to me that it is only since yesterday that your majesty has imbibed a true opinion of us. Your majesty will do us justice. In doing us justice you will no longer treat us as men of ordinary stamp. You will see in me an ambassador worthy of the high interests which he is authorized to discuss with his sovereign."

"Where is the treaty?"

"Here it is."

Anne of Austria cast her eyes upon the treaty that d'Artagnan presented to her.

"I do not see here," she said, "anything but general conditions; the interests of the Prince de Conti, or of the Duke de Beaufort, de Bouillin, and d'Elbouf, and of the Coadjutor, are herein consulted; but with regard to yours?"

"We do ourselves justice, madam, even in assuming the high position that we have. We do not think ourselves worthy to stand near such great names."

"But you, I presume, have decided to assert your pretentions; 'viva vôce?'"

"I believe you, madam, to be a great and powerful Queen, and that it will be unworthy of your power and greatness if you do not recompense the arm which will bring back his Eminence to St. Germain."

"It is my intention so to do; come—let us hear—speak."

"He who has negotiated these matters (forgive me if I begin by speaking of myself, but I must take that importance to myself which has been given to me, not assumed by me), he who has arranged matters for the return of the Cardinal, ought, it appears to me, in order that his reward may not be unworthy of your majesty, to be made commandant of the Guards, an appointment something like that of captain of the Musketeers."

" 'Tis the appointment that M. de Treville had, that you ask of me."

"The place, madam, is vacant; and although 'tis a year since M. de Treville has left it, is not yet filled up."

"But it is one of the principal military appointments in the King's household."

"M. de Treville was merely a younger son of a Gascon family, like me, madam; he occupied that post for twenty years."

"You have an answer ready for everything," replied the Queen, and she took a document, which she filled up and signed, from her bureau.

"Undoubtedly, madam," said d'Artagnan, taking the document and bowing, "this is a noble reward; but everything in this world is unstable; and any man who happened to fall into disgrace with your majesty would lose everything."

"What then do you want?" asked the Queen, coloring, as she found that she had to deal with a mind as subtle as her own.

"A hundred thousand francs for this poor captain of Musketeers, to be paid whenever his services should no longer be acceptable to your majesty."

Anne hesitated.

"To think of the Parisians," resumed d'Artagnan, "offering the other day, by an edict of the Parliament, six hundred thousand francs to any man soever who would deliver up the Cardinal to them, dead or alive; if alive, in order to hang him; if dead, to deny him the rites of Christian burial!——"

"Come," said Anne, " 'tis reasonable,—since you only ask from a Queen the sixth of what the Parliament has proposed," and she signed an order for a hundred thousand francs.

"Now then?" she said, "what next?"

"Madam, my friend du Vallon is rich; and has therefore nothing in the way of fortune to desire, but I think I remember that there was a dispute between him and M. Mazarin as to making his estate a barony or not. 'Twas even a promise."

"A country clown," said Anne of Austria; "people will laugh."

"Let them!" answered d'Artagnan; "but I am sure of one thing—that those who laugh at him in his presence will never laugh a second time."

"Here goes the barony," said the Queen, and she signed a patent.

"Now there remains the chevalier, or the Abbé d'Herblay, as your majesty pleases."

"Does he wish to be a bishop?"

"No, madam, something easier to grant."

"What?"

"It is that the King should deign to stand godfather to the son of Mdme. de Longueville."

The Queen smiled.

"Nothing more?" she asked.

"No, madam, for I presume that the King, standing godfather to him, could do no less than present him with five hundred thousand francs, giving his father, also, the government of Normandy."

"As to the government of Normandy," replied the Queen, "I think I can promise; but, with regard to the present, the Cardinal is always telling me there is no more money in the royal coffers."

"We shall search for some, madam, and if your majesty permits, we will seek for some together."

"What next?"

"Madam, the Count de la Fère."

"What does he ask?"

"Nothing."

"There is in the world, then, one man who, having the power to ask, asks for nothing."

"The Count de la Fère, madam, is more than a man; he is a demi-god."

"Are you satisfied, sir?"

"There is one thing which the Queen has not signed—her consent to the treaty."

"Of what use to-day? I will sign to-morrow."

"I can assure her majesty that if she does not sign to-day, she will not have time to sign to-morrow. Consent, then, I beg you, madam, to write at the bottom of the schedule, which has been drawn up by Mazarin, as you see,

"'I consent to ratify the treaty proposed by the Parisians.'"

Anne was ensnared; she could not draw back; she signed, but scarcely had she done so, when pride burst forth in her like a tempest, and she began to weep.

D'Artagnan started on seeing these tears; since that time Queens have shed tears like other women.

The Gascon shook his head; these tears from royalty melted his heart.

"Madam," he said, kneeling, "look upon the unhappy man at your feet. Behold, madam! here are the august signatures of your majesty's hand; if you think you are right in giving them to me, you shall do so; but, from this very moment, you are free from any obligation to keep them."

And d'Artagnan, full of honest pride and of manly intrepidity, placed in Anne's hands, in a bundle, the papers that he had, one by one, won from her with so much difficulty.

There are moments—for if everything is not good, everything in this world is not bad—in which the most rigid and the coldest hearts are softened by the tears of strong emotion, of a generous sentiment. One of these momentary impulses actuated Anne. D'Artagnan, when he gave way to his own feelings, which were in accordance with those of the Queen, had accomplished all that the most skilful diplomacy could have done. He was, therefore instantly recompensed, either for his address, or for his sensibility, whichever it might be termed.

"You were right, sir," said Anne, "I misunderstood you. There are the acts signed; I deliver them to you without compulsion; go and bring me back the Cardinal as soon as possible."

"Madam," faltered d'Artagnan, "it is twenty years ago—I have a good memory—since I had the honor, behind a piece of tapestry in the Hôtel de Ville, to kiss one of those beautiful hands."

"There is the other," replied the Queen; and that the left hand should not be less liberal than the right, she drew from her finger a diamond, nearly similar to the one formerly given to him, saying, "take and keep this ring in remembrance of me."

"Madam," said d'Artagnan, rising, "I have only one thing more to wish, which is, that the next thing you ask from me, should be my life."

And with this way of concluding—a way peculiar to himself—he arose and left the room.

"I have never rightly understood these men," said the Queen, as she watched him retiring from her presence; "and it is now too late, for in a year the King will be of age."

In twenty-four hours d'Artagnan and Porthos conducted Mazarin to the Queen; and the one received his commission, the other his patent of nobility.

On the same day the Treaty of Paris was signed; and it was everywhere announced that the Cardinal had shut himself up for three days, in order to draw it out with the greatest care.

CHAPTER LXXXVI.

IT IS MORE DIFFICULT FOR KINGS TO RETURN TO THEIR CAPI-
TALS, THAN TO LEAVE THEM.

WHILST d'Artagnan and Porthos were engaged in conducting the Cardinal to St. Germain, Athos and Aramis returned
to Paris.

Each had his own particular visit to make.

On the next day, at daybreak, the court made preparations
to quit St. Germain.

Meanwhile, the Queen, every hour, had been sending for
d'Artagnan.

"I hear," she said, "that Paris is not quiet. I am afraid for
the King's safety; place yourself close to the coach-door on
the right."

"Be assured, madam; I will answer for the King's safety."

As he left the Queen's presence, Bernouin summoned him
to the Cardinal.

"Sir," said Mazarin to him, "an 'émute' is spoken of in Paris.
I shall be on the King's left, and as I am the chief person threatened, remain at the coach-door to the left."

"Your Eminence may be perfectly easy," replied d'Artagnan,
"they will not touch a hair of your head."

"Deuce take it," he thought to himself, "how can I take care
of both? Ah! plague on't, I shall guard the King, and Porthos the Cardinal."

This arrangement pleased everyone. The Queen had confidence in the courage of d'Artagnan, and the Cardinal in the
strength of Porthos.

The royal procession set out for Paris. Guitaut and Comminges, at the head of the Guards, marched first; then came
the royal carriage, with d'Artagnan on one side, Porthos on
the other; then the Musketeers, for twenty-two years the
old friends of d'Artagnan. During twenty he had been their
lieutenant, their captain since the night before.

The cortège proceeded to Nôtre Dame, where a *Te Deum*
was chanted. All the people of Paris were in the streets.
The Swiss were drawn up along the road, but as the road was
long, they were placed at six or eight feet distance from each
other, and one man deep only. This force was, therefore,
wholy insufficient, and from time to time the line was broken
through by the people, and was formed again with difficulty.
Whenever this occurred, although it proceeded only from
goodwill and a desire to see the King and Queen, Anne looked
at d'Artagnan anxiously.

Mazarin, who had dispersed a thousand louis to make the
people cry "Long live Mazarin," and who had, therefore, no

confidence in acclamations .bought at twenty pistoles each,
looked also at Porthos; but the gigantic body-guard replied
to that look with his fine bass voice, "Be tranquil, my lord;"
and Mazarin became more and more composed.

At the Palais Royal the crowd, which had forced in from
the adjacent streets, was still greater; like a large, impetuous
crowd, a wave of human beings came to meet the carriage,
and rolled tumultuously into the Rue St. Honore.

When the procession reached the palace, loud cries of "Long
live their majesties!" resounded. Mazarin leaned out of the
window. One or two shouts of "Long live the Cardinal!"
saluted his shadow, but instantly hisses and yells stifled them
remorselessly. Mazarin turned pale, and sank back in his
coach.

"Low-born fellows!" ejaculated Porthos.

D'Artagnan said nothing, but twirled his moustache with a
peculiar gesture which showed that his fine Gascon humor
was kindled.

Anne of Austria bent down and whispered in the young
King's ear:

"Say something pleasant to M. d'Artagnan, my lord."

The young King leaned towards the door.

"I have not said good morning to you, M. d'Artagnan," he
said: "nevertheless, I have remarked you. ' It was you who
were behind my bed-curtains that night when the Parisians
wished to see me asleep."

"And if the King permits me," returned the Gascon, "I shall
be near him whenever there is danger to be encountered."

"Sir," said Mazarin to Porthos, "what would you do if the
crowd fell upon us?"

"Kill as many as I could, my lord."

"Hem! Brave as you are, and strong as you are, you could
not kill all."

" 'Tis true," answered Porthos, rising in his saddle, in order
that he might see the immense crowd, "there are many of
them."

"I think I should like the man of wit better than this one
of muscle," said Mazarin to himself, and he threw himself back
in his carriage.

The Queen and her Minister, more especially the latter, had
reason to feel anxious. The crowd, whilst preserving an appearance of respect, and even of affection, for the King and
Queen-regent, began to be tumultuous. Reports were whispered about, like certain sounds which announce, as they are
echoed from wave to wave, the coming storm, and when they
pass through a multitude, presage a riot.

D'Artagnan turned towards the Musketeers, and made a
sign imperceptible to the crowd, but very easily understood
by that chosen regiment, the flower of the army.

The ranks were closed, and a kind of shudder ran from man to man.

At the Barrière des Sergents the procession was obliged to stop. Comminges left the head of the escort, and went to the Queen's carriage. Anne questioned d'Artagnan by a look. He answered in the same language.

"Proceed," she said.

Comminges returned to his post. An effort was made, and the living barrier was violently broken through.

Some complaints arose from the crowd, and were addressed this time to the King, as well as the Minister.

"On!" cried d'Artagnan, with a loud voice.

"Onward!" roared Porthos.

But, as if the multitude had waited only for this demonstration to burst out, all the sentiments of hostility that possessed it broke out at once. Cries of "Down with Mazarin!" "Death to the Cardinal!" resounded on all sides.

At the same time, through the streets of a double stream of people broke the feeble hedge of Swiss Guards, and came, like a whirlwind, even to the very legs of Porthos' horse and that of d'Artagnan.

This new eruption was more dangerous than the others, being composed of armed men. It was plain that it was not the chance combination of those who had collected a number of the malcontents at the same spot, but the concerted attack organized by an hostile spirit.

Each of these two mobs was led on by a chief, one of whom appeared to belong, not to the people, but to the honorable corporation of mendicants, and the other, who, notwithstanding his affected imitation of the people, might easily be discovered to be a gentleman. Both were evidently stimulated by the same impulse.

There was a shock which was perceived even in the royal carriage. Then, millions of cries, forming one vast uproar, were heard, mingled with guns firing.

"The Musketeers! here!" cried d'Artagnan.

The escort divided into two files. One of them passed round to the right of the carriage; the other to the left. One went to support d'Artagnan, the other, Porthos. Then came a skirmish, the more terrible, because it had no definite object; the more melancholy, because those engaged in it knew not for whom they were fighting. Like all popular movements, the shock given by the rush of this mob was formidable. The Musketeers, few in number, not being able, in the midst of this crowd, to make their horses wheel round, began to give way. D'Artagnan offered to lower the blinds of the royal carriage, but the young King stretched out his arm, saying:

"No, sir! I wish to see everything."

"If your majesty wishes to look out—well, then, look!" replied d'Artagnan. And turning with that fury which made him so formidable, he rushed towards the chief of the insurgents, a man, who with a large sword in his hand, tried to clear out a passage to the coach-door, by a combat with two Musketeers.

"Make room!" cried d'Artagnan. "Zounds! give way!"

At these words, the man with a pistol and sword raised his head; but it was too late. The blow was sped by d'Artagnan; the rapier had pierced his bosom.

"Ah! confound it!" cried the Gascon, trying in vain, too late, to retract the thrust. "What the devil are you doing here, Count?"

"Accomplishing my destiny," replied Rochefort, falling on one knee. "I have already got up again after three stabs from you; but I shall not rise after a fourth."

"Count!" said d'Artagnan, with some degree of emotion, "I struck without knowing that it was you. I am sorry, if you die, that you should die with sentiments of hatred towards me."

Rochefort extended his hand to d'Artagnan, who took it. The count wished to speak, but a gush of blood stifled him. He stiffened in the last convulsions of death, and expired.

"Back, people!" cried d'Artagnan; "your leader is dead, and you have no longer anything to do here."

"Indeed, as if de Rochefort had been the soul of the attack, all the crowd who had followed and obeyed him took flight on seeing him fall. D'Artagnan charged with a party of Musketeers in the Rue de Coq, and that portion of the mob whom he assailed disappeared like smoke, dispersing near the Place St. Germain L'Auxerrois, and taking the direction of the quays.

D'Artagnan returned to help Porthos, if Porthos needed it; but Porthos, on his side, had done his work as conscientiously as d'Artagnan. The left of the carriage was as well cleared as the right; and they drew up the blind of the window, which Mazarin, less heroic than the King, had taken the precaution to lower.

Porthos looked very melancholy.

"What a devil of a face you have Porthos! and what a strange air for a victorious man!"

"But you," answered Porthos, "seem to be agitated."

"There's a reason! Zounds! I have just killed an old friend."

"Indeed!" replied Porthos; "who?"

"That poor Count de Rochefort."

"Well! exactly like me! I have just killed a man whose face is not unknown to me. Unluckily, I hit him on the head, and immediately his face was covered with blood."

"And he said nothing as he died?"

"Yes; he said, 'Oh!'"

"I suppose," answered d'Artagnan, laughing, "if he only said that it did not enlighten you much."

"Well, sir!" cried the Queen.

"Madam, the passage is quite clear, and your majesty can continue your road."

In fact, the procession arrived in safety at Nôtre Dame, at the front gate of which all the clergy, with the Coadjutor at their head, awaited the King, the Queen and the Minister, for whose happy return they chanted a *Te Deum*.

CONCLUSION.

On going home, the two friends found a letter from Athos, who desired them to meet him at the Grand Charlemagne on the following day.

Both of the friends went to bed early, but neither of them slept. When one arrives at the summit of one's wishes, success has usually the power of driving away sleep on the first night after the fulfilment of long-cherished hopes.

The next night, at the appointed hour, they went to see Athos, and found him and Aramis in traveling costume.

"What!" cried Porthos, "are we all going away then? I have also made my preparations this morning."

"Oh, heavens! yes," said Aramis. "There's nothing to do in Paris now there's no Fronde. The Duchess de Longueville has invited me to pass some days in Normandy, and has deputed me, while her son is being baptized, to go and prepare her residence at Rouen; after which, if nothing new occurs, I shall go and bury myself in my convent at Noisy-le-Sec."

"And I," said Athos, "am returning to Bragelonne. You know, dear d'Artagnan, I am nothing more than a good, honest, country squire. Raoul has no other fortune but what I possess, poor boy! and I must take care of it for him, since I only lend him my name."

"And Raoul—what shall you do with him?"

"I leave him with you, my friend. War in Flanders has broken out; you shall take him with you there. I am afraid that remaining at Blois would be dangerous to his youthful mind. Take him, and teach him to be as brave and loyal as you are yourself."

"Then," replied d'Artagnan, "though I shall not have you, Athos, at all events I shall have that dear, fair-haired head by me; and though he is but a boy, yet, since your soul lives again in him, dear Athos, so I shall always fancy that you are near me, sustaining and encouraging me."

The four friends embraced with tears in their eyes.

Then they departed without knowing whether they should ever see each other again.